PRAISE FOR MICAH YONGO

"A strong work from a very promising new author."
Publishers Weekly

"Yongo invigorates the epic fantasy genre with his original and accomplished voice in the striking and throroughly enjoyable Lost Gods.*"*
Adrian Tchaikovsky, author of *Children of Time*

"Fast-paced and intriguing… with an African-inspired setting that makes a refreshing change."
Anna Smith Spark, author of *The Court of Broken Knives*

"Lost Gods is fresh, fierce, and lush with inspiration from the lands and mythology of ancient Africa and the Middle East."
Cameron Johnston, author of *The Traitor God*

"Yongo's debut feels fresh in its conception and worldbuilding, exploring an intriguing landscape from the points of view of a diverse array of characters of different social strata."
Barnes & Noble Sci-Fi & Fantasy Blog

BY THE SAME AUTHOR

Lost Gods

Micah Yongo

PALE KINGS

ANGRY
ROBOT

ANGRY ROBOT
An imprint of Watkins Media Ltd

Unit 11, Shepperton House
89 Shepperton Road
London N1 3DF
UK

angryrobotbooks.com
twitter.com/angryrobotbooks
Blood will out

An Angry Robot paperback original, 2019

Cover by Larry Rostant
Set in Meridien

ISBN 978 0 85766 785 4
Ebook ISBN 978 0 85766 786 1

Printed and bound in the United Kingdom by TJ International.

9 8 7 6 5 4 3 2 1

For the survivors…

"If thou gaze long into an abyss, the abyss will also gaze into thee."

Friedrich Nietzsche, *Beyond Good and Evil*

PROLOGUE

DUSK

In many ways a bloodtree is a beautiful thing, or so Suryal had always thought; the way its life – so mysterious, so fickle – can span generations, its roots resting beyond time, living out the secret of its seed to mirror the sha of the one to whom it has been bound. Over the years she'd had her favourites, and in better times would sometimes come here to the Forest of Silences just to visit them, strolling unseen beneath the broad elegant canopy of Tutor Maresh's acacia, her steps brightening the shadows as the sun lowered beyond the mount's peak; or at other times gazing upon the sweeping boughs of Master Sol's magnolia as the season changed, its dainty blossoms, ruffled by the breeze, cascading to the ground like flakes of snow.

She thought back on them all, allowing her memories to drift through the centuries to chart the path that had led here to this point. She'd watched, as her kind must, when Qoh'leth had planted that first tree, slicing his palm to soak the seed in his blood, before giving it to the soil to birth the Brotherhood of the Shedaím.

"A strange thing isn't it," Abdiel said, walking beside her, "that all we have been witness to – centuries of conflict, both seen and unseen – should now rest upon them."

With that Suryal had to agree. As much as she'd known it would come to this, it still amazed her to think the fate of worlds could now be tied to the fates of the four trees they'd come here to find; the bloodtrees of Neythan, Arianna, Josef and Daneel: the surviving members of the Brotherhood's last sharím.

"They are young, it's true," she replied. "But the Brotherhood has raised and trained them well."

"It has. Yet there is no training for what comes."

To which Suryal said nothing. She knew Abdiel's words to be true, but there was no helping that now. With the fall of the Brotherhood, and after having been forced by the betrayal of their elders to scatter across the Five Lands, these four, young as they were, were the only ones left to trust in.

Suryal glanced up at Josef's bloodtree as she passed by it, a solid strong oak – straight, unyielding, towering into the evening sky like a sentry to survey the grounds. Beyond it, she could see his twin brother Daneel's, with that slight twisting kink midway up its trunk, and those bright autumnal leaves flickering in the breeze like erratic tongues of flame, making the tree itself seem perpetually on fire. Steadily, she moved into the Forest, Abdiel at her shoulder, continuing further up the slope to find Arianna's bloodtree, which even now remained like no other she'd ever seen: the beguiling way its boughs opened fearlessly to the sky, and the way its blossoms, blooming in every possible colour, continued to shift tone from week to week: one day darker, another day lighter, as changeable as the wind. Finally, they came to Neythan's – the tree that had remained stunted and barren for so long, and that now reached beyond the Forest's canopy, taller than the others, its branches clustering in complex matrices as Suryal came to a halt and stood before it.

"He goes south with Arianna and Caleb now," Abdiel remarked. "To the Summerlands, led by the Súnamite mystic to uncover the secrets of the Magi scroll."

"There is hope in that," Suryal replied.

"Yes. There is always hope."

"And what of the others?"

"Daneel has fled north with the boy, hunted by what remains of the Brotherhood for rescuing the child he'd been sent to kill. Only Josef remains part of the Shedaím now. He does not know that it is dying. He remains blind to what it has become, but loyal to the throne."

"As was said he would."

"Yes. As was said… It is left to them now. They must do what must be done, seek what must be known."

"Yes," Suryal agreed as they stood there, staring up at the pale trunk of Neythan's bloodtree as the dusky sky continued to dim. Even though she knew there was no choice but for things to be this way, she remained uneasy. She turned, surveying the grassy shallow slope they'd climbed, the beginnings of the village loitering beyond the slim stream that bordered the Forest below. The sky was darkening, the night coming on. She looked up once more at Neythan's bloodtree. "I shall wait for you here," she whispered to it, and then reached out to touch its smooth white bark. "But I cannot wait long," she added. "The shadow comes, and shall not abate… The time is short."

ONE

OUTLAW

When Neythan was a boy he'd awake to the sound of the irhzán, a kind of long ended flute with cuttings of willowcane enclosed in the mouthpiece. He'd listen to the burred woody sound drifting up through the morning and gliding along the edges of the dawn as the sunlight nudged above the mountains. The day, just starting, would be silent but for those long meandering notes, wandering haltingly like the storytelling voice of an elder by campfire. His mother would find him listening as he stared out through the window of their hut toward the east where the mountains stood caped in shadow by the sun's ascent, no more than dark crooked shapes against the horizon, the sky behind ablaze, nascent day spreading out from some vast hiding place beyond the blackened ramparts and beckoning him, to see if he could search it out beyond the mountains, to see whether day was a place rather than a time, or both.

"What else do you remember?"

Neythan glanced up from the ground and peered at Filani through the smoke of the campfire as he kindled it. It was late, or perhaps by now it was early. He shrugged. "Little. No more than scraps. In Ilysia it was forbidden to talk of life before the Brotherhood. The

Shedaím was to be our only kin, thoughts of all else were to be buried… I remember once, I asked Josef and Daneel where they'd lived before being brought to the mount. When Tutor Hamir heard of it he beat me so hard I couldn't sit for a week. I was six, I think…"

He tossed another chopped bough onto the fire and poked at the smouldering pile as the flames curled around it. Caleb, still asleep, coughed where he lay on the other side, snoring as usual whilst Filani's niece, Nyomi, slept on her back beside him, undisturbed.

"Strange now I think about it," Neythan said. "How easily it happens, I mean. How quickly you let go. There was a time I'd think only of home, being back in Eram. Not an hour would pass without my thinking of it. The sea. The fish. Mother. Father… A few moons in Ilysia and it fades. A while more and you can scarcely remember their faces. In time they are no more than ghosts. It's as if they never existed at all."

"And yet they did," Filani said. "And still do, within you." She glanced up at him. "The sha keeps all things. It never forgets. I will help you. You will see."

"Help me?"

"To remember."

"How?"

But she just did that thing of pretending not to hear, busying herself with the frayed hem of her skirt. It was beginning to get light again, the sky turning dim emerald; the sun, hours from rising, trying to compete with the moon for what was left of the night.

They'd journeyed for more than a week through the sands of the Havilah to the edge of Súnam after fleeing the elders' temple. And then on through the sweaty clamour of its jungly forests, the ground growing increasingly lumpy from the crowded undergrowth and tree roots until in the end Filani thought it best to untether the animals and leave the unwieldy cart behind. And so they did, and continued on with just the mule and camel as Filani and Caleb rode with the provisions slung across the burdened beasts' backs whilst the rest of them went on foot.

For most of the way here Neythan had distracted himself with the strange sights and sounds of the jungle: the bright sappy leaves and thick lazy insects and flowers and birds he'd never seen before, each stranger than the last, as though everything had grown gaudy and mad in the sun's wild white glare. Tiny sparrow-like birds with shimmering yellow breasts. Long-limbed monkeys climbing through almost luminous greenery. Green lizards. Yellow frogs. Purple ants. Even the dirt was different, a bold silty red, as though worn rusty by the sun's stifling heat as beneath it all the loud continuous croak of insects filled the silence.

Not that it mattered. At night the distractions peeled away anyway, leaving Neythan's mind to wander through the small hours, leaning inevitably toward the memory he'd been trying to avoid. The sight of Master Johann's slim dark eyes blinking slowly as his tired mouth hung ajar, mouthing Neythan's name as he lay bleeding beside him on the dusty canvas of the temple floor. Like a suffocating fish. Hands clutching the wound in his gut, the wound Neythan had put there. The wound that–

"You're shivering."

Neythan followed Filani's gaze down to his bandaged hand where, weeks before, a blind elder had thrust a dagger through to pin him to the floor of the temple of the very Brotherhood that had raised him. His fingers were twitching, again. He held them still with his other hand and folded them into a fist, and then glanced up at Filani watching him.

"I'm fine."

"The one thing you are not, is fine, Neythan."

"It will pass."

"Yes… you have been saying so for nearly two weeks now." She gestured at Arianna, sleeping a few feet away with her shoulders hunched beneath a ragged blanket. "Ten days and she was well. With you the elder's fever persists."

Neythan coughed, as though to demonstrate.

"Your struggle to sleep," Filani went on. "The dreams you have when you do. These things are why you must remember."

6

"I don't see how remembering life before Ilysia has anything to do with it."

"It has *everything* to do with it. You will find no rest until you do. It is as I have said, Neythan. The sha keeps all things... but sometimes it seeks to tell them."

"And that's what this is? My not sleeping?"

Filani shrugged, scraping her teeth with a narrow twig to clean away a lodged crumb.

"And you can help?"

"There are ways..." She turned to the fire. It was warming now, beginning to grow. "Tomorrow, when we come to Jaffra at last, and speak to the chieftain and elders concerning the scroll. Afterwards, when we have rested, I will help you remember." She looked up at him from the flames. "You will not be whole until you do."

They came to Jaffra before noon of the following day. Neythan couldn't help but be stunned by the size of the place. The settlement was broad and sprawling, with narrow streets lined by high walls that turned the city to a kind of labyrinth. Tall palm trees speared the horizon above the pale stonework and straw-thatched roofs. Above it all loomed a high pyramidal tower of whitewashed stone that seemed to mark the city's centre.

"It's a ziggurat," Filani explained. "A way for the priests to speak with gods, or so the tradition goes." To which Neythan nodded numbly, eyeing the surroundings. He'd imagined the Summerlands to be little more than plain and dusty, an unending horizon of white cracked earth lying neat and still and naked as bone beneath a blue and silent sky, perhaps a village here or there, like the Salt Lands they'd journeyed through further north, only warmer. Instead the settlement before him sprawled out, bold and broad, as large as Hanesda probably, and just as busy.

People moved along the narrow, walled streets in both directions. Tall-necked women with gleaming black skin ambled by with baskets and jars of clay propped elegantly on their heads. Others wore long wrap-around skirts, intricately woven, arms swaying slowly as they strode along the road. Children scampered and giggled along the walls. Cattle groaned as they were led slowly through the scrum. Whilst above it all, perched on a yard-wall opposite, a dirty-turbaned old man slapped a drum, his eyes closed, his naked narrow torso swaying as his palms flashed rapidly above the skin.

Every street they turned into was the same, the whole place crammed ready for trade. The market, if there was such a thing here, rather than being gathered in one place instead sprawled out along the various broadways wherever the tall walls were wide enough. Frontages sat splayed with the wares of their occupants – wickerworkers, bayweavers, sandal-makers, spice-sellers – all lining the wider streets on both sides, and then, as they turned into another road, a tanner. Neythan's nose wrinkled at the tired reek of meat as he eyed a pair of scraggly rawhides draped over a bench fronting the house wall.

"You see, Neythan?" Filani said, walking beside him. "The world is bigger than the Sovereignty. There are more lands than just the Five." She smiled, nodding at the surroundings. "As you can now see."

Neythan nodded again, taking it all in – the people, the clothing, the smells – all of it so different and exotic and yet, in a way, strangely familiar too. Both his father and uncle were Súnamites, and although Uncle Sol had rarely spoken of his homeland, Neythan couldn't help but feel a sense of kinship with it, as though a part of him had always been waiting to come here – waiting to return home.

"Master Sol never said how pretty this place was," Arianna said, as though hearing his thoughts. She was at his shoulder, examining a set of peculiarly carved trinkets hanging from a nearby tree. There were more of them along the road, strange objects hanging from the gables of shack doors and houses; little bars of sculpted wood, no bigger than a finger, each one tethered with tufts of feather and straw bindings and bits of bone. Others tied with bird skulls and silver trinkets, or twigs bound together in strange latticed shapes; all hanging like wind-chimes from the rim of doorways or the boughs of cypress trees by the roadside.

"They are tokens," Filani said. "Keepsakes." She pointed at a cradling of twigs with chunks of moss and straw tucked into it, hanging in the shape of an uneven pyramid from the bough of a tree overhanging a wall on the street. "That one is for Talagmagon. She governs the harvests." She pointed to another icon beside it, a column of carved wood hanging by two twisted threads of yarn. "This one is Ishmar, the Rainspeaker. She both commands the rain and speaks through it. In rainy season the priests will interpret her words, tell what sacrifices should be brought to ensure the health of their crops."

She glanced back, saw the uncertain smile on Arianna's face, the mild frown on Neythan's. "There will be many things here that will seem strange to you. But remember, we are all foreigners in another's home. Your own customs were once just as strange to me."

They rounded a corner further up the road into a narrow, cobbled walkway with terraces on either side and the beginnings of a half-built gangway arching overhead. Fewer people here. Filani's fingertips brushed the painted stones of the walls where faded pictograms of black two-headed serpents and what appeared to be a bear chased each other, merging into a winding medley of colour. Neythan glanced over the images, wondering what story they told, and of what god.

"How long since you were last here?" he said.

Filani looked at the painted wall and smiled. "Too long…" Her gaze turned to the street ahead of them, her smile fading as she considered the clutch of shanty housing at the other end. "But not long enough… Come. We are close."

As they stepped into the adjoining street Arianna laid a hand on Neythan's shoulder and nodded. Neythan followed her gaze to an old skinny man ahead of them. The stranger was standing in the road, allowing the ongoing tide of people to pass around him as he stared at Filani and the rest of the group. The man said nothing, his coffee-dark body just turning slowly as he continued to watch them pass by on the opposite side of the road.

In the next street Caleb noticed a woman staring at them, flat-eyed as a goat, before turning to whisper to a friend beside her who duly left off from what she was doing to join her companion in watching them as they walked. Caleb came alongside Filani and leaned down from the mule. "Foreigners not so common a thing here as they are in the Sovereignty I take it."

"We're nearly there," Filani said.

By the time they'd reached the next street a small group had gathered; people who'd drifted idly into their wake or kept pace from the other side of the street, following along, their gazes fixed unabashedly on the strangers.

Arianna was beginning to get agitated. "Why are these people following us?"

But Filani didn't answer. They walked on toward a growing mob – twenty, thirty perhaps, it was hard to tell. Dark sun-baked figures filled across the narrow passage to bar the other end as more climbed along the tops of the walls on either side.

Filani heard the scrape of Arianna's blade pulling loose from the sleeve. She turned to face her.

"No."

Arianna glanced at the men on the walls. The crowd was growing.

"We are near to the heart of the city," Filani said. "This place is sacred. The ziggurat is just beyond those walls. You must draw no weapon here."

"Why are they following us?"

"They are following me."

"You?" Neythan said. "Why?"

The old woman hesitated. "You must trust me in this. Whatever happens, whatever is said, whatever is said of me, you must trust me. And you must not draw your weapons here. It is forbidden. Do you understand?"

Neythan looked at her, then the crowd, and then Arianna, who having eyed the mob once more was frowning doubtfully, offering Neythan a slow wag of her head.

Filani touched his arm. "Promise me, Neythan. No matter whatever is said. I know you do not understand now, but later, you will understand. You must trust me."

The shouts from the crowd were growing louder. Some had even begun to call out to Filani by name.

"There is no time to explain now, Neythan. I'd hoped to explain later. About all of this. But you must not draw your blade."

Neythan nodded uncertainly.

"No matter what."

Reluctant grunt.

Filani turned back to the road. The slanted pale stones of the ziggurat were visible above the wall to their left. Neythan could see where the street's walls widened beyond the mob, leading into a square to accommodate the huge structure's whitewashed steps. The people were chanting loudly now, clambering up onto the walls and huddling beneath the shade of a tall palm tree further along, jockeying for position like spectators before sport.

An old woman stepped out into the road from the foot of the palm tree ahead. Tall. Slim. Dressed in a sleeveless blue ankle-length shift. Expensive colour. A complicated pattern of scars marked her shoulders and neck beneath a thick, heavy-looking wig of narrow beaded dreadlocks capped with an elaborate covering of bejewelled woven yarn. Some sort of ceremonial accessory, Neythan guessed. Perhaps befitting a rank of some kind.

She approached slowly and came to a stop a few paces away. She stared for a few moments as the crowd watched on, and then, even more slowly, drew a few steps closer.

"So, it is true." The woman's lips hung wonderingly ajar as she gazed at Filani. "It really is you."

"I've come to speak with Ráham."

The woman laughed. "I should not be surprised, eh… After all these years…" The woman shook her head, "still the same. Still asking that the whole world listen to your tales and do as you want." She glanced at Neythan and the others. "And I suppose these are the latest to bow their ear to those tales."

"Listen to me, sister."

The woman recoiled, her face twisting. "Sister? Is that what you will call me?" The beads of her dreadlocks slapped gently against her shoulders as her head tipped to one side. "Sister?"

"I know it has been a long time, Sulari."

"Yes. It has." The woman prowled to one side to eye the others more closely, her gaze passing over Neythan, Caleb and Arianna, then lingering on Nyomi, before turning again to Filani with a short sour laugh. "You will die." She said it almost gently, and then nodded. "Yes," more certain now, leaning into the words. "You will die."

"We have found a Magi scroll," Filani said.

The woman hesitated only briefly. "And you thought it enough to bargain for your life?"

"I have come to seek the good of us all."

"Good? And what would you know of good?"

"If I am allowed to speak to Ráham, or perhaps Maríba, or one of the others to explain–"

"You are no priestess now, Filani."

"No. I know, but–"

"Yet you come here, of all places, to bargain with a *scroll*–"

"Not to bargain–"

"After all this time. And after all the trouble these writings have brought us–"

"You know as well as I that it–"

"All the trouble they have brought *me.*"

"I have not come to fight, Sulari."

"No?" The other woman pouted mockingly. "Well. Sister. We do not always get what we want, eh. You taught me that truth well. Remember?" The beads of the woman's wig snapped around as she turned away to face the crowd and raised a hand to address them. "Your eyes did not deceive you, Jaffra," she shouted. "You saw this woman well. She is the one you thought. She is the accursed…" She turned back to Filani, pointing. "You know what has been determined of old concerning her. You all know. Today Ishmar smiles on us, she brings her here to fulfil the debt that is owed."

Sulari lifted both arms and stepped slowly back, her eyes fixed on Filani, teary with hate.

"Please, Sulari."

The first stone was only a pebble but stung as it struck Filani's calf. When Neythan looked up he saw others on the wall with their arms cocked, ready to throw. The crowd on the road began to slowly move up the narrow, walled street, rummaging on the ground for rocks as they came.

"Sulari."

But the other woman was backing away now. "You brought this on yourself... sister."

The dust began to skip around Filani's feet as more stones tossed down at her from the wall. Others were throwing from distance further up the road.

Neythan looked and saw more people filling up the road from behind, creeping forward, blocking the way back. Neythan took Filani by the arm but she pushed him away.

"Stay back!"

Caleb was trying to steady the mule as its hooves pawed and stepped in panic.

Arianna reached for her blade.

Filani turned on her. "No! I told you no weapons."

"That was before this mob decided to play hit the tree, and make *you* the tree."

"And what will you do? Can you put the whole city to the sword? You must live! You must stay back, and live! You cannot die here. Not for me. You must–"

A rock caromed off the back of her head. She staggered, nearly falling, and then turned, groggily waving Neythan back as he again stepped forward to intervene. She stumbled around to face Sulari. The people were closer now.

"Sulari!"

"You knew it would be this way, sister. You knew from the moment you decided to return here."

"He has the eyes, Sulari."

The other woman, still backing away as the crowd came forward behind her, slowed and paused. A round stone thudded heavily

13

against Filani's knee, dropping her to the ground. Nyomi and Caleb had taken a grasp of Neythan, holding him back, his swordhand clasped tight to the handle of his sheathed blade as he stared after Filani on the floor with her headscarf coming loose.

"He has the eyes!" Filani's words were slurring. "Look at him, Sulari!" Her arm was outstretched as she sat crumpled on the ground, her finger thrust back, pointing, Neythan realised, at him. "Look at him."

Stones were beginning to rain down from the wall more freely. The wigged woman had come to a stop, no longer backing away but peering at Neythan.

"Look at him," Filani shouted again.

She grunted as another stone from the street slammed into her ribs, then another from the wall above, bouncing dully off her arm. The dust began to litter with them as they skittled off the dirt like a thin storm of hail.

"No!"

She hunched over as a rock hit her shoulder. Her garment had grown ragged, mingled with dust and blood. Another stone hammered off her leg, splitting the skin, gashing bright red.

"No!" It was his own voice, Neythan realised, screaming as he shrugged loose of Caleb and tried again to move forward but this time staggered, collapsing to one knee, his breath suddenly short. His bandaged left hand twitched and shivered as he wheezed for air. He looked up at the street walls. Everything had turned blurry, and the bricks, somehow, seemed to be filling with black, as though being swallowed from bottom to top by dark water or pitch, running up the wall. He tried to look at the men and women on its ledge but he could hardly see them, suddenly they were no more than eyeless shadows staring down on him from above. And then he saw a girl among them, not dark-skinned like the rest, not a Súnamite, just standing there – white skin, long black hair – holding a goat's skull in one hand as she calmly looked down on him from the high wall as though she knew him and...

Neythan was tugged back from behind, someone pulling him up. Arianna beside him, yanking him back by the shoulders and arm.

His limbs felt heavy, cool knots of stone. The sun's bright glare shone down on Filani's crumpled frame in the street, prone and groaning as more stones and rocks thudded and skidded over her to the bleary roar of the crowd. The sun yawed and swung overhead, swaying like a lamp on a rope and then slowly growing still, the cloudless sky staring down and for a moment seeming to Neythan like some empty endless floor beneath him, waiting for him to drop, waiting to accept him into its still, weightless void… He was on the ground, he realised. Had fallen or collapsed somehow. Vision suddenly narrow. Noise blurring. Just the wide deep blue slowly dimming as a woman's face hovered into view. Sulari loomed over him, the beaded locks of her wig rattling. Her tear-welled eyes stared down on him in astonishment. Finally, a tremulous tight smile toppled the tears that had built as she began to weep.

"Blood of Ruben," she whispered. "Blood of Sol."

TWO

EXILE

Joram used to hear it said that it was a curse to consort with the dead. But then he'd heard men say many things, scrounging for meanings where there were none, as though the world could be shrunk to their fit. Come to think of it, when Joram was a child, Father would teach him a new and meaningless proverb every new moon, the apparent tools of his future trade. A king is a sage with a throne, he'd say, or at least he ought to be. And so when Father found him sticking pins into the eyes of a whimpering broken-legged dog, it can only be assumed he saw it as the latest in a pattern worryingly at odds with his paternal counsel. Several moons before, he'd discovered him urinating on his younger brother, Sidon, whilst he slept. The year before that, Joram had taken to handling his own faeces, smearing it over himself, his face and lips and arms, and then offering it up like muddy cake dough as though he were some crazed beggar. Still, these things never really seemed to concern Father, nor Father's special friends. The boy would grow, he'd say, the boy would learn. In fact, perhaps all Joram had done or ever would do would've been forgiven if not for that waggish grin that accompanied his every misbehaviour, a complacent winking smirk, mocking the covenant between them, the complicity of their shared blood, reminding his father that however deviant or disgusting his son's acts became he could not be other than party to them. He'd always be the one who'd sired him after all. Joram would always be his seed.

And so when Joram tossed his mother's cat from the roof of the crown city's palace it was strange Father did not see the beauty of this. How could he not understand? How could he not see that every misdemeanour was an offering to him, a relishing in the surety of his love, a celebration of how much his son had learned to trust it? How could he not see the way Joram was marking out the measure of their immutable bond, showing it back to him, teaching him of its virtue, rejoicing in what it would endure? Yet Father didn't see. Father didn't understand. But then that was nearly twelve years ago. And time, as Father often liked to say, always has new tales to tell.

Joram parked the memory as he looked out over the rainy moonlit terrain. The ranger was here now. Joram could see the small distant shape of him on horseback, slowly crossing the empty plain as he made his way toward him.

The hour was late. The rain was sideways. Lightning smacked the sky like the lash of a god's whip. So Joram waited, peering out from beneath his shelter as the miserly sizzling of thunder chuntered through the gloom.

"He is late."

Joram shrugged, half ignoring the voice at his shoulder as the man eventually reached him, climbed down from his horse and walked in from the rain.

"You're late," Joram said as the ranger stepped beneath the shack.

The man, soaked, looked up from beneath his dripping hood as though he'd been spat at. "The horse was sick most of the way."

Joram watched as the ranger removed his hood and shook out his soggy hair, then gestured him to the seat opposite. The shack was the only house for miles, a stone-made building, stable-wide, and with a stairway along the outside of its eastern wall that led up to a fairly warm bedchamber and, through a door, a kitchen balcony beside it. The building had been hewn into one of the many rock columns that populated the usually dry plain the ranger had just made his way across. They sat down in the open shelter beneath the upper room as windswept spits of rain gusted in, the canopy shuddering as the stanchions of the gable wobbled and shook with the wind.

Joram leant back in his chair and appraised the ranger. "So," he said.

"So," the ranger said.

"It has been close to half a year, Yevhen."

The ranger nodded.

"Seems as though it's been even longer."

"Yes. Waiting is like that."

Joram smiled. That was the thing with Kivites, always cockier than their station warranted. He watched as the ranger looked out over the soaked desert, eyeing the denuded plain he'd just crossed through the canyon.

"Hasn't rained like this in these plains for decades," the ranger murmured.

"Yes. That's what makes it fun."

"It is your doing?"

Joram's smile widened. "Of course not." Though he liked that the ranger had thought it. "But you can't have come all this way to talk only of weather, Yevhen."

"No. I suppose not."

"Well then. Do you have it?"

"You know that I do. Why else would I have come?"

"Then why so coy? Come. Show it to me."

The ranger shifted uneasily in his seat. "My sister, Kareena. She is here?"

"Yes."

The ranger waited.

"It will be as we agreed," Joram insisted. "A word and she will be well. But not before I see the amulet."

The ranger stared for a long time, weighing the options, and then dipped a hand into the fold of his cloak. He withdrew it slowly, his fingers draped with a thin chain and the loosely dangled amulet attached at the end, swaying gently beneath.

Joram grinned, and then exhaled slowly as he gazed at the polished black bulb. It wasn't what he'd expected. The thing was as big as an eye, neatly cradled by the amulet's gold fixture. "The black pearl of Analetheia. Brought from the royal tomb itself." He stared at it for a moment, savouring the sight, then closed his eyes to centre himself, bracing against the voice's apparent excitement as its presence itched the hairs along the back of his neck.

"Do you know how a pearl comes to be, Yevhen?" Joram said as he opened his eyes and began to walk across the space. He came halfway and stopped, looking down on the ranger, awaiting an answer.

Yevhen offered him a dismal look. "No."

"They begin as sand. A small grain of sand – worthless, inconsequential – until by some happy accident it slips into the wrong place." He gestured, palm upturned, fingers twitching as he stepped forward. Yevhen obeyed and leaned from his seat, extending his hand to proffer the amulet. Joram took the jewel, inspecting it reverently. "Whilst it is in this wrong place – perhaps even *because* of it – the most miraculous thing happens. Over time, over many years, it is transformed, changed, turned from what was no more than a tiny irritant into something costly and precious…" He smiled at the pearl as it glinted dully in the shallow light from the lamp behind them. "And beautiful."

He collected the jewel in his other hand and pocketed it. When he looked down again the ranger was watching him carefully.

"Why so nervous, Yevhen? I have given my word. Your sister shall be well."

"Even so. The bargain… It's been a long time. You said so yourself. I've brought what you asked. I'd rest easier seeing you do as promised… sooner rather than later."

Joram considered the other man's pale silver-blue eyes, the straight and long gold hair. They were common features in this part of the world and yet, even after all the years Joram had been here, dwelling beyond the Reach, they still seemed strange and exotic to him. "Of course," he smiled again. "I understand. Come with me."

They went striding out into the rain as the lightning flashed again, the night blinking, turning the clouds silver and shiny and then gone again, shunted back to blackness like a slammed door as the thunder coughed its echo. Joram led the ranger up the sidesteps of the house to the upper room, walking hoodless to allow the rain to batter his face as the ranger followed behind with his cloak held fast around his ears. When they came to the door, Joram stood to one side, arm outstretched, smiling and extending his hand toward it. Yevhen squinted and huddled through into the upper room, out of the rain.

Much warmer here. An open stove cradled a small fire in the corner, the whole thing built into the wall and spouting upwards into a makeshift chimney. A narrow bed lay opposite. Yevhen looked to it instantly and saw his sister beneath the blanket, her face turned to the wall.

"The fever has worsened?"

Joram closed the door behind him. "A little."

"But not too much. You can still save her."

"Perhaps she doesn't *need* to be saved."

The ranger turned to look at Joram. Joram was looking back, expressionless. The ranger, puzzled, moved toward the bed. He could hear the gasping sticky wheeze of laboured breaths; a throaty, bedraggled whistle. The blankets were wet with sweat, the sodden prone heap beneath lay slumped against the wall. He came alongside the bed, to where his sister's narrow shoulders waited, sighing each breath with effort. He reached out and took hold of the blanket's hem and tugged it slowly back, and then again, pulling away the top of the cover.

Everything slowed.

"By my fathers…" he whispered.

"No," Joram said from the corner behind him. "By *the* Fathers actually."

The ranger, staring down at his sister as she rolled onto her back, didn't hear him, his attention frozen on her. The bedraggled and grotesquely thinned hair, her clammy scalp almost bald; her skin damp and pallid and riddled by a thousand tiny veins; her eyes, once so gentle, now bloodshot and skittish as she gazed up at him, reaching for him, and beneath her trembling extended arm, the taut round bulge of her gut, abnormally full and swollen and…

"What have you done to her?"

"Nothing that she didn't enjoy in the doing," Joram said. "It's only afterwards they have complaints."

The ranger turned and looked at him.

Joram shrugged, smiling mildly, then laughed. "Well I suppose now's as good a time to tell you as any isn't it; my little confession, let's say… You see, it was never *really* a fever, Yevhen."

The ranger felt his chest constrict. He straightened from the bed and turned fully, tugging a dagger from his sleeve. It wasn't until he'd pulled the blade wholly free and held it ready in his hand that he saw the change in the other man; that he was different somehow, his stance, the look on his face, staring back with a gaze too ancient and malevolent for the eyes that wore it. Yevhen gripped the blade tight in his hands and saw the shadows in the corner behind Joram seem to move and grow, like unfurling wings stretching out around him. It was then Joram smiled once more. A baleful, still and sickening smile, grinning out from those swelling shadows.

"I'm sorry, Yevhen," he said, still grinning, "but there was no choice. It was always going to have to be this way."

THREE

ORPHAN

Funny thing, hunger. That hollow niggle at the pit of your gut. The way it weighs down your bones, saps at your breath, sags in your soul like some invisible chain pulling at you from inside. Enough to ruin a man, Daneel thought. By the looks of him, the boy Noah seemed to agree. He sat there, knees hunched to his chest, his childish face sallow and glum as a frog's as he peered out through the night across the city square at the coming and going of the crowds, watching them idle around the market and ogle trinkets of ivory or copper or the fresh baked loaves on the stall table opposite. Understandable really. Probably feeling a little guilty, Daneel thought. Regretful maybe. That potential meal the boy had squandered a few nights before on the way here, when Daneel had woken from sleep to find him coaxing a pigeon down from a bough. Strange really. Had just stood there, the pigeon, less than an arm's length from the child, its little witless head flitting about at odd angles as if trying to hear a song. When Daneel whispered for Noah to get it, the boy's response had been so slow and clumsy you'd think he'd *tried* to let it escape. Kind of thing Daneel would have usually laughed about, but when you're managing to barely scrounge a meal every one or two days, a lost pigeon darkens your mood somewhat. They didn't speak for a while after that.

"You should talk to him."

Daneel started, glanced again at Noah, squatting next to him with his cloak draped over his head. "What?"

Noah turned to look up at him, slowly. The boy did everything slowly, his gaze cold as stone. "He's not going to move far from the bread. You should talk to him. Barter. I'll take the loaves when he's distracted."

That was the thing with Noah. Hardly spoke, but when he did it wasn't for nothing. Smart boy. A little unnerving, Daneel supposed, but smart. And besides, the unnerving part was understandable too. Daneel had helped kill Noah's father in front of him barely a month ago, hunting the man down along with his twin brother Josef on the road out of Hanesda before finishing him off by the shore of the Swift. Not the kind of thing it would go easy with a child to see. Not that Daneel had wanted it that way, which was why he'd turned, in a moment of madness, on Josef, his own brother, to rescue Noah, making himself a fugitive to keep the boy alive.

"Fine," Daneel murmured. "I'll talk to him. You wait until I have his back fully turned to you. Then you take the bread, nice and quick, as much of it as you can hold. Good?"

But the boy didn't answer, just did that thing of staring back in cold dumb insolence the way he often did. Daneel sighed and rose from the shadows to walk toward the baker's stall.

An old city, Çyriath. Very old. Oldest in Calapaar some said. Which Daneel supposed could be true, especially since Geled – a city thought to be of similar age – was now no more than a heap of rubble and scattered bricks somewhere to the north. With Çyriath it was the plainness that gave it away. How boringly featureless the whole place was. Well, with the exception of the Heads of Irsespedon – a palace-sized rock column with the three faces of that god carved into its sides, standing a half acre beyond the city walls where a sprawling cape of pebbly beach met the North Sea. Apart from that, the place was plain. Boring slate-cut houses and mud-coloured bricks and the damp-salt scent of the coastline drifting in from beyond the walls. Even the marketplace was boring, a small square of cobbled paving peppered with chaotically arranged stalls. No order here, not like Hanesda. Josef would hate it here, Daneel thought. Gods. *He* hated it here.

He stood up, pulling the collar of his cloak tight around his neck as he strode out across the paved square. It had rained earlier, leaving a thin grease over everything and making the cobbled ground gleam from the sheltered torches fixed to the walls.

"How much for a loaf?" Daneel called as he reached the stall.

The baker – a gaunt and ill-looking man – looked Daneel over before answering. "Forty shekras."

"Forty?"

The baker shrugged. "No grain from Geled. Prices go up."

"And everyone else starves?"

Again, the shrug. "Sent my man there two moons ago. Still hasn't come back." He nodded to the stall opposite. "Same with Farooq's grapes. Sumac. Cardamom. Almonds. Other things. None have arrived for weeks. Bandits, some say." The man shrugged again, evidently a habit. "What can you do?"

Which, Daneel decided, was a fair enough question. What *can* you do? What would anyone be able to do when they discovered the truth – that Geled was destroyed, and that some otherworldly force was responsible. Daneel thought back on the remembered sight of Salidor, a fellow Brother of the Shedaím, dying in the mud on a cold rainy night with wounds unlike anything he'd ever seen – lacerations, bone-deep gashes, bruised swollen limbs, one-eyed and bloody, gasping his last. "They're coming," Salidor had whispered to Daneel that night, his breath no more than a shallow wheeze. "Strange beasts… Dark beasts." Words that had since echoed to Daneel in his sleep.

"You alright?" the baker said, eyeing Daneel carefully. "You seem a little… Hey! Hey!"

Daneel turned around. Noah, by the stall, had evidently thought it a reasonable idea to stuff his mouth with half a loaf first, before filling his pockets with the rest while the baker spoke with Daneel. Which meant all hope of subtly exiting with neither the baker or, more importantly, any of the other stall owners any the wiser was now unlikely at best. Which meant Daneel was going to have to run, hungry and tired as he was.

He grabbed the baker from behind as the man turned to reach toward Noah, gripping him by the collar and shoving him face first across the table of his stall. The man slid sprawling across the woodtop and off the other end like a tossed doll. And then the other traders were shouting, moving towards them, beckoning to a pair of cityguards who'd come wandering from a sidestreet to investigate the commotion. Daneel snatched one of the loaves from Noah, who was now cradling several cakes of bread as he stared flat-footed and wide-eyed at the approaching mob.

"Come on! This way!" Daneel said, shoving the boy ahead of him through a gap in the stalls behind. They squirmed between the stanchions as the other traders began to follow, hurling abuse, stones and, ironically, one or two heads of cabbage and what looked like the severed leg and hoof of a pig. Daneel managed to grab one of the cabbages as it bounced on a stall ahead of him, before shoving aside an oldish man who tried to grab his shoulder.

"That way, away from the market."

Noah obeyed, sprinting ahead through a narrow street with cotton awnings stretched across it. They turned the corner and ran down the next alley, dancing around an old jewellery maker sat on a stool with her wares against the wall and tall pots of clay stacked in rows on the opposite side.

Daneel heard her yelp and curse as one of the pots toppled in their wake as they rushed by. Then he heard the clatter and roar of the chasing mob as they stampeded through the alley after them.

They scampered down a clutch of steps beneath a stone archway. Daneel limping now, his left calf beginning to cramp from lack of food and his breath hot in his lungs as the chalk-scribbled walls of the backstreet rushed by on either side. He glanced over his shoulder to find their pursuers and bumped into a passerby carrying a bowl of caraway seeds. They both went down, limbs tangled, bowl upended. Seeds everywhere.

The boy skidded to a stop ahead of him, then rushed back, grabbing Daneel by the forearm. Eyes wide with panic, the way they'd been back by the banks of the Crescent a month ago, watching as Daneel came stalking out of the water toward him like some demon from the sea.

Daneel fended him off and glanced back. The mob had gained on them. He climbed to his feet and pushed the boy ahead of him again. Beneath another archway and out into the South Square: a broad paved walkway hemmed in by high terraces on one side and the tall broad-windowed walls of the governor-house on the other. People everywhere.

A troop of young girls with baskets of pine-woven models – boats, miniature chairs, animals. An old woman with colourfully woven fabrics draped over her forearm, shouting their prices to passersby. Turbaned men dressed in white carrying rolled pages under their arms. The scent of pan-fried garlic and peppers assaulting the air as a sea of bodies lumbered about in every direction.

Daneel took Noah by the arm and started into the scrum, pushing his way through to the middle of the square, toward the sheepgate in the wall on the other side where they would crouch to squeeze their way out, when he heard it…

It was like something between a bear and a hawk. A long guttural and urgent screech. Loud and deep. A sound unlike anything he, or anyone else, had ever heard before. Everyone stopped, stilled to near silence by the cry. Their heads lifted almost as one toward it. And that's when the screaming started.

The young girls with the pine models had collapsed against a wall, gazes fixed upwards, baskets discarded, mouths agape, trembling. The turbaned clerics were chanting some sort of unintelligible prayer, heads in their hands and scrolls crunched in fists as they stared up in terror and awe at the thing descending out of the sky.

The babbling whimper of the man at Daneel's shoulder finally snapped his gaze away from it. He grabbed Noah again and began to yank the boy toward the fringes of the square. No reason. Moving to move.

And then it swooped down. Huge. Black. Vast wings. Needle teeth. Dagger sharp. Pincering around joint, bone and sinew in almost the same moment it landed. The brief shuddering tension in the squeeze, followed by the abrupt and sickening give as bone suddenly snapped and crunched and huge black lips peeled back in satisfaction, red with blood. The eyes were whiteless, black as a shark's. Vacant. Unseeing. Indifferent. Screams everywhere. Daneel watched as the thing swung its head, tossing the lifeless body of the man it had snatched when it landed. The body tumbled bonelessly through the air, limbs akimbo, drizzling the crowd with bloodspray as it flew overhead and slammed into a wall. The beast bellowed, jaws yawning, throat cavernous, its broad skull thrown back as though drinking the sky. Daneel had never seen anything like it. The head alone was the size of an outhouse. He watched in awe as it swung it to the side, scything the crowd and sending several cityguards flying in the opposite direction.

And then came the panic.

People squashed in against each other, fumbling and fighting to escape. Daneel saw the creature swing what might have been a claw. Stalls flung away like unwanted toys one or two stallkeepers with them, smacked head over heels through the air.

Still gripping Noah, Daneel yanked him beneath a row of parked grain carts by the wall, crawling beneath them along the side of the square. Women shrieking somewhere over the tumult. Another baleful roar from the beast. When Daneel looked back he saw a second of the creatures landing from the sky, hard to see in the dark, a riddle of bulk and teeth, wings glinting faintly in the torchlight. Cityguards were rounding on it, thrusting with torches and spears. Others scrambling to get away. Daneel saw a severed limb tossed skywards as he climbed out from beneath the cart on the other side, scrambling along the wall for a way out.

"This way!" he cried.

The small grated exit of the sheepgate across the square, barred by the rushing tide of fleeing people. A way out.

"No!" The boy. Afraid. "We should go back through the archway, into the streets."

"We'll be crushed. They're all trying to go that way."

A cityguard had somehow clambered atop one of the beasts' backs, was hacking down with a sword or knife. Daneel watched as the creature bucked, flicking the man off like an insect, then stamping down where he landed.

"Now, boy. We have to go now."

They ran out into the square, shoving through the torrent of frenzied traders and herdmen and street vendors whose wares of carved trinkets and fruits now lay scattered and crushed somewhere in the commotion. A blaze had started somehow, embers lifting from somewhere just beyond the second beast as it slammed its head against the wall of the governor-house, crumbling the brickwork.

An onrusher bumped against Daneel's shoulder, ripping the boy free from his grip.

"Noah!"

Daneel reached for him, then saw the wall of the governor-house beginning to lean and sway above them, crumbs of mortar and dust showering down.

The boy was on the ground, there, amid the rushing chop of legs and hips. Daneel ran in, reached down for him. Saw the boy reaching for him too. Arm outstretched. Fingertips away. An onrusher's knee smacked against Daneel's temple. He reeled, caught an elbow off another, and toppled.

Sea of stampeding shins and ankles around him. Dirt in his eyes. The scrum nudging his ribs as they tried to step across and around. A woman tripped headlong over his back as he tried to get up. He cast about, stumbling, woozy from the blow to the head. Cries from the throng. Screams. He looked up. Stones had shunted loose from the wall. It was going to fall. Was falling.

"Daneel!"

Noah at his shoulder, tugging at his arm, pulling him away.

They pushed free of the crowd. Danced around a dazed bearded man with blood streaming from his head. And ran, sprinting east, away from the archway where most of the crowd were shoving to flee the square, and toward the small narrow grate at the foot of the wall beneath the pillared colonnade as behind them the wall of the governor-house yielded to the black beast's pummelling. The creature slammed its skull against the base once more, then paced back as the wall gave. The boy turned and gawped as the pavilion began to collapse, people somehow still on it, screaming, falling into dust as the whole thing crumpled in on itself like a fast-shrivelling leaf and then abruptly dropped away.

There was a third creature now. Shadowed giants in the dark, ripping, charging, trampling. Coming closer.

Daneel reached the sheepgate. He grabbed the pulley of the heavy metal grating and heaved, hissing with the strain. Two-man job. He gripped the rope, wrapped it around his forearm as he braced his foot against the wall, and yanked again. The grating inched up, the hinge creaking.

The creatures were butting against the wall by the archway now. The boy turned to watch, saw the third grab a mother head first, her children fleeing ahead of her. It chomped down on the woman to the hip as it lifted her whole, fangs sinking into the flesh of her stomach, her head and shoulders buried deep into the beast's maw as her legs kicked impotently, desperately.

"Noah!"

The grate had lifted. Daneel straining at the rope with another man who'd joined to help. Noah looked back for the children. No longer there. Lost in the crowd, or worse.

"Hurry Noah!"

He turned back to Daneel, trembling, crouched and squirmed through the open gate on hands and knees. Others were following behind, pushing through the narrow opening. Noah climbed to his feet outside the wall and watched as they shoved their way through, waiting for Daneel. Waiting. Like the road out of Hanesda all over again, stuck on the shore, shivering from the river and waiting for

Father to climb from the waters and find a way to him. Lost. Alone. Waiting.

Others streamed through the grate, running off into the night once they were clear of it and scrambling down the damp dirt slope beyond the city wall into the nearby thickets.

Smoke was rising from the top of the wall now, the blaze inside growing thicker. The screams were like a song over the night. Daneel came scrambling out through the gate, turning to pull an old woman out behind him, covered in dust, headscarf dishevelled. Others were continuing to swarm out behind. Daneel bounced to his feet, panting, and gripped Noah by the shoulders, checking him over.

"You alright? You hurt? Come now. We've got to get out of here."

"What *are* those things?"

Daneel glanced back to the wall, the people trying to squeeze through the sheepgate to get out, the billows of smoke rising from the watchtowers above. The sounds of terror within.

"I don't know." He took Noah by the arm again, began moving him toward the thickets to follow the others. "And I don't want to find out."

FOUR

SOVEREIGN

Trust no one. Confidantes, friends, subjects, slaves – in the end they will all lie. Or die.

Sidon remembered the day his father, Helgon, told him this as a child, strolling through the royal gardens the day after new moon. Sidon had been distracted by the decorative debris strewn across the crown city's many monuments – coloured ribbons and chains of cidle leaves and daisies, garlanding Pularsi's Peak and the city forum as though tossed there by a giant unruly child. His father's words had been like those decorations to him back then – dramatic, flimsy, a little too colourful for Sidon's taste. But not now. Now Sidon pondered the old man's words like prophecy as he stared down at the clearing beneath him where the meeting had been set.

"Are you sure this is the place?" He tossed the question to the bodyguard at his shoulder as he gazed at the lush red bulbs of pomegranates gleaming from beneath the neatly groomed foliage in the summer sun below.

"If Yaron's man is to be believed," the bodyguard said.

Sidon turned to face him. Casimir was a large man – bulky round shoulders, thick arms, sturdy neck. The kind of man whose occupation lay open to any who saw him – there in the cords of muscle wrapped taut about his forearms like flesh-made rope, there in the thin creases of scar tissue along his knuckles and right elbow; there even in his laconic replies and the implacable stillness with which he held himself – all of it hanging off him like a banner flag telling any passerby of a history of blades and blood. The man's vigilant gaze reeled in from the grove to look at Sidon, who, appeased by his full attention, proceeded to unburden himself. "And is he to be believed?" he asked. "Could this stranger truly be a witness to what happened at Geled?"

Casimir shrugged. "Yaron can be a weasel of a man, but not when he himself is at stake. If he says this man has information about the city's destruction, I will believe him."

Sidon nodded, his eyes drifting to the younger Shedaím standing at Casimir's shoulder. The boy was tall. Lithe. Deep olive skin. An untidy flop of black hair partially obscured his dark eyes. Josef, General Gahíd had called him when he'd been introduced to Sidon, added to the royal retinue the week before to replace the now fallen Abda. "And what do you think, Josef?" Sidon said. "Gahíd tells me you are one of the few to have witnessed the city's ruins with your own eyes. Tell me, did the damage you saw seem like the kind of thing men could have survived?"

Josef regarded him gravely, as seemed to be his habit. "Anything is possible, Sharíf," he said quietly. "There's a chance there were survivors, but more likely there were not."

"Never one for optimism, is Josef," Casimir quipped. "A flaw of his nature. He's been known to spy shadows on the sun."

The younger man shrugged, looking out over the grove. "I see a thing as it is, is all. Men don't always like to do that."

"No," Sidon agreed, "they don't."

Word had come to him weeks ago, a rolled missive in a flute of snowcane, surreptitiously passed to one of the palace servants as he was bumped on his way through the bustling narrow aisles of the crown city's market – the promise of information, but for the Sharíf's ears only, messily scrawled across the rough page, along with the ominous message that had marked the bottom: I know what happened at Geled. Which would have been intriguing enough, but the fact that Geled's destruction was yet to be announced even to the sovereign council only made it more so, as did Sidon's desperate need to show himself a king worthy of his father's throne.

There'd been whisperings of dissent, rumours of opposition among the council, ever since the bedlam of Sidon's wedding night a month ago, when the slave girl – Iani, Arianna, whatever her name was – had revealed herself to be an assassin of the Shedaím Brotherhood and thrown the proceedings into disarray. In the end the whole thing had chased his betrothed – not to mention her family – away from any desire to be joined with the royal house. Throne or no throne, Sidon had been made to look a fool. Naïve, the people whispered of him now. Childish. Too immature to know friend from foe when an enemy of the Sovereignty was staring him stark in the face. But if he could meet this supposed witness of Geled's destruction, and discover the truth of who was responsible without Mother's help, perhaps they'd finally see he was more than just the secondborn son of Helgon, more than just a boy. Perhaps they'd see he could be a king in his own right.

"Sharíf? You alright?"

Sidon glanced at Casimir and nodded, "I'm fine."

"You sure?"

"Yes. Fine… Run me through the plan again."

Casimir sighed. "We wait until he arrives. Most likely through the yard gate to the east." The Brother gestured lazily, only half lifting his arm to point this time. Sidon had asked to be run through things three times already and Casimir, it was clear, wasn't a man accustomed to repeating himself. "He will go to the olive tree – there, beyond the clearing – and sit. Then you and I will go down to meet him, but circling in behind, by the wildflowers and down the lay-path to the west. There, on the other side." Again, the half-hearted attempt at a pointed finger. "Meanwhile Josef here will wait by the thickets along the rise with his bow."

"And you are good with your bow?" Sidon said, turning to the younger man.

Josef inclined his head.

"Gahíd says he is the most talented bowman of his sharím. No easy feat."

High praise indeed, especially coming from Casimir. Either he esteemed Josef highly or was simply growing tired of Sidon's questions and angling for a way to assure him.

Sidon's gaze slid back to the waiting grove and the knots of brierbush that hedged the clearing. The skies were mostly clear; a thin fringe of cloud waited toward the north, hovering above the shallow sink of land bordered by verges of forest on either side. A year ago Sidon would have counted it an easy place to grow fond of. Quiet. Still. Several miles north of the city. Away from everything. And Sidon liked the way the short stocky pomegranate trees lay arranged in those tidy rows, lines of bushy green over pale dust, glittering with the neat bright red of ripening fruit like new moon decorations.

"Someone is coming."

Sidon saw the man the same moment Casimir pointed him out, loping down the slope into the grove on muleback from the opposing treeline in a large tophood. They watched in silence as the man made his way through the narrow gaps lining the foliage and toward the olive tree that centred the grove, Sidon trying to quell the pangs of anxiety suddenly running through him as the man approached. Maybe agreeing to meet had been a little rash after all, especially without Mother. Spiteful as she often was, she'd always known how to handle things like this, and Sidon just wasn't used to keeping secrets from her.

"He's armed," Casimir drawled lazily. "Suppose he'd be a fool not to be." He nodded approvingly to Josef who was already flexing his bowstring before taking it in hand and walking away along the bluff.

"Ready, Sharíf?" Casimir said.

Sidon inhaled deeply, then after a pause looked up at Casimir again. "Yes. Yes, I'm ready."

"Well, alright. Let's go."

They traipsed down the verge, out of the thickets of the forest behind and into the grove. The neatly aligned rows of trees cast hard shadows across the dirt as they passed along their ranks. The quiet felt thick, the gentle wash of the breeze the only song. Ahead, the olive tree's thick foliage peeped above the aisle of bushes as if patiently watching their approach.

"We are nearly there," Casimir murmured as he went slowly ahead of him, leading him along the row until they eventually came to the final bush before the olive tree, rounding it in careful deliberate steps to meet what awaited on the other side.

And there they found him.

The man sat beneath the tree's shade, hunched, elbows on knees atop a short mound where the tree's thick roots and trunk had pushed up the ground. He was facing toward the north as they approached from the west, gazing at the horizon of even-heighted bushes stretching for half a mile in that direction.

Sidon almost didn't notice the subtle way Casimir positioned himself, a pace or two in front of him and almost blocking Sidon's view, as he slowed his pace and lightened his steps, rolling his feet over the dry grit beneath. They were within a boat's length before the man – his entire head caped in the large tophood – turned to see them and rose to his feet, bringing Casimir and Sidon to a halt.

He didn't move. Just stared at them. He was clothed in a plain, baggy smock, belted at the waist where his blade hung. Leather-thonged sandals and scabby, dust-caked feet. Skinny ankles. His face narrow and gaunt.

"You are Sífan?" Sidon asked, then retrieved the letter from within his coat and held it up. "The one who wrote this?"

The man's gaze flicked nervously from Casimir to Sidon before settling on his answer. "Yes… I am."

"So… you are a survivor of what befell Geled. There are not many of you."

"Not many, sire. No."

"Your letter said you wanted to speak with the Sharíf himself."

The man nodded uncertainly.

"Well, I am he," Sidon said. "See?" Sidon took the ruby ring from his signet finger, the one Mother had given him after his anointing just over a year and a half ago, and tossed it carefully to the man. The ring plopped harmlessly in the dust a foot away from the stranger, causing Casimir to visibly stiffen. Allowing the man to touch the ring wasn't something they'd discussed. The sovereign signet was a singular jewel, embossed with the crest of Sidon's line and imbued with the authority of the Five Lands. Its stone made laws.

They watched as the man, Sífan, squatted down, keeping his eyes on them as he pawed around the dusty soil to collect the ring and stand again. He eyed it carefully, turning it this way and that, examining the jewel and the emblem cut there, the gold glinting from the stray shards of light slipping through the olive tree's canopy above him.

"I want you to tell us what you were witness to," Sidon said. "At Geled. What happened there? Who is the enemy?"

The man, so startled he almost dropped the ring, clutched it in his palm and then tossed it back, under hand, landing it in the dirt by Sidon's feet.

Sidon picked it up and returned it to his finger. "Tell us. What did you see?"

"I saw that men cannot fight with gods," Sífan said.

"What?"

"It is not our place. And we cannot do it. They devour everything. Destroy everything. They will take—"

The javelin came from nowhere, suddenly burying itself in the left side of the man's chest as though having materialised out of thin air. Sidon flinched at the sickening bone-slamming thud. Watched the hooded man tossed backwards, almost off his feet, and crashed against the trunk of the tree behind as blood plumed around his shoulder. And then Sidon was abruptly on the ground, chin in the dirt, shoved there by Casimir who was whirling around with his blade out, trying to find who'd thrown the spear.

He craned his neck toward the slope behind them and saw the

figure in the distance, off toward the south where Casimir was scanning the horizon, running between the olive saplings along the high ground shadowed against the coming dusk. Sidon thrashed around, trying to get up. The figure in the distance seemed to be trying to flank them, circle around, which meant there was probably another one of–

A man leapt out from behind the bush beside them at a dead sprint, knee first, smashing into Casimir's chest before the Brother could swing his sword. Sidon watched as they went down, Casimir's blade skittling free across the dirt. The figure – hooded, face covered – rolled with the momentum and got on top.

"Run, Sharíf!" Casimir shouted, as the assailant bore down on him with a blade of his own.

Sidon scrambled. The figure on the horizon couldn't be seen now, probably heading toward him through the immaculately arrayed rows of greenery. Sidon looked to the speared man, pinned to the tree and still breathing, staring back at him now, his hand extended, gasping for breath as he strained to push out words.

"Run!" Casimir repeated.

Sidon glanced about. Looked back to Casimir. Blood. The assailant's dagger lodged in the Brother's collar, the attacker pressing down on the pommel as Casimir struggled to hit and shove him off.

"Run, Sidon!"

So Sidon, finally, did. He headed east through the grove, back toward the verge of thickets and greenery bordering it from that end, pomegranate trees rushing by on either side as he ran through the corridor of pale dirt between.

He could hear the skid of rapid footfalls in the dirt behind him, and snapped his head around to look. Saw the attacker there, maybe the second one too, knees and arms pumping madly to chase him down.

Sidon scrambled up the verge to reach the treeline. He could hear the relentless breaths of his pursuer now. Hear him nearing, gaining on him as the royal drape of Sidon's linen shift cumbered his strides. He stumbled as he reached the summit, almost going down, palming the ground to steady himself as he continued to sprint beyond the thickets and into the brief wood to get away. Gnarled junipers stretched out ahead of him over the lumpy earth, their branches barring the sky. Sidon weaved and ducked beneath a low-hanging bough, then hurdled a tree root as he rushed toward where the wood thinned to reach the horses and–

A sudden dull thud of weight against his ankle swatted out his stride. And then Sidon was falling, tumbling headlong toward the dirt with his hands out to brace himself. He hit hard, palms scraped on grit, sliding in the forest's rubbly dried soil as he went down. He rolled onto his back, mildly dazed, looking up at the looming height of trees as they stretched away toward the sky. And then the attacker was there, standing over him and blocking out the light, a shadowed shape against the bright blue overhead. For a moment the figure didn't move, as though savouring the moment and allowing himself to recover some of his breath. And then, face shrouded by his own silhouette and the wrap of cloth that covered it, he reached up and drew the shortsword from the sleeve on his back.

"Unfortunate, I know," the man said. "But some tales are not meant to be told." He took the weapon and hefted it. Sidon closed his eyes and imagined the blade stabbing down, thrusting hot white pain through his gut or throat. He could almost feel the warmth of his own blood as the cold metal cut in to cleave at tissue and bone. He could even hear the coughed gurgle of his imagined choking, how he'd gag on his blood the way he'd seen men do at the duelling games he'd witnessed as a child before Father put an end to them. And someone *was* gagging, but it wasn't him… He opened his eyes. The man was still standing there, immobile, the long shaft of an arrow protruding from his rag-covered face. The man seemed to look down on him for a moment before slowly collapsing sideways to the ground as the young, lithe Brother, Josef, came into view.

"Come, Sharíf. Come quickly."

He yanked Sidon up by the collar from behind and helped him to his feet as Sidon continued to stare at the fallen attacker lying prone in the dirt.

"Come, Sharíf."

Sidon looked beyond the dead man, saw the second attacker running toward them along the treeline in the distance, and obeyed.

They hurried through the forest, Sidon limping from the weapon his dead pursuer had thrown to trip him. The wood was sparser here, the trees younger, trunks of slim timber barely a man's height and clearing to the arid slopes of an open plain, dotted here and there with tamarisk trees and the odd Karirar – and there, by the watering pool, the young sycamore where they'd tied the horses.

Josef reached it first and then turned to ready his bow, shouldering out of the bowstring and planting down in the dust to set the arrow in one smooth motion.

"On the horse," he commanded as Sidon reached him.

The Sharíf obeyed, clambering into his saddle as Josef stood poised with the longbow.

"Leave," Josef said.

"No. Not without you."

Josef looked at him.

"We've seen two," Sidon explained. "There could be others out in the plains."

Josef nodded, unset from his stance and unsheathed his sword as he approached Casimir's horse instead. "Forgive me," he murmured, petting it softly, then placed his palm on the long broad neck, felt the warm blood pulsing beneath, and took his sword and thrust it hard and up beneath the jaw, crunching through cartilage and bone into the skull. The horse squealed briefly, the sound abruptly cutting off as it stomped and spasmed, before collapsing against the tree, forelegs twitching.

Josef yanked the sword out and put it away, and then returned to his horse and clambered up into the saddle, wiping the bloodspray from his face as Sidon stared at him. Josef nodded behind to the second attacker emerging on foot from the forest. "So, he cannot follow," he said, then yanked at the reins, turning his horse away and toward the city. "Come, Sharíf. Time to leave."

Sidon turned his horse too. Looked down on Casimir's mare

slumped against the sycamore, its eyes rolled upwards and its weight bending the young trunk as blood pooled on the gritty earth. Then he looked back at the attacker, standing at the edge of the woodland watching him. They were beyond the range of a longbow now, and too far to chase on foot. The man's own horse was probably tethered somewhere on the western side of the grove. Sidon saw that his hood had been removed in his rush to catch them, revealing a dark headkerchief, the same colour as the wrap covering his face. He continued to watch him as they turned their horses and began to trot away – the man standing stock still with his feet square as he recovered his breath, staring after them as they rode up onto the road and toward the crown city.

FIVE

JUDGEMENT

It's said Talagmagon built the ziggurat to commemorate the death of her brother, Markúth, when he drowned trying to wrestle a whale in the Summer Sea. Upon finding Markúth's body drifting down the Serpent, Talagmagon took it and burnt the flesh, burying the bones inland and building the ziggurat over the grave with fifty giant stones she tore from a quarry two days south of the burial site.

Neythan listened to the story, drifting in and out of consciousness and vaguely wondering how Markúth had found grievance with a whale in the first place, though the answer may have been at the beginning of the tale. He couldn't quite remember. His head hurt. And the woman's parched voice was growing agitated and jittery as she spoke.

He blinked awake to find himself in some kind of broad wall-less pavilion. White-stone pillars stood in each corner supporting a patterned ceiling whilst the wide gaps between them lay open to an evening sky, stars dotting the expanse like scattered seeds.

"You're awake. Good. That is good."

Sulari's dark face came into view, eclipsing the ceiling where images of an over-sized man swimming with a giant fish sprawled across the pale stonework encircled by floral patterns. "You fell," she said. Her voice was slow and hoarse, wrung out, as though she'd been weeping or screaming for hours, or days. "You are unwell. But the priests will soon be here. They will help you."

Neythan was warm, and cold. The room seemed to be swaying gently beneath him. The air felt too close. "Where am I? Where is Filani?"

"Filani?" Sulari's nostrils flared with contempt as she mopped Neythan's brow with a rag. "Why should you ask of her?"

He tried to answer but his ribs felt tight. The woman's hands went to his shoulders as he tried to sit up, warding him down.

"You must rest. They will be here soon. Let them see to you first."

"I must find Filani."

Sulari stopped mopping his brow. "That woman is not your friend."

He glanced up at her. "And you are? Tell me where she is. What have you done with her?"

"You should not trust what you think you know of her. You should not trust anything she has told you. She is not who you think she is."

"What do you mean, who I *think* she is?"

She was about to answer when another woman entered the pavilion followed by two men, rising from beyond the floor's purview as though from out of water as they stepped up onto the canopied platform clad in similar garments to Sulari's, blue-dyed shifts and smocks with yellow yarn stitching. The woman wore a narrow plaited wig that covered the top and back of her shaven scalp like a horse's mane. Inked patterns marked the sides of her hairless skull, a row of white dots across her brow, whilst loops of gold and small spikes of painted wood dangled from either ear like the keepsakes they'd seen on the streets outside.

She shrugged her chin at Neythan. "So, this is him."

Sulari stepped back from the couch where Neythan lay. "Yes. This is him."

The woman tilted her head curiously as she approached, coming to stand over Neythan as Sulari had whilst Neythan just stared back at her, taking her in; the narrow jut of the wig, the curious and haughty slant of her head evoking, to his mind, a prying and insistent cockerel.

Her skin was rust-coloured, lighter than Sulari's and covered by intricate patterns along both forearms and the backs of her hands, like those Yulaan would sometimes draw on herself back in Ilysia after harvest. Which was strange to see on this woman; the boldness of her features, the thickness of her lips, the accent to her speech: all Súnamite. Not Livian. Not like Yulaan.

"There is no way to tell what he is or isn't," she said finally, staring down on Neythan as one of the men who'd accompanied her also huddled in to observe. The man looked Neythan over carefully as he lay there, examining his broad shoulders and slim muscled frame. He was seemingly fascinated, from what Neythan could tell, initially by his skin – the heritage of his mixed blood – a deep olive that had been darkened further by the Summerland sun; and then the man seemed to be drawn by Neythan's face – the cool hazel eyes, the wide thickened lips, even his dark and slightly kinked shiny hair.

"Maríba will say different," the man said.

"Maríba is old, and dangerously sentimental."

"And high priest," the man added.

"Yes. I had not forgotten."

"You hadn't? A shame. It would explain many things."

The woman sucked her teeth and flipped a palm at the air as the man turned to face Sulari.

"Maríba is on his way, Sul. You must decide what you want to do."

With his ribs still feeling tight, Neythan coughed, the sound tugging Sulari toward him again with the cloth to dab his brow. She paused to look down on him as he lay there, feverish, and then nodded to herself as she watched him shiver. "I want to try," she whispered, then glanced up at the man. "I want to try, Iqran."

"Where are my friends?" Neythan managed.

The man, Iqran, looked down on Neythan, adjusting his colourfully patterned robe where it draped over his shoulder and scratching at the grains of silver stubble on his jaw, bright against his dark lustrous skin like tiny flecks of frost. "They are safe," he said finally. "In truth, you are likely to be with them soon."

"You think Maríba will really send them?" Sulari asked.

"I do," Iqran said, turning back to the older woman. "If you insist on it, I doubt he will refuse you. Still, I will speak for you also, unwise though I think this is."

"Thank you, Iqran."

The man passed his hand through the air in a self-deprecating gesture as he turned and moved away, and then motioned to Neythan. "Come. See for yourself."

Neythan, still confused, glanced to Sulari, who smiled and nodded, then to the cockerel-wigged woman standing by the pillar opposite, who offered no more than a blank stare in response. So Neythan levered his feet gingerly from the bed to the floor, a pale matrix of stone tiles, and pushed himself up to stand, following Iqran to the edge of the wall-less pavilion to lean on one of the pattern-carved columns that propped up the corner.

"Look," Iqran said. "See."

Beyond the floor Neythan could see the streets of Jaffra sprawled out far below in every direction. Shrunken straw-roofed tenements huddled together beneath the sway of palm trees in the starlit gloom. By his feet the sheer drop of the whitewashed stone tower wall stretched down to the torch-lit level beneath, and beyond that, a further broader level; the whole structure built like a narrow and blocky pyramid. And there at the base, a group of Súnamites, small as ants from this vantage point, standing by a small hut.

"That is where your friends are," Iqran said. "For now, at least. What happens to them, and you, will be decided in the next hour."

"Just as it was decided concerning Filani? What you all did to her out there in the street… Why? I want to know why."

The cockerel-wigged woman scoffed. "And I want to go home and have someone rub my shoulders as I sip palm wine, but there will not be time for that either."

Iqran, smacking his lips disapprovingly, turned toward her. "Kishani. Please. This is not the time."

"Actually, yes," she answered, continuing to stare down into the broad square beneath. "Yes, it is."

Neythan followed her gaze. A crowd was entering the square from beyond the terraces, a small tide of torchflames moving along the alley that barred the grounds of the ziggurat. A hundred people, maybe more. Hard to tell from this distance in the dark. Neythan, instinctively, reached for his blade at his hip, clutching at air.

"Maríba is here," Iqran said, turning around to face the others.

The other blue-clad man hurried to the opposite edge of the pavilion and began to descend.

Neythan remained where he was, leaning against the pillar, watching as the crowd neared the outhouse Iqran had drawn his attention to a moment before. Some of them approached the hut, opened the door and ushered the occupants out into the night. Neythan watched three figures exit and amble into the darkness, wrists bound together. A man came forward from the crowd and seemed to adjust the bindings, then walked away as the prisoners followed, tugged along by ropes down an adjoining street.

"Where are they taking them?"

"Do not worry yourself, Neythan," Kishani said. "They will be fine. Most likely."

Neythan turned to face her. The woman, her finger stroking the cursive line of one of the patterns on her forearm, just gave him a thin smile, then walked away, back toward the edge of the pavilion. She reached the first steps and turned, looking at Neythan over her shoulder. "Well… are you coming or not?"

They all walked down the tall blocky steps of the ziggurat together to the level beneath before following the rust-skinned Kishani inside the structure to descend the rest of the way to street level. They moved across the square into the adjoining lane the crowd had gone down, and then on through a series of backstreets. The city seemed different now, the bustling trade of earlier replaced by an eerie quiet – a maze of empty alleys and looming terraces, rising up on either side of the narrow roads like unmanned watchtowers as the walls' pale stonework glowed mutedly in the moonlight. Neythan, beginning to feel better, found himself examining the stonework as he walked, the vivid murals they'd seen earlier rendered colourless by the night, ghosting across the adobe walls like shadows.

"This place is twice as old as your crown city," Kishani said, again glancing at Neythan over her shoulder as she led on. "That is our strength. We know the history that made us."

"You think the Sovereignty doesn't?"

"How can it? You *murdered* your history. Killed the priests. So you could forget your beginnings and pretend at some other story; one without the things that made *you*."

"And you think killing old women in the street is better?"

She snorted. "Nothing here will make sense to your foreign eyes. And you *are* foreign, no matter what tales others here may try to tell you. Besides, Filani is not dead. And if she were, even that would be too kind a thing."

"Why?"

"Because she is an *mgbejime*."

"A what?"

"Enough," Iqran said. "We're nearing the gates."

The priestess, Kishani, continued to march on ahead whilst Iqran and Sulari brought up the rear. As they rounded the next corner the noise of a crowd somewhere began to swell, muted jeers and shouts and the rapid patter of drums ringing vaguely on the air as they turned west into another street. The roads here were slightly broader, and less empty. Old men sat decked in scraggly cotton shifts on doorsteps or leant up against walls, smoking lingerweed and gazing blankly into the small hours as the light from lamps licked at their sinewy rimpled features. Once or twice Neythan spied faces in windows, the glinting whites of moonlit eyes staring out at him and the rest of the party as they passed by.

"There are some here claiming you are Shedaím," Iqran said, coming alongside Neythan.

Neythan glanced at the black man. "You know of the Brotherhood?"

"What your Sovereignty calls rumour or myth, we here count only mystery, a truth lying in the shadows, waiting to be brought to light. You could say belief in the Shedaím is not as uncommon a thing here as in your Sovereignty. Our fathers passed down tales of the things done by your Brotherhood in the time of Sharíf Tsaruth, when your Five Lands tried to invade ours. *Mbakuv*, they call you in the old tongue: Those who walk with shadows, and spill blood."

"Almost poetic."

Iqran looked at him. "I suppose. In a way."

"Makes a change," Neythan said. "To be known, I mean. Something the Brotherhood isn't used to. Not a thing we welcome."

"My people say, nothing known is known truly. And nothing unknown is truly unknown."

"More poetry."

"Perhaps. But there *is* something I *would* like to know. You are yet to ask about the scroll you brought here. A thing like that... there are some in this city who will count it a precious thing, perhaps seek to take it from you."

Neythan glanced sidelong at him. "They're welcome to try."

The man smiled. "You think you will stop them, but you do not know this city, Neythan."

Neythan shrugged. By now the scroll had become to him a token of the things he'd lost along the way. There'd been nights during the journey south that he'd watched the stars alone, sitting atop the Havilah's pale barren sands with the scroll in his lap, repeatedly running his fingers across the mystifying scripts that marked the page for nothing more than the sheer feel of it against his skin. Family, Brotherhood, home – they were all gone now, all that remained was that strange ancient book and the secrets it held: the promised means to explain it all, and perhaps save the Sovereignty from what the Watcher had promised would come. Neythan glanced over his shoulder at Iqran, too tired to explain or lie. "The scroll belongs to me," he said simply. "I went through a great deal to claim it. The hour someone here decides it should not be returned to my hand is likely the hour that both they *and* I die, because I will kill as many people in this city as I can, beginning with those who've made the choice to take it from me."

Iqran apparently had no answer to that, so just slowed his pace to fall back to the rear as Neythan returned his attention to the road ahead and the swelling noise of the nearing crowd. Kishani peered back at Neythan once more like the butt of a joke he didn't understand as a shout erupted from somewhere up ahead. She gestured languidly, nodding toward a bend in the street with a thin derisive smile as she led them around the corner toward the gathering din on the other side.

A broad square. People everywhere, ivory horns to their lips, blaring guttural groans into the night whilst others waved lamps and improvised torchflames in noisy chaotic protest. The crowd was facing away from Neythan and toward something or someone he couldn't see, beyond the riled jostle of heads and arms. The blue-clad attendant who'd rushed from the pavilion ahead of them was standing on some kind of makeshift plinth above and toward the rear of the gathering. He saw Iqran signalling to him and waved back, then took a deep blast on the horn hanging from his leather shoulder strap to quieten the crowd.

"Come," Iqran said, tapping Neythan on the arm. "Follow me."

As they moved forward, shouldering their way through the crowd, Neythan could feel every eye on him, sullen gazes turning to track his path as he made his way through the mob to the clearing beneath the gates. He stumbled out on the other side, shoved the last step by some of the crowd, and found himself before what appeared to be some kind of judiciary. Two men, one woman. Seated in broad wooden chairs. Waiting.

"So. You are the one." The old man, his voice high and gentle, was sitting in the middle with an encompassing bright white turban swaddled around his neck and chin to cover the whole of his head and frame his dark shiny face. He leaned back in his chair, prodding at his gums with a chewstick as he appraised Neythan.

"You must be Maríba," Neythan said.

"I am," the old man drawled scratchily. "And you are brought here that we may come to understand some important questions." The man turned to those seated with him and gestured.

"To be honest, I see no likeness," the woman sitting beside him said.

"And yet Sulari insists it's there," Iqran replied, appearing at Neythan's shoulder. "And as the closest living relative, it is her eye we must trust more than any others."

"That would be true were those 'others' strangers, Iqran," the woman answered. "But I knew Mbiké well. As did Maríba… and grief, it can do many things to the memory given time. Forgive me, Sulari."

Sulari, standing beside Iqran, made a placatory gesture and nodded back.

"There was no comfort for what you suffered," the woman continued from her seat. "No salve. Not then. Let us not prolong this suffering by thinking there is now. This boy is nothing to do with you."

"Filani insists he is," Iqran said, inserting himself once more.

"Filani? You will bring her name before us?"

"Only to say she has made claims concerning him. And Sulari believes her. Grief or not, Sulari is a singer of our songs. How many years have her intercessions kept our crops healthy? How many famines averted by her offerings?"

Some in the crowd murmured assent, tapping rods against stone in a sort of quiet thudding applause.

"These years she has served Jaffra," Iqran continued, "she has known only this one longing, Maríba. She never imagined it could be met. Perhaps Ishmar smiles on her now, for the devotion she has shown to her, and us. Perhaps this boy is brought here as a gift, a healing balm to Sulari's sorrow. Should it be for us to stand against the will of gods?"

Maríba roused a little. "We will not presume to know which god wants what just yet, Iqran. Nonetheless… I have heard you…"

The woman sitting beside the high priest almost swivelled on her seat. "Maríba?"

"I do not say I agree. Only that I have heard him…" He worked the chewstick against a corner in his mouth, eyes still on Neythan, before signalling lazily to a nearby guard.

Neythan watched as Arianna, Nyomi and Caleb were ushered forward and led to the front, standing before the elders with Neythan, making him feel even more as if they were defendants at a trial.

"There is only one way to determine the truth of your sister's claim, Sulari," Maríba said. "Only one true way."

"Yes, Maríba."

"If the boy does, as Filani says, have the eyes, then there will be reason to think he is who you believe him to be."

"Maríba," the woman beside him had turned to the elder once more. "If you think to involve the Sayensí—"

"We will have no dealing with them," Maríba confirmed, and then returned his attention to Sulari. "But *he* will. The boy will go there, along with the book he has brought. Do you understand what I am saying, Sulari? Are you certain this is your wish?"

Sulari's voice was almost a croak. "If it be Ishmar's will, the boy will return. He will be brought back to me."

Maríba studied Sulari a moment longer, and then nodded. "Then may it be as you have said." His eyes switched to Neythan. "You will choose two of your companions to go with you. The other will remain here as guarantee."

"Go with me where?"

"Choose."

Neythan just stood there as the high priest chomped idly on his chewstick, staring coolly back, the silence thickening in the wake of his words. So Neythan glanced to Arianna, who seemed mildly disgruntled, standing with her wrists bound in front of her beside Caleb, whose demeanour appeared more or less the same. Beside them, Nyomi was staring back at him like a wall, her gaze as blank and inscrutable as ever – waiting; watching, just like the formerly riled up crowd quietly observing it all, as though possessors of some hidden stake in whatever Neythan was going to say next.

Glancing at Sulari at his shoulder, her eyes still reddened from tears no one had yet deigned to clearly explain, Neythan turned again to Maríba to speak. "How is it she knew my father's and uncle's names?" he asked.

It was enough to move Maríba to raise an eyebrow and remove his chewstick. "I see... Well... If you do as you have been bid, and go to the Sayensí, and return having read from the scroll you came here with, then you will have earned your answers, and shall have them. But be warned, we will know if you lie when you return. We will know if you have truly read, or not..." Maríba slowly replaced his chewstick. "Now..." the old man announced, waving his hand casually in the direction of Neythan's companions. "Choose."

Caleb and Arianna were both looking at him now, waiting for what would come next like everyone else. He glanced at Nyomi beside them – a woman, even now, who remained little more than a stranger and a mystery. The whole journey to Súnam she'd hardly spoken, murmuring occasionally with Filani but otherwise keeping her words perfunctory and brief – *there is the smell of rain on the air. This is a good place to make camp.* Caleb had tried several times to goad her into conversation – her favourite foods, her feeling on returning to her homeland, what customs they ought to expect when they arrive – before concluding her slow-witted or half mute. They were weeks into the journey before Neythan heard her say anything beyond noting the hours of sunlight left in the day or the position of the stars.

Neythan watched her closely now, the slim muscled forearms, the lightly wrinkled chestnut skin, the narrow face and blank unyielding gaze. Over half a month travelling here together and he still knew almost nothing about this woman, but something about the way she was looking at him now, a sort of still knowingness, as though this moment was something she'd been waiting for.

"Choose," the high priest repeated.

Neythan lifted his arm to point. "I choose Arianna," he said. His gaze darted once more to Caleb – whose eyes lifted to meet his – then back to this stranger who was Filani's niece. "And I choose Nyomi," Neythan said.

"*What?*"

"I will come back for you, Caleb."

"You're going to leave me here?"

"I will come back."

"Neythan, what are you doing?" Arianna said, as the guardsmen took Caleb by the arms and began to pull him away.

"We will come back, Caleb."

But Neythan saw only shock and doubt in the little man's eyes as the guardsmen dragged him back, his heels skidding in the dirt as they took him away.

SIX

BLOODLINE

"I mean, ask yourself. Don't you ever get to feeling, well, I don't know... Like maybe it's time to let go of all that – what shall we call it – *weight?* Father says this, Father says that. Your father's not a god, after all. And he clearly doesn't understand you like I do."

Joram handed the girl another cup of Marin's special brew and smiled. The girl, still uncertain, contemplated the drink like a divine missive, before eventually taking it from his hand and sipping.

"Oh, come now, you're barely tasting it. Beauty like yours deserves to have its fill. Of all things."

She drank more heartily, tipping her head back. She was a pretty girl for a Kivite, all milky pale skin and light freckles, and a thick dance of golden-red hair. Slender shoulders, a little bony, as were everyone's in the Reach, the irremissible price of the barren lands they'd been born into.

Joram deftly hooked his finger into the fold of her twill smock as she emptied the cup, tugging the collar down her shoulder and letting his finger trace the length of her arm. It was always the way for him here Marin would say, and Joram couldn't deny he had the truth of it – his tan skin, his dark hair and lashes, longer than was typical for a boy's, and then there was the liquid hazel eyes too, all making for an alluring and exotic mix, at least to the mousy-haired, pale-skinned inhabitants of the Reach. He imagined it from the girl's perspective, the way his eyes would be glinting tigerishly in the firelight cast by the casket flame sitting on the small table beside them in the tent. The way the warm glow would be bronzing his youthful skin, polishing it with a burnished sheen so smooth that even the most stoic of maidens' breath wouldn't be able to help but catch, like the girl's now did as he moved his hand to cup her breast.

"You see?" he murmured softly. "Wasn't so hard, was it? And don't you feel so much better?"

She nodded slavishly, sighing as he leaned in, allowing his breath to brush her ear. She'd acquiesce now, to the softness of Marin's rug beneath them, the balmy warmth of the air trapped within the thick skins of Marin's tent, the dry, tart smell of the wine. He saw her eyes close as their lips touched, the girl letting go, tipping into herself, yielding to the surroundings and his touch and the strobic play of the firelight against the tent's goatskin walls as he–

"Joram!"

Typical. Joram sighed heavily as Marin burst into the tent, panting. "We've found the perfect one. Perfect this time. Truly."

Peeling his attention reluctantly away from the girl, Joram turned, glaring disdainfully at the interruption as Marin just stood there, dumbly taking up space, looking gleefully at Joram as though brimming with secrets to the meaning of life itself.

"I mean it, Joram. Perfect."

"Marin, you say that every time. You said it last night when I and Isandra here were getting to know one another. You said it last week when we were by Irses' Peak trading with those goatherders on the way back from Bataar. And then several times during last new moon, twice when I was *very* busy. As I am now, come to think of it."

"But the thing is, this time–"

"Out, Marin."

"But Joram–"

"Out."

Marin lingered awkwardly by the tent's entrance for a moment, filling the opening with his broad slumped shoulders and wide gut before eventually turning sheepishly around to walk away.

Joram just shook his head, sighed, then turned to the girl. "Sorry about that…" he reached out to cradle her face. "Now, where were we?" He leaned in and kissed her fully this time, showing her how. She was, if she'd been telling the truth, only two years younger than him at sixteen, but with the life Joram had lived, those two years may as well have been decades. Twelve years here among the Kivites, banished by his own father to dwell among a people who stubbornly refused to build houses or villages or cities, and who instead roamed the largely barren breadths of their ugly scarred lands herding their meagre numbers of cattle or goat or sheep. Such an exhausting and pointless way to live, Joram had always thought, forever beholden to the whims of the season and the paltry pastures that sprouted from Kiv's cold and clayey earth. There were days he thought of going back south of the Reach, just for the sake of somewhere more habitable to live, and forgetting his hopes of becoming chieftain and raising an army to reclaim the Five Lands' throne that had been stolen from him as a child. But those days were fleeting, buried by memories of that last night in Hanesda – being yanked screaming from his bed like a thief and tossed into a walled carriage, before watching his father, Helgon, stand by the city gates like some kind of stranger, receding into nothing as the cart's wheels rolled Joram north along the grim rubbly road and into the night, away from everything and everyone he'd ever called home.

"Go with Marin," the voice whispered, tickling at the nape of Joram's neck as he tasted the girl. "You have the pearl now," it continued. "Everything is possible."

Which was also true. He pushed Isandra from him gently and sat back. The girl stared at him, flushed and blinking.

"Did I do something wrong?"

"No. Nothing. It's not you, it's…" Joram flinched at the absurdity of his feeling the need to explain. "I have to go," he said simply, and then rose to his feet, tugging the collar of his skins back across his chest as he went to the door of the tent, and then stepped out into the cool dark.

Outside was twilit, leaving a gentle blue-green reef over the horizon to the west, out beyond the glow of the tribe's campfires. They'd been camped here for nearly a week now, the herdmen making the most of the pastures by the Kivite borderlands before the season turned, and making the most of the craggy shelters offered by the Seat of Saramak too – a broad and exalted stone plateau at the edge of the world, filled with caves and tunnels and marking the southernmost brink of the Reach.

To the north the Sahadi range spread for miles – great copperstone peaks, capped here and there by batches of green on the rocky inclines too steep for goats to graze. To the south, empty grassplains rolled away to the Wetlands and then, beyond them, the northernmost outskirts of the Sovereignty, and beyond that, the still smouldering ashen rubble that used to be the city of Geled. Which was something Joram hadn't expected – for the smoke to still be there, nearly a moon since the city's destruction. On a clear day you could just catch the vague edges of smog, a tiny smoking pillar in the distance, lifting from the ruin as though from a logger's campfire. Soon he would see it for himself – the ruins the voice had told him of in his dreams – just as everyone would if Marin's claim, this time, turned out to be true.

Joram found him sitting with Djuri and Ola by their campfire, sulking, as Marin was sometimes prone to do. He perched on a small stool, his wide bearish shoulders hunched up to his ears and his vast back, as he faced away from Joram, bending toward the warmth.

"You well, Joram?" Djuri said, glancing up as Joram arrived. "You've an ill look."

Joram sat down by the campfire next to Marin, lifting his palms to the flames.

"Don't alarm yourself, Djuri," Ola said, smiling. "It's his way. Ill as a fish is Joram, shivers in summer, with never a day you don't think him feverish. After a while you grow used to it."

"The beggar calls his scraps a meal," Joram replied. "And you people call five days without rain, summer."

"You see that?" Ola said, leaning toward Djuri sitting next to her as she chewed a piece of dry bread. "That's how you can tell he's salty. Always starts with the riddles and sayings when he's salty, doesn't he."

"You know, I noticed that. Salty or hungry. Always one or the other."

Ignoring them, Joram turned to Marin, flicking the big man's shoulder. "Well? I'm here, like you wanted. So, where's the man you spoke of?"

"Oh, so *now* you've time for us? Now that you've had your fun with the girl?"

"Come, Marin. It's cold. And I can see you want to tell me."

Marin grunted, not bothering to turn from the fire, refusing to answer even though Joram could see he was bursting to, doing that thing he often did whenever nervous or excited – of bouncing his thick knees in a rapid rhythm as he sat there and tried to hold it in. Ola, sitting opposite by the fire and leaning back with her feet propped on a whetstone, spread her hands in disavowal as Joram's gaze swung back toward her.

"Don't look at me," she said. "I was the one told him to wait till you came out from the tent."

"You were, Ola," Djuri put in. "But too excited, wasn't he."

"He was. Too excited." She glanced back to Joram. "But I *will* say with good reason from what I can tell. Marin pointed the man out to me earlier. From what I could see he was carrying the mark."

"You're sure?" Joram said.

"As I can be." She took the mug Djuri, beside her, had offered without looking and swigged. "How's it work anyway, Joram? Seems so simple when you do it. You touch a man, whisper some words, and then just like that he's yours, obeys you like a child."

"Better than a child."

"Yeah, that's what I meant."

"Spooky if you ask me," Djuri said. "Unnatural."

Which was typical of him. Cautious about everything, unlike the ever-curious Ola sitting next to him.

"You touch them first, Joram," she asked, "or do your funny whisper?"

"It's the whisper, I think," Djuri offered. "Did the same to Kareena, probably. Why she doesn't mind being laid up in his tent while he borrows Marin's and works his way through every girl in the clan. How far along is Kareena now anyway? Five months? Six?" He leaned away as he caught Joram's look, mirroring the same open-palmed gesture of innocence Ola had thrown up a moment before. "I'm just asking is all, Joram."

Joram glanced to Ola. "Perhaps if we were to find a suitable man, as Marin here claims to have done, I'd show you how it works. Or perhaps Marin here realises he made a mistake, and failed to find a suitable man after all, but doesn't want it to be known."

"I *didn't* fail," Marin protested.

"Then show me. Show me the man. Show me his priestmark."

"That's the other thing," Ola said. "Why's it only work on priests?"

"You're not helping, Ola."

"You're the one promised to teach me."

"If you helped me get into Magadar."

"I'm here, aren't I? I'm helping."

"You call this helping?"

"Moral support," she quipped, taking another bite of her bread. "And besides, I still don't get this whole Magadar thing. I mean, let's say you manage to get in there, even with those bare arms of yours; now, let's be true about the thing – you're not exactly the greatest fighter, Joram. And Uruq, well, he's an animal when he puts hands on a man. You find a way in there he'll just take that scrawny neck of yours and snap it in two."

"I appreciate the vote of confidence."

Ola swallowed her morsel of bread, flicking back her boyish flop of hair as it fell into her eyes. "What friends are for."

"Well, *friend*, how about you persuade Marin here to move things along – you know, actually *help*, like you promised. Perhaps you'll see for yourself how I'll beat Uruq and become chieftain."

Ola thought about it, twirling a finger through the drab brown strands of hair near her neck, and then she shrugged and leaned toward Marin sitting opposite her by the fire.

By the time they reached the pit most of the herdmen were already drunk, cheering and singing songs as they watched the wrestling contests in the makeshift arena they'd arranged themselves around in a clearing of dirt and shrubs further in from the cliffside.

Joram had wrestled too as a boy, just as every Kivite had, only it had gone harder for him because of his darker skin. He could still remember how people would throw things at him from the crowd, lazily tossing rotten vegetables when they were in a jovial mood, knee-buckling rocks when they weren't. Not that it had mattered; with no family of his own, the wrestling contests had been the only way to earn his first ink markings, of which he now had several, covering his right shoulder and the beginnings of his upper arm – a wolf for the time he'd beaten the firstborn son of Uruq, the chieftain of Shurapeth, to earn admittance to the tribe. Then there was his moon for his win at a summer new moon gathering a year later, when tribes from other parts of the Reach had come together to pit their men and boys against each other for sport and trade. There'd been several lesser victories after that, marked by the neat geometric lines radiating from the moon on his shoulder like rays of light, and then, by his wrist, a small and mysterious ink mark he'd had for as long as he could remember: just five small dots, equidistant from each other, marking the angles of an invisible pentagon just beneath the base of his thumb. It was the only mark he wasn't able to remember when or how he'd gotten it. But then Joram's memory had always been sketchy even at the best of times, and besides, his markings were meagre pickings anyway, and in no way impressive when compared to Marin's.

As he often did, Joram stared enviously at the brute's ink as the big man walked ahead of him through the scrum, leading the way. It was almost sickening really, the way Marin's markings covered both arms like sleeves, leading from his hands all the way up to his untidy and frizzled beard to record his many victories along with the story of his blood. Among the tribesmen of the Reach, Marin's was an old and illustrious line. As a child, most of his right arm had already been covered, tracing a history of victories before he'd ever set foot in his first contest – there, at the top of his shoulder: fights won by his father and grandfather, then lower down around the thick meat of his upper arm, a waterhole his great grandfather had discovered during a drought to preserve the tribe. By his elbow, a battle between rival tribes an earlier forefather had helped to win, claiming good pasture during a time of famine; all of it sketched out across Marin's skin like an elaborate tapestry to commemorate the exploits of his blood from start to end.

It irked Joram sometimes to look at them, knowing the rich history of the lineage he'd been divorced from, and knowing how utterly redundant it all was here in the Reach. No Kivite would be inclined to believe that he – a brown-skinned beggar who'd managed to somehow make himself more – could be rightful heir to the Five Lands Sovereignty to the south. Which was just as well. Anyone who did would have cause to slit his throat on sight. But that, if all went as planned, would change soon. Soon everything would be different.

The men on the fringes of the crowd glanced at Marin's height and the markings on his arms and allowed him through, parting as he led Joram, Ola and Djuri to the front to watch the contest. There were men here from Pelag, Joram noticed. Red-haired and white skinned, paler even than those of Shurapeth. And there, standing by an untidily erected shelter of cowskins and thatching on the far side, some men of Bataar from the western Reach, probably here to barter with Chieftain Uruq, as many often did, for access to the metal mines beneath the Seat of Saramak's cliff.

Joram tapped Marin on the arm. "You see him?"

"He'll be around here somewhere," Marin said, scanning the

gathering. "Shouldn't be too hard to spot. He was big like; the way we wanted."

"And you're sure he had a priest's mark."

"Sure as sure can be. It was that winged one you showed me once, with the coin that looks like an eye, and those funny patterns around it."

"The sigil of Armaros? You're certain?"

"Yeah, that one. Looked that way. But it was small like." He lifted his thumb and forefinger to demonstrate.

"They all are," Djuri remarked. "No one really follows gods anymore do they? Best to leave skin for other things." He then leaned in toward Joram's ear, whispering, "We sure we want to do this, Jorry? Now? Here?"

Joram glanced aside to consider him – the slim hawkish nose, the narrow bony jaw, the inquiring eyes peering out from beneath the white-gold fringe of his hair, watching Joram carefully, as was his habit with everyone. Always careful, Djuri. Like the hunter he was. "You losing your water, Dju?"

"Uruq won't be happy, if he discovers us."

"And if we succeed, and I am able to enter Magadar, what Uruq is or isn't won't matter much will it. Nothing will matter then."

"So you say."

"So I know."

"It's a risk is all."

"Heat makes the blade, Djuri. Can't have one without the other."

"See?" Ola said, nudging Djuri's elbow. "The sayings again. Like I said. Salty."

Djuri held Joram's gaze for a long moment before he finally acquiesced. "Alright then. If you're sure…" He nodded, pointing with his eyes beyond the far side of the circle. "I think that's Marin's man there, across the clearing, standing by the cookfire with a mace."

Joram followed Djuri's gaze. "Keen-eyed as ever, Dju." He nudged Marin beside him and nodded toward the man. Marin smiled to confirm. "Well, alright then," Joram said, and began to work his way through the crowd of jeering, shouting spectators that lined the clearing of dirt the men were continuing to grapple in.

The man, nearly as big as Marin, stood before a barrelled cookfire, his shoulders hidden beneath the thick white pelt of a snowfox to mark his origins – a tribesman of Gabbai, a son of the Northern Reach – leaving no way for Joram to check the man's sigils for himself. He greeted Joram with a dead-eyed mix of boredom and scorn as he approached, jutting his chin questioningly.

Gesturing to Marin at his shoulder, Joram smiled. "My man here tells me you're quite the wrestler."

The man acknowledged Marin with a nod, eyeing the ink on his arms. "I'm not doing any more tonight," he said. "I've had three already, and the gambling's low now. But if your man wants it, he can have it tomorrow. If his clan's name is good it'll be best to wait anyway, make an occasion of it. I've an old name myself. Be a treat for the people, two old clans this far out from winter." He favoured them with another nod to send them on their way, which was polite at least, happy at the prospect of a prize worth having. So Joram stepped in and decided to return the courtesy.

"You misunderstand. I wasn't asking for good Marin here. I'd like to wrestle you myself."

The brute's dull eyes darkened, staring down on Joram as though he'd just asked for his mother's hand. "You?"

"I understand your being scared. Who'd want to lose to a man half his size in front of this many people?"

The man glanced to his companions, then to Ola, Djuri and Marin standing behind Joram, and then broke into abrupt laughter, long and hard, his companions with him, guffawing so hard spittle began to lodge in their beards. And so Joram decided to laugh too, joining with them. It was a pleasant evening after all, a little cool for his taste, as they always were in the Reach, but pleasant.

"You had me, little man, I'll give you that. Had me good. Clever one, bringing your man here over with you to set it up. Clever."

Joram nodded, waiting for the man and his companions to recover before stepping closer. "Is that a no then?"

The man squinted, then waved him off. "You carry on back to

where you came over from, little man, before you overstep with your wit there. It's easily done."

And finally, the voice stirred, its sibilant whisper brushing along the hairs of Joram's neck like a warm feather – it was excited, he could tell. Alert. To the point Joram almost became distracted by the sheer thrill of it, the voice of a fallen god fizzing along the nerves within him. "Son of a dead whore," it murmured eagerly.

Which, looking the man over, Joram didn't find hard to believe; so he smiled, no need for coarseness after all. Truths can be as sharp and damning without it, and the man, as things go, hadn't been all that rude. Not yet. "So, I hear you were the son of a whore," Joram said gently, "which is why I understand your worry. Makes sense you'd be itchy about being shamed in a contest."

"What did you say?"

"I said–"

"Joram, perhaps–"

Joram shrugged Djuri's hand from his shoulder, his eyes still on the man. He was just being honest after all. Polite and honest. "–I said I'm sympathetic. I can see how your being the son of a whore might make you a little fragile about being shamed in a contest by me."

Joram heard the breath go out of Djuri behind him like something deflating.

Opposite him, the big northerner's face had drained of colour, sick with rage, glaring across the warm light of the cookfire.

"He's hard of hearing perhaps?" Joram added, glancing to the man's companions as though they'd have an answer. "Can happen, I'm told. All that rubbing on the ears when grappling, bound to damage something."

Marin was moving forward as the man came around the fire's barrel, bringing him to a halt with a gentle bump of his palm against the chest. "A contest is all he wants."

The man looked past him to Joram, who was still smiling as he stood calmly out of reach, no longer bothering to pretend he wasn't enjoying the man's ire.

"A contest the little rat wants," the man growled. "A contest he'll have."

The man stalked away, stripping off almost immediately, yanking his furs from his shoulders and tossing them to the side. He strode toward the clearing of dirt, shoving his way through the crowd whilst a match between two younger skinny boys was still going on. He pushed the youngsters aside and turned to the gathering.

"New contest," he announced, then pointed to Joram waiting on the fringes. Men sidled out of the way of his pointing finger like parting drapes to reveal Joram, standing there like a waiting aide in some mocked-up drama, gazing serenely back. He shouldered his way out of the beaverskin coat he'd gambled off a Pelagite last month, then pulled the woven shift beneath it over his head to reveal his torso. He watched as the crowd's gaze weighed him from the fringes, appraising his narrow chest, his meagre waist, the relatively bare arms with their sparse inkings.

"Oren, he's just a kid," someone said.

"The boy says he wants a scrap," the man boomed. "We're having a scrap. Set your wagers."

The man who'd protested nodded timidly and waved Joram into the ring before turning to the crowd to take the bets.

"The sigil," the voice intoned. Joram could feel its presence within him now, thrumming comfortingly between his shoulder blades, soft and warm and busy, like wingbeats trapped in his spine. "Touch the sigil once," it whispered, "and with a still sha, and it shall be done. He'll be yours."

Joram was nodding, eyeing the small coin of an eye on the man's upper arm as the announcer set them in their places, positioning them opposite one another in the middle of the dirt-floor arena. Joram could smell the stink of the other man's breath now, and the stale waft of his sweat as he towered over him, glowering down with so much hatred that Joram, for a moment, wondered whether the poor man was going to choke.

"Breathe, Oren," Joram smirked, "it's a much-underrated thing, you know. Calms the soul, lightens the senses."

And that was enough. The man dispensed with the decencies and shoved the announcer out of the way, taking hold of Joram by the throat and lifting him bodily from the ground, legs kicking. And then it was mayhem, Marin and Djuri rushing in, other men racing forward on the upended announcer's behalf, others on behalf of the transgressed ritual itself, whilst others still came for the pure thrill of the fight, punching and kicking and grabbing and grappling as somewhere in amongst the melee, as fists swung and noses bloodied and men screamed, Joram managed to work the knuckle of his forefinger onto the big man's arm and press against the ancient priestly sigil of his clan, stilling his sha amid the chaos as men tussled and stamped and cried out around him. He pressed the knuckle in, felt the man's sha slacken within, felt him yield to his touch like the click of a lock, and knew that he'd be his now – half awake, half asleep, and as obedient as a slave, just as the voice had promised. Just like all the ones before.

SEVEN

REGENT

"So, Casimir is dead. That's what you're telling me."

Sidon just stared at his mother across the table. "Actually, what I was telling you is I was attacked barely three miles from the city walls, by men from who knows where, sent for reasons we have no idea of. *And* Casimir is dead."

They were sitting, at his mother's insistence, opposite one another by a frontage in Hanesda's oldtown – what used to be, in the days of Sharíf Karel, Hanesda proper. Not that Sidon cared. This wasn't a part of the city he particularly liked. Open gutters running along the sides of some of the alleys. Aged whitewash peeling away from sun-dried bricks like diseased skin. Across the street part of the old city wall still stood, ringing the district off from the rest of the city that had since built up around it, as though to keep the whole place caged in the past – not unlike Mother.

"Another Brother of the Shedaím gone," she muttered, her fingers working agitatedly around the smooth brass ball in her hand as though trying to rob it of its shine. "And for what, Sidon? Your pride? All these secrets you keep now… Meeting strangers in groves without me? It isn't right."

Sidon allowed the words to wash over him as he stared at the greying adobe opposite. The walls were marked by scribbles of chalk and the remnants of mocking, ink-drawn likenesses of a jilted Sharíf. If he stared hard enough, he could still make out the shadowed outlines of the shoddily drawn images – Sidon falling from a rostrum at the push of a dainty servant girl; Sidon weeping with his face on the Sharífa's shoulder. The lines were faint and smudged now, scrubbed off by guards in a futile attempt to erase the notorious night of a wedding that never was.

Sidon shifted uncomfortably on his seat and regarded the queen mother as she sat across from him – her dark blue shawl, set back an inch from her hairline to show the chained diadem of gold coin tassels that hung there. The immaculately placed hem of her garment, sweeping its fringe across her elegantly poised shoulder like a regal Haránite sash. No accident she'd insisted on their meeting here, he thought as he looked her over. No, with Mother, everything was always just so.

"So how was Qareb?" he said.

The Sharífa tutted dismissively, waving a heavily jewelled hand. "Don't change the subject, Sidon. You know how that bores me. You didn't tell me about the meeting. I want to know why."

"You were in Qareb. I am Sharíf. You can hardly expect me to wait on your presence every time I have to make a decision."

"A wise Sharíf *waits* for counsel."

"Now you sound like Father."

"If only someone would. Especially now."

"And what's that supposed to mean? *Especially now.*"

The brass ball clicked against her fingernails as she tapped it, knocking out a rapid rhythm. "Oh, don't pretend, Sidon. It's never suited you. You know as well as I what's said of you. There are those among the council who question whether you are able to even sit on the throne."

"Curious that they should feel so free to share these grievances with the Sharíf's mother."

"Would you rather they shared them only among themselves?"

Sidon sighed and looked away, toward the street. They were

sitting by a cobbled broadway opposite a row of apothecaries and dye-makers, old women coming and going, stirring their coloured solutions in clay vats and flapping cloths against the air to ward off the smell. The whole street reeked of mingled sewage and the sharp vinegary scent of the dyes, and yet Mother just *had* to meet here, all so Sidon, he now realised, would be forced to look upon the ghosts of the poorly disguised drawings on the wall and be reminded of his disgrace. "What else do they whisper?"

The Sharífa nodded to herself, pleased he appeared to be laying his sensitivities aside to at least deal with the matter at hand. "Some ask of my position," she said casually, "say a more formal arrangement should be reached."

"A more formal arrangement…"

"Well. You know it's tradition for the queen mother to act as regent until the Sharíf finds a wife…" Sidon cocked an eyebrow: the stiff way she was using their titles, as though she was discussing strangers they hardly knew. "But it is only a tradition," she went on as Sidon leaned back in his seat, waiting for the blow she was clearly preparing to deliver, "not a law. But now, with what happened with the wife that was arranged for you… well…"

Sidon smiled coldly. "So, you want to be *enshrined* as regent."

"Not I, my son. Although, when the idea was put to me, I did ponder it, I was ready to discard the notion out of hand, but now, with all this… The secrets, the irresponsibility. You are young, Sidon. It's not fair for so much to be asked of you. Only natural there will be errors of judgement from time to time. But with what happened at the wedding… things are… *delicate* now, among the council. We must steer carefully."

"And you want to… *help* me steer."

Chalise inclined her head. "As you put it before. Your father always said counsel is the strength of any throne."

"Could be he'd have changed his mind on that one, maybe picked health instead."

"You think this is funny?"

"No, Mother. I don't think any of this is funny."

"Then let me *help* you."

Sidon didn't answer, just looked away again, back toward the street and the old women. Some were sitting on stools now, mashing their pestles into the coloured solutions to mix the garments around in the vat.

His mother sighed heavily. "It's her I blame, you know."

"Who?"

"*Her*... before you allowed that ratty slavegirl to come between us things were fine."

"That's not quite how I'd remember it."

"Well, I don't *remember* you arranging to meet strange men beyond the safety of the city walls before *she* came along."

"And I don't remember you being more attentive to a little miscommunication than the fact of my *life* being threatened and those responsible remaining uncaught."

"So *that's* what this is about? Can you really be so *naïve*, Sidon? You are Sharíf. Your life will *always* be threatened. You're not supposed to make the job easier by meeting people you don't know in places you can't be properly protected."

"The man was a witness to Geled. He was going to tell us what happened, share what he'd seen. And then just as he was about to, the attackers showed up. At that very moment, no less. As though they didn't want for me to learn what he had to say—"

"Oh, don't you see it was a *trap*, Sidon, to lure you from the city. He *had* nothing to say. And you, like a child, fell straight into it. And now another of the Shedaím is needlessly dead. We have only a few of them left, Sidon. You know that. Gahíd told you that."

"And that's the other thing, to have overcome a Shedaím in single combat. Who can do that?"

"You see? You and these wild conspiracies. This is exactly why you need my help. It was a trap, Sidon. Nothing more."

"But if it was a trap, who set it?"

"The same people who destroyed Geled for all we know. Or maybe spies from Súnam, or the Reach, or hired hands from across the West Sea. The throne of the Five Lands is not beloved by everyone." She leaned across the table toward him, voice low. "The Sovereignty was built on the blood and bones of men, Sidon. Order carved from lawlessness by a vision born of the blood that runs through *your* veins. Now, will you spill it so needlessly, for childish conspiracies and an unwillingness to hear reason? You have no wife, Sidon. You have no heir. No siblings. Don't you see that one stray arrow could overturn what has taken centuries to build, cast the Sovereignty back into confusion and war? And for what? So you can meet a man you do not know in a grove of pomegranates, to hear him say things he will have no proof of anyway?" She leaned back again, her eyes still on him, and sighed heavily. "I know you think me… a little overbearing, inflexible perhaps."

Sidon snorted sarcastically, it was all he could do not to laugh.

"But it is only because I am able to see how fragile things are," she pressed on, tapping her brass ball against the table to enunciate her point, "how fragile the throne is. *Your* throne. I am trying to protect you, Sidon. I'm trying to protect your future."

She let him stew silently on the words as he continued to insolently avoid her gaze, staring in the general direction of the old women opposite, but really at nothing in particular.

When she saw his silence was unlikely to relent, she rose to her feet to leave. "You are my son, Sidon," she said softly, adjusting her garment as she made a small hand signal to the guards waiting by the entrance alley to escort her back to the palace. "You are the only son I have left."

Sidon was still thinking about what she had said later that evening as he stood in a corner of the main municipal hall, watching as the crowd bustled and swirled around him. The memorial gatherings held here were things he'd learned to both loathe and love. Years ago, before he was made Sharíf, he'd enjoy the subtle floral aroma wafting in through the windows from the gardens outside. Or gaze at the exotically patterned tapestry that clothed the towering walls. He'd shake the hands of obscure dignitaries whose obsequious smiles were a little too polished and introductions a tad too grandiose; all while the thinly disguised politicking and jockeying of the gathered delegates went, by him, wilfully unnoticed.

But not now. Not tonight.

Not after the ignominy of the last month following the aborted wedding. Or after his life being threatened mere days before in the city groves. And not after the patronising talk with Mother and her failure to comfort or commiserate with him, or barely even show concern that he'd managed to dodge his own death.

So instead he just stood there, listening to the soft insouciant play of the minstrel's strings, wishing the delicate music was loud enough to drown out the chatter and contrived laughter of the attendees who filled the vast and extravagant space. There was Kamal, the crown scribe, with his quick fussy glances and slim lips, and that fastidiously neat beard that looked like something one of the handmaids had painted along his thick flabby jaw. And there, by Arvan's Pillar – Queen Satyana of the house of Halak, leaning against the ancient chalk-pale column as though she owned it, as if it was no more than some pretty and oversized frippery to add to her salon in Hikramesh. Governors, obscure dignitaries, old royalty, merchants, all crowding the space like clucking hens. Sidon was simply tired of it all, standing here amongst a lively throng of the haughty elite, feeling dead and alone.

"So, did you ask her?"

Sidon looked around to find Elias, his chamberlain, now hovering at his elbow like a sudden conjurer's trick.

"Yes," Sidon murmured, turning back to face the crowd. "I asked her."

"And?"

He shrugged. "She seemed more interested in the fact I didn't tell her of the meeting."

"She did not ask further about the attack? For details?"

"Not really. No."

"That is interesting…" The man drew in nearer, the tanned pate of his bald head hovering at shoulder height. "Very interesting… I know this is difficult, Sharíf. Impossibly difficult. But you must consider the possibility that she herself was involved."

"*What?*" Sidon looked at him.

Elias stared back, expressionless.

"She's my *mother*, Elias."

The chamberlain lowered his head in deference. "I understand, Majesty. But she would not be the first to count the throne of greater worth than blood."

"Would not killing her last remaining heir jeopardise the throne further?"

"Perhaps. But these things are never as simple as they seem. Karel the Young, as you know, executed his queen during the Cull."

"That was different."

"Of course, Sharíf. Forgive me. I will say only that I've noticed the Sharífa to be a woman of many secrets and few qualms. Even now, you can look and see that she is not here. A summer solstice, guests gathered from as far west as Tresán and as far east as Kaloom, and at a delicate time for your throne, Sharíf. And yet no queen mother?"

Sidon surveyed the room and saw he was right. "Where is she?"

"I will say only that your servant did observe her passing along the east gallery toward her bedchambers, with another, to take counsel it seemed... I see that your uncle, Prince Játhon, also fails to be present?"

Sidon turned and looked at the old man as if he'd just vomited at his feet.

Elias merely bowed. "But perhaps you are right, Sharíf. Likely there is nothing to fear. There'd be no harm in your going to speak with them, see why they are unable to attend. It may be one is ill, or there is some other sensible reason that detains them... both."

Sidon said nothing, staring at the old man until he bowed once more and withdrew. Ridiculous of Elias to even suggest it. Mother involved in an attempt on his life? He turned back to observe the smiling, drinking gatherers and decided to remain for a while, watching the delegates.

He even made the occasional attempt at conversation before considering he'd rather not be there anyway; what harm would there be in going to his mother's bedchamber? Perhaps they'd talk, make amends. Could be he'd been unfair with her earlier. Like she'd said, he was her only remaining son after all.

Sidon took two goblets of wine and passed along the gallery adjoining the hall, past the hanging baskets of lilies adorning the narrow shield-shaped windows that ran along the broad passage. He turned the corner into a quieter space, then pressed on the second brick from the window's paved sill and watched as the wall hinged open to admit him. Apparently, the palace was riddled with them, these secret passages and tunnels built into the walls, allowing the Sharíf private entry and escape from almost every part of the building – yet another secret Elias had shown him and Mother had not. He exited into the mosaic-floored vestibule on the palace's south side and then went up the stairway there. He'd greet Mother and Uncle Játhon warmly he thought, then call for more wine to be brought to them in her bedchamber, a gathering just for them, just for family. He was framing the words in his mind as he rounded the corner leading to her door, and then stepped in, passing into the high-ceilinged antechamber that came before her room whilst her guards, standing further along the corridor, continued to face away to the centre stairway.

Sidon could hear his mother's voice now, muffled by the walls of the bedroom and the closed door, but agitated; lecturing. Sidon slowed, wary of entering in on her mood. Should've had a servant bring the drinks for him, he thought. That way there'd be a goblet for all three of them. Mother could be fussy about the slightest things when riled, and less welcoming of interruptions. Sidon thought about going back out, commanding one of the guards to bring more wine, but then decided against it. Best to wait, see if Mother calms first before bothering with any of it. He edged toward the inner door and leaned against the jamb, trying to listen.

"I cannot just demand for her not to touch the ornaments, Chalise." Uncle Játhon's voice – frustrated yet quiet, as though straining not to shout.

"Why not? She is *your* wife," Mother snapped.

"She is also queen of Harán."

"An empty title if ever there was one."

"You did not say that when you insisted on my marrying her."

"And why does she have to fondle everything anyway? Those grubby fingers of hers. Makes me itch thinking of them, smearing the marblework. It's an ill habit, you know. She does it with everything – You. The palace. Even Elias."

"This again."

"What? Are you saying you *haven't* noticed it? The old man whispers with everyone."

"Honestly, I think you're being paranoid."

"And I think you're being complacent."

Sidon heard one of them get up, moving to another part of the room, for a moment obscuring their speech with the gentle thud of their steps.

"And Elias is just a decrepit old man," Játhon eventually resumed.

"I'm not saying he isn't. I'm just saying there's something about him at the moment."

"So, basically you're having trust issues. Well. So unlike you, of course."

"He is up to something."

"Well, of course he is. You've *put* him up to something. Come to think of it you've put many people up to many things. Persuading governors, bribing others. Oh, and of course, the small matter of killing your own husband, who happened to be the ruler of the Five Lands."

Sidon's breath stopped. He stumbled back a pace from the door, trying to understand what he'd just heard. He exhaled shakily, the fingers of his left hand seemed to involuntarily slacken, allowing the goblet to drop from his grasp. Time slowed, the wine turning in the vessel to spill as it began to fall toward the floor like the drop of a moulting petal until–

Another hand suddenly shifted into view, catching the goblet, as an arm snaked around Sidon's mouth and jaw to pull him back against the wall.

Sidon tried to swat at the arm and push free as he turned to find… Josef? The young Shedaím put a finger to his lips as he let him go, still holding Sidon's safely caught drink. Footsteps were coming from inside, approaching the doorway and vestibule to investigate the scuffle. The Brother pivoted and shoved Sidon into the coffer by the door, stooping to wipe wine from the floor with his trousered knee before stepping in to follow the Sharíf out of sight.

"What was it?" Mother called out from within the bedchamber.

"Nothing," Játhon answered, apparently now peering out from the bedchamber's door, "just as I said…" The sounds of his footfalls receded again, drifting back into the bedchamber. "Monkeys probably."

Sidon and Josef waited in the confines of the coffer a few more moments, pressed up against each other, until Josef finally opened the door and stepped out. He gestured to Sidon to follow, leading him silently away from the Sharífa's bedchambers and out onto a broad tiled pavilion on the palace's west side to avoid the guards.

"By all the gods, what do you think you're doing?" Sidon blurted.

The Brother regarded him coolly. "I'm sworn to protect you."

"By manhandling me like some kind of puppeteered doll?"

Josef didn't answer.

Sidon began to pace the balcony, shaking, he noticed, his uncle's words echoing in his mind, through his veins, down his spine. *The small matter of killing your husband, who happened to be the ruler of the Five Lands.* Sidon staggered toward the balustrade and leaned there, staring out at the night as images of his dead father drifted up into his thoughts like dislodged debris from a sunken boat – Father's bony long body laid out on the sickbed, the frail emaciated flesh, the gaunt face, those hollow lost eyes staring out to Sidon like an elderly stranger in the last days before he died. *Could Mother really have done that? How? Why?*

"They'd have heard you," Josef said, moving up to the balustrade to come alongside him, "then found you there, listening at the door. So yes, Majesty, I manhandled you. I am sworn to protect you at all times."

"Did you hear?" Sidon cleared his throat, trying to shift the tremor from his voice. "Did you hear my uncle's words, what he said?"

Josef hesitated, then nodded.

"He said my mother murdered my father," Sidon said redundantly. "How can that be?" He turned to face Josef and saw no answer there, and so turned back to the night instead, trying to steady his breathing and make sense of it all. *Mother had killed Father? Why? Why would she? Gods... Was Elias right? Had she also tried to have him, the Sharif of the Five Lands, her own son, killed in the grove beyond the city wall? Was that by her hand too?* He felt as though the balcony was slowly spinning beneath him. The night seemed suddenly colder, alien somehow, as though the lamplit streets he'd looked upon a thousand times before now belonged to another city, another place.

"You may not be safe here," Josef said, still standing beside him, cutting into the growing frenzy in his thoughts as he continued to lean against the balustrade. "I am sworn to protect you, Majesty," Josef insisted. "Only you... I do not think there are any in this city you should trust."

EIGHT

REMEMBRANCE

Luann's brows were spiky and dark, like whiskers, and appeared even darker when they angled in like that, staring at Noah. It reminded him of Mother, her forehead tugged taut and urgent as if by some overzealous tanner, and her dark elliptic eyes still as a cat's. He sighed.

"I don't know. I can't remember."

Luann exhaled in commiseration. She was a year younger than him though to Noah, with her primness, her small sensible voice, had always seemed as though she ought to be a year older. She gave a consoling blink and dipped her head in sympathy.

"We'll try again," she answered. "It was Sharif Kaldan, Kaldan the Protector. He built the Straight Road south from Calpas in the eighteenth year of his reign."

"I thought that was Sharif Helgon."

"No. Helgon the Wise built the trade routes of the north and the Valley Pass."

Noah nodded glumly.

"Many confuse the two though, it's an easy mistake."

If only it was. Luann in her calm precocity had passed the First Judgement two years before. This was Noah's third year of trying. "It took me three tries," his father had told him following his last failed attempt. "And my father, it took him four," though Noah had found that hard to believe. His father's father, Nalaam of Hophir, had died when Noah was still young, but even so he could still recall his quick wit and spry manner, a mind sharper than flint and far too clever to need four attempts at the First Judgement. It was he, after all, who'd brokered the accord between Dumea and Hanesda, writing the tenets to govern their unwieldy alliance and ensure Dumea's survival at the price of his own kingship – it was just about the only part of the histories Noah was able to remember well, and that only because his father had told him this story of Dumea's Last King so many times he didn't need to read it. Noah didn't like reading, which was why he'd thought having his friend Luann speak the histories to him would make them easier to learn.

"Do you remember what else Sharíf Kaldan built?" she said.

Noah looked at her blankly.

Luann gave a slow insistent nod, willing him on. "Think of the name by which he is known," she said.

"The Quiet."

"The other name."

"Kaldan the Protector?"

Luann nodded again.

Noah thought about it. "The Black Wall?"

"Yes, the Wall. And why might he have built it?"

"It was built to protect the north border of Hardeny."

"Yes, and the Iron Valley, but why, from who?"

"Calapaar."

Luann smiled. "Yes. And so you see what that would mean?"

But Noah didn't. He looked off across the green to contemplate. It was getting dark. They were sitting on a rise of ground not far from the Southways Well outside the city walls. They'd have to return soon. Mother never liked Noah to remain too late. Something she'd chided him for more than once. He'd a habit of sitting here, lingering in the bronzed light of the lowering sun as the air cooled and the farmers and herdmen came in from their roams. He'd stay for hours some days, just sitting and watching and talking with his pigeons as they purred, soft *and cautious, that dainty coo that seemed to vibrate from somewhere delicate deep inside, each one graceful and unique. His favourite, Timu, with that small round head and short slim bill and curious, blinking eyes and feathers as soft as silk; the way he could just up and fly – a dart and a hop and a springing into the air, wings aflutter and him tossed up so neatly and easily into the sky quicker than a blink and...*

"Good," Daneel said. "That's good. Your sha is still now. You've found a good memory. A safe memory. Do you feel its safety?"

Noah nodded, eyes still closed. Truth was Daneel's instructions had felt strange at first – *slow your breathing, still yourself, yield to the nothingness* – each word, like a doting father to a favoured child, issuing from the assassin in a kind of soft cooing singsong. Which was what had been hard about it, at least to begin with. Like seeing a bear dance, or hearing one of the burly blacksmiths back home in Dumea croon the high intricate melodies of the Dove's Dirge. The sudden gentleness of Daneel's voice had been too distracting for Noah to follow what he was saying. Until, eventually, he'd felt a new weight to his stillness, and then, when he leaned into it, the way Daneel told him to, his thoughts had opened like a fast-blooming flower, his memories spilling to life within him in an unending torrent of light, sounds, colours and smells – so clear and vivid Noah no longer wanted to open his eyes.

"You're a quick learner," Daneel said. "Give it a while, with a bit of practice you'll learn to rest there, in these places inside yourself, in your sha. But you must build them first, piece by piece. You understand?"

Noah nodded again, his eyes still closed.

It had been Daneel's idea of course, a simple remedy for the nightmares that had started after their escape from Çyriath. After spending a day on foot in open country, lumbering among the thicketed woodland of the Copper Forest south of the city, and then, once clear, toward the long pass that skirted the coastline of the North Sea, they'd been joined by other escapees from Çyriath, some of whom journeyed with them. A young mother and son, an old coiner visiting from the crown city, a crew of clerics and scribes in battered black shifts crusted with dirt – each shocked silent by what they'd witnessed. Only to be shocked again by Noah's screams as they tried to sleep that night in the open country after their long walk south. The next day they were gone, all of them. And so the following night when the nightmares returned, Daneel decided to teach the boy the first meditation disciplines of the Shedaím.

"The sha is a part of a man like any other. Just you can't see it. Like your heart, or lungs, or bones."

"So, it's inside my body?" Noah asked.

"Deeper than that. *You* are inside your body. Your sha is inside *you*. Understand?"

Noah nodded uncertainly.

"My master, back at home, the one who taught me: he once told me it's best if you think of a man as a tree. A man says things, does things. These are the leaves, right? Or the fruit, if it's a fruit tree you're thinking of. But then before a man might say a thing, or do it, he thinks first, doesn't he? So those thoughts are like the branches. But a man's sha, that's more like the roots, buried deep in the ground. You don't see them, but they're the thing that most makes the tree what it is. Keeps it alive. Gives it strength. Like your sha does you. See?"

"I think so."

Daneel read the uncertainty in Noah's face. "Yeah, well. I'm not as good a teacher as my master was. The way he'd always say it is – *if the roots are ill, then the fruit will soon follow* – and I reckon that's what's happened with you. That's why you keep having these nightmares."

"My roots are ill?"

"Your sha. Makes sense if you think about it. You've had a rough month or so. Those things in Çyriath would be enough to shake any man's sha. Then there's been us having to live off the land before that, not eating much, which wouldn't help. Then before that, seeing Salidor that night, those wounds he had. I mean, I've seen a fair few open wounds myself but even I'd never seen any like that. Nothing pretty. And then… well…" Daneel trailed off, not wanting to say it.

"Watching my father die," Noah finished for him. "Watching your brother kill him."

"Yeah… well… Like I said, rough few weeks."

Noah just stared at him for a moment, that blank dumb look he'd give now and then; his eyes flat and still as he thought it over. "And so these… disciplines," he eventually resumed. "They're meant to *heal* my roots? My… sha?"

Daneel half-grimaced, half nodded. "Well… sort of…" He leant back against the broad trunk of the tree behind him, then scratched his head and sniffed. They could still smell the saltiness of the nearby sea on the air, less than a quartermile to the east where they'd tracked south along the Fisherman's Pass the day before. There were villages along the water every few miles, fishing settlements built around small shoddy piers and docks made of rotting planks of oak and pinewood. From here, when they gazed through the trees into the night, they could just make out the mist lifting from the distant water in a slow rising pall. "Be so much easier if Neythan was here," Daneel murmured to himself.

"Who's Neythan?" Noah asked.

"No one. Doesn't matter… I was never good at this stuff is what I'm saying. I could do it, but I learned it slow… See, it's not that the disciplines heal the sha. It's that they shape it… It's like… Let's say you have a tree that lives in a desert. It'll need different roots than one living up in the Wetlands by the Reach, right? The disciplines, if you follow, can help to shape the roots the way they need to be for wherever that tree is. They shape your sha for whatever you might be faced with. See, the way they'd teach it to us, the masters back home, they'd say it's not the things happening around you or to you that cause the problem, it's that your sha isn't shaped right for them. When your sha is shaped right for what you're to face, you can deal with it. When it's not, you're broken – because there's a gap between what's on the inside and what's happening on the outside. A man's sha and life need to be joined, they'd say, and the disciplines, they can help a man to do that. They take away the gap. Or at least they're supposed to, if you get good enough at them. I'm still learning, like you."

"So, the disciplines *shape* the sha?"

"*Everything* shapes your sha. The disciplines are what you do to have more control of *how* it's shaped. Make sense?"

"I suppose."

"Good. The more it makes sense the better you'll be able to get at it. And the fewer nightmares you'll have, and the more sleep I'll be able to get, which is the main thing here. So… ready to try again? It'll be quicker this time, you've already made the road in."

Noah nodded, re-crossing his legs as he shifted upright and closed his eyes once more. He slowed his breathing, the way he'd been taught, and let himself settle into the stillness, let its weight begin to press gently on him until… And there it was, like a waiting friend by a door. Memories resuming, as vivid as life itself.

He was in Dumea again, with Luann, walking back up the hill to the city and then through onto the Southways road by the sheepgate with its fusty odour of dung where the herdmen had ushered in their flocks. On this side of the city, even within the high walls, the grounds were open and mostly empty; sandy dirt pockmarked with shallow, dry tufts of yellowed grass and here and there a hut or bricked house with a fenced pen adjacent where the flocks and herds were kept. Beyond, the Southways road continued, edged by shale and sandstone tenements, each build set apart one from the other and, above them, to the western quarter where the sun's vernal haze settled, the white-edged tip of the library's upper walls, like a flat snow-capped peak, peeping over the roofs.

Noah eyed it as they walked, trying not to think of all he was still yet to learn – these unwieldy knots of knowledge he was to retain of Sharifs and kings and queens and stewards, not to mention the old chieftain lines of Súnam, with their hard to pronounce names and peculiar titles – all so he could claim an honour he wasn't sure he wanted.

That evening as they sat for supper the names continued to roll through his head. Theron the Great, Arvan the Scribe, Karel the Young, Helgon the Wise, King Seth of Dumea, Rivam of Tsahir, Chieftain Se'tani.

"Do you have a favourite?" his father asked as they ate, prompting both Mother and Luann, who'd been invited to dine with them, to look up from their food.

"Of all those I've to learn?"

"Yes, Noah."

Noah thought about it briefly and looked about the adobe walls of the house. The day's remaining light mingled with the lampflame and turned their dusty sediments a pale yellow. They sat together on mats and pillows with a basket of bread each and a bowl of soup in the middle. Noah shook his head.

"You must have a favourite, Noah. You should try to choose one."

Noah pondered for a long while. "I don't know," he said, then, after more thought, adding, "though I know it would not be any of the Sharifs."

"And why is that?"

"Well… they are the reason for the levies."

His father nodded and waited expectantly.

"And… I don't know… I do not like them."

His father smiled. "They were none of them perfect, Noah, that I will grant. But a man seldom is, in each there is always both virtue and flaw. It is this, more than anything, the Histories teach us. Take Karel the Young. There are some who call him a great man, and with reason. He came to the throne little older than you are now, and yet by his end he'd stilled the Sovereignty of the warring faiths that had threatened to tear it apart."

"But he only did that by starting the Cull and killing all the priests, destroying the Magi. He even killed his own wife."

His father smiled. "As you say, and so the same man who is named a hero of some is thought a tyrant by others. And then think also of Helgon the Wise, who, with my father, made the covenant."

"The teachers say the covenant is bad."

"In some ways it is, in others, not. But whether it is or isn't, this same Sharif also built four trade routes, built the Valley Pass, important roads. And so how ought he be judged? And then there is Arvan the

Scribe, Karel's son. He wrote the First Laws of the Sovereignty, some of them not unlike our own here in Dumea; he sought to order the land, keep it from war, extol peace. Most scribes call Arvan a good man, yet he cut the tongues from his own consuls if they transgressed his will. It is the same with all, Noah, virtue and flaw, they are as light and shadow, one never without the other."

"Then why must I choose?"

"Because we are all men, Noah, none perfect, and to deny the virtue in a man because of his faults is to make yourself better than him. Any man who thinks himself so will soon grow prideful. And a man, if he is to be a king, or even a steward, must keep himself from such pride. Lest he, in the end, become a tyrant too. Do you understand?"

He saw from Noah's face that he didn't and so smiled and touched his cheek.

"You will in time, my son," he said, picking another piece of bread to dip in the dish. "But until then," he lowered the sop to the soup and looked at Noah. "You must choose."

Noah considered briefly as he ate and then looked up once more, smiling. "I will choose you then, Father. You are not like the others."

But his father did not smile back as he had expected but instead grew still, his eyes flitting to Mother and then back again. His voice was quiet when he spoke, his eventual smile slow and thin. "Thank you. But none are perfect, my son," he said. "Light and shadow. Light and—"

"Noah!"

Noah could feel that something was wrong, different in some way. And he could hear Daneel's voice calling to him through it all, but faintly, like an echo on the wind, too far to be clear, trying to beckon him away from his memories and back to the world he knew, where hunger waited and where Father and Mother were no more. And he could feel within himself that he could resist, keep his eyes closed, remain here in this place with its familiar homely walls and warm food, where cities did not crumble under the savagery of strange beasts by night. Perhaps if he ignored Daneel's voice long enough, perhaps if he leaned hard enough into the balmy warmth of the Dumean air against his skin, the soft evening sunlight slanting in through the window, the proud, kind smile of Mother as she lifted the ladle to pour more soup into his bowl and…

"Noah, stop!"

So he clung hard, pulling on every detail, willing it all to stay, trying to forget Daneel and the cold dark of the forest and the memory of Father, face down in the sand by a Sumerian river with blades sticking out from his back like an archer's practice board, and decided it was those things that were the dream, an unhappy make-believe he'd imagined but that wasn't really true. It was all mere fiction. This, *here*, in his memories, this was home, this was the world as it really was, the world as it should be.

"Noah!"

The sudden jolt tossed Noah back onto the ground like a thump in the chest. He opened his eyes, reluctantly, to find himself lying on his back, eyes to the sky, the night having resumed and Daneel kneeling beside him, cradling Noah's head in his lap. It was raining now, thin darts of wet light shooting down as they caught the glint of the moon.

"Noah, you must stop. Stop."

Stop what, Noah thought.

"Just let go, Noah. The memory is yours, it will not leave you, but you must let it go. Now."

And so Noah did. Allowing his imagination to slip back from Mother and Father and Luann like a petitioner slowly withdrawing from before a throne – softly, carefully, he blinked and opened his eyes again. Strange. The trees were swaying, but against no wind, each rocking slowly in its own direction as the drizzling rain continued to drop from out of the night. Daneel was on his feet now, watching the trees in amazement. He turned to Noah as the boy stood to join him.

"What is it?" Noah asked.

Daneel regarded him suspiciously. "You didn't feel it?"

"Feel what?"

"The ground. The ground was trembling."

"Like an earthquake?"

"Yes, like an earthquake. You didn't feel it?"

"I was meditating, like you told me to."

"It stopped the moment you woke up. The very moment, Noah."

Noah glanced at the slightly swaying trees again. "Well. That's good that it's stopped at least."

But Daneel was just looking at him now, frowning, watching Noah as if he was some kind of thief, or threat. "Your family," he eventually said. "Who are they?"

Noah frowned back now, registering the accusatory tone. The gentle cooing voice of earlier had abruptly fallen away, as though the earthquake was somehow *Noah's* fault. As though he could've actually caused it. Noah stepped back, suddenly angry. "You know who my family are," he spat. "You hunted them, helped to kill them. Remember?"

Daneel flinched, as though slapped by the words, and then sighed, nodding to himself to accept the barb. He glanced warily at Noah before bending to collect their few remaining provisions – the last remaining loaf of bread they'd stolen from the market stall in Çyriath, wrapped in a kerchief; a half-torn skin of leather they'd been using as a cloak in the rain, the empty flask, Daneel's belt straps, with the sleeves of his shortsword and dagger attached. "We've rested here long enough," he mumbled. He gave the boy another distrustful glance as he handed him the flask and cloak to carry. "There will be more villages further along the coastline," he said. "Best we go find shelter from this rain."

NINE

SERPENT

"Filani did not tell you everything."

Nyomi's words, spoken quietly once they'd unmoored the boat and drifted out onto the river beyond earshot of the bald-headed priest who'd accompanied them. They'd been led from the Elderhouse and through the city in silence, then ushered out through the rivergate to the banks of the Serpent as the priest pointed lazily upstream and shooed them on. He watched them wade through the shallows and climb into the boat, watched them dip the oars and push along into the river's slow current to begin the journey to the Shrine of Sayensí, where the scroll was to be read. Now the three of them, after spending a day confined to separate quarters, sat in the narrow boat – Neythan at the stern, Nyomi at the prow, Arianna squatting in the slim space between – swaying to the mild bob and yaw of the river as the water slid along the boat's hull in the dark like a snake over sand.

"Filani did not tell us everything," Arianna echoed slowly, nodding. "Well, don't be coy, Nyomi. Speak on. I think we'd all agree now to be a good time to share what Filani neglected to say." She turned to the stern. "Wouldn't you say so, Caleb? Oh wait, that's right. Caleb isn't here."

Neythan sighed. He'd known Arianna wouldn't agree with his choice to take Nyomi the moment he made it. "Nyomi knows these lands," he said. "Caleb doesn't."

"Caleb can be trusted," Arianna said, then pointed toward the stern. "*She* can't."

Neythan felt his hand spasm and glanced down at his twitching middle finger and forefinger. He felt tired, too weary to argue. He leaned, angling his attention past Arianna to the woman rowing at the prow.

"Why did you and Filani bring us here, Nyomi, knowing what awaited you?"

Nyomi continued to draw her oar through the water. "We did not know," she said.

"But you knew there was grievance against her," Arianna said. "And now Filani lies either wounded or dead back in that city."

"She is not dead."

"How do you know?"

"I just know."

Arianna laughed. "Ah, well then. Say no more. You and Filani have been such models of truth and honesty after all."

Nyomi glanced over her shoulder from the prow. "We could not tell you everything." Her eyes shifted to Neythan. "Not until they'd seen you with their own eyes. Not until we could be sure."

Arianna turned to Neythan at the rear. "You know, I sense no contrition in her."

"Sure of what?" Neythan asked Nyomi.

"Of who you are."

"Who he is?" Arianna put in. "And what under the sun does *that* mean?"

"There are things you will not understand."

Arianna tossed her hands up. "Bones of gods, Neythan… I'm telling you, if this woman does not start explaining herself soon I don't see how I'll not gut her and toss her over the side."

Nyomi just turned back toward the prow, facing out into the still blackness ahead as the water lapped at the slow steady strokes of the oar. The shore had receded into the night behind them now, the river glinting like liquid pitch in the prow's torch as midges and moths danced around the flame. "I will tell you…" she said eventually, then bowed her head, made some sort of sign over herself, touching her head and chest with the knuckle of her thumb. "But you must understand, Filani was not as she is now. She was young. You must remember this when you think on the choices she made."

Neythan leaned forward. "What choices?"

"Choices she should never have *had* to make…" Nyomi continued to dip the oar as she spoke, but more slowly now, drawing it through the water in long steady strokes. "She too once found a Magi scroll, just as you have. Many years ago. Before all this… It is how she learned of the things to come – the nearing darkness… And it is why she was forced to make a decision in the hope of preventing it."

"What decision?"

"The scroll spoke of ancient bloodlines. Including Filani's – the line of her father, Mbiké, the high priest – a bloodline, according to the scroll, that would be one of only a few able to discover how to prevent what was to come, or withstand it."

"The darkness."

"Yes. The Great Shadow, Filani called it. So, she did what she thought was best… Filani and her sister, Sulari – they were Mbiké's only offspring. And by then they were young women, too old to be taken and taught the arts of war. Filani would have given her own child had she been able. But she was barren, so that wasn't an option either. The others of the priesthood would not listen to her. They doubted what she reported from the scroll, the meanings she discerned, the things it warned of. None would believe her. None would see to what needed to be done. So Filani chose a way. An unspeakable way. A sin she knew would never be forgiven…"

Nyomi downed her oar once more and made the sign over herself again, thumb knuckle to forehead then chest.

"What did she do?" Neythan asked after a few moments' silence.

Nyomi sighed heavily, then let the words spill from her. "She took her sister's children. Sulari's children. Stole them away in the night. Twin boys. Six years old..." Nyomi had grown still now, facing away into the night, her gaze seemingly transfixed by it as the raft drifted slowly on with the momentum of Neythan's strokes from the rear. "In Súnam there has always been talk of your Brotherhood. Rumours. Through her scroll Filani learned of the truth to those rumours. Learned of the Shedaím. Learned of Ilysia. And... took those boys there, to be trained... That is why she was so pleased to find you, Neythan. Grateful to do so. She had not anticipated you."

"Their names," Neythan said. "Tell me the names of the children she took."

"Their names were Ruben... and Sol."

Neythan didn't speak. The words seemed to pass through him, into him, settling to the pit of his stomach like leaden weights. He sat back against the raft's stern, gazing at the smoke as it dragged from the prowtorch.

"Filani told me she saw their likenesses in you the first day she met you," Nyomi went on. "Only she could not be sure. Feared to let herself believe it could be so, after all these years. It is why she sought to bring you to me, to know if I'd see the same likeness in you too. And I did, Neythan. As I do now. As Sulari too saw on the street in Jaffra... You have the likeness of Sulari's father, your forefather, Mbiké..."

"But that is not the reason we brought you here to this place." She finally turned from the prow, twisting to face Neythan and Arianna as the narrow raft continued to slide onwards through the water. The river had grown broad now, the embankments hidden in the blackness on either side, making the night quieter, the sounds of the water as it pushed between the fingers of leaning branches and reeds along the shoreline now muted by the distance. "It's your eyes, Neythan. Filani was the last of our people to have such eyes – the colour of jade and pearl. Sulari does not have them. And yet you – though your mother was not Súnamite – by some miracle you have them... Among the Inchah, the priesthood, those whose eyes are this way are counted seers, Neythan. Like Filani once was."

"You are saying that woman... Sulari... that she is my grandmother."

"Your father's mother. Yes... yes, she is."

"And Filani..."

"Your father's aunt... You will find you have many kin in Jaffra."

Kin.

Neythan stared at the night as though the word was written there, hanging in the air.

"You have a family," Nyomi went on. "Perhaps even a place among the priesthood were you to choose it. The seat of seer is the most honoured among the Inchah. It's why not all will want for you to prove to be who Filani has said you are... You see now why we could not tell you these things, without being sure."

Neythan didn't answer. For a while, no one said anything, the only sounds the papery flutter of moths around the prowtorch and the gentle slap of Nyomi's oar sweeping through the water as she resumed her strokes.

Family. Kin. They'd always felt like borrowed words to Neythan, to be used but not owned, like the rubies and silk the Brotherhood would sometimes give Arianna to wear on her witnessings. To think he had a grandmother, maybe cousins...

"Wait," Arianna leaned forward. "You said Filani learned to read her scroll, understand its writings. If that is true, why bring us here to read Neythan's. Why not read it herself?"

"Because there is a cost... Some say it is a curse for mortals to read from the writings of gods. This is not true. But there *is* a cost."

"What kind of cost?" Arianna asked.

"To read a scroll takes from one's sha, one's very life..." Nyomi gestured loosely at the oil-drenched stave of the prowtorch fixed to the front of the skiff. "Like the wick of a candle. When it's lit, it will allow for things to be seen that cannot be known without it. But that same flame will also devour the wick it is joined with."

"So, you're saying the scroll is like a flame."

"Just so. And the wick is the sha of the one who reads it, being consumed by the light the scroll brings… One can only read so much, after that some become sick and die. Others, their minds grow twisted, descend into madness, or darkness. It depends…"

"On what?" Neythan said.

"On–"

"Shh. Do you hear that?" Arianna hissed.

Neythan lifted his oar from the water, letting the narrow boat drift in silence. Clicks and rustles to the east, beyond the light from the prowtorch. Apparently, they were closer to the riverbank than they'd thought, maybe no more than a few ship lengths.

"What *is* that?"

Arianna shushed Neythan again as the small glint of distant torchflame winked at them from across the darkness, blinking and flickering through the knots of trees and vegetation as the boat continued to drift.

"We are here," Nyomi whispered. "The priest said we'd find no one along these banks until we'd reached the shoreline of the Sayensí." She lifted her oar and dipped it slowly into the water, pulling the boat toward the shore and the distant fires beyond it. Neythan did the same, long slow strokes so as not to disturb the water as Arianna listened for more sounds.

The boat eventually bumped gently against a boulder in the shallows by the shoreline. Nyomi unhooked the stave of the prowtorch, lifting the flame to view the long ridges of rock buried in the dust of the slope rising alongside the riverbank. Thickets of trees stood atop the stone shelf like waiting guards, the forest lying beyond. They dragged the raft to the shore and lifted it up into a pocket of smooth blunt rocks poking up from the water, then proceeded to climb the shallow slope and make their way to the edge of the forest.

"So, what now?" Arianna whispered as she reached the treeline, waiting for Nyomi to reach her with the torch.

Nyomi came alongside, then Neythan, breathy from the short climb. Nyomi stared into the forest and nodded at the small faraway flames moving between the trees, probably a quarter-mile away.

"Now we follow them," she said, and then doused the flame before stepping beyond the treeline into the undergrowth.

They traipsed through knotted tangles of moonlit greenery and treelimbs with little to no light, moving slowly as they allowed their eyes to adjust to the dark. They walked for a long time, an hour, maybe more, trying not to flinch at every graze of a leaf or twig against the knee as they pushed through the undergrowth. No telling what lay beneath the canopy, waiting to bite or fasten to ankles.

After a while the forest fell away, opening into a clearing of leaves, chopped wood, and what looked like the fallen fruits of some kind of tree. Long tubers the size of feet littered the ground, scattered across the clearing like refuse.

"Careful!"

Arianna reached out and grabbed Neythan by the shoulder. He stumbled, his footing suddenly unsure. Glancing back, teetering, he saw the abrupt drop beneath and behind him, his heels faltering atop a cliff edge. Arianna yanked him back from the brink by the collar.

"What is *wrong* with you?"

Neythan looked out beyond the precipice, his fingers twitching again. "I'm fine. I just missed my step."

"You? Miss your step?"

"I'm fine."

"Look," Nyomi pointed. "There."

The rocky gorge, too deep and dark to see to the bottom of, was lined part way down by dots of flickering light where lamps marked out some kind of path below. A pair of other dots moved between them, travelling along their course.

"Well," Arianna murmured. "At least we know where they went."

"Just so," Nyomi answered. She glanced back at Neythan, now standing away from the edge, then looked north along the bluff. "Come. This way... And watch your step."

They went slowly along the cliff edge until they came to a verge. The path down leaned steeply from its crest, bending down into darkness on the other side. Nyomi stepped over the slight rise and onto the path, bracing on her heels as she began to make her way down the cliffside as Neythan and Arianna followed. They walked slowly, the dark trail winding back and forth like the kinked spine of a serpent. It was only as they reached the bottom that the torches appeared, standing on head-high wooden staves on either side of the path at wide intervals.

"Look." Neythan pointed down at the flame-lit dust, riddled with footprints, many of them children's.

"Nice," Arianna said grimly.

Nyomi looked down at the dust for a few moments and then led them on, continuing along the trail between the posts. They proceeded down the declining path for close to a quarter-hour before the lights ran out. They then continued on beyond the lit path. They'd stumbled on in the dim moonlight for a few hundred feet when Nyomi stopped so abruptly Neythan almost bumped into her from behind.

"What is it? Why are you…" Neythan trailed off as he followed Nyomi's gaze, staring up at the enormous structure in front of them.

"How is that possible?" Arianna said quietly as she too stared up at it. "Men cannot build such things."

Most of it was shrouded in shadow, a near endless mass of sediment stretching away in both directions, similar in breadth to the ziggurat they'd seen in Jaffra. Seamless stone scaled toward the sky, passing beyond the small puddle of light cast by the torches fixed to its lowstones until it merged with the night, rendering the structure's height visible only by the abrupt dark that cut across the stars overhead as it blocked them out. But that wasn't really what made them stare. The whole thing was… built? sculpted? – in the shape of a partly submerged head, buried into the earth from the lower jaw down so that the foot of the wall before them began from just beneath the cheek, as though a stone-made giant had been frozen in the act of rising up from the dirt around it. Nyomi moved closer. The ear, the size of a small tree, was directly in front of them. Neythan couldn't help but marvel at the detail, the way the whorls of the outer ear curved in large neat arcs. He looked up toward where the eye might be, walking along the side of the structure without thought as he went to meet the face, but the eye too remained buried in shadow, beyond reach of the shallow light from the lampposts behind. And then they saw it. The entrance – the giant head's mouth, jaws distended, stretched open into a silent scream.

Neythan began to jog, Nyomi and Arianna with him, working their way around to the front and watching the throat's angle open to them. Dry blockish teeth, thick lips, the beginnings of the flared nostrils above, all of it perfectly re-created. They came to a halt as they reached the front, staring down the chasm of the open throat.

"How could men *build* something like this?" Neythan said.

Nyomi began to walk toward it. The open mouth was the height of a city terrace. "We do not say *men* built this," she said quietly. "We say gods did."

She stood beneath the massive high arch of the upper jaw and ignited their torch, and then gazed into the tunnel at the flame-lit interior. Neythan came to a stop when he saw it.

The inner walls of the mouth were riddled with faces. Row upon row of them, carved into the stone on either side and covering the ceiling; each of them fixed with differing expressions. Terror. Ecstasy. Mirth. Anger.

Neythan looked at Nyomi, then glanced behind to Arianna who now stood just beyond the entrance.

"I don't have a good feeling about this," Arianna said.

"And I do?"

But when Neythan turned back around, Nyomi was already moving into the tunnel. The faces, lodged into the rocky walls like an endless crowd of witnesses, stared down on her, receding beyond the light into shadowy nothingness.

Neythan looked at Arianna. "We don't have a choice." He stepped over the threshold and into the tunnel, glancing up at the teeth high overhead and trying not to imagine them suddenly clamping down to lock them in. He looked behind once more to Arianna and saw she'd begun to reluctantly move forward too, following him inside. Neythan nodded at her, and then continued to walk after Nyomi, down into the dark.

TEN

SANCTUM

"Reminds me of a dream I had once," Arianna said quietly, walking beside Neythan as she gazed at the faces on the wall.

Neythan glanced sidelong at her. "*This* does?"

"No need to say it like *that*. It was a dream. We don't choose them."

"Now *there'd* be an idea."

"I saw my mother in it. The dream, I mean."

"I thought you never knew your mother."

"I'd said I don't *remember* her. There's a difference. But in the dream I could just feel it was her. Could tell somehow, even though I couldn't see her face. She was walking ahead of me down a tunnel – dark, like this one – and whispering to me over her shoulder." Arianna's voice leapt into soft maternal sing-song. "*Just a little further, little one. Nearly there. Just a little further…*"

"Strange dream."

"No stranger than the one you told me by the Dry Lake in Ilysia that time. Do you remember? The one where you'd see someone dying?"

"I'd never see them, only hear them, or just… *know* somehow."

"I used to think, the way you told it to me that time… I always thought it sounded more like a memory than a dream."

Neythan thought about it, glancing up at the carved face of a child at the apex of the tunnel's curve above him. The child was grinning, he noticed: the eyes squeezed tight, and thick blocky teeth, like those of a hare, bared in a wide gleeful smile, passing once more into shadow as Nyomi's torch continued forward up ahead.

Neythan's mind had been strange of late: wandering, discursive, offering impressions to him – images, memories maybe, vague and yet, every now and then, randomly vivid too. Meals gathered around a palm tree and campfire, watching the tide drift out along an Erami coastline beneath the milky glaze of a new moon. Laughter and the fiery fresh scent of cooking spices and whitefish as he giggled and playfought with other boys whose faces he couldn't now name. And Uncle Sol's voice, drifting over it all like a song over a dance, regaling those gathered with fishing tales while they all squatted or reclined by the warmth of the flames. The whole thing had felt so real he could almost taste the sea salt, almost feel the gritty rub of the sand between his toes.

"Neythan?"

He glanced aside. "What?"

"I said are you alright? You seem… a little distracted."

"I'm alright." He glanced down at his hand. The bandaging was a little damp from sweat and perhaps the weeping of the wound. To be expected in this heat, but his fingers weren't twitching. "I'm alright."

They continued along the tunnel as the passage steepened and seemed to narrow, drawing the stone faces on the walls in nearer. Neythan tried to ignore the feeling of being watched as they passed beneath the innumerable mute, hollow eyes of the stone-sculpted visages. So life-like, most of them shaped with the thick lips and broad noses common to Súnam, and then some of them, disconcertingly, shaped into likenesses that didn't quite seem human – the jaws and mouths a little too wide, the eyes too small, the teeth slightly too big, each one emerging and disappearing into shadow as the light from Nyomi's torch passed over them.

"What are these anyway?" Arianna said, gazing at the faces.

Nyomi glanced up at them. "Revenants," she answered. "Joybloods."

"Joy what?"

"The Sayensí believe a man can choose to die to himself, and in so doing join his sha with that of another, and of that sum become twice as strong as he was. Two men in one, or three men, or many more." She turned to look at Arianna. "Some believe they can even join themselves to beasts too."

"And can they?"

"They cannot. But it does not stop them from trying." She glanced up at the faces above them. "Or cherishing things that mark what they hope to become… the Sayensí have many strange practices."

"They sound like madmen," Arianna said.

"You would not be the first to say this," Nyomi answered.

"And yet they can help us read the scroll?" Neythan asked.

"Even the madman has wisdom, Neythan."

They came to an alcove at the bottom of the tunnel's decline with a high pillared entrance. Nyomi lifted her torch to view the images carved into the walls. Pomegranates and the strange tuber-like fruits they'd seen on the clifftop were sculpted into the tops of each pillar, with further images cut into the stonewalls on either side. Neythan stared at them – a pair of moons and a near naked woman beneath them, girt around her hips with a sash and standing in profile as she faced a large creature halfway between a bear and a bat whilst a strange array of orbs riddled the sky. The whole thing was framed by rows of glyphs, the same on each wall.

Nyomi passed between the pillars and through the tall entrance without a word, leading them into a narrow, low-ceilinged corridor. Torches lodged in ornately patterned sconces along the walls on either side, spaced at wide intervals between long rows of symbols they didn't know how to read. They passed into another corridor, turning a corner into a well-lit series of long thin chambers lined by rows of clay pots – some tall and slim, others short and squat – resting on long shelves of stone. They slowed; each of the pots were marked in some kind of elaborate ink-written language, the characters unrecognisable. Arianna lifted one from the shelf to peer in at its contents – sand mostly, but then there, beneath all the dross and grit, the dull metallic glint of silver or maybe only iron.

"What are these things?"

Nyomi, further along the corridor, turned and saw Arianna holding the vessel. "*Don't!*"

Arianna froze, her hand poised above the lip of the tall pot.

"Put it back where you found it," Nyomi said.

Arianna exchanged a glance with Neythan, and obeyed, reaching back to the shelf to replace the clay pot.

Nyomi exhaled, and was turning back toward the corridor to resume along its path when she flinched to a stop and turned back again. "No. *Wait.*"

But Arianna had already returned the pot, placing it back on the shelf, which seemed to give a little as she did so. Something clunked and shifted behind the wall, then snapped and rolled into place, triggering the creaking drag of ropes through pulleys. Arianna stepped back from the wall, Neythan with her. He was turning to Nyomi for guidance when the ground suddenly hinged open. They fell, scrambling for purchase as Nyomi sprinted back along the corridor toward where they clung to the sudden opening's edge. But it was too late. The floor dropped abruptly, upending them as they clawed futilely at the stone paving, and then they were both slipping, sliding down into darkness as the dim-lit corridor skidded away and slammed shut above them.

They landed against hard stone in a tangle of limbs, Neythan shoulder-first against a wall before feeling Arianna's weight slam against his ribs in the darkness.

"Bones of gods…"

"Are you alright?"

He let out a tight cough. "Nothing broken. You?"

"I'll live."

Neythan pushed himself up against the wall to lean his back against it, then reached out a searching palm, groping at the air. He could hear Arianna shuffling too, rising to her feet, then scraping, somewhere beside and above him.

"What are you doing?" he asked.

"Flints."

"You have some?"

"I took Caleb's. His lamp too, although I think that may be broken now."

"He loves that lamp."

"I know. He's going to absolutely... ow!"

"What? You alright?"

Arianna cursed. Breathed. "*Fine.*"

"What *are* you doing?"

The scraping resumed, then the click of flints and... "There." Light. Neythan glanced up at the flame on the wall above him. The short stave of an iron torch, caging the fire Arianna had managed to ignite. Neythan climbed to his feet and looked at her as she held her bleeding hand. "It's just a scratch," she said.

He ignored her and reached into the pouch of his hip bag for the fresh bandages he carried for replacing the wraps on his wounded hand. "Hold still."

"I said it's just a—"

"Just shut up and hold still, Ari."

The cut was on the blade of her palm, beneath her little finger. He wrapped around her knuckle and the side of her hand the way Yulaan used to wrap theirs back in Ilysia on sparring days.

"You'd make a good handmaid," Arianna said.

"And you wouldn't." He finished up and turned toward the now partly lit chamber. Long narrow room. Not enough light to see to the end of. The torch on the wall beside them was weak, not enough lime or kindling in the cup cradling the flame. Old, likely not often used. Neythan reached up and lifted it from the fixture anyway, cupping the waning light as they began to move forward into the dark. They stayed by the wall as they crept further in, errant pieces of furniture emerging from the blackness as they went – an overturned table, its top laid on its side, facing toward them like a pitifully improvised blockade. Someone had scratched words over its entire surface with a pen knife, scarring the softwood. Neythan was leaning in to try and read them when Arianna gripped his arm. Neythan looked at her. She took hold of his wrist and guided the lamp toward the wall beside them. Neythan froze when he saw.

Blood smeared the wall, darkened by age, a large blotch of it ringed by splatter as though tossed there from a bucket. Neythan went nearer, lifting the lamp, and saw more, but now etched in neat lines, and then… words, scores of words, traversing the length of the wall like some kind of stonewrought tapestry.

… Only he who hears the dark moon's song shall know those who watch and reach beyond his soul to touch the dusk's cursed grace where sage and fool are one and call from blood the things done and long forgotten as all things speak to those for whom they're meant of hidden paths that cannot be told where shadows mark the ways of men and turn their hearts to that wasting wind which ushers in the night that shall not abate when works of decay cannot turn back the stars for whom the chosen wait who've gazed on death's thoughts and dreams in black fire against which only the sons of ancients stand by eternal laws with oaths of gods and men and living books whose witness shall not be known except by those who yield to worlds beyond time where pale kings have dwelt since the beginnings of all things with sayings by which the intents and acts of men are judged before living and dead as…

Neythan flinched at Arianna's touch. She'd taken hold of his arm again. He turned toward her with the lamp and saw her staring at him, eyes wide, panting, shaking. Panicked?

"You… Need to explain that… Right now," she said.

"Explain what?"

"*Don't*… you… how did you do that?"

"Do what?"

"Don't give me that, Neythan. You started reading that… that…"

She gestured at the wall of writing. "Whatever *that* is." Neythan glanced back at it, but there were only symbols there now, a litany of unintelligible glyphs and elaborate scribbles scrawled in dried blood. He felt his bandaged hand beginning to twitch again. "And that… *language* you were speaking. When did you learn that? Where?"

"Arianna, I–"

"And how did you make the room move?"

"*Move?*" He looked beyond her, saw the shape of the upended table, still visible at the fringes of the lamp's light behind them, but now close to twenty feet away. It had moved across the room. Or they had? He looked back to Arianna, confused.

"How?" Arianna hissed.

"Me? What do you–"

"And how did you… Wait… Gods, what *is* that?"

She was looking off to another corner of the room. Neythan turned to follow her gaze. He could hear it too – the sound of breathing, haggard and low. He lifted the lamp but who or whatever was making the sound was beyond it, shrouded in gloom. Arianna drew her sword and took hold of Neythan's shoulder as they moved forward with the flame. Neythan could feel himself trembling now, could feel that same cold gut-deep feeling he remembered from the temple in Ilysia, the blind elder staring down on him like a wolf over caught prey. He stretched the lamp out in front of him, willing the shrinking flame to hold out.

"There," Arianna whispered.

The light flashed over something like flesh. They stopped. Neythan brought the lamp back to it. A limb, ash white, outstretched on the ground, leading up to the scrawny taut stomach of a child. And then…

"Gods above…"

Neythan froze there, trying to make sense of what he was seeing. A girl sat there, legs sprawled out as she not so much leaned against the wall as *into* it, her torso somehow encased in the stone. Submerged. Above her navel the pale flesh had turned sallow and grey, and above that, was completely consumed, her chest hidden in the brickwork along with her left arm whilst her right arm, shoulder and head hung limp from the wall as though from a guillotine's headlock. The girl's ragged, shallow, breath hissed out pitifully, struggling through leaden airways. She seemed to be whispering something, her lips trying to form around laboured wheezy breaths as her head hung. Neythan leaned in, trying to hear. Some kind of chant, the sounds unintelligible yet repetitive.

Neythan was about to move nearer when the girl's head suddenly snapped up. Tired bloodshot eyes, suddenly wide and alert, locked on Neythan, staring into him as though into a hole she'd lost something in. The same girl, Neythan realised, he'd seen in Jaffra on that wall when the city had turned on Filani with stones. But that made no sense. How could she be *here*? Why? Who was…

"You shouldn't be here," the child whispered, peering at him through the stringy drapes of her straight black hair, hanging across her pale face. "You shouldn't have come."

Neythan just stared at the girl's sweat-polished face as she sat there in the halflight, watching him. He then followed her gaze as she looked down, towards her sprawled legs and bare feet where a goat's skull rested against her outstretched ankle.

"Neythan." He flinched again from Arianna's touch, who in turn lifted her palm placatingly. "Neythan, what are you looking at?"

He looked back for the skull but nothing was there, and the girl was gone, a starving dog in her place, whimpering as it lay against the wall.

"You shouldn't be here." A man's voice, coming from somewhere behind them.

Neythan felt the sharp prick in his neck as he turned to find its owner. Then saw the tall shadow, standing by the door.

"Neythan?" Arianna's voice.

He glanced at her, saw her looking back at him puzzled, hand reaching lethargically toward her own neck, her fingers coming away bloody as her gaze turned dull and sleepy. Which was strange, because Neythan felt sleepy too, despite the blood, despite it all – the girl in the wall, these musty sepulchral chambers and the lamp in his hand. He watched it fall from his grasp and clatter on the ground. Watched Arianna slump to the ground too, in front of him, wondering why it all seemed to be happening so slowly, as if underwater, everything turning blurry and dim and somehow unreal. So he joined her there in the dust, so sleepy, and let the dark's cool tide wash over him like a welcome friend.

THE NARROW, ON THE STONE ROAD AND SOUTH OF THE SUMMER SEA

The month of Melek. The second year of Sharif Sidon.

"So, what's your story?"

"Story?"

"Everyone always has one, don't they? A reason why they are where they are, the road that's led them to it. You're asking me to trust you. The least you could do is help me understand why you are doing all this."

"Suppose you could say I'm a product of the times, the ways of men."

"Just sounds like a busy way to not answer the question."

"Could be. Could be it's also true."

"You're expecting me to take your word for it?"

"Maybe… Men, if you think about it, really think about it, their chief trouble is they use things they know in seeking to understand things they don't. They've not learned to know things any other way."

"And that's a problem?"

"It can be. Often is."

"When?"

"Well, that's the other problem. They don't know how to tell the difference between what they know and what they don't... Ignorance. Like a plague. It's his greatest affliction."

"You speak as though you're not one of them."

"Hm. Could be I've learned to think of it that way."

"Then why are you here? Why are you trying to do all this; trying to help them?"

"I have hope."

"Funny... You don't strike me as the optimistic kind."

"Well, there you have it then."

"What?"

"That plague again. Thinking we know what we don't."

ELEVEN

RULE

"There," he whispered. "Did you hear that?"

"Ola, please."

"Don't *Ola please* me. I heard it. We must be close now."

Joram sighed. He turned, tapping a fist on Marin's shoulder, who'd become distracted watching the gleam of moonlight on the water. The brook ran unusually thin in this part of the forest. "You paying attention, Marin?"

Marin turned and nodded numbly.

"I definitely heard *something*," Ola insisted.

"What did it sound like?" Djuri asked.

"Scratching, like the time we had rats in the granary."

"I hate rats," Marin said.

"You and me both."

"Listen," Joram interrupted. "I'm saying I'll go over by that clutch of trees, across the clearing there. If you three wait a while then follow – Djuri this way along the east, Marin and Ola the other way – it might be we'll know the truth of what you say you did or didn't hear."

"I *did* hear," Ola said.

"Fine. Now, perhaps we ought to take a look? Good?"

"Good."

"Marin?"

Marin's gaze had wandered back to the stream. It was so shallow, no more than a wet glaze over the sloping silt underfoot.

"Marin?"

Marin, eyes still on the stream, nodded; which Joram found concerning. He'd seemed distracted for almost the entire way here, daydreaming, pondering. Scared perhaps. To be caught here, trying to enter the Magadar uninvited – a privilege almost only ever extended to those whose arms and shoulders were thick with ink from neck to knuckle – would mean death.

Joram, a little nervous himself, clapped Marin on the back and turned to look at the others. "You ready?"

They stared back at him grimly.

"Alright then," Joram said, pulling the strap of the sack he was carrying his offerings in onto his shoulder. "Let's go."

"But what about *him*?"

"*Gods*, Marin."

"What? I'm nervous. And you haven't explained who he'll be going with."

Marin, along with the others, was looking at the dull-eyed brute squatting next to Joram in the undergrowth. Ola, for her part, had seemed comfortable enough with his presence throughout the journey here but Joram had been able to tell for a while that the man's docile and occasionally drooling, vacant look had been bothering both Djuri and Marin for at least the last day or so, and in the case of the latter probably longer. Which was fair enough. Joram had never held a man's sha for this long before, and although he felt confident the man would remain sleepily obedient, possessing him for this long was still new, and anything new would always provoke doubt, especially with Marin.

Joram reached out and touched the man's sigil again to be sure, feeling for his sha. Oren, his clansmen had called him, although even if Joram hadn't heard them shouting his name as he hid him in

Marin's tent in the nights following the scuffle at Saramak, chances were he'd have been able to learn it himself by probing his sha. In the end, it was surprising how brief the search for him turned out to be – three nights of roaming about the camp bellowing his name, and a few jaunts around the outcrops surrounding the Seat of Saramak, and his clansmen were satisfied to move on, unwilling to linger any longer whilst their herds continued to grow restless for new pasture. As far as they were concerned, he was either dead, drunk or, most likely, with a woman. If it was the latter, he'd have to find his own way back to them. Otherwise they'd give it a month before lighting fires for him and making a few songs. Which would do, Joram supposed. If all went to plan Oren would be back at the Seat within a day, with little to no memory of the past week he'd been duped through.

"He's fine," Joram decided, after probing him a little. "He's still well under. Nothing to worry about."

"Makes me nervous," Marin complained. "It's like he's looking at you sometimes, but he isn't. It's spooky."

"I'd have thought you of all people would be comfortable with it," Ola said.

"What's that supposed to mean?"

Ola opened her mouth to answer, but then stopped, apparently thinking better of it.

"What do you mean?"

"Nothing."

"Here, wait now… Have you ever done that to *me*?" Marin asked, nodding to Oren's docile frame as he continued to squat beside Joram, staring at nothing.

Joram didn't answer.

"You have, haven't you."

"Did I say I have?"

"I can tell by the look on your face."

"What look?"

"You're smiling." He turned to Djuri and Ola. "Djuri look at him. He's smiling."

"Forget about it," Ola answered. "It's nothing."

"Easy for you to say. It's not your head he's been messing around in."

"He tried once, funnily enough. I asked him to. Wanted to see what it'd be like. Didn't work though. Not suggestible enough, he says. That right, Joram? Suggestible? That how you put it?"

Joram ignored her and peered through a clutch of cedars to the west, trying to plot the path he'd take down the slope and through the wood. It was a cloudy night. Unlikely the moon was going to be enough to see properly with, and there'd be no risking lamplights once they neared the bottom if they wanted to avoid being seen. In the end they were just going to have to find their way and hope for the best.

Joram breathed deep, exhaled. "It's time. And you needn't worry about big gentle Oren here, he'll be coming with me. You just make sure you don't lose your footing, or your offerings. None of us can afford to be empty-handed when we reach the altar." He looked them over a final time to see if they were ready. "Alright. Let's go."

Moving off in different directions, they each began to make their way down through the oaks and cedars toward the basin and the waiting volcano beneath them.

It was archaic really, a contest to the death, but it had been that way for centuries, or so Joram had been told; the annual gathering at Magadar providing the arena for the fights that would determine who'd be chieftain for the next year to come.

Joram worked his way along a gulley beyond the stream with big Oren following behind him, staying low as they scampered through the knot and tangle of the trees toward the volcano's foot. From here he could just make out the dark volcanic rock, a wall of night beyond the trees, with craggy edges glinting faintly in the beclouded moonlight. Joram slowed as they reached the bottom, checking the sack on his shoulder and scanning the dark for guards. He was about to move southwest to track around the mountain's arc when he heard the whistle from the other direction, a short hollow hoot, just as they'd agreed, so as to imitate a forest owl and not arouse suspicion.

"Well, well. Looks like they've found it, Oren."

Joram adjusted the sack of offerings on his shoulder and began moving towards it, skirting northeast around the mountain's blackstone foot as the duped Oren followed behind.

He found Djuri, after another whistle, crouching by the base of a wide tree stump, gazing into a lamplit clearing where men were wandering around, chopping heat-seared meat they'd dragged off of an altar onto a nearby bench of stone. Joram almost stumbled over the dead guard, covered in leaves with an arrow lodged firm through the left eye, lying beside where Djuri squatted.

"Good aim," Joram remarked, crouching beside him. Which did no more than provoke an unhappy and anxious glance.

"This had better work, Joram. The things we've done… We'll be quartered seven times over if they find us."

"It will work," Joram answered. It had to. It's what the voice had promised. "Have you seen Marin?"

"He heard me. He's on the other side of the clearing with Ola. He'll come out when we do I think."

"Good. That's good."

The altar lay in a brief clearing beyond a break of gum trees and thickets fifty feet away, surrounded by priests handling the meat, prodding the chunks of beef and lamb as they hissed and sizzled in their fat on the altar, whilst a chief priest stood a pace or two away, mumbling chants and supplications to the sky. Beyond them, Joram saw others standing or sitting close by – a pair of them upwind from the altar, clothed in rags of fur and with identically tonsured scalps: the pates of their pale shaven heads daubed white and red from the tops of their skulls to their foreheads and down the bridge of the nose. Each held torches whilst others sat on benches repeating the chants of the chief.

"I think it'll be best if I do the talking," Joram murmured.

"Funny. I was about to suggest the same thing."

Joram could feel his heart pounding as he stepped out from behind the stump and bushes and walked slowly into the clearing with the sack in his hand, Oren at his shoulder. Only as he stepped clear of the undergrowth did he see their full number, perhaps as many as thirty men, bowing and rocking and chanting in their skins and ragged scarlet robes.

The chief priest saw Joram first, followed by the rest, their gazes turning eerily as one toward him as their chants died. Joram walked slowly, his arms spread wide, and came as close as possible before lowering the sack to the floor. The man, beardless, couldn't have been more than thirty years. He eyed the bare skin of Joram's forearms cursorily before addressing him. "You should not be here."

Joram, blood thundering through his ears and chest, breathed deep again and gestured to the sack on the ground. "I have brought a gift." He nodded to Djuri, who placed his own sack next to his as Ola and Marin emerged from the bushes on the other side to join them. "We all have."

Gesturing sharply to one of the congregants, the chief continued to watch Joram as a shaven headed boy came forward to take the sacks. They all watched as the boy reached in and pulled out a thick slab of raw meat and lifted it to the priest, and then, somewhat showily, to the other congregants, parading it like the results of a hunter's first kill.

"A generous offering," the priest remarked.

"May the gods show us favour," Joram answered, bowing his head.

The boy had already taken the sacks over to the priest by the altar, who immediately began to toss the pounds of flesh onto it, each chunk hissing in the flames as they slapped onto the fat-greased stone. The priest looked at Oren and Marin, now standing next to each other just behind Joram, and glanced over the ink markings that covered their arms as Joram stepped aside to allow him to get a better look at their sigils and the stories of their lines, and, most importantly, Oren's priestmark.

"The gods *do* show favour," the priest said, catching sight of the small winged eye on Oren's shoulder before returning his attention once more to Joram. He again stared at him for a long moment before eventually inclining his head and motioning toward a craggy pocket at the foot of the mountain behind them. "And they show you your path… Go."

Joram bowed, and then, with the others, moved toward the mountain's foot, following the white-daubed boulders marking the path up. They moved quickly, stepping from boulder to boulder until they reached a verge where the path turned in and opened a tunnel through the rockface into the cavernous interior on the other side.

"Gods old and new…"

They stood on a ledge overlooking the vast cavity. The walls, huge dam-like blockades of red rock, stretched up toward the opening where the cloudy night stared down from above. The whole place like a massive enclosed ravine and then there, at the centre, the huge mythic structure all their childhood tales had spoken of – a colossal stone monolith, streets wide in every direction, dominating the space and reaching to the broad opening above like some kind of god-made tower.

"Magadar," Joram whispered as he stared up at it – god-fort in the old tongue – the giant column of stone that had lent the yearly contests their name.

The others remained speechless, gazes cranked to the sky, trying to digest the incomprehensible scale and magnitudes around them before eventually unlocking from their frozen stares to venture down to the ground and across the yawning chasm's floor. By the time they'd finally made it to the column their perspectives were warped, stretched and bent by the volcano's huge dimensions. The gathering crowd of people toward the column's foot seemed meagre and distant.

"Takes some getting used to doesn't it." Anika, an elder of Shurapeth and one of the few who'd spoken up for Joram as a child when he'd fought for admission to the tribe, had sidled up to him almost without his noticing, jolting him from his trance. There were close to a hundred people here, less than half a tenth of the tribe – the heads of clans, elders, and the most highly esteemed hunters and warriors, all here to try their hand at claiming the seat of Shurapeth, or watch as others attempted to.

"Beautiful, some might even say," Anika added. She inhaled as though breathing in spring's first rose and planted her great tribestaff in the dirt, making the talismans at the top rattle as she turned to face him with that annoyingly wry, maternal look she always seemed to favour him with.

"It *is* beautiful," Joram agreed.

"My forefather scaled the face of this column, near two hundred feet of sheer cliffside, handholds so small a child can hardly clasp them. Clawed his way up there at the risk of every limb, the risk of his life, to claim the Seat. The last true chieftain of Shurapeth."

Joram craned his neck to stare up at it.

"Quite something isn't it, at least more so than those who've claimed themselves chieftain since."

"I'd forgotten your dislike of the contests."

"It's not the contests I dislike, Joram. It's the lies that are told against the old ways to make them. Some say four hundred men died here, fell from the wall and splattered their skulls here on these rocks beneath like cracked eggs." She gestured, prodding the tribestaff vaguely in the direction of the bed of serrated edges that covered the ground at the vast column's foot. "A thing that never happened, Joram; a thing that would never be allowed. Just like your presence here. Why *are* you here?" She glanced behind to the others standing with him. "Why are *any* of you here?"

"The priests allowed us passage like everyone else."

"Nothing with you is *ever* like everyone else, Joram. You are here for mischief."

"I'm here to contest the headship of the tribe."

Anika stared at him. "You're an outsider."

"I'm of the tribe. I've a right as everyone else."

"You've no ink. You're not a warrior. Gods, you're barely more than a child, and you want to stand before Uruq?"

"I do."

She just stood there, staring at him for a long while, before eventually moving away to inform the rest of the gathering. From there, Joram watched it all play out the way the voice had told him it would – the confusion, the debate, the arguing – before the elders finally acquiesced to their law, determining that any man or woman at the Magadar was permitted to contend the headship.

Moments later Joram was being conducted to the casket-shaped cage at the foot of the column by Gurat, another of the elders, who, despite his clear dislike of Joram, at least had the probity to check the rope before hinging the cage's front open for Joram to step inside.

"Hold tight," the elder advised as Joram ducked to enter. "It is not always a smooth ride."

And then Joram was being winched upwards, staring down on Ola, Marin and the others as the rope tugged and lifted him away from them and toward the waiting Uruq atop the column's vast height.

He clung to the bars of the cage, holding tight as it gently swung with each winch of the pulley above. After a while he could see the counterbalance – a door-sized boulder – passing along his axis several feet away as it lowered to the ground to aid his ascent. Some of the crowd that had been at the column's foot had migrated to the walls now, climbing the stepped paths to seat themselves above the purview of the column's peak. Joram watched them, and then looked out to the overwhelmingly broad angles of the volcano floor as it widened beneath him. The people that had remained there were barely visible now, no more than specks.

Joram reached into his pocket for the black pearl, nervously rolling its smooth orb between his fingers until the cage finally shuddered to a halt, the rope's knot bumping against the scaffolded pulley-guard above as it reached the top. Slowly, the cage swung in from the edge of the column to a sort of plinth, and an elder waiting there. Tall. Grey. Stubbly hair and beard.

The man assessed Joram grimly before moving forward to unhinge the door and help him out. It was as though Joram could feel the height all around him now, a thinness to the space, as though the air itself had somehow become more precarious. Joram couldn't help thinking back on it all as the elder led him across the choppy terrain – the planning, the waiting. Twelve years languishing in the

Reach, the hungry and cold nights, the things he'd had to do to fight his way into the tribe, the things he'd patiently and painstakingly learned, and endured, all so he could reach this moment atop a two-hundred-foot-high crop of rock in a volcano. This was it. There was no going back. This would be everything.

He could feel the persistent knock of blood through his ears and chest as he caught sight of Uruq waiting for him beyond the rugged terrain in an evenly planed rink of polished stone. The arena's floor was perfectly smooth, the stone almost ice-like, the work of gods as was often said.

Uruq was heavily armoured, decked in cured leather shinguards, wristguards and a solid looking breastpiece. He stared contemptuously at Joram, watching him enter into the rink, and then, noticing he'd come dressed in nothing more than woollen garments and an overcoat, pulled a face that could almost have been pity. Perhaps in some small way it was, but smeared beneath smug smiling disdain as he watched Joram walk with the elder toward him at the centre.

The choice of weapons lay on the arena floor. The predictable options – axe, a spear, a sword. Uruq squatted to claim the axe, of course, thumbing the worn metal stained with the gritty coppery residue of old blood. Joram crouched to pick up the sword, which didn't look much better, leaving the elder, as the contest's overseer, to take the remaining spear.

"The Magadar is simple," the elder began. "Two begin, one will fall. He who remains, will be chieftain." He swung an arm, indicating those gathered along the walls of the volcano to spectate. "And he shall lead Shurapeth." The elder then planted the spear hilt down like a staff, gazing out beyond the column and across the empty space between it and the volcano's high walls to where the people had gathered on the stepped paths to observe the contest. "It is time," he announced, and then directed each man to stand at opposing ends of the arena.

The voice, when it finally came, almost made Joram jump, which was something he hadn't done since he was a child.

"There shall be a cost," was all it said, allowing a silence so distracting to open in the wake of its words that Joram almost failed to notice Uruq moving toward him. The man walked slowly, nonchalantly swinging his axe in one hand as he strode across the polished empty space, his great grey-flecked beard and head pushing toward him like a bull as his thick arms drew the axe up.

Joram gripped the sword and held out the bladetip like a torch, trying to ignore the way Uruq was smiling at the tremor in his arms. The man was drawing closer, step by slow menacing step, almost dragging the axe as he lumbered forward.

"I'll be merciful," he murmured, smiling. "And quick... Maybe."

And then...

Nothing.

The moments that followed passed by in a hazy blur, strung together by stretched fragments, isles of clarity amid a shimmering fog – the hot sting of Uruq's axe as it bit into Joram's flank, shoving through his attempted block to draw blood. Uruq's crazed eyes, bearing down on him like a madman, his bloated sweaty face inches away and locked in angry grimacing mania as he leaned down his ample weight, pushing the belly of his axeshaft against Joram's sword. The noise of the crowd seemed to swell and shrink, swaying like a pendulum as Joram fell to his knees. And then he was on his back, gasping for breath as the axeshaft pressed in on his windpipe. Joram clasped the other man's weapon with both hands, trying to keep Uruq from burying it in his throat. But it was no use. Joram could feel it coming, sinking in, the beginning slow crunch of cartilage as the shaft crushed down on his neck, the burn of bile in his lungs, the hammered thump of his heart as he began to give way to delirium and black out.

But when he came to again there was only silence. Deathly silence.

He was crouched, down on one knee with one fist against the floor, staring at the glossy whorls of copper and grey rock trapped within the rink's perfect smooth pane. And that was when he noticed the blood, there by his pressed fist, whether his or another's he couldn't tell. So he tried to get up, still woozy, a little out of breath, and see more. Rising to his feet, he felt a strange ache gathering around his ribs and back, as if his entire torso had swollen and was beginning to bruise. The crowd were still in their places on the wall, but silent, and still, staring across the void toward the arena; toward him. It was only then Joram noticed the heat in his fist, and unclenched it, allowing the black pearl to roll free from his palm onto the smooth stone floor. It sizzled a little like the meat that had been tossed onto the altar from their offerings outside as it landed, without bouncing, onto the rink. The amulet and chain were gone now, somehow burned away, leaving only the jewel. *But why? How?* Still dazed, Joram crouched and reached out to gather it, then slowly tried to straighten and rise to his feet once more. Which was when he saw what everyone else had been staring at.

He moved toward the heap of tangled garments and splayed limbs lying on the ground a few yards away. Uruq's axe lay discarded, several feet from the crumpled mass, beyond what may have been an outstretched arm. Joram could hear himself breathing now, tides of air sweeping in and out as his thoughts scattered loose within him, rattling to the tumultuous thump of his own heart like dust atop the skin of a beating drum.

The strange angle of the body, face down and with a cruel grim twist to the spine. The legs positioned at odd slants, the toes of one almost touching the ear. And then the pool of blood beginning to gather on the other side beneath the outstretched arm and axe.

Joram prodded at the knotted heap with his foot, redundantly checking to see if there was any life left under the piled folds of clothing. When he saw no movement, he placed his booted sole onto the meat and pushed, rolling the body. Limbs flopped and splayed, tangled and awkward, as the body tumbled slowly onto its side. Joram stared, momentarily fascinated by the muddle of blood and swelling that used to be a face. Uruq's face. He stared for a moment longer before noticing the elder standing opposite at the edge of the arena's rink, watching Joram with stunned, fearful awe.

"My gift to you," the voice said then, suddenly close, near as a lover, resounding from within and over Joram as though entombed in his ears. "They will listen now," it added. "They will listen to anything we say. They will listen to all we have been waiting to say for so long."

Joram looked at the elder's face and studied the expression there. And suddenly he could feel the thrill of it lifting him, guiding him away from Uruq's bloodied prone flesh and to his feet as the elder, standing before him, stumbled back as he moved.

Joram opened his palms to him, holding his arms out on either side. "What needed to be done is done. We are brothers now." He looked beyond him, gazing out again to the shocked silent crowd along the walls as he lifted his voice. "I am the brother of you all…" He walked from the rink, toward the cliff edge of the column. "You have called me outcast. Alien. Stranger. Names I bore without complaint because I knew why you used them. I've always known. For fear. Fear of what you don't understand. Fear of the unknown. Fear of change. The same fear I see in your eyes now. And the very fear that has imprisoned you, kept you bound, scrounging and foraging in lands that refuse to feed you, whilst *your* lands, the lands of your fathers, feed the bellies of the oppressors who stole them from your forbears three hundred years ago.

"The Five Land Sovereignty is a thief. A bandit that now calls its theft law. But theft does not cease to be what it is when enough time has passed. What was done then cannot now be counted law by those who have benefitted from it, and who *continue* to benefit from it, whilst we starve and shiver in these wastelands."

Murmurs from the crowd, people recovering their tongues as they listened to what he was saying. They were hearing him now; for the first time in all his long years of being here, they were *really* hearing him.

"The Sovereignty is a *thief*," he pressed on. "A bandit that takes as it wants. It took your lands, and everyday takes the food due your children whilst they shiver and die, and all the while it calls these things law. Nature. The way things ought to be. But it is not, brothers. This is not the way things *ought* to be. This is not the way Markúth desires it to be.

"It is the sins of your fathers that have visited you. It is they who forgot Markúth, they who forgot their god. They who ceased to acknowledge him at their harvests and wedding feasts. They who allowed their hearts to grow cold toward him, until he was no more than an icon on their doorposts, a sigil on the arm or at an annual ritual, and for some even less than that…

"You have forgotten him. But he has not forgotten you. He sees your suffering. He has heard your cries. And he beckons you once more to embrace him, trust him. Give place to his ways and become his people again.

"This is why he has sent me to you – an outsider. To teach you his ways, show you his paths. And he has promised, that if you follow me this day then what you have witnessed here shall be the fate of your enemies, the thieves to the south who took the lands that rightfully belong to you."

Joram stepped beyond the rink onto the outer edge of the column, spreading his arms.

"You are not a horde of scattered tribes and beggars. You were not born to dwell in cold, famine and disease. You were born to live and breathe in strength, as a nation, in your own land, just as Markúth has willed it. That is the law *your* god gives you. That is the way things are *supposed* to be.

"So, brothers, will you cast off your fear to follow your god? Will you go with him to take what belongs to you? Will you turn and embrace the lands you were born for? Tell me, brothers… What do you now say?"

TWELVE

GIFT

"We're not far now," Daneel said. "Just over that crest in the road."

But Noah didn't mind. The journey had been pleasant; breathing in the gentle waft of sea salt air from the coastline beside them, watching as gulls called dissentingly to one another in the sky. Noah liked the way their cries mingled with the soft claps of the water as they sauntered overhead, before diving from their lazy revolving orbits to snatch prey from beneath the waves. And it felt good, being out here in the warmth, bellies full from the fish Daneel had speared and cooked that morning. The disciplines that Daneel had been teaching him were working, calming his anger, thinning his fear, helping him sleep. It was the best Noah had felt in a while.

He looked ahead along the road as they reached the crest and saw the settlement Daneel had been speaking about: a small sunny fishing village of huts and shanties, assembled about a sandy cape along the western tip of the sea.

"Balaam's Corner, they call it," Daneel said. "Named after the lastborn of Theron the Great. Right here is supposedly the place he chased the last of Calapaar's armies into the sea at the Battle of Suns, nearly two centuries ago."

Noah had never heard Daneel speak of histories before but it was the first thing he'd said in days that didn't amount to an instruction, so he decided to make an effort. Talk back. It was a good day after all. "I was never good with history."

"Really? Thought that was all they speak of in Dumea. I was stuck there once, for about a month, with my brother."

"You did well to survive it."

"You're not fond of the place then, though it's your home?"

Noah shrugged. "I don't know. It's never really felt like home… I think I always hoped to leave one day."

"How? You're the heir."

"Maybe I would forfeit. Dumea is not like other places. Just because you're born the son of the ruler doesn't mean you will one day become one. You must complete trials. Judgements, we call them."

"Judgements," Daneel quipped drily. "Sounds fun."

"It's tradition. Back home they say it goes all the way back to when Dumea was first settled by the Seven Families during the Forty Year Famine, back before the Cull. It's how they chose their kings."

"*Chose* the king? Interesting notion. Most places no one chooses that first king but the man himself, then he goes about with a sword and a few other men persuading everyone else to agree."

"Father would say that's what makes Dumea different. They decided from the beginning they didn't want to kill each other over who should be king; and so set the trials instead, made it so whoever would sit on the throne would be worthy of it in better ways than how well they can swing a sword."

"Very civilised."

Noah shrugged and glanced back to the water, thinking of Father.

"So how does it work then?" Daneel asked. "These contests."

Noah looked at him. "You really want to know?"

"It's as good a thing to hear as any. We've time to kill."

Noah, squinting up at the sky, sighed. The sun had passed behind a long strip of clouds, drifting west from across the calm waters of the sea. "You have to be a part of the Seven Families," he replied.

"The ones who began the city. They're like a kind of royalty now – Hophir, which is my bloodline. Then there is Tsahir, Tarabi, Hadjíf, Dossad, Naeem, and Yousani. Old lines. If you belong to one of them you can take the Judgements, as long as you're of age or younger than the steward's firstborn... me."

"And so... what? Whoever completes these Judgements first becomes heir?"

"It's more like as long as I don't fail them, I become heir. As the steward's son I'd need only to complete the Judgements better than the least from among those who chose to take them with me. As long as I wasn't the worst, I'd be made heir. The Families, they always wanted to favour the ruler's son, just didn't want to make it a birthright. Didn't want whoever was heir to become lazy."

"So, they test you, to make sure you deserve the throne."

"Not a throne anymore, just a stewardship. But yes, they test you. You learn the Histories first, then the scribes test you. Few years later, you learn the Philosophies – the Sayings of Sufjan, the Proverbs of Ycothar, the Fables of Markúth, that kind of thing, and again, the scribes test you. Then, lastly, the Laws, which always takes the longest because you have to spend a year serving with one of the vassals, travelling with them wherever they go. Hanesda, Qareb, Sippar, Hikramesh. Wherever."

"Sounds tedious."

Noah just shrugged again. "I'd have taken the Second Judgement next year, or probably the year after. It's always taken me longer than the others to learn things."

"And yet you've been quick to learn the meditations." Daneel was looking at him peculiarly now, the way he had back in the woodlands along the coast a few days before when he'd had to shake him awake from the memories Noah had found when Daneel had begun to teach him the first disciplines. "It's unusual for someone your age," Daneel added. "Very unusual."

Something about the way he said it felt like an accusation, again, so Noah looked at him, trying to read Daneel's intent, and then when he couldn't, just turned back to the road ahead and let the silence open up between them once more as they came into the village.

Sunny dimples glinted along the soft moving pane of the water beside them where a boy and his father were wrestling a skiff onto shore. The beach was narrow, the sand hard and compacted like grit. Noah could see people gathered further up on the seafront, sheltered beneath large open stalls with thatched-roof awnings whilst children milled around on the beach bare-chested or chased the waves as they climbed the shore. Away from the beach, a short slim man in a cotton shift and pale turban was leading a pair of oxen and an oxcart toward them. Daneel smiled at him as he passed, eyeing the grain sacks piled on the cart as he went by.

"We need to find some food," Daneel explained, "and an animal to ride on… We'll need more than just our feet to get south."

"Is that where we're going?"

Daneel shrugged. "Probably. For now, at least. But first we need to find some food. And a mule."

They walked into the village, heading along the main road away from the seaside. Wooden houses mostly, built with charred planks and shingles to protect against the salty air, and some of them propped on stilts like a wharf to guard against the tide. The settlement was bigger than Noah had expected somehow, and better organised – houses set in rows and streets, branching off the main thoroughfare whilst gutters ran in narrow grooves behind the terraces. Two wells sat on a shallow mound in the middle of what appeared to be some sort of village square or crossroads. Daneel took his bag off his shoulder and undid the drawstring, then took out his flask and handed it to Noah.

"May as well make yourself useful," he said, and nodded at the mound.

"Where are you going?"

"To try find us something to ride out of here on." He glanced down. "And, if we're lucky, maybe something new for our feet."

He walked away, south along the dirt road toward a house backed by a large fenced yard as Noah watched. After he was gone, the boy glanced down at his battered sandals. Clods of dirt and dust had caked together into a dark grime wedged between his toes. He considered them for a moment, and then wandered over to the wells where a pair of girls kneeled by the bricked wall, bending over the edge of the largest one and peering down into its deep round hollow.

"You shouldn't do that," Noah said absently, and was almost startled by how quickly they turned to regard him. "It's the walls…" He explained when they didn't answer. He gestured awkwardly to the crumbled mortar and heavily eroded bricks along the well's lip. "So close to the sea, bricks like that, they always get weak."

"We know," the taller one said. "We live here." She leaned heavily on the words. She was pretty, Noah thought, freckles dotting her snub nose and olive cheeks like delicate sprinklings of cinnamon. Her teeth were small, slightly gapped in the middle; and her hair – thick, black and curly – bound beneath a patterned headkerchief like someone five times her age.

Not knowing what to say, Noah just stood there, scratching awkwardly at his neck and trying not to stare.

"Yusrah dropped her doll in like an idiot," the girl announced to break the silence.

The girl's younger sister, or so Noah assumed, hung her head, pouting. "Wasn't my fault," she stretched out the words, almost turning them into a melody.

"Was. And now Papa will blame me because of *you*."

Yusrah, the younger girl, looked up at Noah and smiled. "Will you help us get it out?"

"Don't be stupid. He can't help us. Look at him. He's a beggar."

"I'm not a beggar."

"Yes, you are. Look at your clothes. Look at your shoes. If you're not a beggar then what are you?"

"You wouldn't believe me if I told you."

"Come on, Yusrah. Papa says we shouldn't talk to beggars. We'll come back later."

"Wait." Noah walked toward the well. "If I was to help you, would you bring me some food?"

"Thought you said you weren't a beggar, blockhead."

"I'm not begging, blockhead. This is what's called a trade. Do you want my help or not?"

The smaller girl, Yusrah, giggled, revealing gummy gaps where front teeth should've been, whilst her older sister just tilted her head, regarding Noah speculatively.

"Well? Deal?"

"Fine," the girl said. "Deal."

Noah put the flask down and reached out his hand. "Good. I'm Noah."

The girl looked doubtfully at Noah's outstretched hand before placing her own briefly into it, barely pressing his palm before withdrawing back to herself. "Dina," she murmured.

"Nice to meet you, Dina."

"And I'm Yusrah."

"Nice to meet you too, Yusrah. So, let's see about this doll."

Leaning gently on the wall, Noah looked down over its ledge into the well – a bricked hole about twenty feet down with a circle of shadowed water at the bottom. Which was good. Not too deep, an advantage of its being so close to the sea. He could easily see the wood doll bobbing in the water by the wall, buoyed by its timber limbs and the air still trapped in the wool of its clothes.

He took hold of the overhang where the bucket-rope was wound and pulled himself up to stand on the wall, then took hold of the rope with his other hand, holding himself steady as he tugged to angle the bucket slowly toward the wall.

"Careful," Yusrah whispered, tiptoeing to watch.

Noah yanked a little on the rope, tipping the bucket to lean its lip toward the water. Then tugged again, quick and delicate, to edge it onto its side. The bucket skimmed beneath the surface, slanting as it drank the well's water in before Noah took the slack and guided it the rest of the way, sweeping beneath the doll in one smooth motion to collect it into the pail as Yusrah squealed in excitement. Noah hopped down from the wall, then proceeded to draw the bucket up from the well and hand it to a bouncing, grinning Yusrah.

"Thank you, thank you, thank you."

Noah laughed. "You're welcome."

She took the doll – a faceless, smoothly carved figurine, jointed at the knees and elbows by string and clothed in a plain woollen rag – and hugged it to herself.

Noah looked at Dina and opened both palms. "No foul, no blame."

To which Dina, apparently impressed, smiled more genuinely.

"So, about this food…"

She seemed about to answer, but then froze, her eyes flitting to something behind Noah where–

The blow came from the side, thick coarse knuckles and a backswinging hand. Noah was suddenly looking up from the ground, splayed on his back, watching a single gull arcing across the blue sky overhead as the side of his head throbbed.

"You stay away from them, you little mutt."

The man stood over him – thin, wiry, bare-chested, and with a rag tied around his skinny stubbled neck. Noah could see the bones of the man's heavily tanned chest as he reached down to grab him by the collar.

"No, Papa. He was helping."

But the man ignored her, yanking Noah roughly to his feet.

"You think you can touch and take whoever you want, stranger? Is that it?" the man hissed, the stale reek of beer gusting into Noah's face as the man held him up.

"No. I was just–"

The man thumped him in the stomach, folding Noah over his fist before shrugging him off to fall, wheezing, back to the ground. The girls were screaming as the man stalked around to Noah's front to kick him in the ribs. He was winding up to swing his foot when Yusrah rushed in and grabbed him by the wrist.

"No Papa. My doll. He got my doll for me. Tell him, Dina."

But Dina wouldn't. Instead the man just swung his arm, shaking the little girl off and flinging her back against the wall of the well, bouncing her skull off the bricks. She dropped to the ground unconscious as Dina started screaming again, which only seemed to draw the man's ire further. He turned around, his finger jabbing in her face.

"You *see*? You *see* what you've done?"

The man's arm was already lifting, cocking back to swat Dina by the time Noah, curled up on the ground, managed to twist himself around to see. He reached out instinctively, as though his arm could somehow reach across the space between them to block the blow, somehow stop him, stop everything, somehow stop it all – all the things he'd seen and that filled his head and felt too much – and for a moment it was as though they were all there, surrounding him. Those winged beasts in Çyriath, tearing apart stone, mortar and bone as they roared at the night. His father's body lying face down in the sand with twin blades sticking from his back as he bled to death on a lonely beach. The broken body of a dying stranger gazing up at him in the rain like a forgotten friend; bloody, bruised and gashed as viscera glinted in the campfire's light from the cuts along the man's face and arms and thigh and too much and stop it all and stop it all and stop it all and…

Noah felt the swell and surge through his chest, channeling up from somewhere within as though the tangled mess of his guts and innards were trying to expel themselves. It rolled up into his shoulders and along his outstretched arm like a wave, shuddering against the bones of his elbow and wrist like a trapped storm that needed to get out and then…

He blinked as the drunken man suddenly shot forward, tossed away like a leaf in the wind. The thick wooden pole of the well's overhang exploded as the man crashed through it, shattered wood splaying everywhere as he vaulted skywards before landing thirty feet away on the dirt road, the well's bucket dropping back down into the pool of water below.

Everything stopped.

Dina, who'd been kneeling and wailing by her unconscious sister, was now staring at Noah. Eyes wide, trembling.

Noah looked at her. "I…" but she flinched as he moved.

"Witch." She whispered it at first. Like a query, a sound she was testing on her lips. And then, still trembling, her arm lifted to point at him, the word dropping from her like a heavy stone, dull and certain. "Witch."

Dazed and wheezing, Noah tried to gather himself and rise, but saw her flinch again, and so settled himself back to the ground instead to look at the sky. He felt too weak to get up anyway, and overhead was so calm and bright. The clouds had moved on, letting the sun back in, and he could see that the gull was still there too, circling in slow lazy arcs as though nothing had happened. And then Daneel was suddenly there, leaning over Noah and frenziedly patting his arms, checking him over and trying to tell Noah something but the boy could no longer hear. Everything seemed so muddled and heavy now, slowed and sluggish as though he'd been plunged beneath the waves out on the cape. So Noah blinked again, looking wearily at Daneel's silently moving lips as the assassin reached down and shovelled his arms under him to lift him up, hoisting him into his arms from the ground and turning to carry him away.

THIRTEEN

BONES

The disguise was Josef's idea. Baggy hoods of dyed burlap, a mess of dark reds and deep blues with tassels of gold-stained horsehair dangling from the hem. Just a few of the many gaudy items Josef and Sidon had managed to filch from one of the closets used by the palace's actors during their new-moon dramas. Bright coloured bangles, polished brass anklets, stained woodbeads, multicoloured turbans that looked as though they'd been dragged through the gluey sap of a honeycomb and then tossed into a vat of jewels.

"Hardly inconspicuous," Sidon murmured as he looked down into the chest of inordinately brash trinkets and garments they'd dragged to his bedchambers from the performers' vault.

"The only people who draw attention to themselves are those who've nothing to hide," Josef answered.

Sidon glanced at him to see if he was joking. The Brother looked back, expressionless. Silly thought, Sidon decided. Josef never joked.

He breathed deep as the noise swelled beyond the window. Outside, the sounds of celebration were already gathering – cheers and singing and the gentle rhythmic bounce of bells and flutes.

"I've never understood it, you know, the Feast of Bones," Sidon remarked as he lifted a yellow scarf from the chest and pulled a face. The whole thing was tinselled in sparkly red stones, like someone had taken a vessel of frosted blood and tossed it over the fabric. "Almost feels like a kind of mockery to me." He held the scarf up for Josef's scrutiny – *yes? No?*

"The scarf is fine, Sharíf. But why do you say that?"

Sidon gestured at the ugly clothing. "Apart from the obvious?"

Josef allowed a thin smile.

"Almost a whole three weeks of festivity – food, drink, dancing – every year, and for what? To celebrate Gilamek? Memorialise a fiction our fathers fought to destroy?"

"It's just a tradition."

"In the name of a god."

"When it started maybe. Now, it's just a way to celebrate harvest. Besides," he drew a whetcloth over his dagger and slipped it into the sleeve on his belt beneath his clothing, "it will lend a good cover to us tonight, make it easier to follow the queen mother."

His mother. Sidon marvelled at the thought of it even now. He'd had days to digest what they'd heard outside her bedchamber but even now it made no sense. Helgon the Wise, Ruler of the Five Lands, the Seventh from the First Father and king of the Sumerian Riverlands, murdered by his own wife, Sidon's mother, for reasons that still remained unclear.

Sidon grunted as he glanced at the assortment of scarves and garments Josef had strewn over his forearm – garishly coloured fabrics with chaotic patterns and dyed stitching, they looked as though they'd been tossed together by a drunken seamstress. "You're really going to wear those?"

"The bolder the disguise the better. Although you'll perhaps do better to leave those here." Sidon's ruby jewelled signet and the patterned gold thumb-band he'd received at his anointing glinted in the lamplight on his right hand. Sidon glanced down at them and frowned. "They are the marks of a Sharíf," Josef explained, "easily recognisable, which is not what we are aiming for tonight."

Sidon made a wry face as he removed the rings and placed them on his sidetable, then changed his mind and put them in a purse to keep with him in his pocket.

"Are you sure about this, Sharíf?"

Josef's eyes were still on him, coolly measuring, and for a moment Sidon wasn't sure how to answer. Ever since they'd overheard Uncle Játhon's apparent disclosures about Mother's part in Father's death the world had seemed slightly askew, tilted somehow. Even now the notion of it seemed unthinkable, ridiculous, like the make-believe stories Mother would tell him as a child.

"Sharíf?"

"Yes," Sidon finally answered. "I'm sure."

Josef's gaze lingered on him a few moments more before he turned to the sidetable and picked up the brush dipped in face paint. "Very well then. Now... hold still."

An hour later they were standing amid the Feast of Bones watching a parade of giant puppets saunter and jig along the main street, propped up on stilts manipulated by costumed men whilst a band of skimpily clad women strutted behind. Coloured ribbons trailed from small arced scaffolds on the dancers' backs like wings, fluttering as they twirled and pivoted along the road. Sidon couldn't help but feel tense, so close to the parade and crowd without a troop of cityguards to protect him, just Josef. He stared at the tall ambling effigies – bulging heads of upholstered wood and dyed cotton, hanging lanterns for eyes – wandering like slow drugged giants along the main thoroughfare west of the palace.

"I don't like them," Sidon said, but Josef, beside him, didn't hear. Too busy scanning the crowd.

The street was filled with revellers – dancing, drinking, shouting, dressed in gaudy colours and kooky wigs like exotic Summerland birds. Almost everyone had painted faces, as did Sidon and Josef, daubed in black and white to resemble a skull. Laughing women with peacock feathers in their hair twirled and twisted to the music, the metallic blue-green sheen of the pinions glistening in the halflight cast by the torches on the wall. Beyond them, further along the street, a gang of bare-chested young men sat hoisted on shoulders, pounding the air with clenched fists as they sang at the sky. For a moment Sidon thought he'd been recognised, and froze, watching as one of the youths turned his skull-painted face to look directly at him. But then the boy just grinned, and resumed blaring out his drunken song with his companions as Josef took Sidon by the arm to usher him along through the din.

The Sharífa eventually emerged from a gate to the palace gardens by the far wall, just as expected, dressed in something elegant and green beneath a dark hoodcoat, flanked by two similarly hooded guardsmen.

"Shedaím," Josef shouted into Sidon's ear, pointing toward his mother's bodyguards as they moved across the street.

Sidon leaned toward the brother to ask how he knew but Josef was already moving to follow them, angling around the crowd as the queen mother and her bodyguards turned into an alley on the corner. Sidon went after him, the pair with their hoods up and heads down as they went across the road to enter the passage. Murals of giant sunbirds covered the alley walls on either side, faded purples and pastel blues, smudged dark by patches of ash from the passage of torches and oil lamps. At the other end the space opened into a short cobbled broadwalk that led west to the city baths, and tonight was a den of activity. There seemed to be more people here than in the main street, packed in against each other like fish in a bucket, prancing and romping to a shuddering rhythm of whistles and pandrums as a troupe of musicians danced and strutted along the near wall as if it was a stage. The smell of cooking meats and spices assaulted the air, wafting from the bank of spits and grills that lined the wall opposite. Sidon watched from Josef's shoulder as men tried to inch a barrel-laden cart through the dancing scrum.

"There."

Sidon pointed as he caught sight of the queen mother, patiently pressing her way through the tide of dancing people alongside the cart with the guardsmen. He adjusted his hood and felt for the blade at his waist as Josef took him by the elbow and stepped into the throng.

The noise was deafening, a wall around them. Raised arms and jigging elbows, heads bopping as they faced toward the musicians on the wall, and a half naked man who'd managed to climb up there, buttocks bared, a wineskin in one hand as he urinated into whatever grounds or bushes lay on the other side.

Welcome to the Feast of Bones.

Sidon felt Josef's hand tug him forward again, this time out of the thick of the crowd and toward the margins. More space here. Beggarly vendors loitering on the fringes with baskets of wood figurines and clay statuettes, each painted into skeletons and clothed in brightly coloured rags.

"There she is." Josef pointed toward the far end where the Sharífa and her guards were still pushing their way through the crowd toward an alley along the opposite wall. Sidon went briskly along the side of the broadwalk, Josef ahead of him, skimming through the broken edges of the multitude – gaggles of inebriated men playing sticks against the wall with members of the cityguard, youths scrawling on the brickwork with chalkstone behind them. Sidon and Josef drew level with the Sharífa and watched her enter another alley before starting into the bustling throng to follow. They pushed and shoved their way through, came out the other side, and stepped into the narrow passage.

They moved along the alley in silence, ducking and weaving between the wild sprawling limbs of vined plants that climbed the walls. Josef slowed and motioned to Sidon as they reached the end, then crouched to glance around the corner. No one there. A tall locked gate, smothered by more plants.

"Can you open it?" Sidon whispered.

Josef reached into his garment and fetched out a small roll of cloth and undid the bind, allowing the array of complicated utensils pocketed within it to flip open. He took two out and handed the roll to Sidon to hold, then hunched over the gate's lock. Soft click as he unhitched the latch and slowly eased it open, allowing the gate to glide on its hinges to reveal the garden behind.

Tall rows of neatly kempt bushes ran in twisting corridors like a kind of labyrinth, lit by standing torches throughout.

Josef stepped in first. "Stay low," he cautioned, and then led Sidon along the hedged aisles until they came to a brief opening of tidily cut grass and polished benches, centred by a perfectly circular pond. They were in the gardens of Kamal, the crown scribe, Sidon realised.

"I never knew there was a back way into here," he whispered. "These are the grounds of–"

"Shh. Look."

The queen mother, still hooded, suddenly strolled into view and sat on the near bench, facing away from them to watch the pond. A few moments later she was joined by General Gahíd and Uncle Játhon, the latter offering the Sharífa a goblet of wine as he lowered to his seat. Sidon shuffled to the front of the hedge, holding his breath as he strained to hear them.

"What about that Calpasese girl?" Játhon was saying. "The one who came to Kamal's banquet last year, when his niece was born."

"Nephew," Chalise corrected.

"Whatever."

"I didn't like her," Chalise replied. "Too prideful. And she has a funny smile."

"Really? A funny smile? Could you *be* any more picky?"

"It's an important choice."

"Perhaps the Sharíf could be asked?" Gahíd offered.

Játhon leaned forward on his seat and stared witheringly at him. "Forgive me, Gahíd, but have you lost your mind?"

The general sipped calmly on his wine.

"Perhaps you should explain yourself, General," Chalise said.

"You will listen to him speak on this?" Játhon hissed.

"The boy will know what he likes," Gahíd answered. "If you learn that, you'll have him. A man's ear often bends to a pretty face."

"He's a boy," Chalise murmured.

Gahíd shrugged. "They've the same habit."

"You've other things to concern yourself with, General," Játhon said. "Namely, Geled."

"Yes, about that…"

"What?"

The general leaned in and answered but Sidon couldn't quite hear. He was about to turn to Josef again, ask if there was a way they could get closer, when he felt the Brother stiffen beside him.

"We have to go," Josef whispered. "Now."

"What? Why?" But he saw the answer almost as he asked. One of the hooded guards had appeared on the periphery, beside the circular pond, and seemed to be looking in their direction.

Josef took Sidon by the arm, tugging him back toward the hedgerows as the guard, beckoning to the other Shedaím, prowled forward like a stalking wildcat.

Josef and Sidon started running once they'd rounded the corner, rushing through the twisting path of hedgerows to find the way out. Sidon could hear the scampering footsteps at his back as they reached it, and then pushed through into the narrow alley with its hanging plants and sap-greased walls.

Stray fronds of light from the street up ahead, casting long ghoulish shadows along the alleyway as they ran up it. They reached the road and spilled out into the crowd. Drums hammering. The exultant blare of horns. There seemed to be more people now, the crowd brimming against the wall so that Josef and Sidon almost couldn't press their way through. Eventually they managed to squeeze into the glut of bodies, Josef's hand gripping Sidon's arm again as they shoved their way through the clamour.

Flutes. Bells. Jumping elbows and arms. Staccato drumbeat and a pair of women wearing black-painted large-beaked birdmasks. Josef pushed between them, the pursuers closing in from behind. They could hear their shouts now, carrying faintly, muted by the din. Up ahead, the stick-playing cityguards glanced about like spooked geese as they roused from their games by the opposite wall. The pursuers from the garden surged through with drawn blades held aloft, shooing and shoving people out of the way. Sidon, panicked, tugged frantically on Josef's arm.

"Josef! Josef!"

The Brother finally turned and, seeing the guards, warded Sidon back as he stepped in to meet the pursuers. The crowd was still dancing. Sidon saw the wink of steel, the quick darting thrust of the blade. Saw Josef shift, pivoting his hip as he chopped down on the first man's attack and sunk his dagger into the ribs. The man went down, a girl next to him screaming as the crowd continued to jump and gyrate, trampling and stumbling over the attacker as he fell into the crush of bodies.

Sidon looked toward the escape, then back again. Saw Josef stiffen and wince. The Brother swivelled suddenly, swung his elbow, slamming it against the temple of another attacker, then grabbed the man by the skull as he slumped and jabbed a dagger through his throat.

More screams now.

Josef breathing hard, grimacing as he reached to his flank and tugged out a bloody fingerblade. He shoved Sidon away as he tried to step in to help.

"No. Go. Go. That way."

The alley wasn't far now, barely a cart length. Guards were continuing to spill out from the alley behind and wade their way through the frenzy toward them. A youthful reveller flew aside as a soldier shoved him out of the way and drew his blade. Some in the crowd were trying to escape by climbing up onto the wall, fleeing the soldiers' shouts and the glint of steel.

Another soldier lunged at Josef, who, despite the crush, managed to sway out of the way, nailing the other man with a knee to the ribs as another attacker appeared from amid the mob. Josef turned to engage him, caught his wrist, twisted, dropping the blade free.

Sidon saw another coming at Josef from behind as he tangled with the first. Sidon screamed but it was no use, his voice swallowed by the music.

The man came in and stamped on Josef's calf, dropping him to a knee as others crowded in and blocked his view.

"Josef!"

Sidon hurled himself forward, trying feebly to reach over the heads and backs of the jostling scrum. But it was too far. Too late.

The dagger was already there, glinting in the firelight like the silvery shimmer of a fish as it thrust forward through the chaos to sink into Josef's back and–

Suddenly, the attacker was reeling. Sidon looked up. The birdmasked woman. She hit the attacker again, and then thrust her hand repeatedly into his gut as though digging for change. The man folded over her buried fist, then fell as she yanked it free, slick with blood. Sidon was being pulled away before he could make sense of it, dragged back from behind with a blade at his neck until moments later they were in the alley, out of the crowd.

His assailant shoved him against the wall.

"You come with us. Or you die. Your choice."

Sidon glanced aside, saw the other birdmask dragging a wounded Josef free from the panic and into the alley with them, and nodded. And then they were being marched along the alley, shoved into the back of a large horsedrawn carriage, the two birdmasks climbing in after them before they were driven away.

They were free of the crowds, rolling south along a sidestreet in the direction of the oldtown district when the women finally removed their masks to reveal themselves.

Súnamites. Short cropped hair and dark smooth skin.

"Ironic, isn't it," the first of them remarked. She eyed them briefly as the carriage continued to trundle south through the city, and then turned her gaze out to the busy streets rolling by beside them. "The festival, I mean. I'm told it was named after the story of a god who died from a song so sweet he couldn't resist listening." She reeled her gaze in from the roads and alleys passing by, the crowds beginning to thin as they continued to travel further away from the palace and marketplace. "Yet a song he knew to be cursed, and that would rot the hearer's flesh for as long as he listened, right down to the bones. Which makes you think, doesn't it? The kind of thing a man will count to be worth his life." She looked them over. Josef, sitting beside Sidon as the carriage swayed and rocked, was still bleeding, leaning against the sidewall and breathing heavily.

"My man needs help," Sidon said.

"Strange too that they call it Gilamek's Song though," the black woman said. "Seeing as he only died from it, never sang it. They wouldn't do that among my people. They'd call the song by its singer. But then that's just one of many strange things about your ways. You do not like so much to give names to the women in your tales."

"Where are you taking us?"

"Somewhere safe, of course."

"Why? Who are you?"

"My name is Imaru, and this," she gestured to the woman beside her, "is Luavese."

"What do you want?"

The thin smile again. "Well. First, we want you to keep from dying in a sidestreet in your own city. After that? Well. We will have much to talk about. The Five Lands are not what you think they are, Sharíf, and neither is this city of yours. As, I think, you can now tell. There are many things happening here you do not understand. But you will, Sharíf. For us."

Sidon looked her over, the glossy dark sheen of her skin, the clear wide eyes and the way she sat there, calm and smug as a queen lounging in her throneroom. "You mean, for Súnam," he said.

The smile broadened. "You will not understand it now, Sharíf, but in time you will. You will see, in the end, that Súnam is your only hope."

FOURTEEN

MAGI

Neythan could feel the familiar bite of bindings against his skin. The thick ropes, coarse with wiry bristles where the twine had frayed, chafed against his wrists and ankles, keeping him stretched out and fastened down on the wooden slab.

"What do you think it means?" Arianna wondered as she lay on the slab beside him.

Neythan glanced over and saw her staring again at the copper icon on the wall – a clash of sheet-thin polygons, vaguely man-shaped, with carefully painted-on eyes on the piece that appeared to be its head. "Who knows?"

It was hard to tell how long they'd been here. A couple of days perhaps. Neythan had watched the beam of sunlight angling in from the small window somewhere behind them take its slow path across the room that many times, creeping along the grimy ledge that skirted the far wall where a clutter of instruments and tools he didn't recognise lay spread out – implements of flint and ivory and metal, small wooden dishes, what looked like a banana leaf smeared with various blobs of dried paste and sediment. A couple of times people had entered the room from a door behind them – a pair of women their first day here, after they'd awoken, morning probably, carrying ornate brass kettles of incense dangling from chains they held in their hands and their every step marked by the soft tinkle of bell-tethered anklets as they swung the kettles and filled the room with their sweet smoke. They'd walked around Neythan and Arianna on their slabs afterwards, sprinkling them with some kind of aromatic oil flicked from the dipped leaves of what looked like a hyssop branch as they muttered and chanted some unintelligible song. Since then a small brown-skinned woman had come in at intervals to feed them – boiled plantains, soup, slices of mango and guava, a peppery rice stew mix neither Neythan or Arianna had been able to identify – and each time the little woman, her face covered with a kerchief, had patiently and wordlessly spooned the dish into their mouths and given them water as they lay there, waiting to learn what would happen to them next.

"For the record, this is your fault," Arianna said.

"Really? That's what we're going to do now? Discuss fault?"

"The whole going into the giant stone head thing? Bad idea. Those were my words."

"It's a temple."

"Whatever."

"We need to find a way out of here."

"You know, I think it's a sign for something, but I don't know what."

"What?"

"The icon on the wall."

"Weren't we just talking about the temple?"

"We were talking about the icon first."

"We need to be talking about finding a way out of here."

"No, actually what we *need* to be talking about are these little episodes you keep having. Seeing things? Dizzy spells?"

Neythan sighed heavily. She'd been intermittently harassing him about it for almost the entire time they'd been stuck here. "*Again*, Ari? You really want to do this now?"

"You made that room *move*, Neythan. You were reading the

symbols on the wall. You were speaking in some kind of… other tongue. It's all connected."

"And I don't remember doing any of it… I remember reading, yes. Vaguely. But I don't remember anything else."

"What about the words. Do you remember any of *them?*"

Neythan sighed loudly, staring at the ceiling. Bronzed light was washing through the muslin draped across the window overhead, flooding the little room in a warm bright light.

"Just try, Neythan. Please."

Neythan thought back on it, the way the blood-script glyphs on the wall had seemed to somehow move and coalesce, morphing and shifting like drops trickling down a pane, into some kind of temporal meaning. "I… It was more like a riddle than anything else… Something about a… a dark moon's song? Sons of ancients. Eternal laws… Pale kings… I don't know, Ari. I can't remember any more than that. A moment later you took me by the arm and then the next thing I know I'm waking up here, in this room, and wondering why I can't move–"

"Wait," Arianna hissed. "You hear that?"

"I don't hear anything."

"*There.* That… I think there's someone coming."

Neythan glanced aside to the bucket beneath Arianna's slab, still empty since being slopped out a few hours before when they were fed, which meant it was too early for anyone to be returning with food. They'd been kept to a meal a day since arriving here.

They closed their eyes, feigning sleep, as the latch behind them clicked and lifted, then listened to the familiar crunch of the hinge as whoever was entering opened the door and stepped inside. The figure passed by them slowly, pausing for a moment between their prone bound bodies on the wooden slabs before moving to the room's other end to put something heavy down on the table and then walk around.

"I know you are both awake, of course, so you may as well stop pretending." A man's voice, deep but gentle. They opened their eyes to find a dark-skinned Súnamite standing opposite them. Tall.

Angular beneath his hooded smock and coat. His face was wide and taut, his cheeks almost skeletal, as if there wasn't enough skin to cover the bones beneath. He removed his hood, revealing a shiny hairless scalp that made Neythan feel he was looking into the face of a skull.

"I am Teju," the man quietly announced. "I am master here, of the Sayensí order." His eyes, large and severe, flitted fastidiously between them as his long fingers, poised tip to tip to form a cage, tapped solemnly against each other.

"You must be here to release us?" Arianna quipped.

"Does that mean you wish to leave then, before gaining what you came all this way to acquire?"

"You know why we are here?"

"We found the scroll amongst your things. Not the kind of thing one brings to a place like this without reason. Of course, we know why you are here. What *you* should know is there is a reason you were not able to read it. Well, many reasons in truth." The man had moved to the shelf skirting the side wall, littered with its strange collection of tools. He glanced over them, eyeing them like trinkets at a bazaar as he talked. "I suppose, in a way, it could be said it's not really your fault. The Sovereignty, you see – what a name for a place, as though it is some kind of answer to something." He turned from the shelf momentarily to look at them. "It is *not*." Then resumed his perusal of the shelf's items. "That place is the reason you cannot read the scroll. Or the reason you have not learned to."

"So, that means you plan to help us then," Neythan asked, "show us how to read it?"

"Well, that depends on whether you are going to help me."

"You? How can we help *you?*" Arianna replied.

The man turned from the shelf to face them for a moment, and then began to slowly stroll to the room's other side, passing through the beam of light from the window. "I was once of the priesthood, you know. In Jaffra. Did they tell you that? No, you needn't answer, of course they wouldn't. I am too inconvenient a truth. Not to be spoken of. They do not like to look upon difficult things there. They prefer only what they know, only what is familiar. In a way, precisely why I was cast out. I was exiled, you see; for, of all things, simply trying to heal a man."

"And why would they do that?"

"Because I cut him open." He paused midstride to register their response, his long fingers tapping and motioning in time to his words. "Yes. With a blade not unlike those on the shelf over there. A little cleaner though. I will have to speak to the others about having them washed."

"But why?" Arianna asked. "Why cut him open, if you hope to heal him?"

"Oh, a method I'd learned from some relic I'd found by a temple ruin further inland," he said casually, "west of the Serpent, although…" he turned and glanced at them again, "no, I don't suppose you will know it. You do not seem as though you would be familiar with these lands."

"A relic?"

"Hm? Oh. Yes. I shall explain about them later, perhaps. The point is I'd cut a man open to heal him, remove his sickness, but those backward, primitive minds Jaffra's priesthood is rife with decided to intervene. Had they let me alone to finish what I'd started the man would have lived, but instead he didn't, and they decided they'd blame me for his death, and blame my methods, all because their minds are too narrow and stubborn to understand." Teju let out a small bitter laugh. "*Tsung*, they call us now. Barbaric. Savages. But then I suppose that must always be the way of things, hm? It is always the older brother who shall oppress the younger, and misunderstand him. Always the old ways that will set themselves against the new. Nature's oldest game, and yet it needn't be; if only they would understand what we do here. If only they would listen. That is something you may be able to help change."

"*Us?*"

"Yes." The man pointed a long slender finger in Neythan's direction. "You, in particular… Neythan."

"You know my name?"

"And Arianna's too, yes. I know many things about you. That is why we kept you here, so we could go and learn of who you are, why you have come. I know the priests of Jaffra think you a seer, some of them at least. And I know it is they who sent you here to test that claim. You mustn't be alarmed. You came here with a Magi scroll, as I've said, an uncommon thing. *Very* uncommon. It was natural we would seek to learn of who you are, and I, for my part, am glad that we did. It has allowed me to learn how we might help each other." He stopped strolling and stood square to them now. "The bargain is simple. If I teach you to read the scroll you will be judged a seer. If you are judged a seer you will be joined to Jaffra's priesthood, perhaps even the high priesthood. You will be able to speak for this order, show them what we are."

"And what exactly is that?"

"Explorers. Learners. Perhaps teachers, if we could only be given the chance. As you will soon see."

"And you are certain you can teach us to read it."

"It is not as simple as that, Neythan. I must teach you why you have *failed* to read it. Only then will its secrets become open to you. So…" His fingers opened to them in a flourish, offering his request. "Do you agree?"

Neythan turned to Arianna.

"Well, don't look at me."

"No? With how you just got through telling me how all this is my fault, I thought I'd invite your counsel."

Arianna looked from Neythan to Teju; covenants, agreements, trades – strange how often they found themselves in these kinds of predicament. "Fine," she said, then addressed Teju. "If you are what you say you are, and help us, *and* release us, we will be agreed."

The man bowed his head. "We ask nothing more."

"So, tell us then," Neythan said. "Why can't we read the scroll? What does it have to do with the Sovereignty?"

"Isn't it obvious?"

"You mean, because they killed the priests?"

The man huffed, making a cutting dismissive motion with one

long hand. "Well… yes. Fine. That is part of it, but it is not nearly the whole. It isn't what they did, it is *why*. Yes, so some of the priesthoods had become corrupt, it is true. But *all* things corrupt. Thrones. Crowns. Even *brotherhoods*. But the Sovereignty does not seek to destroy *them*, only the priesthoods. A man should ask questions, he should seek to know why."

"For power," Neythan said.

"Yes. Power. As men endure, so does what is in them. The priesthoods were powerful. Very powerful. They could tell men what things are, *why* they are, how they came to be. You give a man a story of the world and his place in it, and he will listen. You give him a good enough story and he will even fight to defend it. It will be a god to him, a thing he will worship, and protect. You change that story, you change the man. You own the story, you own the man."

"Which is why the priesthoods were destroyed?"

"Yes. But it is not why they *could* be destroyed… We have priests here, in Súnam, who hold stories too, but our stories are told in song – easier to remember that way – both for the one who is to sing and those who are to hear. But each singer is different, how they sing is different, as is how they tell the stories through their songs. Perhaps they make one part of the story bigger than another, or change the words to make it clearer, or skip parts and return to them later."

"You're saying the priests here are corrupt too?"

"No. They do not lie. They *interpret*. They allow *how* the song is to be shared to change, but without changing the song itself. I'm saying that *is* the work of a priest. The days of our fathers are not the same as ours. If a song is to be sung, a story told, it must be told to those who are to hear it, in the way that best *allows them* to hear it; understand it, make use of it. That is what gives the songs their power. That is Súnam's way. We hold our truths *here*." The man patted his chest. "But in your Sovereignty, your stories are not sung, they are written. They are as dead things, fixed, the words unchanging, inscribed for a generation whose home is now the grave. Traditions instead of truths. And tradition, if left alone, can become a dangerous thing, a sort of rot. Soon men lose sight of its meanings, and then other men come and decide to clothe it with their own. In this way you keep the words, but change their meanings. Here, we change the words, keep the meanings. That is why your priesthoods fell."

"I'm sorry," Arianna put in. "But what does all this have to do with reading the scroll?"

"In your Sovereignty, you have learned to kill your priests and honour your scribes. So now in your lands men's minds flourish whilst their sha dies. But to read a Magi scroll, a man needs *both*. *You* did not see this, *could* not see it, because your way is the way of the Five Lands. You see only what it sees, what it has *taught* you to see… It is why you thought this," Teju had walked to the table at the back of the room, lifting the scroll he'd evidently brought in with him when their eyes were closed, "is a book. When in truth, it is a library."

Neither Neythan or Arianna answered, waiting for Teju to elaborate.

"I'm going to untie you, Neythan," he said, putting the scroll down. "If you *are* a seer, and you are of the Shedaím, you will not need to be taught to read this. You only needed to see what not to do and why. You have already learned the disciplines of the sha, the meditations. This will be like that. The only difference is instead of journeying into your sha, you will journey into the sha of the things in the page."

"*What?*"

The man undid the tether of the scroll's vellum cover and unrolled some of the page, then stepped forward to present it to Neythan. "Look. See the page, ignore the markings. The words are not important, and they are written in a tongue you cannot understand. What else is there?"

"Shards," Neythan answered. "Bone, stone, metals – woven into the page. I'd thought them keepsakes, to mark or explain what the words and symbols are saying."

"Of course you did." The man smiled. "Written words always the focus, as I said. It must be *they* that are the primary thing, the thing the shards are there to help explain, when in truth, it is the other way around. What if I was to tell you each of these shards is a book?"

Neythan looked at them – a slice of bone, no bigger than a fingernail, and beside it a similarly sized piece of rock, both sealed in some kind of resin and stitched into the page like garment jewels. "I'd say I don't see how that can be possible."

"But all living things have a sha, Neythan, some stronger than others. But a sha nonetheless." It reminded Neythan of Master Johann and his lessons back in Ilysia to watch Teju, his fingers dancing excitedly through the air as he laid out his truths: how life flows through all things, but at differing speeds with each – flesh and blood the quickest, then bone, and then more slowly through wood, rock and metal. It was mostly familiar fare, drawn from the Shedaím disciplines or something like them. "But now, suppose a thing – maybe a staff, a piece of wood, or metal, any old relic – is able to… witness things, capture them *within* their sha," Teju continued. "You understand the sha keeps all things, forgets nothing. These shards in the page have been treated, prepared, to preserve some of their witness and allow the rest to fade. So that the one who looks into them, will see what they are intended to see – what the author hoped for them to see."

"You mean Qoh'leth. The name on the scrollcoat. The father of the Brotherhood."

"Yes. And father of other things besides. As you will perhaps in time come to understand."

Neythan tried to take it in as the man stepped away to place the scroll back on the table behind him.

"You don't understand, Neythan. But you will soon. You will learn to use both your mind *and* sha to read the scroll's contents. Now… I am going to untie you. Are you ready?"

Neythan nodded.

The man came toward Neythan's slab and unbuckled the knot beneath it, letting Neythan's wrist slide out. Neythan grunted and flexed his fingers, working his muscles loose from the tension of the bind as the man moved around the slab to loosen the rest of his bindings. Slowly, he sat up on the slab, and then stretched, setting off a chorus of clicks in the bones of his neck, shoulders and arms.

"What about Arianna?"

"If you do as you've been asked you will both go free." The man stepped aside and gestured to the table and the scroll waiting on it. "Think of them as memories, Neythan, locked into each relic on the page."

Neythan got up, approached the table and slowly lowered to the stool next to it. "Memories..." Teju had stretched the page out to fill the table, displaying the strange symbols and glyphs Neythan had grown so accustomed to. He hesitated, gazing at the exotic lines and scribbles. "I was told there is a cost for the one who reads from it."

"Yes. Of sorts."

"What kind of sorts? What will happen to me?"

"Well, if you go about trying to read whatever wild tree or rock you come across, you will likely die. They are untreated, all of their memories still in them. Thousands of years old. Often older even than that. There's only so much the mind and sha can take. But if you keep to properly treated relics like the ones on this page, then yes, you will still need to be careful – too much of anything can lead to decay – but there should be no risk of that for you. You need only be sensible. And you have the disciplines. They will help you with the relics."

"Relics..."

"Yes. Centuries old, often. There are many of them, not only in the scrolls. Usually a sword, or staff, or jewel. Something like that. A keepsake that can be preserved from generation to generation. We have some here, and use them to learn things, new practices, like the method I told you of earlier of how to heal men of certain sicknesses, things that are not yet understood, but once were. But what makes a Magi scroll so precious is that it is filled by shards taken from *many* such relics, hundreds of them, and all of them treated. A man who owns a scroll such as yours can own the secrets of the world. You will understand this once you have read. So..." The man nodded at the page.

Neythan glanced at Arianna, still lying on her slab on the other side of the room watching him. He looked back to the scroll's page, his fingers hovering over the small pieces of relic littered there, some as small as a crumb, the largest the size of a coin. "Which should I try first?"

Teju stepped around the table to stand next to Neythan and began to trace his finger over the glyphs.

"You can read these symbols?" Neythan asked.

"Some of them… This one," he pointed to a small piece of silver near the top. "The goblet of Yoaz, son of Abiram… the courts of our king… And something to do with your Shedaím Brotherhood, I think. Seems to have been a gift from Qoh'leth himself." His finger drifted further down the page. "This one is bone, which is good. Bone often makes for an easier shift. Najjib son of… Romesh… and something about a banquet in Qalqaliman. And then there's this one. Qoh'leth's spear… The Battle of a Thousand Banners, which would be interesting no doubt… and then it says something about a… pale king."

"Pale king?"

"Or something like that."

"Then I shall read that one."

"You are sure? Perhaps the bone shard will be best to begin with. Stone is the worst, wood is better, but bone is always the easiest to shift into."

"No. The spear. It will be the spear."

The man opened his hand in a *very well* gesture and stepped away. "Well then, all you need do is touch it, then simply do as you would when you meditate, but instead give yourself to the shard on the page, and let *its* sha guide you."

Neythan nodded and looked down at the thin piece of wood ensnared in the vellum, half the length of his thumb and slick with the dried resin encasement. He looked at Arianna once more and then puffed out his cheeks. Then, when he had sat there long enough, he reached out toward it and touched the splintered tip, tentatively at first, his fingers roaming the brittle coarse timber of the shard until he could feel a warmth beginning to build along it, the shard yielding to his touch. And then it was happening; he doubled over on his seat as he felt the strange gravity open inside him, like being swallowed from within, until finally he let go, falling from himself into it, the world sliding away like shed skin as he dipped inwards to the void.

He sees it all, the generations passing over him like a rough breeze; kings and Sharifs, mountains, rivers and skies; the terrains of the Five Lands and the world itself all blinking through him as quick as light until he wakes standing on a rampart overlooking a smouldering plain of bodies and armour. He is taller than himself. The spear is no longer a wooden shard but whole in his hand, upright in his grasp like a staff. The small yellow standard of Sumeria flaps from the bolster like a flag. Beyond it he sees Karel, the first Sharif, founder of the Sovereignty, a man dead for more than two hundred years but now standing before him. The waning sun glitters in his eyes as he surveys the carnage below. He is speaking but Neythan cannot hear, the words slippery, dulled by the shift as though caught in the wind.

The Sharif turns to face him and gestures toward the battlefield, sweeping his arm to the gathering twilight where the standards of a thousand priesthoods lie scattered over the hills. Neythan can see the place where the crown city will be built and the twin rivers running west toward the lowering sun. He sees the jarring absences; the lack of those broad whitewashed walls and terraces and tall barbicans in the places he knows they now are. Instead the land stretches out toward the horizon, naked and empty, shorn of the conquests that will await Karel and his offspring in generations to come. Neythan turns back as a soldier approaches the Sharif with head bowed carrying several leather-coated scrolls. The soldier is old and small, a cloud of white hair ringing the back and sides of his tanned scalp like a horseshoe as Neythan realises he knows this man, recognises him. But how can that be? How can he be here? The pages of vellum are tightly rolled in the old man's arms. Karel inspects the names written on their covers and nods. And then turns to Neythan, speaking again. Neythan hears him this time.

"Here," he says, offering the scrolls. "Take back what belongs to you.

We will not destroy these with the others. They shall be preserved… and you will teach me their use."

Neythan's arms reach out, thicker and stronger than his own, to receive the scrolls, cradling the rolls of vellum in broad palms. He looks down on the scrolls' ornate coverings and then reads the name that is his but isn't.

"Qoh'leth," he says.

But the words dissolve away as he speaks them, the stitched lettering coming loose and smearing like runny ink along with all else – the sky, the battlefield, the colours of the Sharíf's armour and garments – all blurring into each other as the twilight and the Sharíf all dim and then slip away, spilling from him like vomit as the stony echo of the room's walls and the inscription-scarred table and the gentle ashy scent of the lamp in the corner and everything else abruptly resumes around him.

Neythan fell from his seat, panting, braced on his hands and knees. He could feel the strain and age of the relic. The shard was too old, its memories yielding to decay. He tried to sit up but couldn't. There was a new weight to everything. The air felt hot and thin as though parched by the spicy singe of a cookfire.

"Did you see?" Teju said.

Neythan gulped a long dry breath as he gathered himself and coughed, wiping flecks of bloody spittle from his palm where he'd covered his mouth. "Yes," he said. "I saw." He looked up at Arianna still tied to the wooden slab on the other side of the room. "I saw Elias, Ari… I saw Sharíf Sidon's chamberlain."

FIFTEEN

PROGENY

"Can I have some?"

Joram started and glanced down at the little girl staring up from his knee, bone-white skin with blotches of colour rosing her cheeks and gathering at the tips of her tiny earlobes. It would be warmer the further south they travelled, he knew. Warm enough to flush her short chubby limbs bronze and brighten her hair.

He bent to hand her a crust of bread, grimacing a little from the bandaged wound on his hip. "Of course you can, little one," then glanced up to scan the dull grey cast of the horizon.

There were hundreds of them now – men, women and children, scattered across the span of the shallow ravine like an abandoned flock. Even Ola had been surprised at how fast word had spread, and how swiftly and eagerly the multitudes had amassed in response to it – bands of tribesman clutching slings and bows and sacks of herbs and teas, bandits from Gabbai and Bataar who'd wandered out from their mountain roosts to see if what they'd heard was true. Even those belonging to the hilly homesteads of Shurapeth, close to the borderlands, had come out, unfazed by their chieftain's death at Joram's hand, seemingly drawn more to its manner than its fact.

From what Joram had been told, the way he'd dispatched Uruq had involved a show of strength and speed so unnatural and "beyond the ways of men," that many were beginning to call him a son of the gods, or, for some, even Son of Kúth, after the month for which Markúth was named. Joram decided he liked the moniker; apt, he thought.

He glanced down once more to the little girl beside him, wondering whose she was and where she'd wandered over to him from. She seemed to be frowning a little, the smooth curve of her forehead crimped into little lines of displeasure beneath the mousy bangs of her hair as she chewed.

"You don't like it?"

She wagged her head slowly and squinted her eyes. Couldn't have been more than six years old, five maybe. It was always hard to tell with Kivites when they were this young, prone as they were to malnourishment. So he squatted down to her height and smiled, watching her chew. Then slapped the rest of the crust from her hand, dashing it into the dirt a few yards away where a stray dog rushed over to quickly gobble it from the ground. Joram's smile dropped abruptly as he straightened to look down on her. "The thankful always eat first," he said, then walked away as she rubbed her slapped knuckle and began to cry.

"Bad omen," Ola said, coming alongside as Joram began to stroll through the assembly toward his tent, "teasing the young like that." The dog, now trotting behind them in the hope of more food, barked as though to agree.

"A dog craps in the wrong place and a man will call it an omen," Joram answered.

"Well. Sometimes it is."

Joram smiled, browsing the gathering. With the witnesses at Magadar having been mostly warriors and elders of the clan, it wasn't difficult for either their families or those of the other warriors they'd inevitably told to become first to join Joram's army. More difficult, and just as crucial, would be galvanising the other tribes of the Reach to add to their numbers. The Five Lands spanned territories too vast for many Kivites to comprehend. To win and occupy the whole of it would require more than just Shurapeth, but for now, Joram was pleased to have the heads of the tribe with him.

"There's more than I thought there'd be," he said.

"Word is there'll be more to come soon enough. Especially when they see this." Ola nodded at the ruins. The rubbly, broken-down walls of what used to be the city of Geled, the northernmost outpost of the Five Land Sovereignty, spread for a couple of miles in both directions. "I mean, gods, Jorry. A city of the Sovereignty, razed to dirt like this... How did it happen? And how did you know? There's people here saying *you* did it, you know, somehow pulled down the walls with your own hands."

Joram smiled at that. "Imaginative."

"Yeah, well. Kivites, aren't we. We learn to be that way. But you still haven't answered the question."

There were times Joram considered telling Ola everything: the voice that whispered through his bones, the dreams it gave him – of fires shimmering along smoke-clogged corridors of shadow with dark and monstrous shapes circling overhead, and him, there in the midst of it all, hurrying down narrow alleys and sidestreets toward some hidden destiny that awaited him. A door. Always there. Always the same.

"Well, Joram?"

"What?"

Ola was just looking at him, her blue eyes glinting in the sun as she awaited his answer.

So Joram just sniffed and spat, glancing away to the untidy riddle of tents skirting the rubble. "Where are Djuri and Marin?" he asked.

"They've gone into the ruins with the others, scavenging. Probably just their way of avoiding you for a while I reckon."

Joram grunted. "I see..."

"They'll come around soon enough. Seeing what you did to Uruq at Magadar... It's the kind of thing to make *any* man nervous. And it's not as if you gave us much warning."

"I told you I'd defeat him."

"Not like *that*, Joram. We'd no idea you could even *do* that."

Neither had I, Joram thought. "You're not nervous though?"

"Of you?" She shrugged. "Don't know. Suppose I should be shouldn't I… But no, I guess not. Maybe I've known you too long. Besides. When I think back… I don't know…" She glanced up at him again, her snowy-gold hair pressing across her slim face in the breeze. "You've always said these things, Joram. Right from when we were small. I remember you'd go on forever about the Five Lands and how you were the rightful heir. I'd want to slap you sometimes with how much you went on about it. Thought you were mad. We all did. I mean, what would the son of a Sharíf be doing up in the Reach anyway, scrapping for food in the mud? I'd almost forgotten how you used to say these things. But now, being here, I guess it all starts to sort of make sense…"

"There will be other cities like this, Ola. Further south. Markúth will see to it… He'll see to all those forgotten things I used to say."

The dog, still walking with them, yipped in agreement, crumbs from the bread still dusting its lips and its mangy head bobbing shyly as it sniffed the ground. It glanced up at Joram sadly, as if in apology, a single watery eye commiserating with how much there was still to do.

They would begin moving south by noon, a few days from here to Çyriath the voice had said, depending on the strength and pace of the people, then maybe half a day to forage among its ruins for tools or weapons before continuing on toward the banks of the North Sea and the surer footing of the Stone Road. They'd reach Balaam's Corner a few days after that. Maybe Hanesda a week or so later. But he hadn't told Ola or anyone else about that yet, even though he wanted to. In fact, looking at her now, walking beside him as the breeze continued to tussle her hair – so relaxed, and, unlike the others, unafraid despite what she'd witnessed him do – he realised there was so much he wanted to tell her.

"Come," Joram said. "I want to show you something."

They continued around the dilapidated remains of the city to the eastern fringe of the settlement where Joram had pitched his tent. The land lay in grassy ridges here, levelling up like a pair of giant steps. Joram came to the tent and stood at the entrance, looking around to make sure they wouldn't be disturbed, and then, beckoning Ola to follow him, he stooped to step inside.

Kareena lay huddled under a heap of blankets, covered from head to toe and, from what Joram could tell, facing toward the skin and wool wall with her shoulders hunched, fists probably buried to her chest to keep warm against the fever. Joram was moving toward her when the voice roused sluggishly to life, tingling feebly across his shoulder blades.

"*No time,*" it said.

Which Joram didn't understand, so he just stood there, waiting to hear more.

"*Fading… Now. Must be now. The stone.*"

"Joram?"

Joram flinched at Ola's voice.

"Are you alright?" she said.

"It's Markúth."

He felt her hesitate, but only briefly. She stepped toward him. "He is speaking to you?"

"His voice. Yes. It is why we are here, Ola. It is what has guided me."

"What is it saying?"

"It says it must be now."

"Well… What does that mean? *What* must be now?"

Joram closed his eyes, breathing slowly as he leant against the tentpost and tried to focus his sha.

"What does he want?" Ola asked. "What must be now?"

Abruptly Joram felt sick, fatigued. "I think it wants to shift. I think it's… I don't know, dying somehow. Maybe."

"Dying?"

"Or something. I don't know. It needs to shift, join itself. That's what it's saying."

"What do you mean 'shift'?"

"Bring me closer to Kareena on the bedmat."

"What's going–"

"Please, Ola. Just help me. I don't think there's much time."

She came forward and took Joram by the arm to lead him over to the girl. They kneeled by her bedmat as Joram slowly reached out to pull back the blankets. He suddenly felt so weak, trying to keep hold of the fading voice within.

"Joram. Where is she?"

He opened his eyes. The bedmat was empty. A clump of pillows and bags lay piled up on the mat atop a patch of sweat where the pregnant girl should have been. Joram could feel the voice, pinching agitatedly at the nerves in his back, making the muscle beneath his eye jump. He hauled himself to his feet.

"Find her. We have to find her."

The words tumbled out breathily, the ground beneath him seeming to tilt one way then the other as he staggered out of the tent.

Outside. The settlement behind them. The sun high overhead, peering down sleepily through thick clouds onto the choppy terrain. The gorge was shallow but craggy, covered by pale rubble and patches of stalky wildgrass and dirt paths spreading through its jagged slopes like veins. Not ideal footing for a half-delirious and heavily pregnant young girl. Ola came past him and squinted at the soft tilt of the terrain, the way it angled ruggedly up for about a quartermile before you reached even ground.

"She couldn't have got far."

Joram, preoccupied with the voice, barely heard her. He could feel its panic like a grip around his chest now, tautening along his ribs as it scrambled for a way out. The stray dog just sat there watching patiently, its eyes fixed to Joram as though awaiting a command.

"Find her," Joram said.

The dog, to his surprise, bolted, running up one of the slope's dirt paths as though to do exactly that.

Joram looked at Ola, who was staring anxiously at him now, puzzled.

"Your voice," she explained, wonderingly.

"What?"

Ola stepped back, her eyes wide. Afraid, Joram realised. "You sound… different," she said. "You don't sound yourself."

Joram understood. He could feel the pressure of the voice within him, wanting to take matters into its own hands, trying to claw its way out. Joram reached into his pocket and felt for the black pearl. It was hot to the touch again, a ball of solid heat against his skin, stealing his breath, weakening him, strengthening him, just like at Magadar.

"Stay here, Ola."

"Joram?"

"Stay. Don't let anyone come up after us."

He knew. He could feel the voice's plan taking shape within him as he strode up the shallow slope, its presence sharpening with his every step. The heat of it ran all over his body, scrambling against his nerves. It was going to leave him early, before the agreed time. It somehow needed to.

The dog was barking. Off somewhere where Joram couldn't quite see. He pushed himself up the slope, further along the path to where the grasses shortened, exposing rocks and dry pale earth amid the sedge. The land sloped down momentarily, descending then rising again to where the dog's barks grew louder. Joram strained as the voice pulled at him again, agitating for the stone like a caged madman. But they couldn't yet. The girl would be too far away, and they didn't know where she was.

He saw the dog's red-brown rear and wagging tail off to one side next to a solitary tree stump, the wood as old and white as bone. The muscles of the dog's short hindquarters were tense and shuddering as he whined and barked and pawed with his forelegs at the dirt beyond Joram's line of sight as Joram took hold of the jewel again, this time holding it, letting its heat burn against the flesh of his fingers as he willed himself on to where the dog had settled. *Nearly there. Almost there.*

And then there she was.

Sitting there, her back against the stump and her legs sprawled, panting and sweating in the cool air. The parturient bulge of her gut dominated her upper body, pushing up against her breasts. He watched as her eyes slowly turned to him – empty, haunted, bloodshot.

"Please," she whispered. "Please."

Joram took out the pearl and looked at her, ignoring the sharp sting of the heat as he held it before him. "You will be free soon," he said. "You will swallow this, in a few moments, and it will make you free. Do you understand?"

"I want it to stop."

"Yes. It will stop soon. You will swallow the pearl. It will soon be ready."

She looked doubtful but there would be no time for threats and cajoling, no time to persuade her. Joram could already feel the shift beginning to creep along the edges of himself, drawing him inexorably on toward its precipice like a slow-moving current approaching the calm drop of a cliff. His vision flattened, the yellowy greens of the sparse tufts of grass sprouting from around the foot of the stump, the tiny buds of dandelion emerging from among the weeds, the crash of dusky yellows and blues across the sky, all of it waning, fading into pallid shades of grey as though the world around him had begun to drain away. And then he could physically feel it, the layers of consciousness peeling away within him, shrivelling into something icy and dense at the pit of his gut like a ball of liquid metal. He dropped to his hands and knees, but there was no resisting it now. It was coming, preparing to leave him. He could hear the girl crying out, the dog barking furiously, fearfully, a chorus of shrieked gnarled yips and soft remorseful bleats, but it all felt distant and muffled, as though happening a world away. He shivered at the sudden chill along his limbs and spine, the inward sense of rupture, the abrupt and increasing aloneness as the voice unpicked itself from the cords of his mind like tightened strings snapping from an instrument. And then it was all rushing up within him, thoughts, feelings and memories spewing up his throat and out of his mouth like vomit, like a scream he could no longer contain.

When he came to, he was still there, poised on hands and knees. He blinked. The girl was still there too, whimpering by the tree stump, her legs still sprawled out but her arms now hugged to herself, her hands clutching her elbows above the bold swell of her gut. The dog was gone, hiding somewhere, whilst on the ground in front of him lay the substance. Joram moved back onto his haunches to give it room, staring at it. Like sodden mud or faeces but darker, steaming in the cool air.

The pearl.

Joram remembered he was still holding it, clutched between thumb and fingers in his left hand. He reached out tentatively and saw the streak of black sludge twitch, keening toward the dark jewel like a plant to light as Joram brought it near. The girl groaned and whimpered as she watched the substance move.

"Shh, it's alright," Joram managed, his throat coarse and dry, his voice scratchy. "It's going to make you stronger," he told her. "You'll see."

He placed the pearl carefully on the ground next to the sludge whilst the girl watched him. It stirred immediately, slithering toward and then over the pearl like a snake consuming an egg. It shuddered as it came into contact, then continued to move over the jewel, pulsing slowly as it did so, like heartbeat, like breathing. The substance then began to thin out, sizzling loudly as it melted into a small black puddle before drawing up into itself once more. It hissed as it shrank, hardening into a perfect black sphere. Joram leaned forward and picked it up. So beautiful, the smooth glossy dark of it, a perfect jewel, a neat ball of night.

"Your brother, Yevhen, is dead," he said to the girl. "But I know you've a little sister. I know where she is. So, you will swallow this, or you will watch me do to her as I have done to you. You will watch her take your place. Do you understand?"

The girl didn't speak but Joram could see she'd heard him. He waited a moment to watch the words take hold, breaking her from the inside as the dull weight of resignation stamped the fear from her eyes.

Then he handed her the pearl.

She regarded it without expression as he held it out to her, and then took it and put it into her mouth.

Joram took out a blade. "Swallow. You'll only need one eye to watch me keep my promise if you refuse."

The girl obeyed.

"Good," Joram whispered, then slowly let himself collapse to the ground. The girl would do the same soon, he knew. She'd convulse and writhe and cry out and scream for a day or more, and then she'd be well again, or at least as well as she could be considering what waited in her womb. So he allowed himself to lie there on his back, gazing up at the wall of cloud above and waiting for his strength to return, and trying not to let the fear overwhelm him as the new solitude set in. The voice would be gone forever now, joined to what waited within her. Now, for the first time since he was a child, Joram would be truly alone.

SIXTEEN

TRUTH

Sidon had never seen anything like her. The long-boned limbs, languidly splayed in elegant angles as she sat in the cushioned chair opposite, her arms spread cruciform across the back as she regarded him coolly from across the small room like a jeweller eyeing a stone. Josef stood by Sidon's shoulder with his hand on the pommel of his sword, but the woman didn't seem to care. She sipped nonchalantly, then considered the goblet in her hand before placing it on the table between them and leaning back to resume her pose. It was her skin Sidon couldn't help staring at. Dark as a plum, and shiny. And then the way her head tilted at an angle atop the long strong pillar of her neck as she looked at him, as though he were a game she was still deciding whether to play.

"So then," she said. "Here we are."

"Yes. Here we are."

She favoured Josef with a brief glance, still nursing the wound in his flank as he leaned against the jamb of the door watching her, and then she looked to the diminutive Elias sitting next to Sidon on the couch before returning her gaze to the Sharíf himself. "Do you trust them?" she asked, nodding at the bodyguard and chamberlain.

"Elias is the one who first advised me of my mother's deceit. And Josef has saved my life twice in the last ten days. So yes, I would say they are the *only* people I trust right now."

"Good. Always best to be sure of these things, especially if they're to remain here as we speak."

Sidon fidgeted impatiently. Imaru had laid out her wishes following her rescue of him during the first night of the Feast of Bones. They would meet. She would set forward her intentions, and Sidon would agree. The latter, she claimed, was not a demand, just a simple stating of how any reasonable man would respond to what she was going to share.

"So," Sidon said. "What do you have, Imaru?"

She smiled. "Your mother is preparing herself."

"Preparing herself? For what?"

Imaru pursed her lips, her eyes – the whites luminous against her dark skin – locked on Sidon's as the sun shone across her close-cropped scalp like gleaming metal. "I think you know."

"She wants my throne?"

"She does." She brought her arms in and leaned forward. "But the question is why."

"Actually," Elias answered, "if you are who you've said you are then the question is why you would want to help? What interest can the throne of Súnam have in serving the Five Lands?"

That, more than anything, had been the thing that had unsettled Sidon the most. Imaru, a self-confessed daughter of Súnam's queen, here in the Sovereignty, apparently for nothing other than benign or benevolent purposes, or so she had so far claimed. He watched her closely as she considered Elias's question, the smooth geometries of her face seeming to rearrange themselves slightly as she turned her attention to the chamberlain. "Geled," she announced, and then sat back again, allowing the word to just hang there in the taut quiet that opened in its wake.

Sidon tried not to let his surprise show. Geled's destruction was yet to be announced even to the sovereign council despite the weeks that had passed; mostly due to Elias's advice. With the council so divided, it made sense to wait until they knew more about the enemy responsible. And yet here was this foreigner, making reference to the fallen city.

The chamberlain rose to his feet gingerly, glancing at Sidon as he slowly ambled across the room to the window on the far side. Sidon looked back to the black woman, whose smile had resumed, before standing to join him.

It was a while since he'd been this far up Kaldan's Tower but the view still both awed and consoled him nonetheless, stretching beyond the city's walls and the tiny pale knots of terraced housing far below, and out onto the lush even plains of the Sumerian lowlands where the twin rivers ran west from Hanesda's watergate. Before dusk on a clear day he'd sometimes even glimpse where they joined, the smooth gleaming sweep of the Swift curving in toward the Amber as the sun lowered to meet them on the horizon. But not today. Too cloudy. And too early in the day besides.

"It would make sense for Súnam to fish for weaknesses," Elias murmured, leaning in toward Sidon as he looked out at the horizon, "perhaps try to confirm where the Sovereignty's vulnerabilities lie before planning an attack of their own."

"But then why save me from my mother's men at the Feast?"

The old man shrugged. "Hard to say. Perhaps to gain this audience with you, take advantage of your mother's plotting."

Sidon thought about it. It would make sense in part, but he couldn't help feeling there was something more. Something the woman wasn't telling them, or at least not yet.

"Geled is destroyed, isn't it," Imaru called out from her seat behind them.

Sidon turned back from the window to face her, leaning back on the ledge with his elbows. "Is it? And how would you know that?"

"The same way I know your mother is not to be trusted. We have those who listen and whisper for us just as you do, in your lands as well as our own. They say Geled is destroyed. And they say there is corruption in the throne."

"And you think one is linked to the other," Sidon said.

"You don't?"

Sidon pondered, trying to decide whether to trust her or not. *What did she really want? Why was she here?*

"You don't trust me," she said, as though hearing his thoughts.

Sidon snorted a laugh. "In the last week I've learned my mother conspires against me, and I've survived two attempts on my life."

"I'd like to think I had a hand in helping you survive the last."

"So now I should trust you?"

"You don't need to trust me, you need only trust the truth." She stood too now, her movement triggering Josef to change posture by the door. Sidon lifted a palm to him, waist high, gesturing calm.

She glanced at Josef, noting his swordhand still resting on the pommel of his blade as he favoured his right flank and the wound he'd sustained there. Imaru smiled again, holding her hands out to her sides like a surrendering prisoner.

"You think I am your enemy, but I am not."

"And why should I believe that?" Sidon replied.

"Because the reason we rescued you the other night is we want you to live." She stepped forward and stood square to him. "There is a war coming, Sharíf – one our seers have long foreseen and warned of. A war greater than any that has come before it. I am here because if the Sovereignty does not get its house in order it will mean the fall of us all. The Five Lands. Súnam. The whole world."

"What are you talking about?"

"Prophecy. I know you do not see as we in Súnam see. I know you do not believe. And I will be honest with you, Sharíf. Not all among my people believed the words of our seers either. But when word came to us of the swift and sudden destruction of a Sovereign outpost to the north, their warnings soon became worth heeding. They have foretold an enemy rising from the north, and if this enemy is as they say it is, then neither Súnam nor your Five Lands will be strong enough to face it alone."

"So, why send you?" Elias asked. "A daughter of the queen. Why not a messenger, or emissary?"

"You must understand, the Sovereignty cannot afford to be

weakened by infighting and squabbles over its throne, Sharíf. Not now. And Súnam cannot afford it either. I have been sent here to do what you cannot, to find and remove those who oppose you, before it's too late." She looked at the chamberlain. "They did not send me here to persuade you. And I am not just a daughter of the queen. I am the general of Súnam's armies. They sent me here because I am the best."

Sidon pushed off from the window ledge he'd been leaning on, thinking. "Alright… Suppose what you say is true…"

"My king–"

Sidon cut Elias off, giving him the same gesture he'd given to Josef moments before.

"Just. Suppose…" Sidon repeated, still watching the black woman. "What would you want to do?"

"Your mother controls your spies. Controls what you hear. But she does not control what *we* hear. We know of at least one among your council who has been plotting with her, to help take the throne from you when the time comes."

"Who?"

"The governor of Qadesh."

"You mean *Yassr?*"

"Yes. That is his name. Yassr son of Ussur."

"No. Yassr wouldn't. He mentored me as a child, taught me the histories. He *welcomed* my anointing when I took the throne."

"And your mother carried you in her womb for nine months and birthed you out. Now *she* wants your throne."

Sidon looked at Elias. "Do you think this could be true? Yassr?"

The old man hesitated, the permutations moving over his heavily wrinkled face like shifting winds. "Anything is possible, Sharíf," he said finally.

"There will be others," Imaru added. "And this Yassr will know who they are. You said it yourself, attempts have been made on your life."

"And you're saying he could be responsible? Or Mother?"

"I'm saying we visit this Yassr, Luavese and I – your bodyguard too if you prefer – and we ask him."

"Just like that."

"Yes. Just like that. Your Feast of Bones will continue for another two weeks. There are dignitaries and councilmen here from almost all the Five Lands. There will not be a better chance to uncover your betrayers and remove them. So yes, we begin with him, and learn of the others. Just a few questions."

"And if he doesn't want to answer?"

"We persuade him…" The woman's smile returned. "But you needn't worry. I'm very good at that. But if we are to do this we must begin today. The Feast will be over by the end of the month. And we do not know how many others the Sharifa has turned."

Sidon paused, looking first to Josef and then Elias before answering. "One condition," he said, turning his attention back to the black woman. "I am to come with you."

"*Majesty…*"

"I have to hear his words for myself, Elias. I have to know – by my own eyes and ears – that this is… real. That he has betrayed me. So…" glancing back to Imaru. "You will ask your questions, but you will bring Josef and I with you."

"I understand," Imaru replied, and then returned to her seat to collect her goblet. "If I were in your place, I would want the same."

An hour later they were walking through the streets of the Green District, a borough of broad roads and large houses surrounded by spacious walled grounds toward the city's southern quarter. The area was split by a paved main road that led to the Square of Faroukh, a wide rectilinear space hedged in by audaciously scaled houses and gardens. A stone plinth centred the square at the road's end where the last parade of the Feast would conclude on the festival's final day. Workmen everywhere, attaching festoons of coloured flags to the walls, scattering coins and rose petals across the thick stone steps of each house along the main road, whilst others trundled along the streets pushing wheeled carts stacked with sumac and cardamom and baskets of okra brought up from the Summerlands. Sidon,

Imaru, Luavese and Josef followed behind a pair of men carrying logs, delivering them to the square's plinth to erect a scaffold.

"Busy place," Josef commented.

Imaru, walking with Luavese slightly ahead, glanced at him over her shoulder. "All the better. No one will be disturbed by our being here."

"So you hope," Sidon quipped.

"So *we* hope," she said.

Sidon still didn't trust her, but if Yassr turned out to be as she'd said, then in some ways he'd have no choice but to do just that. Uncle Játhon, he knew already, was part of it; so too General Gahíd. Which probably meant at least some of the cityguard were part of it too, since they were mainly Gahíd's men. But what about the palaceguard? How far did the rot spread? And could it be stopped?

"There," Imaru said. "That's where he's staying."

They stepped up the blocky stone steps into the grounds, a brief patch of green split by a paved path within the walls, leading up to a main house flanked by stone-pillared pavilions. It was like the governor's house in Qadesh but smaller, galleries running along the length of it on one side and a pair of ribbed columns supporting a small porchway before the main door that backed the grassy courtyard.

Sidon led them along the path and up the steps, entering a tiled lobby as a pair of guards scrambled hurriedly to their feet at the door to acknowledge him.

"More like a roofed court than a house," Imaru remarked as she eyed the space within. Faded murals of striding horses adorned the walls in russet and blues. A rich looking rug covered a corner of the room, surrounded by benches and couches and small tables.

"Sharíf, is that you?"

Sidon turned toward the familiar voice.

"Ha. It *is* you. What have I done to deserve this gift?" Yassr came ambling over with his arms wide and corralled Sidon into an iron bearhug against his ample gut, almost lifting him from the ground. He laughed as he released him, padding his shoulders and arms as he looked him over. "Ah, Sharíf. I swear you grow taller and stronger by the day. But why surprise an old man and come unannounced? I'd have set a banquet. And who are your companions?"

"Perhaps there is somewhere we can talk, old friend."

"Of course, my king. Of course. We will eat. And wine. We need wine."

"Please, Yassr. There is no need–"

"Nonsense. Wine. Food." He clapped loudly, summoning a servant girl from an open doorway across the other side of the lobby. "Ah, Sajida. Good. We have visitors. The *best* visitors. Bring them some of the summerwine I had brought from Calpas." He turned to Sidon. "You will love it, Sharíf. Like nothing you have ever tasted."

A few moments later Sajida and another girl were serving platters of fruit as Sidon and Imaru reclined with Yassr on the couches surrounding the rug. Josef stood awkwardly a few paces away whilst Luavese waited by the door, observing the tubby old man as he guffawed and ate and laughed.

"You know," Yassr drawled, eyeing Imaru, "I have often wanted to go to Súnam. Beautiful place. It's all I hear from my merchants, they speak only of the people, how welcoming they are, and of course, the food. Ah, *always* the food – the best spices, the best fruit – it's all they tell me."

Imaru smiled easily. "Perhaps you will one day come to Nubassa, or Tor; should you do so, I will make certain you are welcomed appropriately."

Yassr grinned, almost leeringly. "I like the sound of that." Then turning to Sidon. "She is wonderful this one. Where did you find her?"

Sidon put down his drink. "Actually, she found me."

"Oh?"

"In fact, it's why we are here."

"Is that so?" He took a handful of grapes from the servant girl as she offered her platter, tossing one into his mouth. "Well. Please, Sharíf. Speak on."

"She came here because she'd heard of you, Yassr."

Yassr's grin widened, turning to Imaru. "Well now. Is *that* so?"

The black woman inclined her head, still smiling. "You could say your reputation precedes you, governor."

Yassr let out a throaty cackle, his fleshy neck and ears reddening as his thick gut rumbled with amusement.

"I heard so much I decided I had to come and see for myself."

"Do not be shy, young one. Tell me, what did you hear?"

Imaru, reclining on one elbow on the low bench, sat up, curling her legs beneath her as she turned to face the governor and leant in. Sidon had to give it to her, she had a flair for the dramatic. She was still smiling, her chin perched on the heel of her palm as she continued to lean toward the governor, blinking slowly. "Well," she said, her voice lowering, almost intimately so. "Put simply, I heard there is a governor who wishes his Sharíf to no longer be Sharíf."

Yassr's smile remained for a few moments before eventually turning to puzzlement, as though waiting to understand a joke he needed someone to explain.

"Yes, I know," Imaru went on. "I was shocked too. And yet they continued to tell more, about this governor who secretly wished his Sharíf dead. Who was scheming and plotting against him, to see it so. What's more, and this is the part that will really stun you – this governor was plotting with this Sharíf's own mother, to see him removed and her placed on the throne in his place. Can you imagine?" Imaru grinned.

But Sidon wasn't laughing, and neither, now, was Yassr. The colour had drained from his face, paling his thick fleshy neck and the top of his head where parts of his scalp were showing through his thinning white hair. He looked around, saw Sidon staring flatly back, and drew breath to call out – to the guards, perhaps to the servant girl, Sidon couldn't tell – but by the time his lungs had filled Imaru's penblade was already at his throat. She frowned mockingly in disappointment and tutted. "Now now, governor. Don't you know it's rude to spoil a good party?"

Yassr looked to Sidon. "Sharíf, please."

But Sidon felt cold. "Deny it and I'll have her gut you right where you sit."

"Which would be a shame," Imaru added. "I *love* this rug. I wouldn't want to spoil it."

"You're going to tell me who else is involved, Yassr. Do you understand? You're not going to lie, you're not going to deny it. You're just going to tell me. One chance. That is all."

Sidon watched the older man sift through his options as the threat sank in, pressing through his natural instincts for affront and disavowal, before finally settling into something more resigned and desperate instead. "I'm sorry, Sidon. I'm sorry. Please." He spluttered clumsily, the words becoming cumbersome in his haste to expel them.

"Tell me who, Yassr?"

The fat man swallowed anxiously, the penblade still poised at his neck. "I do not know all those involved. She did not tell me. I know Kamal, the crown scribe, is part of it."

Sidon nodded to himself. "Of course." It had been his grounds he and Josef had spied Mother, Játhon and the general in. "Who else?"

"Fatya, the governor of Tirash."

"Fatya? She hates my mother. She's *always* hated her."

"A facade, to hide their true intentions from you. I was the one your mother sent to her, to make her part of what was to be planned."

Typical Yassr, a blustery but weak man. Now the dam had been cracked the rest would spill. Sidon leaned toward him. "And why would Fatya agree?"

"The Sharífa promised to bring her into your family. Make her royal. The girl you were to marry in Qadesh, before it was disrupted, she is a cousin of Fatya. Chalise would have bought Fatya's vote on the council by the marriage. Had you wed she'd have overturned you already. The Sharífa has many votes in hand. That is all I know, Sharíf. Nothing else. Please, I beg you. It is Gahíd you should speak to."

"Gahíd?"

"He has been helping her, carries word on her behalf. He is the one who will know more."

Sidon digested the governor's words. "How long has this been going on?"

"I don't know. I don't know." The man was almost whimpering now, sweat pouring down his cheeks.

"When did she send you to Fatya?"

"It was nearly a year ago now."

"A *year?*"

"Yes, Sharíf. I remember because it was just before the last Feast, the ending of summer."

And shortly after he'd just been anointed Sharíf, Sidon thought to himself. Which meant Mother had been plotting to kill or remove him from almost the moment she'd killed his father. Sidon's jaw clenched with the new knowledge. He glanced up as the servant girl re-entered with another platter, carrying more fruit, and froze at the door.

"Just a game," Imaru said. "We're just playing. Why don't you run back to the kitchens and wait until we're finished?"

The girl hesitated for a moment and then turned around and hurried away with the platter.

"Do you want to live, Yassr?"

The man's neck jiggled as he nodded, forgetting Imaru's penblade which she had to hastily move out of the way. "Yes, Sharíf. I want to live. I want to live."

"You will not speak of this," Sidon said. "You will tell no one. You will let my mother, and everyone else, believe all is well. Do you understand?"

"Yes. Yes. I understand."

"Good. Because if you fail to keep this promise," Sidon stood and inclined his head to Imaru, adjusting the folds of his garment as he readied to leave, "she will find you, and come for you when you sleep. You will find no mercy should it come to that, Yassr. She will spill your intestines in your bed. And you will know, as you die, that the judgement was just. Because you dared to betray your Sharíf."

SEVENTEEN

WILD

Noah stirred awake in the back of a trundling cart stuffed with fragrant chaff, a bizarre mix of dried meadowgrass and dill from what he could tell, like the herbal teas his mother would sometimes give him back in Dumea when he felt feverish, which explained the familiarly warm and bitter pinch in his nostrils that made him want to sneeze. He coughed, pushing up onto his elbows to shake the stuff out of his hair and clothes. It was noon, or maybe later. It was hard to tell. The sun had hidden behind a pearlescent wall of cloud overhead. Beyond the back of the cart, a long dusty road twisted through a dry hilly terrain of grit and shrubs, receding in their wake as they continued to roll south. Noah looked around, glancing at the wall of rock on his right as it rolled by, stone-coloured lizards the size of his hand scurrying over and through the cracks; and then on the road's other side, a steep verge edging the road, dropping away onto a rubbly slope before swooping up again to join the wide treeless savannah where a small pack of jackals trotted along in the distance, tiny against the backdrop of the vast mountain behind them. The only sounds were the breeze, the crunch of the cartwheels and the rattle of the tracestrap against the cart's sidewall.

Noah turned to find Daneel at the reins, sitting on the driver's bench as a horse lumbered forward ahead of him, pulling the cart along. "Where are we?"

Daneel glanced lazily over his shoulder and slid Noah a tired look; apparently they'd been riding for a while. "So, you're awake. Long sleep that one, even for you."

"How long?"

"About a day."

"A day?"

"Thereabouts."

Noah blinked in confusion, rubbing his head. There was a dull ache gathering around his temples.

Daneel twisted in his seat again to look at him. "You don't remember?"

Noah shook his head.

"Huh…" Daneel returned his attention to the road ahead. "Well, I'd suppose the simplest way to say it is you somehow tossed a grown man into the air like he was little more than an oversized pebble. Broke his arm while you were at it."

"What?"

Daneel nodded. "I know. I'll be honest, when I saw it happen I was of a mind to half believe I'd imagined it. But then there's the others, all seeing the same thing – the man's daughter, screaming her little head off; then you've got villagers who'd been watching the whole thing through their windows, coming out from their houses to gawp and say their piece… Which was why I thought it best to be on our way at that point. On account of how they were all calling you witch and mystic and wanting to stone you and all. You're welcome, by the way. Me saving your life and so forth. It does need explaining though; what you did, how you did it… Needs explaining."

Noah leaned up against the cart's sidewall, trying to piece Daneel's words together with the jumble in his head – the grizzle-jawed drunkard screaming at him by the well, the sudden shocked silence of the whimpering girl, watching on as the stunned man shot up into the air, dashed skywards like a flung stone as Noah's hand had reached out across the short space as though to touch him. Somehow *did* touch him, or at least felt as though he did.

"I don't know how," Noah murmured. "It just happened."

Daneel grunted. "Had a feeling you might say that. Thing is, what you did, I don't think it's the first time."

"What do you mean?"

"The night I first taught you to meditate, when I tried to get you to break off from your memory but you wouldn't. Because you were pulling too hard. You remember?"

Noah rubbed his neck, remembering.

"I think it happened then too. I felt it, some kind of tug on things. A tremor, in the air, in the ground. I don't know. *Something...* Point I'm making is, I'm thinking maybe the meditations, you learning to feel and use your sha, maybe its triggered something, you know?"

"Like what?"

"I don't know. Just something. Released something maybe. We'll have to make sense of it, see if you can learn a way to control it. Last thing I need is you tossing people into the sky because you've gotten a little overexcited or eaten something that didn't quite agree with your bowels. We'll need to lay low where we're going as it is, not draw attention."

"Where *are* we going?"

Daneel peeled another sidelong glance over his shoulder. "I told you already..." then turned back to the road. "We're going south."

"But to where?"

Daneel shrugged. "Sippar maybe. Or maybe further, as far as Hikramesh or Qalqaliman if we can, somewhere like that."

"You said we would leave the Sovereignty, go north, then across the West Sea."

"We tried. You saw those... *creatures*, in Çyriath. North is no longer safe. We've been over this."

"You'd *keep* us safe. That's what you said."

"I said I'd keep you safe from the Brotherhood, those who were sent after you. I don't recall saying a thing about giant winged beasts that drop from the night like… Well… Like nothing I've ever seen or heard of… What we saw in Çyriath… I don't know a thing about how to keep you, me, or anyone else safe from that. We go north, maybe we find more of those creatures. Maybe they've a nest of them up there for all we know… Geled. The foothills where we found Salidor. Now Çyriath. Those things, whatever they are, they began up there and have been making their way south ever since. Could be if we'd carried on toward the Reach we'd be dead already. The further south we go, the further away from them we get. Maybe we settle in a city down there, place with fortified walls and a large cityguard. Somewhere like that."

"I won't go."

"Listen to me, Noah–"

"*No.*"

Daneel flinched, his shoulders tensing as he jerked away just a little. From him, Noah realised. Daneel was wary of *him*. The thought seemed so absurd Noah almost wanted to laugh, and for a moment he thought he might, could feel the giddy hint of it tipping to the surface of him like an overfull vessel about to lean – but instead only a gasp came out, as if the air in his chest was too heavy to heave. Because suddenly it was. Everything was. And now, suddenly, he could feel it, the weight of it all, his fatigue, Çyriath, Mother, Father, Salidor, blood, dead, gone. Because they were all gone, weren't they. Everything was gone. His family was gone. And home was gone. And everything would always go. Take from him. The world would. The world was.

"Noah? You good?"

And for a moment it was as though he couldn't breathe from all the loss, as if it had all accrued into some invisible and silent tangled mass, pressing down on him, suffocating him from inside out. He gripped the sidewall as the cold thick weight of it expanded inside, welling up into his throat and chest and eyes, pushing out into a sob and hot stinging tears until he finally broke, whimpering and wheezing as he hugged his knees to himself in the back of the cart, trying to breathe.

Daneel had stopped the cart now, was clambering into the wagon with him, clutching his shoulders as the chaff and cart began to shudder beneath them, the trace strap rattling against the sidewall as the ground trembled and quaked. "Noah? Noah. Look at me. Look at me."

And so Noah did, staring out at those dark eyes through the air he was drowning in as Daneel held him by the arms and told him he was there, he was there, he'd always be there. That it was alright. That he just needed to breathe. Just breathe. Nice and slow. That's it. It would be alright.

Slowly, Noah felt the weight yield, allowing his chest to fill with air. He let go of the cart's sidewall and watched the chaff resettle to the planked floor. He blinked in confusion. Looked to Daneel.

"Hey, now… Hey." He patted the boy's head awkwardly, and then shifted, climbing back onto the driver's bench. "Come sit up here. We need to get going where we're going."

Noah pulled himself up and climbed over to sit next to Daneel on the bench as he tugged gently on the reins to move them on again. Overhead the clouds were parting, the sun's light winking through in radiant shafts that dappled the savannah to the west where the jackals continued their stroll.

"I didn't mean to be all… I don't know…" Daneel groped for the words, sighed, and started again. "I *will* keep you safe. I just… need to work out the best way how is all. Truth is I'd rather not stay in the Five Lands either. But we *do* need to move south."

Noah sniffed loudly and wiped his nose on his sleeve, his voice jolting softly out like a stammer. "I'm… I'm scared."

"Well, that's alright, boy. It's alright to be scared. It's a sensible thing. Sometimes it can even be useful. And besides, I'm scared myself, but I'll keep you safe. Like I promised. Alright? I'll keep you safe. Me and you. Who else have we got now after all?" He patted the boy again on the shoulder and then rubbed his back. "It'll be alright."

After a while a strong breeze picked up, kicking dust from the road so Daneel and Noah had to cover their eyes, or turn away and look instead toward the savannah and the small balls of tumbleweed rolling across the endless plain in the wind. A common thing in these outlands, even during summer. All that open space, it was as if the wind would just pass through sometimes for the fun of there being so few things to interrupt it. The brief gust died almost as quick as it came, whittling away to a gentle calm breeze and then, a few moments later, to nothing at all, the air still and warm beneath the beclouded sun and wide sky. The road ahead began to lean west, working around the clutch of monolithic columns that flanked along its eastern side. Noah found himself looking up at the giant pillars of rock, fascinated by the way the ridges ribbed across in layers, the stone piled slice by slice into monumental heaps. He could just make out the faraway movement of animals along some of their heights: mountain cats or goats probably; or maybe more jackals like the ones in the plain; or those great-eared mountain hares his father had told him of once, darting from ridge to ridge amid the dry sprouts of grass cropping up in the creases between the rocks.

"Can I ask you something?" Noah said as he watched it all, his thoughts drifting as he observed the way the columns' broad blunt peaks cut across the sky.

"Sure."

"How many people have you killed?"

Daneel turned to look at him on the bench, and then back to the road. "Not as many as you'd think. The Brotherhood I was part of, I was new to it in a way; when we met, I mean... I mean... I'd spent almost my whole life with them, but only training, preparing. But when you and I met, I'd only been sworn a matter of weeks."

"Do you kill when you are training?"

Daneel nodded soberly. "We do... We did. It's how they prepare you, how they make you ready to be sworn."

"Were you scared, when you killed the first time?"

"I was. Very. My first witnessing – that's what they call it – I was sent to a city called Calpas. A port town well north of here, to the far west of Calapaar by the Summer Sea. Nice place. Pretty.

Nice food. Nice fish. They had me and my brother shadow a man who was already sworn. You help him. Clean his weapons, fetch his food, that sort of thing. And then you watch him do what he does. You watch him kill. That first time watching, it was strange. Didn't really feel *real*, you know? It was as if it was happening to someone else, just a story you were hearing, like when they tell tales over the campfire at night and you imagine it all in your head."

"They never did that in Dumea," Noah said. "My father would tell me stories sometimes, but they were boring mostly, about histories, things our forefathers had done, or other people's, and never over campfire."

"That's a shame. One of the villagers in the place we grew up, he had the best tales," Daneel said, "scary ones mostly, and he was good at telling them. Jaleem his name was. We'd beg him to tell us a new one every night but he never would. Only at new moon. We'd all crowd around him, waiting to hear. We'd look forward to it, but be scared out of our minds too; and that's what this felt like, that first witnessing in Calpas. Some cleric or other, or it might have been a prince's aide. I forget…

"We sat in a shed in the corner of the market square for nearly half a day. Full summer. Nearly baked alive in that shed waiting for that cleric. When he finally showed up we woke the man we were shadowing. He put an arrow through that cleric from about a hundred feet away, right through his heart, and that was that. All that waiting and then it's over in a blink. Makes you feel strange afterwards, like there was something you'd failed to notice or understand. But before it happens – waiting in that shed, and then spotting him and waking up the one who was to do the deed – those few moments before it happens, it's like your heart's about to explode from your chest. You feel so scared you think, in the moment, that maybe you could die from it, die just from the fear, the nerves." Daneel laughed a little. "Sounds silly doesn't it."

"No. It doesn't sound silly."

"Sounds strange at the very least. Like some kind of… Wait… Do you hear that?"

Noah listened. A low-level rumble, humming through the ground and broad rockface beside them, but not like before, not a quake. This was something subtler, quieter. Daneel hopped up onto the driver's bench and twisted, looking back at the crest in the road behind. He waited, continuing to stare at the incline, and then saw the galloping troop of horses and riders come driving hard over the crest, sprinting down the road's steady slope toward them. He let go of the reins and put a hand to the pommel of the shortsword at his waist, could feel Noah move toward him, his hand reaching out to grasp the flank of his smock.

"Who are they?" Noah asked. But Daneel didn't answer, putting out an arm to ward him back and shift the boy behind him, away from the empty side of the road as he returned to his seat and snapped the reins to speed the horse into a gallop, before proffering the leather straps to Noah.

"Here. Take these."

Noah glared dubiously at Daneel before reluctantly taking the reins, and then watched as Daneel climbed from the bench into the cartbed, holding the sidewall for balance as the cart gathered momentum.

Behind them, the riders were gaining. Five? Six? Noah couldn't be sure, watching the road between panicked glances over his shoulder.

"I think they're here for us," Daneel shouted, lifting his voice above the noise of the wheels as the cart began to bounce across the road's cracks and rocks.

The men were close now; hooded, dressed mostly in black; flat, wide turbans and scarves to cover their faces.

Noah snapped the reins hopefully, the horse's pace bridled by the weight of the wagon, the riders already nearly upon them, standing on their stirrups as the hooves of their black sleek steeds hammered angrily over the dust.

Noah heard Daneel shout something behind him, then heard the thud as the first of the riders leapt onto the cartbed. He flicked a panicked glance back, saw Daneel and the rider wrestling, swordhands gripped at the wrists as they staggered with the bump and sway of the carriage.

Noah almost missed a bend in the road, distracted by the scuffle; pulled hard on the reins and leant into the turn. Dull thump of flesh on dirt as someone toppled from the wagon, the riders swerving aside as the body tumbled in the dust.

Noah glanced back to find Daneel still there, leaning on the cartwall shouting instructions. Noah squinted, trying to hear through the chaos; the bone-jarring shudder of the wagon, air whipping across their faces like a storm.

Daneel was still trying to be understood when another man leapt onto the cartbed; a third drawing alongside the carriage on horseback and angling toward Noah at the reins.

Noah swerved; pure panic, bumping the rider's horse with the cartwall, almost shoving him down the verge.

The road was curving to the east ahead of them, swinging around a shallow bend edged by a vertiginous drop where the lane narrowed, the whole thing shivering in Noah's vision as the bench shook with the rampant pace of the wheels.

He snatched another glance to the rear. More riders, galloping madly through the riled dust in the cart's wake; some levelling crossbows, trying to the steady their aim.

Noah turned to warn Daneel but still couldn't be heard above the din, the assassin straddling an attacker in the cartbed, thrusting mercilessly with his blade into the squirming man's ribs.

A rider fired as the wagon bucked, the arrow whizzing past Daneel's ear. He shoved the attacker's body from the cart to lessen their weight, and then, seeing another man take aim, dove onto the cartbed, gesturing for Noah to do the same.

Arrows thudded against the sidewall like heavy hail as Noah ducked to hide by the footrest, clutching the reins as Daneel scrambled across the cartbed to avoid the next volley.

The road ahead was beginning to straighten, the slope levelling out. Rows of cacti fencing the narrowed lane on one side, the blur of the rockface racing by on the other.

Noah battened down a surge of anxiety as he felt the horse start to tire. Likely they were miles from the nearest city, scrubland and outcrops for days in every direction. No cover. Nowhere to hide.

Daneel was shouting to him again, probably yelling for him to stay down; but Noah could feel the scrape and thud of his movements in the cartbed; could feel Daneel, against all sense, rising to stand up.

Noah clasped the footrest, grimacing against the wild rattle of the bench and wheels beneath him before eventually peeping above the cartwall. Daneel was upright, tossing daggers at the riders behind. Noah watched as a blade hammered into one of the men's chests, knocking him from his horse.

By the time Noah had pushed himself up the other man was gone too. Daneel was leaning over the sidewall, trying to snatch at the throatlatches of the riderless horses sprinting beside the wagon.

There were more pursuers on the road behind: a band of three in the distance, dressed in similar hoods and scarves to the others, but then out ahead of them what looked like a girl. Slight, hoodless, riding hard toward the next bend to catch them with a riderless horse in tow.

Noah shouted to Daneel and pointed as the girl drew alongside, galloping along the narrow gap between the wagon and the road's edge. He adjusted his grip on the reins, readying to steer the cart toward her, to push her from the road or force her in behind – until she looked directly at him.

"You need to come with me," she shouted. "Both of you."

Noah blinked at her, looked to Daneel, then glanced back to the riders behind, who were quickly gaining.

"You don't know what you are involved in," the girl shouted. "You have no idea. You must come with me now."

Daneel, no time to think, reached out an arm to Noah, who left the reins to grab it, nearly toppling as he rose to his feet. The girl was leading the empty horse in close to them, trailing it behind her as the road began to bend south.

Daneel leant Noah out beyond the sidewall, holding him as he reached for the reins of the trailing horse; Noah's fingers flexing, almost there, inches away, just a little closer. Just a little–

The wagon rocked as another rider leapt into the cartbed,

swinging at Daneel as he tried to hold Noah steady. The man's blade smashed down into the timber as Daneel swayed out of the way, jolting Noah over the side, down toward the rush of dirt and rock racing beneath the wheels to–

Someone grabbed his arm.

The girl, leaning back on her horse to grip his wrist whilst his foot, hooked atop the ledge of the sidewall, held him up.

"Hurry! I can't hold you."

The rush of rocks and dirt beneath was a blur, hurtling by like a speeding river to the thunderous roar of the wheels and hooves.

Noah took hold of the girl with his other arm, levered himself up, then pushed off with his foot, jumping across the short gap to climb onto the back of her saddle. She glanced back as he took hold of her waist to right himself; short dark windswept hair, half veiling the sunlit flash of her eyes, looking beyond him to the chaos still ensuing in their wake. Noah turned, following her gaze as Daneel kicked the other man from the wagon before turning to leap out across the rushing void and onto the remaining horse. He landed on his stomach, clawing for purchase as he clung on, then heaved himself upright and grabbed the reins.

"Your name is Noah," the girl shouted.

Noah turned from Daneel to face her. "You know my name?"

"I saw you," she said, tapping her head, then looked away before Noah could ask what she meant.

She let the horse slow a little, allowing Daneel to come alongside before pulling a sort of shorthanded spear from a sleeve by her right leg – flintheaded tip, the shaft thick but no longer than her arm. She gestured for Daneel to move ahead, out of her way. Daneel glanced at her, confused, but then saw the spear and obeyed, speeding further up the road. She lifted the spear, cocking it at her shoulder as she aimed, and then tossed down hard at the wheel where it dug into the ground, shunting the spokes with its shaft and bucking the cart. She snapped at the reins and raced ahead as the cart jumped violently and tipped onto its side, yanking at the mare that had been driving it as it turned over to bar the road.

"It'll do for now at least," the girl said, looking behind as the riders came to an abrupt halt at the upended wagon. The sun had come out again, washing the men in light as their horses stepped and jostled restlessly behind the improvised barrier, receding behind Daneel, Noah and the girl as they continued to race ahead. "My name is Tamar," the girl said once they'd moved clear. "I'll get you both safe now," she added. "There are things you must see, and someone you will need to meet."

EIGHTEEN

OMEN

"But that makes no sense."

"I don't dispute that," Neythan said. "But it *was* the chamberlain I saw."

He and Arianna sat on a bench opposite Caleb in the small room.

Caleb stared flat-eyed at him and grunted, rubbing his wrists. They'd removed the bindings only an hour ago, shortly after Neythan and Arianna had arrived back in Jaffra to visit with the elders following their release from the Sayensi's shrine. Not that any of that mattered to Caleb. Since being ushered into this room to sit with him whilst the elders conferred regarding Neythan and Arianna's findings, Caleb had been alternating between levelling Neythan with a cold, grumpy stare and gazing off to one of the featureless corners.

"Look," Neythan said. "I'm sorry about leaving you here to wait."

"Against my advice, I might add," Arianna put in.

Neythan glanced sidelong at her beside him on the bench.

"What? It was."

He sighed and returned his attention to Caleb. "Thing was, I thought it better to take Nyomi so she could guide us. She knows these lands better than any of us can."

Another monosyllabic grunt, then, "And where is she now?"

"We don't know."

"Don't know? What, she get bored of your company? Decide to make use of her superior knowledge of these lands and take herself off for a stroll?"

"We were separated, in the shrine," Neythan explained. "Whole place was like some kind of maze or trap. When we came out, she couldn't be found."

"So, what's the plan now? Wait here for her? See if she'll return to visit Filani?"

"You're sure Filani's alive?" Arianna said.

Caleb shrugged, scratching at the old wrinkled scar tissue that covered his face. His brief captivity had aged him somehow, made the burns on his cheeks and neck seem more pronounced. "She was the last time I asked about her. She breathes, and little more than that, so they tell me. She has not woken since they stoned her in the street."

A pause. The chatter from the street outside filled in the gap. They were in an enclosure of wood, rectilinear walls of thick pine beams lined one atop the other and welded fast with some kind of daub. The warm air wafted out through an opening above where the cabin tunnelled up into some sort of spout, leaving a bright patch of sunlight in the middle of the room's dirt floor. A cookhouse of some kind perhaps.

"So… what's the plan?" Caleb asked again.

"I don't know."

"Oh?" Caleb's eyebrows hopped up – exaggerated, sardonic – his gaze switching between them. "No plan this time? No blind quest to this place or that, to discover some obscure and futile truth?"

"*Caleb.*"

He looked at Arianna. "What? You don't tire of it? Well, let him leave you imprisoned and alone in a foreign land, bound hand and foot, see if it dampens your enthusiasm somewhat."

"He didn't choose this, Caleb."

"*And neither did I*, Arianna. Neither did I. Shall I tell you what I *did* choose? I chose to make a bargain with *him*. To find *you*. And in return he was to find the people who murdered my family. A simple agreement, no? And yet lo, here we are – you are found, yet my family's killers are not. Instead I'm left to rot in a Summerland shack while the pair of you go off searching for 'truths'. So, if you're expecting me to slap my thigh and ready for another trek to wherever he says next with nothing but a wink and a smile, then perhaps that fever of his has gone to your head too."

Neythan's hand twitched again, as if triggered by Caleb's mention of the fever. The wound was healing well at least, ever since Teju had treated it with ointments as he and a few others from the Sayensí sat in the boat with them on the way back, but the other symptoms had continued to prove more stubborn – the sudden bouts of fatigue, and, more recently, even melancholy, a deep cold shadow creeping across his sha. Then there was the struggle to concentrate sometimes, his thoughts foggy, trailing off on tangents like fluff snagged by a breeze.

"What would you have me do, Caleb?" Neythan asked. "Go back north, to the Sovereignty, where we are likely still being hunted by whatever remains of the Brotherhood?"

"Be better than staying in *this* dung hole."

"It's not as simple as that, not anymore."

"What do you mean, *not anymore*? Why the bones not?"

"Because he has family here," Arianna interrupted.

Caleb balked. His mouth opened again, shaping on a response, and then folded as he just sat there, frowning in puzzlement.

"Yeah," Arianna continued. "Nyomi dropped that one on us before we reached the shrine. Neythan is the grandson of that priestess out there, the one who set the city to stone Filani."

"*Sulari?*"

"One and the same."

"That madwoman is your grandmother?" He stared at Neythan, then nodded as he looked him over. "Then again I suppose I shouldn't be all that surprised."

"Glad to see you've retained your sense of humour," Neythan replied drily.

"You think I'm joking; the stunts you've pulled? And why do we only discover this now? Nyomi couldn't see fit to mention this little detail before?"

"Believe me," Arianna replied. "I let my thoughts be known on that too."

"You believe her?"

"She said it was why she and Filani brought us here," Neythan said. "She explained many things, said my bloodline is one of only a few that may be able to withstand what the scroll warns of."

"How?"

"I don't know. Not yet. But it apparently means I have kin in this very city."

Caleb thought on that, staring at the sunlit patch of dirt in the middle of the room between them before looking up at Neythan. For a moment his gaze even seemed to soften a little. He knew what it could mean for Neythan.

"Still," Arianna said. "Caleb is right."

"I often am… Right about what though?"

"Going north, to the Five Lands. If what Neythan saw in the scroll is true then Elias is something more than just an old man."

"What are you saying?"

"I'm saying we already know he is involved in all this. If he happens to somehow be more than three centuries old too then we need to get to him, understand what he knows, understand what he *is*. He could be the root of it all."

Caleb sat back and muttered a curse under his breath. "So, now you are infected with his madness too."

"Oh, I take it you'd rather stay here then," Arianna replied. "Since you've enjoyed the hospitality so much?"

Caleb offered her a wan smile. "Take it you'd rather eat cow dung, since you're so used to being full of it?"

"Look," Neythan said. "The reality is we cannot stay here, and we cannot be safe if we go north. But the bigger reality is that none of this ends until *we* end it – the Brotherhood, the Watcher's prophecy, all of it. We need to find the chamberlain." He looked at Arianna, who nodded back, and then back to Caleb sitting hunched opposite him on the bench.

"What? You want to pretend you care for my opinion on the matter? Please. You stopped caring what I thought a long time ago."

A day later they were travelling north, journeying toward the Havilah and back into the Sovereignty despite Caleb's reluctance, equipped with fresh provisions by Jaffra's elders – three strong horses, a packhorse, enough food and water to cross the sands of the Havilah, along with tools, weapons and utensils. Apparently, although the priesthood remained split on the veracity of Neythan's lineage, there were enough among them who believed him to be who Filani had claimed to warrant their aiding him with supplies. Especially since he'd managed to read the scroll – a fact Teju, who'd returned to the city with them to debate with the elders, had been more than happy to confirm. Before leaving, Neythan had visited with Filani and stood over her as she lay unconscious on a bed within the cool shade of a mudbrick hut. Gazing down on her, he suddenly saw it all; the past half year laid out clearly before him as every conversation they'd shared took on fresh meaning, became whole, pieces of a puzzle clacking snugly into place. The way she'd watch him sometimes, the way he'd look up from some chore or sundry task – packing their victuals, feeding the mule, preparing wood for a fire – to find her steady watery gaze on him, probably wondering inwardly, he now realised, whether he truly was what the faint nagging sense within her had suggested. All along, her every glance in his direction had been the scratching of an itch, a contemplating of their shared blood.

He'd stood in the mudbrick hut for close to an hour in the end, just thinking about it, until Sulari, his apparent grandmother, had come in to stand beside him, pleading tearfully for him not to leave. For a moment he'd even thought about it – probably he had cousins in Jaffra he was yet to meet, maybe great-aunts or uncles too. But in the end what would it all mean if he left what needed to be done undone? The darkness the Watcher had warned of was coming, preparing to usurp them all: the Sovereignty, then Súnam, and perhaps even the whole world. He alone was the one who had discovered a Magi scroll, and it was to him the Watcher had come to warn of the approaching darkness. If Nyomi was to be believed, the answers of how to stop it all lay in his blood. There would be no hiding place if he failed to go, not even for his as yet unknown kin.

They travelled for nearly a week seeing no one, first through the jungled forests of the Summerlands' northern borders and then on into the rocky plains of the Desert Pass, south of the Narrow Sea, before heading north into the Havilah, skirting along the dry plains and bluffs bordering its sands to the west. Only the occasional crop of rock formations interrupted the arid calm – a sea of endless dry land, pale and wide, stretching out beneath the silent and cloudless blue above.

They were beginning to run low on water when they finally reached the Straight, a long slim river that split the Havilah from the Salt Plains north of it. A boatman could sit in the Straight and traverse the entire breadth of the land from here, let the current carry him east to Qalqaliman and Hikramesh, then continue north to Sippar and Qareb and eventually the crown city itself. But Neythan and the others would not have time for that, or even the means. They had the horses after all, each of which would be strong and swift once watered.

They filled their skins and the wooden cask they'd been given back in Jaffra, and then continued on to the river's narrow to cross the brief bridge onto the other side before continuing east along the riverbank in search of whatever fishing villages inevitably lined it.

"What allows a man to live for more than three hundred years anyway?"

Neythan glanced at Arianna on her horse beside him as they resumed their journey. "You been pondering that the whole way here?"

"You haven't?"

"For the first day or so maybe. After that, I realised, what does it matter? We're going to have to find him either way, and likely won't know the answer until we do."

Arianna shrugged, riding tall on her horse, those green feline eyes of hers glinting like twin emeralds from beneath her dark hair as she squinted back at him. "Doesn't make it any less worth wondering about. Three centuries. Think how many *trees* he's outlived. Even bloodtrees."

"To live that long would be a curse," Caleb put in grumpily, and then shrugged when the others turned to look at him. "Think about it. Everyone you've known or loved, dying, while you persist. Cities changing, others being built, nothing being the way you can remember it once was." He shook his head. "You ask me, it'd be about as eerie a feeling as you can have, like the world is conspiring around you, without anyone else being able to see it but you. You'd be a living ghost."

No one spoke for a while after that, continuing east along the river in silence as they passed a pair of large stone figures, upended and lying face down in the dust, buried in the crest of the slope opposite the river like murdered bodies in a shallow grave. Adramelec and Armaros probably, Neythan thought. The twin gods, and the only ones he remained able to consistently remember from Jaleem's lessons in Ilysia, and that purely because of how Daneel and Josef would pretend to be them when they were all small.

"You've a dark mind, Caleb," Arianna eventually said, still thinking on the little man's previous remark.

"So I've been told."

"Except there's nothing to say the chamberlain's the only one though is there," she added.

"What?"

"He could just be one of many other ancient ones couldn't he, all three centuries old or more."

"Thanks, Ari," Neythan said. "I was beginning to feel bored, as if we didn't have enough problems to consider as is."

"Pleasure."

"Do you two see that?" Caleb was pointing toward a short

column of stone ahead of them by the river. It was sculpted, Neythan realised as they neared, a block of rock about the height of his horse, shaped into the form of a man's head, like a smaller and less dramatic version of the massive stone mound they'd come across when journeying to the Sayensí. Cruder workmanship, the facial features blunt and undefined, the likeness vague, unlike the bizarrely precise rendering they'd witnessed in the Summerlands. It faced inland, away from the river.

Neythan climbed down from his horse to examine the horizontal grooves cutting across its base and traversing the neck area and jaw.

"Almost looks Súnamite," Caleb decided.

Neythan could see the likeness too – the thickened lips, the small ears.

"Look," Caleb said. "Over there."

Beyond the rise in the land opposite the river, smoke was wafting up.

Neythan climbed back onto his horse and rode up the dusty slope to see what was on the other side.

"So, *there's* the settlement," Caleb said, coming to a stop on the crest beside him.

The land dropped down into a shallow basin with a brief smattering of houses and sheds, wooden mostly, a marker of how far south they were. The trend in most parts of the Sovereignty was to build in stone, but here, by the Straight where the weather was warmer – as with the territories of Harán further east – wood was often thought to be the more suitable material.

"The rains must be heavy here in their season," Caleb suggested as they looked down on the settlement at the bottom of the slope before them. "To have built so far from the river I mean, and on this side of the hill. Probably what the grooves were for at the base of that head back there: to mark off where the water level can come to, so they know how to build."

"Fountain of knowledge, aren't you," Arianna said.

"Well, it's not that hard to look like one opposite the pair of you, is it."

Once they'd descended the hill into the settlement it wasn't hard to see the merits of Caleb's words. Most of the houses were built on logwood perches, propped atop thick stilts like cabins on a pier. More stone heads stood amid the relatively large village like watching sentries, stationed at corners and crossroads, each scarred by the same fine grooves along the base to mark the seasonal waterlines. Caleb wandered a few paces ahead on his horse, scrutinising the streets for somewhere to stable the horses and perhaps settle for the night.

"So, are you going to talk to me about it then?"

Neythan turned to Arianna riding beside him and frowned. "About what?"

"The fever. *Your* fever. You've said almost nothing about it the entire journey."

"And yet you never cease to ask," Neythan answered, scanning the surroundings as they continued along the street. The way the platforms exaggerated the heights of the houses made him feel like he was wandering through a city built for giants. And then there were the stilts themselves, dug into holes and anchored in place by the boulders that had been nestled around the foot of each one.

"Neythan?"

He shrugged. "I'll be fine. What does it matter?"

"It matters if you're going to put me or Caleb in danger because you're too stubborn to admit how weakened you might be. Just tell me, Neythan."

Neythan thought about it, trying to find a way to explain as the horses continued to walk them on down the main thoroughfare. "What I told you back in the shrine is part of it," he said. "It's like, sometimes… I maybe see something, but it might not be there. Or not fully there maybe. Like a piece of a dream, but in the day."

"Like those fungi Jaleem would offer sometimes, back in Ilysia."

"I wouldn't know. I never took any."

"You didn't?"

"Did you?"

"Felt rude to refuse."

An amused grunt. "Well, maybe it *is* like that. I wouldn't know. It's only in moments though, the rest of the time I'm fine… And, well…"

"Well, what?"

"I don't know. It feels like they mean something, these things I see… Like some kind of message. Like I'm being told something."

"Being told what? By who?"

"I don't know, Ari. It's just how it feels. But like I said, they don't happen often… and I'm not always sure if they're happening when they do. It's hard to be certain."

Arianna digested that without answering.

There were people in the next street, villagers ambling along the road: a man dressed in a pale ankle length shift and, incredibly, the skin of a bear's head, hanging from his own like a hood as the rest of its hide dangled down his back and dragged in the dust. He was herding a toddler along ahead of him as he clutched a second child in one arm, and what appeared to be some kind of cutting utensil or trowel in the other. An older man moved along the road in the other direction, wheeling a basket of logs on a small cart, and passed by the man without comment, whilst others milled around, chatting, or perched on the raised wooden porches supporting every house, letting their feet dangle over the open space beneath. One or two woodmen, carrying measured lengths of timber for some kind of scaffolding, glanced disinterestedly at the visitors.

"Wonder where they're getting all the wood from?" Arianna said. "I haven't seen that many trees."

She was right: there were no trees in sight and even the grass was sparse, mostly limited to random tufts of dry weed or brierbush sprouting from between the rocks that footed the houses' stilts and scanty rushes like thinning hair along the sides of the roads. Meanwhile someone somewhere was playing a stringed instrument, plucking softly to a familiar melody.

"You hear that?" Neythan asked.

Arianna nodded and glanced around. "I feel like I've heard the song before."

"Jaleem used to play it sometimes, back in Ilysia, at evening when the herders were bringing the flocks back in."

"I remember."

"I think I've found somewhere," Caleb said, trotting back toward them from up ahead on his horse. After their lack of reaction he added. "You know. For us to stay?"

"Sounds good," Arianna replied. "Neythan?"

But Neythan wasn't listening. The music was strange. The melody disjointed, its rhythm erratic, as though the strings were being plucked by the hands of a drunkard.

"You hear that?" he said again to Arianna.

"Yes, I told you I heard it."

"No, I mean the words. I never knew the song had words."

"What words?"

But Neythan was already turning, flicking his reins to move along the road in the direction of the music as the verses continued to bounce along to the choppy rhythm of the strings.

"There's a season for the sun, and a season for the rain,
a season to have fun, and a season to feel pain.
But as the seasons turn, and wintry nights rob the days,
there's a music to their churn, and a rhythm to their ways…"

The road curved, bending away from the river beyond the crest behind them to accommodate the shape of the land. It seemed to be leading up toward a hill. Neythan could see a cluster of houses on a crest ahead of him, surrounded by a fortified wall and gate.

"If a man should turn his ear, beyond the clamour of the waves,
he'll hear secrets of the earth, and the paths of hidden ways,
the dancing of the fool, the quiet thoughts of the sage,
one is made from the two, in the turning season's maze…"

"Neythan, where are you going?"

Neythan ignored her, continuing forward on his horse. The

song was growing louder now – a man's voice, but strange, twisted somehow, almost a growl.

"So cast your sheets to the wind, turn your troubles into play,
let the song of madness sing, let the storm have its way."

He turned off the road, moving through the shadows as he passed along one of the slim gaps between the houses. He was close now, very close, the singer likely just around the next corner.

"For a man is only a man, a day is only a day,
neither shall last forever, nothing remains the same."

He came to the end of the passage into a space on the other side. More thin grass sprouting from the gravelled earth beneath like whiskers. The music and singing had stopped, abruptly. A smallish child stood by one of the stilts on the far side, facing away from Neythan. Copper skin. Black cropped hair. Scrawny shoulders and back, his ribs showing through the skin of his bare gaunt torso.

"Who was singing here just now?" Neythan asked. "Where was the music coming from?"

When the boy didn't respond Neythan climbed down from his horse.

"Boy. The music," he said, walking toward the child who stood motionless, apparently captivated by whatever was on the ground by the foot of the nearest stilt.

Neythan was a few paces away and about to call out to the child again when the boy turned around. Neythan froze.

The face. The boy's face.

It was covered. Encased in the dirty pale bone of a goat skull.

"Neythan, what are you doing?" Arianna had followed him through the gap between the houses to the yard. "Neythan!"

Neythan glanced behind toward her, and pointed at the boy.

"What? What is it?"

But when Neythan turned back the boy was gone, only the skull was there, its blank hollow sockets staring up at him where it lay on the ground, nestled in the thin patch of grass beneath the stilt-propped porch of the wooden house.

"How did you know?" Caleb said, coming around the corner of the gap behind Arianna.

"What?"

Caleb nodded at the building ahead of them, standing on the porch above the stilt where the goat skull lay. "This is the place," he said, "the inn I found. This is where we'll stay."

NINETEEN

BOND

Caleb had seen this place and what he'd find here a hundred times. It was like a well-worn song, with notes that sounded in his own thoughts before the minstrel's hand had conjured them. He stood at the grassy lip of the brook, here where it was at its stillest and widest as the familiar emotions of sorrow, pain and despair played through him like an aroma before the sight, their melancholy presences floating to the forefront of his heart and mind just like the bodies in the water. There, just beneath the surface, submerged and still beyond the gentle cross-currents of the gurgling creek that ran by the back of the house. That creek had been a stream of frolicking and teasing and fun, and even teaching. In its waters he'd taught his children to swim, and even fish, snatching those silvery slick-quick bodies into baskets from the spray-spitting air just above the rush where the brook turned to a river. This place had been his home. The one place he could always return to, and be safe, with his family. But now their bodies stared up from just beneath the brook's pane, floating, buoyed above the black hollow of the depths that gaped beneath. Tiny stray bubbles trickled sparingly up to the surface from their nostrils and mouths and clothing, the last snagged remnants of air, like life, making for a surface these sunken bodies could no longer reach. Their faces deathly white; their bellies and limbs swollen by the water; their eyes, open, lost and still. His wife and two of his daughters, their pallid images quivering beneath the soft ripples by the bank as the daylight flickered over them in glassy refractions. Like a picture, he thought, an unreal and horrifying picture.

Then he was staggering up a grassy incline. The gurgling wash of the brook behind him had silenced. As he climbed, he could feel his chest tightening, laden with the inevitability of what he knew he wouldn't find, laced by the hope that somehow this time he might. The two – futility and hope – tugged at him with each stride as he stalked laboriously toward the hill's zenith. Searching. The hill came to its crest, the homely wood cabin, so familiar, so right, now sitting to one side, sullen and empty. And that's when he saw it, just as he always did. The hole in the ground, that small and neat void carved into the grassy slope, both mocking and beckoning to him. Was she there? Would he finally see her?

He hurried toward it desperately. He saw its gape open to him as the angle changed with his approach, and, tricked once more by that fiend Hope, dared to look, gazing down into the hole beyond the interrupted grassroots poking from the walls of soil and dirt, their pale filaments exposed and abandoned. Down deep into its darker and shadowed depth where the earth turned damp. Down to the dirt floor where his lastborn's grave might lie, hoping this time that maybe he would find her, but, just like all the other times, he was instead greeted by the cruel void of what was not there. An empty, staring blackness. Hollow. Endless. Nothing. Unbearable nothing.

Neythan awoke, sweating, his damp bedclothes clinging to his skin, bunching the bedsheets around his armpits and knees as he lay on his bedmat, trying to calm down.

He sat up, the dream's sensations and images still running through him. It was like being back at the Sayensí temple, reading the scroll: the same bewildering sense of displacement, of having been plunged into a foreign reality, immersed in memories and thoughts that were not his own.

He closed his eyes, breathed, stilling his sha.

Why did I just dream I was Caleb?

Neythan looked across to where the old man was sleeping and saw Caleb writhing on his bedmat, murmuring breathily. Neythan watched him for a few moments before another thought hit him.

Did I just dream Caleb's dream– the very dream he's dreaming right now?

Neythan got up, still groggy, and crept slowly across the room to sit on the floor beside Caleb's bedmat.

He could hear Caleb whimpering now, calling out a name, a name Neythan recognised.

Caleb flinched as Neythan inadvertently touched his arm. Awake. "What are you doing?"

Neythan sat back. "Sorry…" He blinked, fumbling for an answer. "You were weeping," he explained. "As you slept. And talking."

Caleb just watched him for a moment before turning to face the window. "You're mistaken… Do not trouble yourself. My breathing can become uneven sometimes. You're not the first to notice it."

Neythan nodded, but he could still feel the residue of the dream, stained to his thoughts like sunspots. He hesitated, sitting cross-legged by the bedmat, before finally deciding to say the name. "Yva."

Caleb whipped around, pinning him with his gaze.

"You called the name as you slept," Neythan explained.

Caleb, still staring, said nothing, and then shivered a little, stung by the gentle caress of the breeze as it passed in through the window, tugging a flip-flap from the tails of the curtains on its way to chilling his sweat-covered limbs.

"I remembered the name, Caleb. You told me of it once. The name of your daughter?"

Caleb's shoulders slumped and shuddered as he seemed to recede into himself, drawing his knees up to his chest to hug his calves. "She was my youngest. Of three. All daughters. All…" he exhaled, the breath cracking in his throat, "beautiful… She was five when they killed her, along with the others. Tuya, Natasha, and my wife…" He trailed off, staring to the other side of the room. It was early. Barely day. Still dark outside. Arianna lay curled up on her bedmat in the opposing corner, still asleep. Caleb's eyes wandered toward the pale dimply walls of the inn's bedchamber above her, shadowed by dark trails of mould aggregating in the corners where the plaster lay thin against the timber outside it. "So strange isn't it…" he continued, a sudden distance inflecting his voice. "How all the blood we spill… the killing… how, you don't really *feel* it. When you kill. Even as you look into their eyes, watch their life ebb away… you see the pain, the fear. But that is all. You only… *observe* it. There's nothing there, nothing to reach *you*. But that day looking at my family… it was as if *I'd* done it. Like a punishment…" Caleb turned and looked directly at Neythan now, his eyes watery, gleaming from the stray shards of moonlight sneaking in through the curtain's flimsy thin fabric, "because I should have felt something all those other times. *Something…* And now… now I did…"

"I'm so sorry, Caleb."

Caleb snorted and looked away, rubbing a sleeve over his nose and eyes. Something closed in the old man then. When he next spoke, his words came out flat and hard, like a merchant counting payment. "They drowned them. Left my wife and two of my daughters in a stream behind our house and then hid the body of Yva, my youngest… Yes," Caleb caught the look in Neythan's eyes. "My lastborn killed and hidden as if I were a betrayer."

It was the Shedaím way, one of the many reasons it was so rare for its Brothers to turn away from the covenant. Betrayal meant they'd come for you; betrayal meant there'd be no mercy for you *or* your family when they did.

"They even dug an empty hole on my plot, just to make the point. So I'd know it was them. I see it all…" Caleb's hands were clenching in his lap as he spoke now, "*here*," he tapped hard against his head with his fingers, "when I sleep. The same dream, over and over, sometimes once a week, sometimes once a month, or every few days, but always the same. And no matter how many times I dream it, I'm always hoping, in the dream, it will be different. I'm always hoping, as I come to that hole, that she'll be there."

"We *will* find those responsible, Caleb."

"When?" Caleb snapped bitterly.

Neythan didn't answer, the silence that opened passing between them like an unwelcome smell.

Neythan tried to shift the angle of the conversation. "You never told me of… how they didn't bury her. Their hiding the body like that."

"And why would I tell you? How should I?"

"I am your friend, Caleb."

Another contemptuous huff. "Are you? I've journeyed the length and breadth of the Sovereignty to keep the agreement we made, and yet I feel further from knowing the truth of what happened to them than I did at the beginning."

"I will keep our bargain, Caleb. I've not forgotten the–"

"*Bargain?* Our *bargain* was to find Arianna. Our *bargain* had a finite end. A goal. Clear and specified. Our *bargain*, my side of it, has already been *met*. Yet here I am, Neythan. Here I am in some obscure inn crying in my sleep because they are *still* not avenged. You," Neythan saw Caleb's finger accuse him through the gloom, "covenanted with me to find who did it. I even hoped to uncover *why* they did it. But instead we traipse here and there, a scroll in our hands, for the sake of a Sovereignty which allowed the murder of my… my…" Caleb's chest heaved and gasped, trembling with rage. "You claim to be my friend, yet you left me in Jaffra. Left me there and freed Nyomi, a stranger, instead."

"I told you. She knew the land. We needed to get to the Sayensí, to read the scroll, know what to do next."

"Scrolls be hanged. Sayensí be hanged. If you were my friend we'd be looking for the people who murdered my family. The people who did this to me," Caleb gestured at the burn marks on his face and arms, the shiny seared skin glistening in the half light. "We'd be looking for them *now*."

"Caleb–"

"In truth we'd have probably *found* them." The breeze, thickening outside. "Instead, you know where they are? They're probably sitting on sovereign councils, or retired in the eastern foothills of Harán without a care in the world, seeing out their days like a private king." The wind snapped with Caleb's words, the curtains leaning toward the outside, sucked by the sudden draft. "Wine and quail for breakfast." Neythan saw what the curtains were doing and shifted, half-turning toward them. "Perhaps prime honey steaks for lunch," and as he watched, a shadow seemed to grow there like wetness filling on a kerchief pressed to a puddle, "whilst I am forced to stay here and sit on my grief whilst you... Look at you. You're not even *listening* to me."

Neythan stood slowly to his feet. "Caleb–"

"I know what you will say. You talk endlessly of it – of scrolls and quests and prophecies and all other things that to me just," the shadow had enveloped the curtain now, blocking out the light and darkening the already dim room further, "simply."

"Caleb!"

"Don't. Matter–"

The curtain drapes tore from their fastenings, sucking out through the window as if whipped into the path of a storm. Caleb toppled back onto the bed, startled by the sound, as *something* came through the window.

Neythan froze as the thing moved in, dark, vaguely translucent, its flesh composed of shadow. It moved slowly, its motions seeming to merge seamlessly into one another as it stepped through the window in a crouch, and then, as its foot passed the threshold of the sill and lowered toward the floor, shifted and changed; the foot, somehow, now the creature's head, keening up like a charmed cobra as it suddenly flickered into solidity to reveal itself. Dark-skinned body, long and skeletal and taller than Neythan by half a foot. As it breathed Neythan could see the bars of its ribcage expanding and retracting beneath the taut sinewy skin of its chest, and then... the face... that face.

The goat skull.

Neythan reached in a panic for his sword, leaning in its sheath against the wall behind him. Suddenly, the creature broke off from its slowness, bursting across the short distance between them and gripping Neythan tightly by the wrist with its cold bony fingers. It yanked, flinging him across the room and into the opposing wall with a force that emptied his lungs. He bounced from the plastered wood and landed on his chest, gasping for breath and groaning as he tried to push himself up from the ground and rise to his feet. He'd managed to get to his hands and knees when he suddenly noticed it. There, just beyond the creature. Caleb on the bedmat, just sitting there, mildly puzzled, peering inquisitively toward the window as if at some strange intrigue that awaited there, as though the creature's presence and what it had just done hadn't even happened.

Neythan was about to call out to him when he saw the rest. Standing next to the bedmat where Neythan, moments ago, had been, the creature had resumed its ghostly translucence, allowing Neythan to see through the liquid shadow of its body to what lay behind.

Unable to make sense of it, Neythan, for a moment, stopped breathing. It was him, there on the other side of the room by the door to the bedchamber, standing as he had been a few moments ago and looking, as was Caleb, toward some distraction at the window. Neythan barely had time to comprehend what he was seeing before the menacing shadow flickered solid again, obscuring his view.

Neythan reached for Arianna's sword but he couldn't grasp it, his hand passing through the handle as though he was made of air.

The creature was marching toward him again.

Neythan came in to meet it and feinted, reversing his stance, before leaping fist first at its chest. The creature blinked back to transparency before the strike hit, tipping Neythan forwards, reeling off balance with the unchecked momentum of his attack as he stumbled on *through* the creature toward the frozen image of himself, still standing there, staring at the window on the other side of the small room. Neythan braced instinctively, guarding his head with his forearms as he careered toward his past self as it gazed at the window for an enemy that had already entered the room.

He jolted to an abrupt halt before the collision, the icy clasp of the creature's hand clamping to his neck, the chill of its iron grip pressing right through him, into him, as though it had taken hold of his bones. He watched the image of himself across the room turning slowly toward him, reaching for the sword by the wall in a slow visual echo of what had already been just moments ago. But it felt vague and distant now, almost arbitrary, like watching a tossed pebble fall to the ground again. Inevitable. All of it felt suddenly meaningless and implacable – the dank mattresses and bedmats, the moon-gilt window ledge and cool blue shadows filling the room, all receding from him, glazing over, darkening and falling away like he was a sinking stone beneath deep and muddy waters. And then he felt the bone-deep cold of the creature's grasp turn to fatigue, sweeping its drowsy weight over and through him until it seemed to be the only thing that mattered, until the world itself seemed no more than a cold unerring silence. A void. Gone. No sight. No sound. Nothing.

TWENTY

ENEMY

Neythan awoke before a wide and silent coastline; the ocean, as calm as a pond, glowing from beneath its waters as though its depths had somehow swallowed the sun. For a while he just stared at it, entranced by the strange and preternatural hue, the luminous tint of the water, the seemingly immeasurable breadth of the coast, gleaming beneath the darker yet cloudless firmament above like an unending vat of molten lava. From here, the shoreline was only just in view, obscured by the craggy edge of a chalkstone cliff overlooking the seabed far below. He scanned the beach, gazing at the eerily even line between the sand and water, as smooth and straight as if a builder had set it, and running almost perfectly parallel to the sunless grey expanse overhead. Maybe ten or fifteen miles out from the shore, the beginnings of a peninsula rode the horizon to his right, shimmering atop the still shining waters like some kind of mirage as it curved in from a hidden bay too small and distant to be seen.

"Beautiful, isn't it."

Neythan flinched, startled by the sudden voice. But when he tried to turn in search of its owner he realised he couldn't move.

"Not for everyone though, of course," the voice continued smoothly – masculine, feminine, Neythan wasn't sure. He was too busy trying not to panic, fighting down the terror of the abrupt paralysis that seemed to have overcome his limbs, shoulders and neck. He tried to focus on the shore to calm his breathing – the way the strange luminous sea was just sitting there, waveless and immobile, like an unending breadth of sunnily glowing ice – but he couldn't. He kept blinking, his eyes smarting from the warm salty air as it wafted in on a silent breeze from the still neon horizon. "It's the reversal, more than anything, that disturbs people," the voice was saying. "The light coming from beneath, instead of above. It takes some getting used to for most. But I've always liked it this way; I suppose you could say I've never been one for convention."

"What is this place?" Neythan managed, and tried to move again – an arm, his fingers, anything – but to no avail. Only his lips and eyes seemed able to move.

"You don't like it? I thought it a view you might appreciate, breaker of laws and covenants that you are. Think of it as a place *between* places. Like steam, or vapour: neither water nor air, neither here nor there, just somewhere in between."

As strange and arresting as the sea was the sky above it – grey and grim and yet mostly clear. Neythan could see a few thin scuds of cloud passing low along the horizon, grazing the peninsula like far away ships in the otherwise featureless, gaping void. Neythan could feel his breath faltering, jumping in his chest as he tried to comprehend the view.

"You don't understand," the voice said. "Of course, you don't. Forgive me. I am not always the best teacher, and I did not expect to be explaining it to you. You have been here before, after all."

"I have?"

"Yes, Neythan. You have."

The use of his name jolted him, interrupting his attempts to calm himself and gain control. He glanced again at the glowing sea beneath, trying to manage his breathing, but there was nothing about these alien surroundings that was in any way familiar. "I have *never* been here before," he answered. "I don't even know where here is."

"Where, yes… always the question isn't it. Although I often wonder if those who ask know what they mean, and if they don't, how they expect to learn an answer. Is 'where' a place, for example, or perhaps just a state of mind, or even a time? And can this 'where' even be a thing anyone other than the questioner himself has been to, or ever could go to? How to confer a man's history onto another, after all; have him see and feel all that the other has, and do so with the same mind, so that their 'where,' when they come to it, might be one and the same?"

Neythan blinked, confused. He was starting to feel ill, and his mind, somehow being lulled by the strange fluorescent waters and dim bruised sky, was beginning to feel foggy, his thoughts squirming frustratingly from his grasp like scummy bait fish. "This is some kind of dream," he said, speaking more to himself than the voice at his shoulder. "This is happening within my own mind."

"Or mine. Or perhaps even some other's. Does it really matter? The point is, how can you expect to tell. Consider the ant, Neythan. Do you suppose it knows what land it is in? What city?"

But Neythan was barely listening now. He could feel the panic beginning to rise within him as he glanced at his wrists. There were no bindings there, nothing physically holding him in place, and yet his limbs, deadened by some inexplicable apathy he just couldn't shift, simply wouldn't move.

"Exactly," the voice said, taking his silence as assent. "Of course it doesn't. It is only an ant. It will have its own understanding, limited though it may be, of 'where' it is. But we could never call that understanding the truth, could we?"

"I don't know," Neythan said. "I don't understand."

"Of course, you don't," the voice seemed almost melancholic, disappointed even. "You're just a man, after all. Truth, to you, is as a continent to an ant. So, tell me, Neythan, how should a man speak to an ant of *where* that little creature is? How should I speak to *you* of it?"

Neythan had no answer. He could feel the bizarre ethereal world around him, or perhaps even his perception of it, beginning to bend, filling with a sudden and puzzling menace. And now it seemed as though the horizon, endless as it was, was somehow widening further, stretching out into an endless abyss and leaning toward him like the closing maw of some immeasurable and malevolent throat.

"What do you want with me?" Neythan managed. "Who are you?"

"Ah, but I have had so many names, Neythan. And for centuries after you are buried and gone, I will have many more. But these things are far from simple to explain, at least between you and I, and they are not as important as you might think."

"You're going to kill me?"

The voice laughed. "You think I'd go to all this trouble for that?"

"Then why can't I move? Why am I here?"

"To correct an error, help you see more clearly, to find your path."

"My path?"

"You wish to oppose me, prevent what is coming. But only because you have been misinformed. Deceived."

"So, it is you... You are the one the Watcher spoke of, the darkness that comes. You are to destroy the world."

"Please. Nothing so grand as that. Change it perhaps, yes. But for the better."

"By destroying lives."

"Perhaps. Why not? Did not your precious Brotherhood abide by this same reasoning? Sometimes lives must be taken, but for a purpose, a greater good. You have killed by this same law yourself, Neythan. We are alike, you and I."

"No. We are not."

"No? Why not?"

Neythan recalled the ghostly shadowy figure that had snatched him from the bedchamber he'd been standing in mere moments ago, and then the blind elder who'd attacked him back in Ilysia weeks before. Even now he could feel the nearness of her, her blade in his hand, pinning him to the temple floor as she bore down on him like some grisly avatar of the undead. "You... you are evil."

"Evil?" The voice almost spat the word. Neythan could hear the chilly amused derision smoking off its tone. "You believe there *is* such a thing?"

"I've *seen* such a thing. I *know* there is."

"Really? And were the soldiers you killed in Qadesh evil, when you were pursuing Arianna through the city on the night of the Sharíf's wedding? They were merely men doing their duty, nobly following the orders given to them to protect the people and the city they serve. Or how about the boy you murdered when rescuing the Súnamite, Filani, from her captors? Little more than a child, barely older than you are now. And what of the men in Godswell all those moons ago when you discovered your murdered friend, Yannick? Were they evil too, for coming upon you in a room filled with blood, and Yannick on the chair with his throat open? But then perhaps you will speak of how you refrained from killing them, leaving one with a cracked skull and the other to lose his arm. They are both beggars now, you know. Just a slower kind of death."

"No... That was different. It wasn't like that. You're twisting things."

"Am I? Or have *you*? Do you think you are the first, Neythan? Do you imagine yourself to be *special*? The hero of some kind of story or song? And should that make you a judge, able to decide between right and wrong, good and bad, pure and *evil*; all so you can render sentence with your sword? I told you, we are alike, you and I. But you will refuse to see it. You will refuse to see the truth, as all your kind do. You will choose instead to think your cause greater than others, to imagine you possess the right to live above the very law you have set for all else, all so you can call others evil and worthy of death and in so doing think yourself, the bringer of it, to be some kind of *saviour* – a hero in a story... No, Neythan. These are childish thoughts. You are not the first. You are not special. You are telling yourself the same tale every ruler and warmonger has told from the beginning of time until now, and yet you do not see it. Just as Sharíf Karel did not see it..."

The voice sighed and paused. Out on the sea the beginnings of the first waves seemed to be showing – slow and shallow, and as gentle as the voice which eventually resumed.

"In many ways, you remind me of him, you know," it said. "You remind me of the things he too once told himself when he began this precious Sovereignty you men so adore: a story in his thoughts that allowed him to do terrible things, just like you. I helped him, you see. Karel. Helped him to conquer the lands he overcame, taught him to find the resources that would enable him to do so, until, when he decided I'd shown him enough, he betrayed me. Stole from me what was rightfully mine."

"You? You helped Karel to his conquests?"

"And his sons… Oh, you are surprised? Perhaps you thought it was the virtue of their cause that allowed them to succeed?" Another wry derisive laugh. "No, Neythan. It was me.

"How do you suppose the great Karel, and then his sons, overcame the armies of so many lands greater than their own? How was little Sumeria able to colonise the vast territories of Eram, Calapaar, Hardeny and Harán? By might, hmm? So strong and courageous were they? Or it was by numbers perhaps; when Calapaar alone had more men at their disposal than almost all the other four lands combined… No, Neythan. I will tell you the truth, as the Watcher has failed to. That Karel became king of kings was by the hand of a smith. Yes, a mere smith. Not so glorious a notion, I know. They will write no songs of a lowly smith. Tell no tales of him. And yet he it was who learned how to cast steel. A metal stronger than any other of the time, and that remains so to this day. Harder than bronze, able to be set in a longer blade. Before then a sword was barely more than a dagger, and a bad one at that. By this smith's hand, Karel invented a better blade, and then forged them by the thousands and had the armour of his men shaped from the same metal, claiming an advantage his enemies did not possess and were never able to overcome. Karel had fewer men, but better means, and by those means he took possession of more territory than any other man has before or since. All because of a clever metalworker…

"Understanding, you see, Neythan. Knowledge. Ingenuity. The mind to imagine a thing, create what is yet to be. This is the skill that rules the world. Not might, nor strength, nor numbers. *Understanding*. And it is this skill that was given to men. Yes, *given*. You were not *born* with it. You were *taught* – by those wise and ancient enough to know the ways and secrets of this world better than your kind ever could. It was us – sons of light – who were your guides, Neythan. Or at least those of us who were willing to condescend to you mere sons of dust. Yet, did we know your thanks for our benevolence? Did our showing you the secrets of the earth, its precious stones and metals, secure your gratitude? No. Only your greed. And then your betrayal. You betrayed your gods. You stole from us. And now the time has come to repay what is owed."

The waters were stirring now, surging and lapping at the shoreline as waves began to gather and break, as though spurred by the voice's words. Neythan stared at them as they washed across the coast, swelling and curling to life like harbingers of an approaching storm. "So, you are going to destroy the world for vengeance," Neythan said, to the sea, to the voice.

"Destroy? Is that what the Watcher told you? No, Neythan, I told you already. I do not seek to destroy the world. I seek to change it, to *cleanse* it. You merely stand in the way of progress. As your father did."

"My *father*? What do you know of my father?"

Another laugh. "A great deal more than you it seems. They have been lying to you, Neythan."

"Who?"

"Everyone. The Brotherhood. Filani. Nyomi. You do not know the truth of your own blood, yet seek to meddle in things beyond what you understand. But I am not unreasonable, Neythan. I know you did not *choose* the Shedaím as your forebears did. You were too young, and now you suffer for their sins. But I am a fair soul. That is why I brought you here, to offer you the choice that was never granted you as a child. The choice to leave all this behind, go your way, leave off from your pursuit of Elias. If you take this choice, I shall let you be. I will even protect you. What will befall others will not come near you. You will live old and grey, and your children after you, exempt from all that is to come.

"But should you spurn this offer, generous as it is, and refuse my hand by continuing to pursue this course, then I will take everything and everyone you care about from you, piece by piece, one by one, and you will know, this time, that their fates came to them of your *own* accord, by your hand. You will know, this time, that you are to blame. And then, of course, you will die, a victim of the shadow we have given to you.

"And so you see the choice, this time, is yours, Neythan. You can choose to live, and I will free you from Irsespedon this very moment."

"Irsespedon?"

"Ah, of course, you cannot see him, can you? I often forget the limitations of your kind, but then I suppose that is what makes him so effective an enemy, especially to men. After all, what adversary is there greater than a thought, or a feeling, a thing unseen? Give a man a foe and he will fight. Men are born for war. But how can a man overcome an enemy if that enemy lies within himself? He who has slain a thousand is undone by the disease of his own body. But even the one strong enough to withstand the sickness of his body cannot overcome the disease that abides his mind, that corrodes his very *sha*. There are no bulwarks you can set against that, Neythan. Your blade and all your great skill will not help you. It is a battle no man can *ever* win – no hope of victory, no means of triumph, and no relief. A war that can only be lost, or, should one find the strength to do so, endured. A slow death, Neythan, just like those men at Godswell. It shall be a fitting end should you choose your course and refuse what I offer… You've felt it already, haven't you? The shadow of Irses. The shadow on your soul. A torment that plagues you even here. Look, see for yourself. He is all over you. See your true enemy."

Neythan felt the tightness around his neck abruptly loosen, his muscles unclenching to release his head and shoulders and allow him to look around. He turned first toward the voice to find its owner but there was no one there, just the endless bluff running parallel to the shoreline and the glowing sea. So he looked down, hoping for a way to free himself from the seat he'd been frozen to – and then saw it.

His gut turned cold as he looked on in horror and bafflement at the thing consuming his body. He was almost entirely covered by it: a thick, wet, black mucus, swallowing him from toes to navel, and *moving*, he realised; breathing even, as it clamped along the length of him in a boneless slimy gunk, sucking and gnawing at his flesh as if to embalm him from the outside in. And then he saw its eyes – still, baleful orbs, staring up into his. With the ensuing shift of perspective he was able to make sense of the creature's body: the warped python-like jaws, grotesquely distended to accommodate Neythan's thighs and lower torso, and the weird fleshy tendrils that extended from them like tongues, merging into small fungal stems to syringe his flesh, burrowing and bubbling and wriggling within his skin like hungry maggots. And then there *were* maggots, squirming and writhing on the open sores of the creature's dark, membranous head, and along its outstretched tongues, its body, and Neythan's body too, wriggling and crawling and tunnelling into his skin as though racing toward some hidden home within him. And Neythan couldn't stop them, couldn't move, could only sit there buried in the creature's ever tightening grip as its cold black eyes stared up at him, corroding and sucking as he tried to recoil. Tried to scream. Was screaming. Howling to the dull slate sky as its few stars began to slowly grow and then smear and bleed their light, trailing bright hot streaks in their wake like incandescent tears–

"Neythan? Neythan, wake up."

Neythan blinked. He was back in the inn's bedchamber, Caleb sitting on the bed to one side whilst Arianna, now awake and standing in front of him, held and shook him by the shoulders.

"Neythan?"

"Ari…"

"Gods, Neythan…" She exhaled and stepped back. "This thing

that is happening with you… You were babbling again, just like you did back in that shrine in Súnam."

"Wait," Caleb said, "you mean he's done this before?"

"Are you alright, Neythan?" Arianna asked.

Neythan gazed around the room – the plain walls, the frayed worn bedmats and dusty wooden floor – as his hands worked frantically, patting his body down and slapping at the ghost of the creature he'd seen consuming him.

"*Neythan?*"

He looked up at her again. Scared, he could see. She was as scared as he was, watching him tremble and breathe. "I'm alright," he said. "I'm alright."

But the way he kept looking around the room, to the walls, the window, as if expecting the whole thing to shatter or move, wouldn't allow her to believe it. She came forward and took hold of his chin, turning his head toward her, his gaze to hers. "Neythan, what is it? Tell me."

But Neythan shrugged her off, his hands still working, but more calmly now, as though smoothing out the folds of his garments after having sat for too long. "I'm fine," he repeated, then stepped toward the window to look out through the muslin covering its narrow sill, and breathed, just breathed – "I'm fine." – and then continued to stare out at the night, the fingers of his wounded hand twitching as he leaned on the window's ledge and watched the empty moonlit streets.

THE NARROW, BY THE STONE ROAD AND SOUTH OF THE SUMMER SEA.

The month of Gan. Second year of Sharíf Sidon

"You must try."

"I *am* trying. This isn't exactly easy, you know."

"All things are difficult before they are easy. You will be expected to know these things if you become one of them… Come. We'll do it again."

"From the beginning this time."

"Yes, the beginning. So, you see here the five dots, each at the angle of the one shape. This is the mark of Markúth, the Father of Fathers, the shape is him, unseen, invisible, and yet there. The dots are his five children. Yirath–"

"The one who rebelled."

"Yes, the firstborn. The one who rebelled. He is god of war. After him is Gilamek, who was worshipped in the riverlands of Sumeria, before the Cull. He is god of law. Then Irsespedon, the god of death, worshipped in Calapaar and, some say, beyond the Reach. And then Armaros and Adramelec, the twins – the god of knowledge and the god of land."

"So Talagmagon was not a son?"

"No, she was sister and wife to Markúth. She *birthed* his sons, and their daughters too. She is first of the Mothers as Markúth is first of the Fathers. She fought with her daughters against the Fathers in the Godswar."

"Ishmar?"

"That's right, her firstborn, she governs the rains and orders the seasons whilst Talagmagon governs the moon. Her second born daughter, Ganasaresh, is goddess of all living things – the animals, insects, trees. And then there is Asmadai, the goddess of fertility, and Arioc the lastborn, the goddess of the sea, and of jest and song."

"She is the one who is always writing or singing in the pictures, and seems to sometimes look like a fish?"

"Yes. In Súnam they say she is the sea, playing and singing always and never still."

"But that she grew bored one day and came onto land to teach men to sing and play too, just as Adramelec and Armaros taught them to build."

"You see? You are learning. All waiting is learning… When the time comes, you will be ready."

TWENTY ONE

BIRTH

Joram stared at the stone altar, moving his hands across its face to trace the smooth curved lines of the image carved into it as he walked along its length like a visiting pilgrim. He'd seen variations of the same a hundred or more times as a child, mocked up by one of the royal clayworkers back home in Hanesda to teach him their shape – *look, see the wide-set horns and low base: the altar of Adramelec. See how this one's narrower, with a rounded table: the altar of Talagmagon.* After a while, and the not-so-light swat of Father's cane against his back whenever he got one wrong, it became second nature to recognise each kind of altar on sight, and know which of the defunct priesthoods it had belonged to. There were so many of them, these faiths and traditions with their strange rituals, outlawed centuries ago and yet clung to by rich men in secluded forests with a lust for something they didn't know how to name.

Sometimes Father would even take him out of the city into one of the surrounding forests, his younger brother Sidon too, to see one of the ancient monuments the royal clayworkers had modelled. Joram always loved that, being in the forest, out in the wild and away from the fuss and confines of Hanesda's narrow streets. He loved the way the breeze passed through the leaves, the sound so like rain he'd look up half expecting to be met by a sudden downpour, only to find the foliage illumined by the sun, and here and there where the canopy parted, thick pillars of day shining down into the forest's underbed like gleaming blades whilst little Sidon – with his ruddy knuckles and chubby pouting face – whimpered and whined to go back within the city walls.

"We going to stay here all day?" Gurat fidgeted impatiently, standing a few paces behind him with Ola, Djuri and Marin as Joram examined the altar.

"This altar," Joram answered, fondling the emblem cut into its wall, "is older than the Sovereignty itself."

"As we will be by the time we move on from here."

"And I thought you said you were interested in learning, Gurat."

Gurat caught the sudden hardening in Joram's tone and cleared his throat. "I am... But the people..." The elder gestured toward the gathered multitude, waiting patiently in the shade of a giant boulder in the plain two hundred yards away.

Joram glanced toward them. "Will wait," he finished for him. "They seem content enough anyway. And if you want, as you claim you do, for what they and you witnessed at Geled to be more than a mere novelty, you will do as I say."

Gurat nodded. Geled had changed things for everyone: all that crumbled stone and charred wood, a whole city razed to the ground as though stepped on from a great height by some kind of giant, which, in a sense, Joram supposed it had been. The people had looked over Geled's remains for several hours before moving on, sending others back north to the Reach to admonish the sceptics who'd so far refused to come, and to invite them to see for themselves that Joram's words were true. Since then their numbers had been growing daily – men, women and children joining them as they continued south, new devotees to the coming revolution. At last count, Djuri had told him there'd been as many as three thousand fighting men.

"So, what do you want me to do?" Gurat asked.

"Simply place your arm on the altar."

Gurat stepped forward and rolled his sleeve up to the elbow. "Here?"

"That's right."

"And the cut will be small?"

Joram grinned. "An elder and leader of your people, yet so squeamish."

"You said it would be small."

"And it shall. The covenant requires only a little blood." Joram stepped toward him, up onto the stone ledge footing the altar. "Are you ready?"

The other man nodded. Ola came forward too, placing a comforting hand to Gurat's shoulder as Joram unsheathed his dagger. He took hold of Gurat's wrist and held the blade poised, lining up over the man's forearm to be sure of making the right mark.

"Bones of gods, Joram, just go ahead and do... Argh!"

Joram plunged the blade in, puncturing skin and tissue as he forced the metal into the muscle and then drew the blade up along the man's forearm. Gurat screamed and tried to pull away, reaching out his other hand to shove Joram back right as Djuri, standing behind him, snagged it. Gouts of blood splashed across the altar as Gurat jerked, trying to free himself. So Joram yanked the blade out and shoved it direct into the elder's throat instead, just above the collar, before pulling him face first onto the stone, choking and spluttering like a strangled goat. Djuri and Ola moved around to the other side to hold him down as his arms twitched and waved, his torso bucking now, writhing like a caught fish as his eyes rolled and then fixed on Joram, attempting to speak. Joram rolled the man onto his back and leaned in, trying to hear Gurat's words as he gasped and gagged. He waited for several moments to catch what the man would say – always best to respect the wishes of the dying after all – but it was no good, the words unintelligible. So Joram shrugged and took hold of Gurat by the jaw instead, leaning in closer.

"I know. I lied. But it is to a good cause. Your sacrifice is going to change the world, Gurat. By your blood the people and their god are bonded. Now, it's really best if you don't struggle. You are going to die. You *are* dying. There's nothing that can be done for that. So, we may as well make it as painless as we can, hmm?"

The man's body slackened, his strength waning in resignation. His eyes slid desperately toward Ola, a fellow Kivite, who was standing nearest.

"Oh, you mustn't blame her, Gurat. This is about the future. Ola sees that. I'll be sure the people see it too. I'll make sure they remember you well."

Then Joram took the dagger and ripped it from the man's throat, sending ribbons of blood spurting upwards, before plunging it down a final time into the man's chest with both hands. Gurat stiffened from spine to toe, wheezed, and then went limp.

Afterwards Joram told the people that Gurat had offered himself willingly. No harm in enriching the memory of him a little, adding some dignity to his death, and besides, as impressed as they'd all been with the ruins of Geled, Joram didn't quite yet feel himself established enough in their eyes to risk the reprisals of Gurat's clansmen if they were to be told the truth. This was a crucial moment, and he was without the voice after joining it to the pearl and the child growing in Kareena's womb. Thankfully Ola, Djuri and Marin corroborated his version of events without batting an eyelid, allowing Joram to burn Gurat's body on the altar that same hour and offer up imprecations on behalf of the people to bind them to him by blood, before going on to bind them all in covenant to Markúth – a gift for when he arrived.

"I want to learn of him," Ola said later. She was riding beside Joram as they led the people east toward Çyriath. They wouldn't be far from the city now. The altar, Joram knew, lay less than an hour from its gates.

"Who?"

"You know who."

Joram glanced at her to see if she meant it. "Are you sure?"

"When we began all this, all I hoped was for you to become chieftain, and for me to be made your priestess – the best cuts of meat at new moon, maybe a pretty boy for company every now and then, or a pretty girl. But now… I never expected to see the things we've seen. The things you've shown us…

"I am sure," she finished simply, and then turned toward the road ahead. So Joram took her at her word and said no more, riding on in silence and watching the land. It was mostly flat now, punctuated here or there by brierbushes and shrubs and the occasional juniper as they began to near the coast of the North Sea. The nameless dog that had come to Joram at Geled's ruins trotted on ahead of them, ears flattened against its small tawny skull as its tongue hung agog, panting as it moved along their path like a watching scout before occasionally pausing to sniff the air.

And then they saw it. The city of Çyriath, spread across the landscape below as they rode along an overlooking bluff.

Marin, who'd reached the bluff first, whistled. "Bones of Gods…"

"I don't believe it," Djuri whispered beside him.

They looked down on it, riding along the gentle verge before walking the horses down a crease on the slope and leading the people toward the city's edge. When they arrived at the gates, no one spoke for a long time before Joram himself finally broke the lull.

"Magnificent, isn't it," he said quietly.

Ola, transfixed by the sight, said nothing, but it scarcely mattered. Her silence, like that of the thousands of Kivites standing behind them, was comment enough. Çyriath was a ruin, just as Geled, on the way here, had been.

And it was beautiful. Scattered piles of rubble heaped along the lines of the city borders. Exquisitely gutted buildings with torn-off roofs and broken walls, their brick and mortar innards splayed open to the elements like the bones of a ravaged tomb. And then, Joram's personal favourite, the gate watchtower, the base of it still intact, standing there like the stump of a chopped down tree whilst the rest of it lay scattered across the city in clumps of brick, wood and stone. Joram looked over the devastation, trying to imagine what it would have been like to witness firsthand: the screams of terror as the tower's prodigious height suddenly crumbled – generations of brick-made assurance pulled apart and tossed skywards, raining down over the city boroughs in a deadly hail to bury the panicked denizens as they scrambled for cover beneath.

"You were right," Ola murmured beside him as she climbed down from her horse. "It is just as Markúth has said."

Joram smiled as he watched her stagger forwards, stepping across the threshold of a levelled wall. He tried to imagine it from her perspective as she moved around the dishevelled fringes of the ruin – generations of barren scrublands and intermittent famine to the north, the sum of Kivite ancestry since the birth of the Five Lands and the only thing she or any other Kivite had ever known, and now, all of it rendered null and void by their presence here, tens of miles south of the Reach, standing before a sovereign city that was not only defeated but utterly destroyed. Joram saw it play over her face, the bewilderment, the incomprehension, trying to reconcile what her eyes were seeing to everything she'd ever thought possible as the history and future of her race pivoted within her.

"We will make camp here tonight," Joram said, "among the remains. There may even be supplies we can salvage."

But she barely heard him, her head wagging slowly as she stared at what appeared to be a broken monument of polished stone, upended and lying across a street beyond the mound of rubble that had once been the city wall. "How can this be?"

"By the hand of Markúth, just as you said. Just as he has promised us."

She turned to look at him, startled, just as she'd been at Geled. And it was surprising how thrilling it was to see her this way, standing here with that look on her face, all her usually brash poise suddenly undone.

"We will see even more than this when we go south, Ola. We will see great and terrible things. Beautiful things."

Hearing the restless murmurs of the crowd standing behind them, Ola's gaze broke from his to survey the pale-skinned multitude of her countrymen, gawping in disbelief, their eyes roving over the ruins as they tried to accept the fact of its collapsed walls and demolished structures.

Joram stepped up onto a wide mound of rubble beside one of the doors of the city gate that now lay prostrate atop piled bricks and snapped slabs of stone. He lifted his hands as he turned to address them.

"Brothers. Sisters. You see it with your own eyes – first Geled, and now here. The work of our god, who will grant you these lands and more if you remain devoted to him. I told you the Sovereignty is not invulnerable. Its walls *can* break. Just as the walls of Hanesda will break when we go south to strike at the heart of the Five Lands… Go into the ruins, salvage what you can. Weapons, tools, grain if it can be found. We will rest here tonight, and begin south tomorrow."

The people hesitated for a few moments, like supplicants before sacred land – which, in a sense, Joram supposed they were. Slowly they started to step over the piles of rubble and stone to make their way into the wreckage as Joram turned toward the city where a shallow pillar of smoke lingered on the skyline from somewhere deep within the ruins.

"How, Joram?"

He turned back to Ola, still standing there on the pile of rubble trying to make sense of it all.

"How did you do this?"

"I told you. Not I."

She came toward him, striding down the heap of broken stone and up onto the mound to stand in front of him, a little closer than usual. "I want you to teach me," she said again, her gaze unwavering, not even a hint of doubt in her eyes. "I want you to teach me it all."

That night they lay together atop a blanketed bed of rock as they stared at the stars. The people had set up in haunts of their own, making dwellings of whatever safe crevice or corner they could find. Fires glowed amid the jagged terrain of the debris, beneath paved stone lean-tos and half collapsed terraces and municipal buildings with partially torn roofs. So many Kivites in one place, surrounded by stone and bricks, their fires setting a gentle amber hue over the ruined cityscape as though to augur the new world they would become.

"You know, I think sometimes that maybe I always believed you," Ola said, "part of me, at least, but that I was scared to allow my own thoughts to hear it. Because maybe that would mean I was mad, or something… I don't even know if that makes sense."

"It does, Ola. It makes sense."

"The thing I still don't get is why you'd even *be* there, in the Reach – the heir to the Five Lands, scrounging meals like a beggar?"

Joram sighed, lying on his back as he took in the vastness of the night above, countless glistening stars spangled across the cloudless expanse like motes of cinder frozen in space and time. He inhaled deep, let the breath out. "That's a long and complicated story."

"Well…" She rolled onto her side, cradling her face against her palm as she turned to face him. "I'm a good listener."

Joram smiled wryly and looked back to the constellations above. So clear. The night sparkling like black frost. "Do you know the story of Yirath?"

"The god of war."

"You ever hear how he came to be given the name?"

"Rebelled against his mother, Talagmagon. Began the Godswar."

"That's how the scribes' tales tell it in the Riverlands of Sumeria to the south. But in Harán the priests had a fuller way of sharing the tale. Some would even say a better way. They have the older manuscripts in the East after all. Or at least they did before the Cull."

"So, you're a scribe too now?"

"My father taught me as a child. He'd have the scribes show me the writings of every dead priesthood, their altars too. Wanted me to learn the history as well as it could be learned."

"Why?"

"We repeat what we don't know, he'd always say. Point is, in the eastern telling of it, Markúth is not the benevolent father in the story who comes to rescue his sons from his wife and sister, Talagmagon. Instead he is a cruel and angry tyrant. Yirath turns on *him*, not Talagmagon, to protect his brothers… I suppose you could say it's a tale I've always been fond of." He glanced down at the clay lamp between them. The oil was low, the flame beginning to gutter and wane at the spout.

"So, your father was… cruel?"

Joram shrugged. "He could be kind. Patient. But only when he was sober. When he was in his cups, he became a different man… There were days he'd beat me bloody with a practice sword for holding it wrong. Other times he'd lock me away in a room and leave me there, maybe for a day or two, sometimes longer, only returning to allow me out once he'd put down the wine. It got so you didn't know which side of him you were going to see next. So, I'd try to do things, to help him… I don't know… *remember*. Help him see we were still father and son. That I still trusted what we were despite the things he'd done, the things he'd *do*. But he didn't understand. Just punished me worse instead."

"Sounds like he was a brutal man."

Joram shrugged again. "Perhaps, in a way, we *all* are, or must learn to be, at least sometimes. Back then there was a part of me that was glad when I was sent away to the Reach, but the truth is now, when I think back on it all, I'm not sorry for what was done."

"You're not?"

"We are here now. Had things not happened as they did, we wouldn't be."

"You'd be on a throne in Hanesda, having choice fruits handed to you on a dish."

"I'd be a young and feeble Sharíf, instead of the ruler I am soon to become, the ruler Markúth had always destined for me to be." He looked at her, enjoying the way the light from the lamp played in her eyes, turning their clear aquatic blue into something else, gold and luscious, like honey.

She blinked, and then flicked away the fringe of her hair, glinting like soft strands of burnished metal, as if she was some kind of celestial being, fallen from the starlit night above. "Will you tell me more about him?" she asked. "How Markúth speaks to you."

"He speaks to everyone, Ola. But he only chooses those who decide to hear. Just as he chose me, to find for him a place. A home." He rolled to face her now, turning from the sky to mirror her posture as they lay on the thin bedmat. "Hold out your hand."

She obeyed.

Joram reached out and took it. "The gods have their world, an older world," he said. He cradled her palm, placing her hand over his. "And then ours lies over it, like a veil. See?"

She nodded.

"So, suppose you are a fish," Joram said. "The water is not only your home, it is your world. What can a fish know of lions, or bears, or eagles? Such beasts exist, yes, but how could a fish ever come to know that they do?"

"I don't know. I suppose it can't."

"Exactly. Not unless it leaves the water, its very world – something it would have to die to do, only then would it know that these things are real."

"You are saying the gods are like lions or bears, and we are as fish?"

"I'm saying they – and others – are as eagles, and that the only time a fish sees an eagle is when he is taken by one."

"Alright…"

"So, now imagine *you* are the eagle, and suppose there is something very precious at the bottom of the sea. Something you want. A pearl perhaps… An eagle cannot swim. A little, perhaps, but not enough to abide there, in the waters. Not enough to dwell. The eagle can visit the sea, dip into it, but he cannot go to the bottom to claim the pearl. So, what is the eagle to do? What he wants is on the bed of the sea, but what he *is* keeps him from being able to take it."

"He must speak to the fish, ask one to get it for him."

"That's right. He must find a fish who is willing to hear. Who is able to listen. A fish that is unlike the others. One that is different."

"Like you."

Joram smiled. "Yes, Ola. Like me."

"So what place does the pearl have in this tale of yours?"

"It is a gate, the thing that will allow the eagle to be changed: to clothe itself as a fish and enter the water. The pearl is what will allow it to swim without dying, so that it can one day dwell in *both* worlds."

"A god made flesh."

"Yes, Ola. A god made flesh."

She turned her hand, allowing her fingers to play over his palm now. "You are a good teacher, Joram."

"The story is not mine, it belongs to those eastern priests, although in *their* telling of it they make the Watchers the eagles, and the gods, bears. But I prefer my version."

"What is a Watcher?"

Joram was about to answer when they heard the dog from the foot of the heap where it had settled to guard them, barking, followed by the shouts of men. Joram bolted upright, scanning the dark, and saw torches hovering in the night: a pair of men, climbing the broken steps of the crumpled porch where Joram and Ola had come to rest and stare at the stars. It wasn't until they'd nearly reached the top that Joram recognised one of them as Marin.

"Joram. You need to come quickly."

"What is it? What's going on—"

"It's the girl. Kareena. Her waters have broken."

"Already?"

"Already."

They got up and rushed down the steps. It had been mere days since he'd explained to Ola, Marin and Djuri about the girl and the child – what he'd done, why he had her travelling with them – which was easier to divulge once they'd witnessed Geled for themselves. Whatever their qualms, they'd now seen with their own eyes the validity of what he was trying to do, and the proof of its power. They knew now that the ways of Markúth were real, and that sacrifices –

like Gurat's – had meaning. As did this child, but only if it survived. It was not due for another moon or more.

They stepped carefully over the rubble to each solid level as the torches illuminated their way; then followed Marin across a brief paved platform – probably a ledge or balcony, now broken off from whatever palatial building it had once belonged to and settled instead on the ground. They turned through a narrow gap in the wall, fractured tablets littering the mounds of rubble beneath them, inscribed with images and writings. Probably lawstones, preserving the First Laws for public display.

"This way," Marin said.

Shrieks erupted as they turned the next corner and crossed the street to the makeshift shelter on the other side. Djuri was standing there as they arrived, leaning against a wall of the hollowed out terrace they'd set the tent against. He looked tired, his clothes and hair covered in bloodsplatter.

"Joram…"

It was all he managed before another scream split the night, a loud mournful howl that seemed, to Joram, to scrape along his very blood. He made to move around Djuri but he stepped toward him, placing a hand on his chest.

"You don't want to go in there, Joram."

"Out of my way, Dju."

Joram shrugged him off, was going toward the shelter's entrance when the women came rushing out. Midwives, covered in globs of blood, chunks of gore hanging from their clothes and aprons like offal. Joram stared at them, then heard another sound coming from within the tent: a low guttural thrum, like the quiet rumble of a faraway storm.

"Joram…" Djuri tried. But he wasn't listening now, his feet carrying him inevitably on and past Djuri toward the tent like the drift of a tide. He came to the entrance and drew back the drapes, peeping into the shadowed space within before stepping through into the interior.

Dark. Dim-lit lamps in every corner, set in bowls away from the thick goathair walls. The space was a mess – upended stools, a collapsed table, torn rags and strips of clothing – all of it scattered across the ground like the aftermath of an explosion, flickering in the shallow light cast by the lamps' flames, and all covered in blood.

There was bloodspray on the floor and walls, spreading out from an epicentre around the bedmat that centred the room like the frozen ripple of a giant raindrop in a pool. Joram's eyes were drawn toward it, taking in the deep slick red and the mingled odour of urine and faeces hanging fresh over it all. He saw it then, although it took a moment to understand what he was seeing. Kareena's half naked body lay on its back atop the soaked bedmat, splayed open like the remains of a gutted fish. A long gash ran from throat to groin, revealing the curved bars of her ribcage, split apart at the breastbone and spread wide. Trailing from the corpse's chest were grotesque clumps of entrails and viscera.

Joram considered turning to leave but somehow couldn't, transfixed by it all: this dense, frenzied carnage of flesh and smells assaulting the shadowed space, and the way the lamps, sitting in their little claypots that cornered the room, continued to emit their small dogged flames, as though the violent eruption of bone, blood and meat had been little more than a passing breeze, a blip in time's illimitable expanse.

He almost didn't notice the slow sifting of shadows in the corner, and then, once he'd turned to look, the insectile way the thing hiding there unfolded from its crouch, smooth pale limbs disentangling as the small figure emerged from the dark into the shallow cast of the faltering lamplight. Joram stared then, at the bone-white flesh and slim arms and legs, the streak of long black hair, membrane slick, hanging straight and greasy down the face like a grisly veil. It was only once it had moved to the centre of the room to regard him that Joram understood what it was – standing there naked, covered in blood, breathing slowly, patiently.

"You're a girl," he whispered.

"No. I'm not a girl. I am a god. I am Markúth."

TWENTY TWO

FEALTY

Sidon had been weaned on tales of his father, Helgon the Wise, and his masterful command of the Sovereign councils. He had read the royal records, the excitable fervour and eloquence of the writings of Kamal, the chief scribe, when he described the throneroom deliberations, the annual feasts, the new moon festivals, and all the other notable occasions upon which the great Helgon the Wise had held court and rendered proceedings an extended homage to his own oratorical skill. Which was why standing here now, at the edge of the Judgement Hall as Kamal prepared to announce him to the council and usher him in, Sidon couldn't help feeling uncomfortable.

The cincture girding the waist of his garment felt too tight, as did the snug collar hugging his chest, bangled by amethysts and rubies hanging from the ceremonial pendant that felt too heavy around his neck. And beneath it all he could feel himself sweating, warm pockets of damp soaking his armpits and lower back within the stiff fabric of his tunic as he prepared to address twenty men and women of the sovereign council, along with his mother, the Sharífa, who were arrayed in rows along the curved steps of Pularsi's Forum like a waiting panel of judges.

Especially Uncle Játhon.

Sidon – walking stiffly across the forecourt towards his highbacked throne as Kamal announced his titles – watched his uncle now, lounged on the bottom step of the forum as though he owned the place, gazing across the mosaic-floored rink to Kamal as the portly scribe rose to address the other members whilst Sidon sat down. Sidon had never liked Játhon – his languid charm, that dainty epicene swagger, sauntering about the court of the Judgement House, or the forum, or on occasion even the throneroom itself to delay or sway the sovereign decrees. And always with that unmistakable hint of amused contempt, a flicker of condescension, as though somewhere within that prettily groomed skull of his, he deemed himself more than what he was regarded to be, more deserving, perhaps, of the very throne he was sworn to serve. Sidon's throne.

Sidon peered across the court at Játhon's neatly kempt fingernails, the polished skin, the manically trimmed beard and hair, the earthy-sweet waft of spikenard and oils that swirled around him whenever he entered a room, and that Sidon could smell even from here. And suddenly, thinking back on his every interaction with the man, it was just so obvious – the self-regard, the vanity, the arrogance. The man was born to betray, and offer you one of his cocky genial smiles and a bow of the head whilst he was at it.

"Who else among the court is my uncle aligned with?" Sidon murmured to Yassr sitting beside him. "Who else could be connected?"

"Majesty," Sidon could even hear the sweat in the governor's voice, "as I said, I couldn't possibly–"

"An *educated guess*, Yassr. That's all I'm asking."

"I suppose… Well, he speaks with Nikram of Parses often. Perhaps too Yosephan, the governor of Calpas. And of course, his wife, Queen Satyana of Hikramesh, and the other members of her father's house will no doubt have influence. And you already know about Fatya's involvement."

"I do," Sidon nodded, making a mental note of each as Kamal, the crown scribe, continued to drone on from the lectern at the centre of the forum floor. Sidon glanced across to his mother, sitting in the other high-backed seat opposite the council several paces away in her heavily jewelled ceremonial attire.

They'd announce the war today, if it could even be called that. Close to two moons since the destruction of Geled and they were still none the wiser about who was responsible, or how. Meanwhile councillors and vassals, wise to the notion something was being kept from them but uncertain as to what, had taken in recent days to accosting Sidon at every opportunity to request a private audience or ask for some other inane favour whilst they weighed him with their gaze. Several of them sat here now, hunched on the tall block steps of the forum's arena: Sufiya, the governor of Qareb, and Fatya of Tirash next to her, with her loose-fitting caftan and fleshy shoulders and neck. Tubal, son of Xanti, governor of the High Eastern province of Kaloom, whom Imaru – who, concerningly, hadn't been seen or heard from for over two days now – had promised to investigate. The governor perched upright on the next tier up from Sufiya and Fatya like a waiting peacock, all jewelled knuckles and gold-bangled wrists, and the silken train of his oversized robes glinting softly in the sun whilst Governor Elia of Qalqaliman sat on the middle-tier beneath him, waiting, as was everyone else, for Kamal to conclude his typically pompous and longwinded address so the proceedings could begin in earnest.

"...and so now, Sharíf Sidon son of Helgon, the eighth of his line, King of Sumeria and lord of the Five Lands, blood son of the first King of Kings, the great Karel the Young."

Kamal swept out a deferent arm, welcoming Sidon to the lectern and moving aside as Sidon rose, came forward, and took hold of the rostrum's shelf. He clutched nervously at the sides of the lectern as he stared down at the old scarred stone and cleared his throat.

"Men and women of the Sovereignty," he began, reciting words he'd spent days rehearsing. He glanced at the gathering. Twenty-two members in all, the heads of every citystate of the sovereignty, laid over from the Feast of Bones and sitting there before him like grumpy bullfrogs. He coughed, decided to begin again. "Men and women of the Sovereignty…" then hung on the silence, waiting for his mind to clear and for the quiet to offer up the rest of what he was to say. But it didn't. He glanced back down to the lectern, trying and failing to remember the rest of his speech, and imagining already how his mother, seated on her throne behind him, would be spinning this in her mind, another piece in the scale, a mark against him, an opportunity for her to insist on his inadequacy and immaturity and the need for her regency to be confirmed forthwith. Closing his eyes, he tried a final time to recall the words, the carefully plotted sentences he'd written to himself and then memorised, each one painstakingly crafted to mirror the noble, penetrating verve of his father's speeches, as depicted in the crown chronicles of Kamal. But when he looked up once more to the gathered council and their flaccid unimpressed faces the memory of it all melted within him. So Sidon cleared his throat.

"There is no simple way to say this…" he murmured woodenly instead. "So, I shall just say it… Geled has been destroyed, razed to the ground… And we are yet to know by whose hand."

The words came out rushed, and abrupt, like a heavy ornament dropped thuddlingly to the ground. For a moment no one spoke. Some glanced around at each other, and then eventually began to murmur, conferring to make sure they'd properly understood what had just been said.

"Sharíf…" Fatya ventured.

Sidon gestured for her to speak on.

"Just to be sure, you're saying Geled, the northernmost outpost of Calapaar, has been destroyed?"

"That is correct."

Interesting the look that came over her face. Stunned, of course, but something else too. Part of him, in spite of his duress, almost wanted to revel in her surprise. This woman whom he knew had been scheming against him, now blindsided by this new knowledge.

"Why were we not told about this before?" she said.

Which was strange, Sidon thought, seeing as he was yet to announce when he'd first received the news. He looked at her.

"You're being told of it now." He saw something fracture in her expression then, as though suddenly realising she'd done something wrong.

"Of course, Sharíf. I am… a little startled by the news, as we all are, no doubt."

"Indeed," Játhon confirmed, glancing up at her from his seat on the bottom step.

Which, Sidon felt, was also curious. He glanced behind to Yassr and Elias by his throneseat, who seemed as dumbfounded as he was, and then to his mother sitting stoically on her regent's seat, staring expressionlessly toward the gathered council.

"That is understandable, Fatya," Sidon said, for something to say.

"Majesty," Tubal offered from the back, "when did these things happen?"

"Although we cannot be fully certain, the first reports came to us just under two moons ago." This time the alarm on Fatya's face was clear, and notable enough to draw Sidon's attention even as he was addressing the governor of Kaloom. "The Sharífa received the tidings personally," Sidon said, gesturing to his mother behind him as he continued to watch Fatya, who seemed not only surprised but angry now. That was it. Suddenly it made sense. Mother hadn't told her. Here they were, conspirators in a coup against the Sharíf's throne, itself a fraught enterprise, and until now his mother hadn't bothered to tell Fatya – clearly skittish about the whole thing – of this coming war, despite having known about it for the last two months at least. Sidon could almost see the doubt and confusion welling up in Fatya, tipping into the stiff tense way she was holding herself, and the growing anxiety on her face. Sidon glanced around the rest of the gathering, trying to gauge each councillor's response.

"And what of the people?" Nikram of Parses said. A small and swarthy bald man, sitting on the top step. "All dead, are they?"

"Quite possibly," Sidon answered.

"Forgive me, sire," the man said simperingly, bowing again to acknowledge his Sharíf. "But what do you mean, 'quite possibly'? Surely they are either dead or they are not."

Sidon had expected this to be a gruelling ordeal, but now, observing the responses of the council as they hung on each new morsel of information, and watching as measure and countermeasure was being calculated between them as they tried to weigh up what each already knew, he was intrigued. He stepped away from the rostrum, nodding to Elias as he returned to his seat to permit the chamberlain to answer.

"Men were sent north to investigate nearly six weeks ago and have not yet returned," Elias said. "We'd hoped to learn more about the enemy before addressing you, but it is possible those who were sent are either captured or dead. But, from what we presently know, we do not think there were survivors to the attack on Geled."

"Not one?" Nikram persisted.

"None." Elias dropped the word like a stamp. "Only rubble. And it is now thought a similar fate may have befallen Çyriath."

"Çyriath is destroyed too?" Fatya was almost squeaking now. Tirash, the city she governed, was reliant upon Çyriath for cedar wood and seedgrain in winter. "Many of our rice fields and wood trees surround that city. You're saying they are compromised?"

"What Elias is saying," Uncle Játhon intervened, standing to his feet and walking to the centre of the forum to turn to address his fellow council members, "is that the Five Lands has an enemy whose name and face we're yet to know."

Sidon, continuing to watch them all closely, noticed the way Játhon glared at Fatya as he said it: a warning. But Fatya was unperturbed. She shuffled forward on her seat and thrust out her palms, irate. "What then?" she spat defiantly, glaring back at Játhon. "Men have been sent. What else?"

"What else," Sidon answered, "is why we are gathered here, governor." He rose to his feet, emboldened by the fractures he was observing amongst those he knew to be plotting against him. "I desire for every major city of the Five Lands to ready their cityguard and prepare for war, stockpile weapons and food supplies." Sidon glanced to Elia, the governor of Qalqaliman, perched on one of the middle tiers in the corner. "And I desire for Qalqaliman and

Hikramesh to raise their armies and ready to join my troops under the command of Gahíd, here in Hanesda."

"Are we not perhaps overreacting?" Yosephan, the governor of Calpas, a typically calm and mild-mannered man, and yet even he seemed rattled.

Sidon looked at him. "Better we do," he said, "rather than regret that we failed to."

He met Gahíd later that evening by a sheltered reflecting pool in Hanesda's southern district. The streets beyond the walled off pool were calmer here, populated by students of the scribal school, strolling from there to the surrounding municipal buildings. They sat together on a bench near the water, watching the pool's dark, glassy surface mirror the night sky as a gentle breeze played with the leaves of the palm tree shading them. Gahíd looked like a man who'd been sitting there for a long while by the time Sidon arrived to join him, his bearded blockish head bent toward the water, staring; his thoughts, apparently, elsewhere.

"I loathe the Feast," he said grumpily as Sidon lowered to sit beside him. "The new moons too. Brings out the baser elements… Celebrating bones… Death is always a game to those who aren't close enough to know its shadow."

It was a strange thing to say, but then the general had been growing increasingly morose ever since the betrayers had escaped the temple in Ilysia. Sidon decided to be direct, he would need the man's full attention for this. "It's funny you should say that, Gahíd. It appears someone is trying to kill me."

The general looked at him. You had to hand it to the man; if he was jarred by the revelation he didn't let it show.

"I know, general," Sidon continued anyway. "I find I'm becoming less patient these days, artlessly so. But then who has time to dance around such things when their life is under threat?"

"Who indeed, Sharíf."

Sidon grunted. He'd expected more of a response. "It's my mother who is behind it," he added. "She wishes to steal my throne. But I know there are others involved. My uncle, Játhon." He glanced aside to him again. "You…"

"I suppose you are expecting me to apologise?"

Sidon stared at him. Had he the means or ability he could have killed him right then and there. Shove a blade right through his smug craggy face and watch him bleed out. He cleared his throat and glanced toward the paving edging the pool instead. "I want to know who else is involved, Gahíd."

"First of all, it is not your mother who desires your throne. It is Játhon."

"My uncle? Why?"

"Why? Is it his motives you seek, or mine?"

"Your reasons differ?"

"I would think so. There are enough to go around."

Sidon flexed his fingers and glanced over his shoulder to the shadows where he knew Josef would be hiding. "I'm going to uncover all this, Gahíd. It's my throne. My birthright."

"And you think men should care about your birthright?"

Sidon glared at him. *Where was this coming from?* "They should care about their vows to the throne. They should care about the order of the Sovereignty."

Gahíd scoffed, unmoved. "Listen to yourself. You almost sound as if you believe it. Let me tell you what is real, Sharíf. Men speak well enough of what other men should or should not care about, but it does not shape their will, not really. It merely decorates the truth, often unhelpfully."

"Really." Sidon turned on his seat to face him. Fine. Gloves off. "And what *is* the truth?"

Gahíd just made a sound in his throat, halfway between a laugh and a grunt. "Time was, men followed kings, Sharíf. Real kings. Souls they believed ordained by gods to their thrones. But that time has passed. Your forefathers saw to it. And now it seems to me you have come to the throne of thrones in their stead with no understanding of what it is or how to wield it, an ignorance your uncle, for example, does not share. For all his flaws – and there are many – he at least knows what the Sovereignty is; what its throne is. He sees with eyes wide open, Sharíf. And men will always seek to be led by those who can see where they are going."

"Ah, so that's it – you sing the same old song as the rest of them then. I'm too young. I'm a child. I can't be trusted. So boring, Gahíd. I'd expected something more… I don't know – interesting. Especially from you."

Gahíd peered at him then. "You're still not listening, are you? You think this is about your age? Karel was your age when he became king of Sumeria, and not much older than you when he first marched on Calapaar. What makes one a boy or a man has nothing to do with how many years he's walked this earth, it has to do with how open his eyes have become in the time he has walked it."

"And you think mine haven't."

"I *know* yours haven't. You're as blind as a wolf pup at the tit of a dying mother. Even here, now, bleating on about birthright like some whiny child. Yes, Sharíf. I have become impatient too. As you say, who has time to dance around these things. The order of the Shedaím, *my* order, creaks from its roots. Elder Safít, the betrayers – they gutted it like a fish from the inside out. Most of the Brothers are dead, Sharíf. Almost the entire eldership are dead. And you wander around sulking, because one of them pretended to be someone she wasn't and hurt your feelings."

Incensed, Sidon leaned in, his voice low and cold. "It was you wasn't it, in the grove? You're the one who tried to have me killed, who sent those men."

"So what if I did! You think I am the only one? It could be that Súnamite dog you have befriended seeks the same ends for all I know. It would not surprise me, given as you are to being duped by the fluttered eyelids of any woman who glances vaguely in your direction."

That did it. Sidon, against all judgement, lunged at him, swinging his fist toward the general's jaw. Gahíd caught his wrist with ease, then pushed both it and Sidon away with a hard, sharp shove. A blade was at Gahíd's throat before Sidon had hit the ground.

"You will defend this boy, Josef?" Gahíd grunted, bracing away from the poised blade's cold bite at his neck.

Josef leaned forward from out the shadows behind them, lowering toward their bench as he spoke. "Is that not the vow you yourself gave me? I am sworn to protect the Sharíf. As you too are supposed to be."

"Do not waste your breath, Josef," Sidon spat, climbing to his feet. "It seems vows have become meaningless to him."

"No, Sharíf, they have become meaningless to you," Gahíd snapped back. "So what, your father died. So what? You think the whole world should continue to weep for you? You sit on the throne of the Five Land Sovereignty. You are surrounded by riches and resources from here to Hikramesh. And what do you do with them? What have you *been* doing with them? There is a war coming. You think you are fit to lead men in facing it? You are weak. Your mother has *manipulated* you. Used you. Plucked and pulled your strings like a skilled court minstrel. And you have allowed her to do it. Allowed her to control you."

"No. She did not give me–"

"A *chance*? You see, Sharíf? It is you who has decided you are too young. Not us. You. From birth the gazelle knows it is hunted, knows to find its feet and run. It does not wait to be taught. This is the throne of the Sovereignty. There are only sharks here. If you are waiting for your hand to be held, and for those sharks to teach you, then you do not deserve the throne granted to you by your blood. Do not blame me, or anyone else, for seeing the truth of it. Because what we see is you strolling about your carpeted halls and summerwine banquets as though you've been robbed by the world. You allow yourself to be tricked by your own vanity and deceived – by Arianna, by your mother – and then expect to be counted worthy of the fealty of men because of a *birthright*? Birthrights are not for the godless, Sharíf. And the godless are what we are. Godless is what the men of this city that surrounds you are. What the men of the Five Lands are and have been ever since the Cull. They do not want stories of destiny and bloodlines and prophecies. They want strength. And they want the one who sits on the throne to have it, if they are to follow him. Or else they will look for another. Your father understood that, his father before him understood that. *Játhon* understands that. But you, you will speak and think and act as a child and then complain when those who have observed you, call you one.

"I lack the stomach and time to indulge this pampering. I must rebuild a Brotherhood. I cannot wait for you to decide to wake up and start being what you are supposed to be. You want to kill me for that then go ahead, but do not have the gall to think all this has come upon you by any means other than your own weakness. Or *do*. I care not. It is children who think that way after all. And a child is exactly what you are."

Sidon continued to glare at him, the general grimacing as Josef clutched his chin and held the dagger to his neck, waiting for his command. And Sidon could feel himself wanting to give it, wanting to wave his hand and watch Josef slide his blade across the craggy-faced man's throat, leaving him to gag and choke and bleed. Sidon teetered there, on the edge of saying yes, and for a moment thought that he would, but he didn't. Instead, he breathed out, then offered Josef a barely perceptible shake of his head, ordering the Brother to relinquish him and step away.

Sidon, slowly, returned to the bench as Gahíd worked and stretched his neck and rubbed his throat.

"Your tongue has grown bold, Gahíd."

The general shrugged. "My master warned me of it long ago, a price of gathering age. I doubt it will be shrinking back any time soon."

Sidon nodded, thinking. "Perhaps that is not such a bad thing."

Gahíd cocked an eyebrow and glanced sidelong at him.

Sidon looked back at him, weighing it up. He needed allies. He needed the Shedaím. He needed a way to understand the ways the council were shifting around him, and Imaru, as helpful as she'd been, was no guarantee, and hadn't been seen for two days. So he sat there, weighing it all in his mind and trying to imagine the path he would take if he was more than the petulant child Gahíd had accused him of being; the path he would take if he was more like his shrewd father, Helgon the Wise, instead.

Sidon, belatedly, sighed. "I find I don't want to kill you, general… Perhaps…" Sidon hovered over the thought. "Perhaps I want you to help me."

Gahíd looked at him as a man might a talking donkey. "What?"

"Maybe… Perhaps, there may be some merit, only *some*, to a few of the things you have said."

Gahíd, for a moment, just stared at him, and then broke into laughter, almost doubling over on the bench as he coughed out a long hacking roar before finally righting himself and leaning again against the back of the seat. He sighed and looked to Sidon. "Gods, boy. You could have as near killed me with those words better than Josef's blade."

"I'll help you rebuild the Brotherhood. The sovereign throne shall always need it. *I* will always need it. And perhaps I do need to become… stronger. We both do. The blind elder deceived you as the girl, Arianna, deceived me. And now here we are, sitting amid the ruins their lies brought to us. It could be we *both* ought to help each other become stronger, general."

Gahíd's smile dampened as he thought about it, rubbing his beard. "You expect me to believe that?"

"These days, I try to keep from expecting anything from anyone, which seems to be a habit you and I now share. Yassr has told me you do not trust the chamberlain."

"Yassr's lips are looser than a camel's."

"But does he lie?"

The general settled back against the bench and eyed him carefully. The torches on the wall evidently hadn't been properly doused with lime and were already beginning to wane. "No, Sharíf. He does not lie. Not this time."

Sidon turned toward him. "Will you tell me why?"

Gahíd, perhaps seeing in Sidon a burgeoning opponent to his

enemy, decided to indulge him. "Your uncle's aims are simple. The chamberlain's are not. Játhon wishes to destabilise the throne so he can take over. Elias, he seems to have other interests."

"What interests?"

"I don't know. That's why I don't trust him. But it has been clear to me for a while he is planning something more than just placing your uncle on the throne."

"But what makes you think that?"

The general shifted in his seat. "It was given to the Brotherhood to hunt a hidden society we have come to know as the Fellowship of Truths. An alliance of men and women, apparently spanning the Sovereignty, who are opposed to the throne. But the command to hunt them was an edict that came to us by Safít, the blind elder, before we learned the truth about her betrayal. By the time we discovered her deceit and death, half of the Brotherhood was gone, along with several of the men belonging to this Fellowship we'd been sent by her to kill – Governor Zaqeem, Tobiath of Dumea, Hassan son of Nalaam, the steward of Dumea – all men that Safít, as Eye of the Brotherhood, had named to us by her visions. Following Hassan's death, Elias seemed to change, arguing with the Sharífa, pushing for members of the sovereign council itself to be killed, claiming them to be part of the Fellowship of Truths without any evidence to support it."

"So, you began to suspect his motives."

Gahíd nodded. "But *only* suspect. What made me *know* not to trust him was Safít's death. He knew of it before I'd told him …" The general looked Sidon square in the eye. "He should not have known that. There should have been no *way* for him to know it, except by me. Looking back, I can see that he and Safít were of one mind from the beginning; they were the ones often pushing for the deaths of those belonging to the Fellowship…" Gahíd shook his head, staring into the reflecting pool again. "And now I see him in corridors whispering with council members…"

"He is conspiring with others among the council, for his own ends?"

The general shrugged. "Perhaps. Perhaps not. All I know is there is something about that man. He is not as the rest of us. I do not trust him. No one should."

TWENTY THREE

LEGACY

Tamar was a strange girl. Firstly, there was the way she wore her hair – short, barely long enough to cover her ears, and tethered here and there with knotted strings that bound parts of it into scruffy locks. Then there was the rapid agitated way she had of saying everything. Daneel had never heard anyone talk so fast, or even move so fast, her motions often resembling, to him, the quick stuttery manner of a squirrel. And then there were the sorts of things she said, often at the oddest-seeming moments, as though answering to a conversation that was running in her head that she'd assumed everyone else was listening to, or even could.

"I mean, you ever laugh so hard you can't breathe? Like you think you might die from the laughing. Like that sort of laughter that stretches your lungs until there's no more air you can even take in and no more sound to even laugh with and you just have to sit there shuddering and quivering like some sort of mad person, so you're laughing this sort of dry soundless cackle until whatever part of you decides on laughing or not decides you've had enough, and your insides finally let go from their death grip and whatever the thing was you found so funny in the first place? You ever laugh like that?

Because you should. Everyone should laugh a laugh like that at least once a moon, I think."

Noah, as confused by her as he was, seemed to like her. Daneel, not so much. But it didn't matter. He had found the things she'd had to say about the men who attacked them on the road interesting. Strange, but interesting.

"So, what you're saying is they're godworshippers," Daneel said as they continued south on their horses.

"Yes, yes, that's what I said," Tamar replied. "Followers of Markúth. They do all of it, the sacrifices and the blood lettings and the rituals, and they go about hunting for all the things that used to be around way back, I mean *all* the way back. Things from back before the Cull. And they try to collect them and understand them and try to see how to find more."

"So, what did they want with *us*?"

"*Him*," she'd said, pointing at Noah, who'd by then switched horses and saddled himself with Daneel. "They want *him*."

"Why?"

"Because he's a nudger. They'll want his blood, want to use it, to make babies who can be nudgers too, or maybe make themselves into nudgers if they can. I'm not sure. People go back and forth on that, everyone thinks different on it. Everyone thinks they know, but they don't. Like there's this one oldie, Gev, back south, where we all stay, thinks he knows everything, always. Says they use the blood to make babies into nudgers only. Says he's sure of it. But how can he be sure of it? He's not seen them do it himself has he."

"What's a nudger?"

"Gods, you're slow. I just *said*." She thrust her finger emphatically at Noah again, before going on to explain how the followers of Markúth had been around for decades, the extant remnant of one of the priestly bloodlines from before the Cull – which Daneel had no trouble believing, the Brotherhood had been involved in hunting the remnants of priesthoods for just as long. Tamar went on to explain that she was a "seer", herself part of a clan of others who were similarly gifted, but that she couldn't tell Daneel and Noah where that clan was, not until she trusted them, and not until they'd discovered the priestly bloodline that Noah was part of and that had conferred his gift. Which, apparently, was very important to do. Because the followers of Markúth would not be the only ones hunting him, there were disciples of other gods too – Gilamek, Yirath, Talagmagon, Armaros. Which, again, Daneel had no trouble believing. And so, being eager as he was for Noah to learn how to control himself, Daneel had agreed with Tamar to search out the boy's bloodline. Which was how, despite their concerns, they found themselves journeying to Hanesda.

Daneel had been to the crown city only twice before; first during a witnessing, he and his brother Josef accompanying some third sharím member of the Brotherhood to spy on a cleric from Kaloom. The second time here had been more eventful, arriving with Josef after two weeks in open country, journeying from the piled rubble far to the north that used to be Geled, to report on the ruins they'd witnessed there. They'd met the Sharífa herself that day, bowing in the throneroom to deliver the news as Gahíd and the other members of the queen mother's retinue looked on. But it was still that first time here Daneel always remembered the most – the shock of the slim clustered streets and high terraces; the great stone walls of Kaldan's Tower, reaching to more than twice the height of the city walls to overlook the surrounding plains like a stone-made god. Then there was the loud petty gripes and bickering of the marketplace with its endless array of trinket-filled stalls, wares and workers – potters, tailors, axel-makers, spice-sellers, and a hundred other kinds of trade Daneel wouldn't know how to name, all arranged in crowded rows and lots that seemed to extend in every direction from the crown city court for nearly half a mile. It was the busiest place he'd ever known, which was why he was astounded to find it even busier than he remembered as he arrived with Noah and Tamar through its famous high gates.

The main road teemed with people, multicoloured banners and boards seeming to mark every street, draped across doorposts and walls and flagpoles like the windswept debris of a storm. Makeshift signs stood on every corner, announcing banquets and parties as barrelmen tried to shuffle their way through the endless crowd with casks of wine and beer propped up on their shoulders.

Daneel steered his horse off the main thoroughfare and into one of the slimmer lanes branching off it, following Tamar. "The Feast of Bones," she said, pitching her voice above the din as she leaned across her horse to them. "Didn't even realise we were in the month of Gan," she added. "You forget how much time passes when you're away from the cities."

Neither Daneel or Noah bothered to answer as the girl directed them around another corner and toward a chalk and ink mural at the far end of the next street. Someone had scrawled the beginnings of the familiar concentric patterns of a Sumerian starchart on the wall, marking the constellations of the night against the time of year. Daneel hadn't seen one since Ilysia, and found himself gazing over the carefully sketched circles and lines as they passed, reading the months off like a mantra as he recalled Jaleem's commentaries on each. *The month of Kúth, named after Markúth, the father of fathers and god of the sun. The month of Rath, after his son Yirath who rebelled, making himself the god of war. The month of Gil, named after Gilamek, of whom the old faiths said handed the first truths to the priesthoods to become god of law—*

"There," Tamar said, interrupting Daneel's thoughts. "That's the house."

Daneel glanced to where she pointed. "You're sure?"

Tamar frowned at him, scrunching her freckled nose. "Yes. I'm sure, Daneel."

The house was small, stacked atop several others at the end of the narrow road and led up to by a cramped stepway. They brought their horses to a halt by one of the bannered flagpoles on the street a few feet away and then tied them there by the halter rope before climbing the steps to the door, where Tamar knocked.

An old man emerged a few moments later dressed in a coarse woollen mantle, the fabric frayed by age and use, blurring the polygonal patterns of red and black stitched into it. He was slim; sinewy; with a wispy shock of white hair, bright against his crinkled bronze skin, and lips so thin and rimmed by wrinkles they almost seemed non-existent, a crack across his face. He was opening his mouth to speak when his eyes slid to Noah and stopped. He seemed about to say something, but didn't, then welcomed them inside instead.

The room was cool, heavily shaded by the walls, a pair of small windows either side of the door allowing what was left of the sun's light, after squeezing through the high terraces outside, in from the street. A chair and table stood in the middle of the room, and there was an oak-carved bench in a corner on the far side next to another doorway that likely led up to a roof area with a cooking bench.

The old man hobbled to the chair and gestured for the trio to sit opposite him on the table and corner bench.

"It has been a little while, Tamar," he said as he slowly lowered to his seat, grunting at the loud click of his knees. "And this time you bring friends. Or are they strangers?"

"They are both, Sarwin."

The man grunted, looking Daneel and Noah over.

"It's the boy," Tamar explained. "He's priest's blood."

"Is he now. Well…" He scratched his chin and leaned back in his seat, examining Noah. "And how much has Tamar told you of the bloodwar?"

Noah glanced around, then shrugged. "Not much."

"No. I don't suppose she has. She's a habit of that, saying a lot but not saying much. Well…" The man muscled himself forward in his seat to rise again. "I suppose we'd better get to it then. Come with me, all of you."

He led them into the passage at the back of the room, then through a stringbeaded drape and down some steps to an underlying corridor that split in two directions: one was filled with daylight pouring in at an opening beyond its corner, probably leading up to the roof kitchen; the other passage was shadowed. Sarwin took flints and lit a claypot lamp on a shelf and showed them through to another longer stairway and then to a small door at the bottom.

Noah almost gasped as the old man opened it and ushered them inside. A narrow, low-ceilinged room, the length of a Hardenese longboat, and stacked from top to bottom with scrolls, piled in rows of stone shelving dug into the walls, or on the many wooden scaffolds that jutted out across the chamber's short width.

"Most people know only of the priestswar which began the Cull," Sarwin said, ambling ahead of them into the space to light lamps on the wall, "or the kingswar that followed it, when Karel and his sons began their conquest of the Five Lands. All they teach in the scribal schools, you see. And if you're not a scribe you've only your kin to rely on for what went before – which is not always a bad thing by the by, depending on your kin." He paused at a scaffold and squinted up at the cluster of scrolls on its top bank. "No... they'll be the chieftains," he muttered, then resumed walking. "There've been four wars written of though, uh... what's your name again?"

"Noah."

"Huh. Noah. Decent name."

"Thank you."

"There've been four wars, Noah. The godswar was first, although there are some who'd say that was really several wars. Markúth, Talagmagon and their children battling the Watchers. Then Markúth and Talagmagon battling each other. Then Markúth battling his sons, and his sons battling each other." Sarwin turned, nailing Noah with an arched peering look. "I'm assuming you're not so primitive as to not believe in gods, boy."

Noah, not knowing how to answer, just offered the man a thin smile.

Sarwin grunted. "Good. Well, that one was first, the godswar. Then you've the priestswar. Which, if you take the long view, as I do, was always going to happen. Men are born for war; when the faiths fractured it was inevitable it'd end in conflict. Then came Karel, wanting to clear up the mess, do away with the faiths altogether. Some agreed with him, many didn't, so you have a kingswar, and eventually a Five Land Sovereignty, as we see today. All very tidy, until you understand that not all of the priesthoods were destroyed, and even those that were, were not always destroyed completely. Some escaped to Súnam. Some hid up in mountains, lived off shrubs and mountain cats and whatever else they could find. A king's hardly going to send men up mountains for weeks at a time to find one or two stragglers is he; not when he has lands to conquer, battles to fight. And so they persist, these priestly lines, and eventually they gather men to themselves, resume their practices and traditions, or perhaps create new ones. And then, over the centuries, they grow and learn of each other; and the same disputes that began the priestswar and ended in the Cull repeat themselves all over again. Warring priesthoods, each with different histories and bloodlines. The bloodwar."

"How have you come to have all these?" Daneel asked.

"The writings? Oh... well, I was a scribe once. Royal scribe. Never chief though. Never that. Wasn't well liked enough, you see, and at the time I'd a little habit with the wine. But still, I was an underman in the time of Sharíf Kostyatin. I was there when he cut the treaty with King Nalaam, in Dumea, back when–"

"You were?" Noah put in.

Sarwin stopped. "No one ever tell you it's rude to interrupt, boy?"

"Sorry. I didn't mean... I'm *from* Dumea. Nalaam was my father's father."

"He *was?*" The old man stared at him, then glanced to Tamar. "You knew of this?"

Tamar smiled cringingly. "*Sorry?* But then who'd think to ask a thing like that? I mean, who thinks a boy's likely to be a son of kings, or stewards, or whatever it is they have over there now? I'm sorry."

"Sorry?" The old man grinned. "This is wonderful. Perfect." He looked at Noah. "Dumea, that treaty, is the reason I was tossed from my place as scribe, you know. The library there... When I saw it, and then read the writings kept there... They wanted me to pretend I hadn't read them, you see, or assume them false. But how, when they are written as well as any other record? If they are false then so is all else – the histories, the royal chronicles. And that, in short, is what landed me here, an outcast with a cellar of books.

"But that's not important. You are of the line of Dumea's stewards.

This explains a lot. Yes, now I will know where to look."

He drifted toward a shelf in the wall behind another row of scaffold further in and began rummaging through the piled scrolls.

"This is a rare writing," he murmured as he plucked a long battered roll from the shelf and patted it down, brushing the dust off of the worn leather scrollcoat. "They no longer pass it on to the scribes to be copied, not here in Hanesda anyway. A crime. Being eaten by moths, but they don't care. Things that went before being devoured, and they pay it no mind. May as well walk a road and forget the way you took."

He handed his lamp to Tamar and placed the scroll on a table to stretch it out.

"Now. There was a rumour, among those of us who find interest in these things, that the priesthoods began by the blood of gods; that some of the Fathers took women, sired sons – half man, half god. And that these offspring subdued tribes, forged nations, began the priesthoods. Some say they were as gods, kings *and* priests in their time; *pale kings*, as some called them."

"Strange name," Noah said.

"Yes. Yes, it is. But an apt one. It was the way they looked, you see. Or so the writings say: 'Men whom even the sun could not touch.'" Sarwin chuckled drily and continued to unroll the page, searching as he talked. "It's written that their skin was as pale as bone, their hair too, even among those born to Súnamites. Can you imagine? The same features as any other Súnamite, yet with that pale skin and hair. It was how they were recognised, the truest mark of what they were – divine seeds, the sons and daughters of gods. *Godkings*."

"Godkings?"

"Yes. They are the ones who first taught men what kings are. Ordained to rule, with the power to do so. Our thrones now are shadows of what they began." The old man's eyes glittered in the dim light as he glanced up at Noah from the page, warming to his topic. "What I and a few others have learned – from much study, I might add – is that their power is carried in their line, and can sometimes be found in those belonging to it. Not as pure as those first ancestors, but there nonetheless, in the blood. Priest's blood, some call it… Bring the lamp closer, Tamar. Yes…" He unrolled more of the page, shuffling the pin to reveal the writings, his finger tracing along the scripts as he continued to search.

"What are you looking for?" Daneel asked as he leaned over Tamar's shoulder to examine the page.

"One of the bloodlines I always found fascinating was that of Ashkanaz," Sarwin replied. "An old line from Kaloom, in the High East. A line, when you go back far enough, that may have belonged to the lineage of Anak, who is said to be an 'ancient one' in some of the older priestly writings." He glanced up at Daneel. "A son of the gods. A pale king." He shuffled the pin again. "More light, Tamar… See, the interesting thing is Ashkanaz was both a godking and scholar. Learned, knowledgeable. He began one of the first orders in the east – *the disciples of the sons of light*, he called them – later destroyed during the kingswar. His offspring, following the Cull, became raiders until they later discovered a silvermine in a valley a few miles east of the Silk Pass. As you'd imagine, you discover something like that, and have the wherewithal to guard it, your line changes. And so it is as you follow it in the writings; a few generations later they are clerics. Scribes, like me. Ah… here we are. This is it. Look here, Noah."

Noah followed where Sarwin's gnarled pointing finger hovered above the page. Some kind of genealogy apparently, like the ones Mother would always try to make him study back home in Dumea for the Judgements. Noah placed his finger on the page and read. "Tarabi son of Sayeed, who begat Ruasi of the tophills, who begat Zayed of the Yellow Valleys of Kaloom, who begat…" Noah slowed, "Naseer of Kaloom… that's my mother's father."

"Then your mother was Yasmin, daughter of Naseer," Sarwin said, nodding to himself, "and she wed Hassan son of Nalaam, the steward of Dumea."

"Yes."

"You carry the blood of an ancient, Noah. There are those who do, and it leaves no gift in them. It is not passed to every generation. But, every so often, one born to a line such as this… it can manifest… and this is a strong and ancient line…"

"He's a nudger," Tamar announced brightly. "I *knew* you were." She tapped her head with a finger. "I saw it, like I said. You're like me, Noah. You're a gifted."

For a moment Noah remained as he was, his eyes fixed to the list of names etched into the scruffy yellowed page, not knowing what to feel.

"You should know there are others," Tamar said. "We even have a home together, a place that's safe, where the priesthoods don't find us. You don't have to be alone."

"You also don't have to decide anything right now, Noah," Daneel warned. And then to Tamar, "He has a lot to take in. Go slowly now."

"You could come with us too if that's what you're worried about. If you've nowhere better to go. The three of us could go there together. Better than wandering desert roads being chased by godwhippers. Wouldn't be so bad, eh, Noah?"

Noah looked up at her from the scroll, and then to Daneel, thinking. After a while he looked back to Sarwin who, now the scroll was open, was busying himself with his own curiosity, continuing to peruse and read. "What happened to them, Sarwin?" Noah asked. "The godkings. The pale kings."

Sarwin blinked, his watery eyes fishing up from the page to regard the boy at his shoulder. "Oh, well they were wiped out centuries ago, Noah. By the Watchers, when they came to return the gods to the Aeon, the world that is their home. They tested the Fathers and the Mothers one by one, causing them each to fall by their own lusts or pride, and then destroyed their offspring."

"So, there are none left? No pale kings?"

Sarwin paused, apparently pleased by the question, and pondered it, his eyes glazing over dreamily. "I would not think so, Noah. But I suppose it is not impossible that one or two might remain, hiding somewhere… Perhaps biding their time."

An hour later they were outside again, moving through the crowd to where they'd tied their horses by a pole on the opposing street. Someone up ahead had decided to have themselves driven along the city's tight crowded lanes in an oversized rickshaw pulled by two men. Daneel could see the tall cartwheels and wide carriage over the heads of the crowd, taking up too much of the road ahead and backing the whole street up. He watched as some nearby jostled it, shoving disapprovingly against the sidewalls to rock the wheels.

"We'll take the long way," Tamar said. "It'll be quicker." And led them back in the opposite direction, against the tide of people and, eventually, into a calmer street on the other side. They'd work their way around the block, and then back along the next street to where they'd tied their horses.

"How many of you are there, Tamar?" Noah asked. "Where you stay, I mean."

"Not many. Nine. It'll be ten with you." She glanced up at Daneel walking on the other side of him. "Eleven if the lump comes."

Daneel ignored her, his gaze, as usual, vigilant, scanning the surrounding medley of alleyways, tenements and passersby.

"There aren't many of us *anywhere* I'd wager," Tamar resumed. "That's why I came for you. If any of us see one we always come. Because someone always will. If not us then one of the priesthoods – either Gilamek's lot, or those followers of Markúth who chased you on the desert road, or whoever. They're always hunting, all of them. They never stop. Lately it's been getting worse, actually."

"Have they ever caught any of you?"

"I was captured once, as a child. Snatched from a bazaar in Hikramesh when I was with my mother. They put me in a box and carried me out of the city like some stray farm animal."

"How did you get away?"

"My father. He's a seer too. It's how he found me. He and Mother came to where I'd been taken and got me out."

"So, your parents are there too, at this place you'll take us?"

"No… Not Father. The ones who snatched me managed to grab

him as we were trying to get away… Couldn't go back for him, just me and Mother. She's not a gifted."

"I'm sorry, Tamar."

She shrugged, affected a smile. "Eleven, twelve years ago now," she said. "But I know he's alive. I see him sometimes, in here." She tapped her temple again as she had in Sarwin's library. "The problem is whenever I see him it's always… I don't know. Blurry. I can never tell where he is. But Mother says I'll find him one day. I'll find my father, Jaleem."

"What did you say?"

Tamar glanced at Daneel, obviously startled as he hadn't seemed to be paying attention. "I said I'll find him one day."

"No. You said a name. His name."

"Jaleem… Why, do you know him?"

Daneel stopped walking. "You know, now I look at you I can see it."

"You *do* know him. How? Do you know where he is?"

"I think he's…" Daneel trailed off, looking past her.

"What? You think he's what? What are you looking at?" She followed his gaze, turning around to the corner of the street ahead of them. "What is it?"

"We need to go," Daneel said. He gripped Noah by the arm and started backing away down the street, back the way they'd just come. "We need to go right now."

Tamar frowned at him, then, looking back, saw armed men approaching – a small troop of cityguards, carrying maces and swords, led by a tall, lean youth so similar looking to Daneel it was uncanny.

"This way," Daneel called back to her over his shoulder, and then scampered into a narrow alleyway. They ran through, hurrying along its shadowed corridor until they came out onto another road on the other side and sprinted north, nearing the concourse by the palace gardens, a broad stretch of pebble-strewn road set back from the street and gated by iron-wrought bars.

Noah tugged Daneel's arm. Apparently, the boy had been here

before, perhaps with his mother and father when he was last in the city.

"There will be too many people," Noah said. "We should go the other way... Trust me."

The three of them headed along the carriage lane in the other direction, rushing past shoulder high walls decorated with hanging baskets of white flowers and stems of lavender.

Daneel could hear the barked commands of his brother, Josef, behind him. He turned, moving into another narrow passage running between two compounds opposite the gated concourse. The walls were fresh painted, smudges of slaked lime rubbing off onto their shoulders and hips as they squeezed their way through. Eventually the passage turned into an enclosure; high walls, a small opening for the gutter. Dead end.

Daneel cursed.

Noah pointed.

Daneel looked, and could've kissed him then for spotting it – a rope tossed over the top of a nearby wall, hanging down from its height.

He bent in front of it, cupping his hands, and nodded for Noah to step up onto the cradle he'd made with them to reach the rope. The boy obeyed, placing his foot into Daneel's palms and bouncing as Daneel hoisted him up. Noah reached and grabbed the rope, and then hauled himself over the wall to drop down onto the other side.

"Tamar."

She nodded, following Noah, and stepped onto his hands just as the first guard came rushing around the corner to barge into Daneel, sending them all sprawling, landing together in a heap on the ground, Daneel and the guard grappling as another soldier arrived with a mace.

Noah watched through a gap from the other side as Tamar turned to him and waved frantically for him to run away, before jumping onto the back of the man wrestling with Daneel.

Dull crunch as Daneel pulled and twisted, yanking the man's elbow out of joint and drawing his shortsword as he rose to meet the next oncomer.

Noah shifted behind the gap, trying to find Tamar who was now battering down the limp-armed man with her fists.

More soldiers entering the space.

Daneel on the other side, parrying with his blade as two others engaged him. He dropped to a knee, slashing across the first's thigh as he rose to parry the other's blade in one smooth motion.

Noah was already climbing back up the wall, his foot lodged in the gap, stepping and reaching up to grasp the top. He pulled his chin up in time to see another soldier fall to the ground, bleeding as Daneel cut a third man down. He was a blur of steel and motion now, spinning and slicing and hitting as Tamar beat on any man who managed to be dropped without being killed.

And it was then that Noah saw him, the face that would remain, for him, unmistakable until the day he died.

Josef.

Daneel's brother. The man who'd put his blades into Noah's father's back out by the Swift beyond the city walls. He came strolling around the corner to enter the alcove, watched as Daneel dispatched another guard, and then slowly stepped in from the passage.

They stopped, eyes meeting across the enclosure.

"Hello, Josef."

The brother smiled thinly, looking over the chaos of bodies piled on the ground. "Really, Dan?" he said. "Of all places, you come here, to the crown city? If you were so eager to die you need only have told me. We could have settled this back by the Swift and saved us both a lot of time."

Daneel flicked blood from the blade of his shortsword and shrugged. "And where'd the fun be in that, brother?"

"Same old Daneel."

"It's why you love me."

Josef grunted and drew his blade, warding back the other soldiers arriving into the space. This would be between just the two of them.

Daneel steadied himself, holding his shortsword out as he stepped forward to meet his brother, glancing to the increasing number of armed men filling up the periphery. Which was perhaps why he didn't see it right away, how Josef had somehow lifted from the ground, hovering a half inch from the stone-tiled paving beneath them. And then he was struggling, swinging and kicking his limbs, trying to free himself from the baffling grasp the air around him had apparently taken as he began to drift slowly back, and then, more quickly as he flew across the confined enclosure and into the soldiers behind. It was only then Daneel understood. His eyes shot to Noah, the boy's chin propped atop the wall he'd scaled, poking above it like a prisoner awaiting the headman's blade.

"What are you doing, Noah? I told you to go. *Go.*"

Noah ignored him, heaving his knee onto the wall's ledge to haul himself up and balance on the wall. He stood and reached with both hands, stretching out their trembling bones and joints toward the other guards, who, for a moment, just watched him, puzzled.

"Noah, *no.*"

The first guard spontaneously lifted from his place, feet kicking at air as he shot toward the opposing wall as though yanked there by an invisible cord of rope. The others watched, befuddled as the man slammed hard into the stone, before they then turned as one like a crowd in a gallery to face Noah on the wall, who was now sweating and panting from the exertion.

Noah, trembling with fatigue, reached toward the rest of them, feeling the energy build along his joints and crackle through the bones of his wrists and knuckles as he tried to contain the thunderous shudder riding along his limbs. And for a moment he felt as though he couldn't, that his arms were about to come apart, that they would flay and split open, spilling out muscle and tissue and bone along with the illimitable bubbling something channeling out from within his chest to his hands and beyond to pummel the air. And so he almost didn't feel the sting of it, the arrow that sliced through his shoulder, but he felt the impact, knocking him off his feet and tossing him back beyond the wall beneath him into the waiting emptiness behind. As he fell, he instinctively tried to reach out again, but couldn't, his eyes gazing up to the sky's cloudy bright expanse and the wall he'd fallen from, his fingers twitching impotently through the rush of air to the receding stonework for a way to save himself, but he could find no way, and so let himself fall, plunging down onto the cool shadowed dirt to slam onto the grit of the street on the other side.

TWENTY FOUR

MIRROR

Looking at him, Sidon couldn't help but be sceptical. The prominent ribs, the scrawny dip to his flanks lower down, the bony hardness of his limbs and, of course, that skin – so thin, bruised in places, and with an unappealing blotched pallor not unlike worn vellum. The boy looked a little small for his age too – eleven? twelve? – and evidently malnourished. Hard to believe he'd somehow repelled several of Sidon's cityguard without swinging a blade.

He stepped away as the boy began to rouse from his sleep, grimacing like a startled pup as he opened his eyes. He blinked at Sidon from the bedmat, then winced as he tried to rise.

Sidon sat down by the table the servants had brought in, leaning languidly, elbow propped as he plucked a grape from the assortment of fruits in the dish beside him. "I'm told you are a boy of unusual talents. *Unnatural* talents, my men say." He tossed the grape into his mouth and chomped. "They're calling you a pagan, you know. A mystic."

The boy croaked. "Who… Who are you?"

Sidon gestured lazily at the surroundings. "I'd have thought that would be obvious, given the circumstances."

The boy glanced around – the sunny coral flush of the smartly brocaded walls, the intricately tiled windowsill beside the raised slab beneath his bedmat, the ornate murals of Sidon's forebears reaching to the ceiling on every side. Sidon watched as the boy, growing increasingly flustered, took it all in, even levering himself up to look out of the window and ogle the exotic assortment of trees and flowers that filled the royal garden's enclosure beneath.

"You're the Sharíf aren't you. Sharíf Sidon, son of Helgon."

"Not as obtuse as you appear."

"And this is the crown palace," the boy added, somewhat vacantly, still staring out of the window as though having woken to a dream; as if Sidon, sitting patiently in the room with him, was no more than a fiction of his own making.

"Right again," Sidon answered, trying to draw the child out of his daze. "But you, I think, have more pressing matters to worry about. Like the fate of your friends, for example."

That, predictably, got the boy's attention. "Where are they?"

"They are safe, for now. How long it remains that way will depend on how willing you are to cooperate, and how... Don't pull at that."

The boy, startled, apparently hadn't noticed himself itching and pulling at the bandaging on his shoulder.

"A flesh wound," Sidon said. "You were lucky. Either the guard was an exceedingly poor shot or, as he has suggested, you were somehow able to... well... *deflect* the arrow. Which, curiously enough, brings us to why you are here. Now, the general here–"

The way the child – noticing Gahíd for the first time, sitting quietly on the opposite side of the room – flinched was almost comical, and yet saddeningly pathetic too. Already Sidon was finding it difficult to believe this boy could have done the things the men were claiming. But then Josef, who was just about the only person in the world Sidon could say he wholeheartedly trusted, had claimed it too. Sidon exhaled patiently and took another grape from the dish.

"What is your name?"

"Noah. My name is Noah."

"Good. That's good. Now, the general here thinks it may be that you can be a friend to us, Noah. I myself am of a less sure mind. But Gahíd says he knew of your family, a noble family he assures me. Is this true?"

Something in the child's manner seemed to change then. "It is," he said, somewhat impudently, biting off the words.

Sidon glanced to the window. Gahíd had assured him the archer would have a clear shot as long as the boy remained on the bed, and the man was supposedly one of the general's best with a bow. "Gahíd thinks because of this you will prove a trustworthy soul, should it be required of you. Is this also true?"

"Was it you who had them killed?"

"Excuse me?"

"My parents." Something wolfish about the boy's eyes now, menacing even. "Was it you?"

Sidon just looked at him. For a moment it was like he'd found himself sitting across from an entirely different person, the nervous skittishness suddenly gone, replaced instead by a cold calculating malevolence, gazing out at him through level, still eyes. "No. It wasn't," he replied evenly. "But I am interested in those who ordered their death. They are the same people seeking to steal my throne."

"Why did they order it?"

"That's what I intend to find out, among other things. The question is whether you are willing to help me. If not for the sake of your parents, then for the sake of your friends – the girl, whatever her name is. And Daneel."

"He is here?"

"He's close by."

"I want to see him."

"He's busy right now. But you will see him soon enough."

Josef sat opposite his shackled brother across the table, staring at him as he stared back, their gazes locked like players in a game. The girl, he would come to later. The guards had locked her in a vault of an inner room beneath the palace. But for now, blood came first.

"I take it I'll have to do the talking as usual," Daneel quipped.

Josef placed his hands on the table, palms down. "Always a game with you, isn't it, brother."

Daneel yawned, looked about the room. The far wall was inset with an elaborate image spanning almost its entire length: Sharíf Kaldan in profile, seated atop a giant upright scroll – often symbolic of the First Laws – with a scale before him, receiving merchants from the High East; the Sharíf, oversized, the merchants reduced to half his height even while he was seated. A typical rendering.

"If you're waiting for some kind of apology, brother, you'll be waiting a long time."

"You transgressed the covenant, Dan."

"So, we're going to do *this* again, because from what I remember we've had this talk already. We did not agree, as I recall."

"It's hard for anyone to agree with an oathbreaker."

"Hard for anyone to agree with a fool too."

"I'm not the one sitting in shackles."

"You know, part of me wondered what it'd be like if we saw each other again. Perhaps time'd change things, I told myself, make you more reasonable. But we don't even get by the small talk and you're already on about Brotherhood this and covenant that."

"Selfish. Lazy."

"What?"

"So easy to care only of yourself, isn't it – your own thoughts, your own feelings – and pay no mind to anything bigger than that, anything bigger than *you*."

"You expect me to care about all those meaningless rules they made for us?"

"You are a betrayer."

"So what. I betrayed the Brotherhood. I refused its laws and creeds and its claim it should tell me what to think, feel and do. You act as though I've murdered a mother with child for looking at me wrong."

"You don't get it."

"Get what? That I learned to look in my own mind for what thoughts should be there? If you ask me, you're the lazy one, just blindly following whatever decree they pass down to you."

"It is not lazy for a man to care for something greater than himself, to yield his mind and heart to something beyond them. You treat devotion as some dirty word, because you cannot comprehend what it is to give yourself to something that will outlive your own fleetingly fickle thoughts and flesh."

"Be simpler to just have a child if that's what you're after, Josef."

"I suppose you would know, seeing how gifted you are at thinking and speaking like one."

Daneel scoffed. He tried to gesture with his hands but they jarred from the shackles, rattling the chains. "Why are you so angry? You ever ask yourself that? What should it be to you what another man does?"

Josef's fingers began to tap an impatient rhythm on the table. "You weren't just *another man*. You were my brother."

"*Were?* So that's the way you play it then. And you say *I'm* the one who doesn't know what he's talking about?"

"Shut up, Dan."

"Why should I? So you can pretend to yourself that you're in control of things, just like when we were children?"

"That's not what this is."

Daneel laughed, mirthless and mocking. "Please. That's *always* what this is. You just don't like that I'm finally telling you. Always has to be your way. That's what bothers you."

"You. Are. A *betrayer*."

Daneel just smiled. "But that's just it, brother. That's what you're not understanding. I don't care. I don't care about the Brotherhood. I don't care about their decrees. I don't care about the creeds or disciplines. I don't care about any of it anymore."

"You don't get it."

"Just because I don't care about betraying them doesn't mean I don't get it. If anything, it means I finally do. I get exactly what they are now, what people like that are. And you want to whine and mope because I betrayed them? Because I woke up and you won't?"

"You're the one who refuses to wake up. You didn't just betray *them*."

"Ah, here we go. I betrayed the covenant, I betrayed the disciplines. I betrayed my training. Predictable, brother. All so predictable. I can probably say all you will say before you even–"

"*No*," Josef exploded from his seat, standing over him, arms straight as he leaned on the table to bear down. "You don't *get* it. You didn't just betray the Brotherhood. You betrayed *me*."

Daneel, surprisingly, fell silent, just staring up at Josef, watching the rage smoke off him as he stood there, his arms tense and stiff, leaning over him. Josef seemed to remember himself then. He pushed back from the table and flopped back down into his seat as though defeated.

Neither spoke for a while, staring off into opposing corners of the room until Daneel eventually broke the lull.

"You're right," he said quietly. "I *didn't* get that…"

Josef looked up at him from his seat, meeting his eye, and nodded his acknowledgement. It was the closest either one of them was going to get to an apology for now.

"So…" Daneel said. "Why don't you tell me why we're here, Josef?"

"Put simply," Sidon said, offering Noah some fruit from the dish. "I want you to become part of my bodyguard."

Noah took a couple of grapes and fed them cautiously into his mouth. "But I'm just a boy."

"Apparently a fairly special one, although I'll admit that's something I'll want to see proof of at some point. But yes, you and Daneel. I want you both to join my bodyguard, at least until all this is over."

"All what?"

Sidon sighed, exchanged a glance with Gahíd in the corner, who seemed to be growing just as perplexed as he was. It was getting dark outside. The servants had been in to trim and light the lamps on the walls, setting another one down on the floor beside Sidon.

"Noah. I'm beginning to feel you've not been listening… I'm saying I am surrounded by men ready to obey my orders, but I cannot trust them. I cannot be sure who among them belongs to my mother. Already, my life has been threatened more than once."

"Do you hate her?"

"Sorry?"

"Your mother. The Sharífa. You say you feel it's her who's been trying to kill you, and take your throne. Which I don't think makes sense really. Why would she do all you've said she's done to turn these people–"

"The council."

"Yeah, the council. Why would she work so hard to turn them against you if all she's to do is kill you anyway? She should do one or the other, shouldn't she? Seems a lot of extra work to do both."

"Huh." Sidon sat back in his seat. It was a fair point.

"And the other thing is, who'd she *get* to kill you anyway? Who'd she know to do so? Because she'd have to know them well wouldn't she. To trust them enough. Because if you're to kill a Sharíf it's not the sort of thing you get just anyone to help you do. And most people wouldn't know that many who'd know how to do it."

Another good point. Sidon looked over at Gahíd, who raised his eyebrows – approving, impressed, surprised. Sidon had felt foolish having shared so much of it with a child – especially *this* child – until now.

"Her brother, Játhon," Sidon answered. "My uncle. He is prince of the land of Calapaar, and governor of its largest city, Tresán. We think he's one of her allies. He'd know men skilled enough, I think."

Noah nodded simply and fished another grape from the dish Sidon had now handed over to him. "What about Tamar?"

"Who?"

"The girl. My friend. Where is she? What will you do to her?"

"Whatever you please. She is safe too. If you agree to help me."

Noah seemed to ponder it for a moment. "You say the ones trying to kill you are the same as killed my parents?"

"Yes."

Again, the simple nod. "I'd like to know who they are, why they did as they did."

Sidon again glanced to Gahíd in the corner, who stared back expressionless. "Very well," Sidon said.

"And I'd like for my friends not to be harmed," Noah added, "to be let go."

"We can do that too. If you agree to help, Daneel will be pardoned of his treason. It will be as though it never happened."

"There's something else," Noah replied. "I want for us to be kept safe, from what is coming. From what we saw in Çyriath."

"Çyriath? You were there?"

"Yes. Daneel and me."

Both Sidon and the general had leaned forward on their seats now, peering at the boy. "Listen to me, Noah. I want you to tell us what you saw there. I want you to tell us it all."

"So, you agree to join the Sharíf's bodyguard?" Josef asked.

"I do," Daneel replied.

"Good... As for what you have described..." Josef had begun to speak and then stopped, groping for words. "The Sharíf must be told."

"And I'm happy for him to *be* told," Daneel answered.

It was true night now. Outside, a deep indigo shroud had layered itself down over the sky. Josef had lit several lamps around the room, and then a candle on the long table between them.

"How long ago were you there, in Çyriath?" he asked.

"A few weeks. Long enough for those things to make their way down here were they to come this way, depending how long they remained in the city after we fled."

"We'll have to hope they stayed awhile."

"They were like something from out of one of Jaleem's scare tales, Josef."

"Master Johann never liked for him to tell us those."

"No, he didn't. But Jaleem would tell them anyway."

Josef stared at Daneel for a moment without speaking, then

pushed his chair back to stand. "Come then. It's time we went."

"Went where?"

"To the Sharíf. We must tell him what you saw: what is coming."

Sidon was moving toward the door when the servant knocked to open it, stepping aside to allow Josef to enter, trailed by his twin brother, Daneel. Unsettling to see them together like that, almost mirror images of each other: the same thick dark hair and tan skin; the same mildly aloof way of standing, as though bullishly waiting to be entertained or impressed; only a slight twist to Daneel's lips and a difference in the shape of his jaw – sharper, narrower, and unshaven – to tell them apart.

"It is agreed then?" Sidon asked.

Josef bowed. "It is. But there is–"

"Good. The boy too. Which is just as well. They may be needed sooner than we'd like. There is something coming, from the n–"

"–north," Josef finished for him. He glanced at General Gahíd seated in the corner, and then the boy he'd once sought to kill in obedience to the general's decree. The child was sitting up on the bedmat by the window, looking at him, his eyes dreary, yet cold. "The child told you," Josef said. "He has seen the creatures too."

"Yes, he has. Which means we need to tell the captain of the cityguard to prepare the–"

Josef saw the flash before they heard the sound, a rapid burst of flame outside the window, gouts of smoke abruptly lifting from the moonlit cityscape beyond the window as the deafening crash of a falling wall echoed across the night. The ground and walls shuddered with the impact. And then came the shouts, confused shrieks from the streets as distant fires began to flicker above the terrace roofs to the north.

"*Sharíf!*"

Sidon shrugged Josef off, continuing to stare out at the gloom as the shape of something hung in the sky above it all, a thin long shadow staining the night.

TWENTY FIVE

SHADOW

Neythan had dreamt of the Great Dry Lake back in Ilysia again, and of sitting there with Arianna, cosied up beneath a spangled sky and clear full moon, the way they would as children. They'd perch at the lip of the crater, feet dangling over the edge, torsos bent forward, straining to look over the yawning chasm of crag and stone hiding its dark vast worlds beneath their heels. And he'd remembered, whilst dreaming, how they'd always thought of it that way – how the Lake, to them, had seemed like some colossal wound in the earth, veiling a realm of myth and shadow like a drape before a show that was yet to start. They'd tell each other they knew things the others couldn't – that the Lake is a pathway, the Lake is a door, and that one day they'd cross that great void from here to there, to where all the things they'd ever dreamt or imagined and all the firelight fables they'd ever been told were no longer fables at all but real; words made life, thoughts made flesh. As though myth was merely a harbinger, foreshadowing some secret place they'd always known to be true, a world beyond seeing, beyond time, but there, at the edge of things, if only they could be brave enough to forgo their fears and descend into that waiting abyss below to witness it for themselves.

Looking back, it was a wonder they never tried to, never dared each other beyond the cliff's ledge and down its steep crevices to where they imagined gods and Watchers and dark fleshless things dwelt, breathing the same air as them. And yet they never did, the disciplines of the Brotherhood always too tight around them, too loud in their minds, a law within their bones. Which was why it was strange, in the dream, when instead of sitting serenely at the edge of the world with the crater waiting far below, the Lake's shadows morphed to life and reached up toward them, ensnaring their ankles and pulling them toward its hungry black maw to drag them down into its dark waiting void.

Not the kind of thing to dream about the night before seeking to kidnap an aide of the throne from within the crown palace itself; which was why Neythan kept it to himself, another secret to add to the rest, along with the strange visions and the aches and spells of fatigue that seemed to be growing increasingly frequent.

He stared up at the night, a cool glittered abyss overhead. No clouds. An uncommon thing this time of year, especially with the way the mist could sweep in from the Swift during the small hours.

"There," Arianna whispered, crouching beside him and pointing ahead. "That's the chamberlain's room, out at the furthermost tip of the west wing."

Neythan eyed the long jut of the palace's wing, stretching across the forecourt and propped up by a row of ribbed pillars beneath it, lined by a stepped portico that ran almost the entirety of its length.

After having arrived here the week before, they'd spent the last several nights watching the palace – the routines of the guards and servants, making their patrols, emptying slop buckets by the latrine, bringing spices and meats into the kitchens, or grains. Even the gardeners had their routines, ferrying their chests and baskets of blood lilies and lemon blossoms, or the gathered clippings of acacia into the palace to presumably adorn the walls and corridors within. Watching it all, spread across time – moments into hours – had been like watching some kind of vast and complicated organism; eating and sleeping and excreting according to its own set cycles.

"Alright," Arianna whispered. "Someone is lighting the lamps in his chamber. The servants will tend to his table soon, bring his wine, some fruit, maybe a letter or two. He'll arrive not long after that. We should move now." She nudged Neythan with her elbow. "You ready?"

"Yes," he lied.

Caleb, beside him, made a grunt of assent.

"Alright then. Let's go."

The good thing was that Neythan had done this before, that time slipping into the palace to collect a strange jewel from the neck of a corpse in the tombs beneath the foundations: a peculiar black pearl set in an amulet, like nothing he'd ever seen before or since. He hoped this time things would be simpler.

They worked their way down to street level from the terrace block they'd been watching from, and then moved through the night time roads and alleys toward the courtyard's outer wall.

The palace loomed above the borough, dominating the surroundings despite its relatively moderate height – the Governor's House in Qadesh, the library in Dumea, even Kaldan's Tower splitting the horizon to the southeast within the walls of this very city, all reached higher than the crown palace whilst failing to rival its overall sense of bulk and heft. Glancing at the shadowed shape of it to their right as they approached the grounds at the rear, they moved north along its outer wall. The streets were still occupied despite the late hour: what looked to be a small bald-headed coiner, clutching his hammer and mint with his elbow as he scurried along within the corridor of light cast by the torches lining the walls; a mother and small boy – six, maybe seven – walking slowly with a pile of firewood shelved in their arms whilst the old men and women sat atop the low walls bordering the street, puffing on their flutes of snowcane with crinkled pouting lips.

They reached the northern wall of the courtyard, higher here than the southern side that fronted the palace's forecourt, and continued until they were out of sight of the loiterers in the street. Once clear, Arianna tossed her hook-tethered rope over the top, tugged it taut, testing the grip, and quickly hauled herself up, walking up and over the wall to drop deftly into the royal courtyard on the other side and wait for the others to follow. As predicted, the yard was empty. Most of the patrols would be within the building itself at this hour or guarding the forecourt on the palace's south side. Hurrying, they moved toward the gallery at the lower part of the wall. The end of the southern wing was set in levels, a windowed gangway leading to a laundry room and then a set of stairs from what Arianna could remember. She climbed in head first, squeezing through the narrow gap and over the ledge to alight within the palace walls. No lamps here. No need. Clothes were seldom washed at night. So she stood to her feet, waving the others through to join her.

"Come. This way."

They worked their way up through the levels of the wing by the stairways cornering each floor, hiding behind walls to wait and then go as patrolling guards conducted themselves according to their usual routines. When they'd reached the top, they knelt on the steps and waited, eyeing the corridor.

"The door on the right," Arianna whispered, "the third one down. That is the chamberlain's bedchamber."

A pair of guards stood at the other end. Others could be heard closeby, patrolling the level beneath. Arianna was already positioning her bow, setting the smooth long shaft of the quarrel to the string, when they heard the loudening voices of the men below, nearing the stairway.

Pointing first to herself, Arianna gestured to Neythan before signalling to Caleb to keep his eyes on the guards at the other end of the corridor. Neythan nodded and slipped his dagger from his belt as he followed Arianna down the steps to meet the men approaching from beneath. She slowed as they reached the bottom, crab-stepping with her back to the wall as she edged toward the corner. They could see shadows flickering against the opposing wall, growing with the approaching guards' every step as their ribald chatter and japing neared. Neythan could hear himself breathing now, his fingers twitching unhelpfully against the handle of his blade. Worryingly, he was beginning to feel weak, his arm tremoring, his knees like water as he sidled carefully down the steps along the opposite wall while Arianna waited by the corner with her blade.

One of the guards muttered a parting joke to the other and then began to climb the steps. Arianna, watching the man's shadow shrink against the wall as he neared, nodded at Neythan, making sure he was ready.

The guard, his sword tucked into the sleeve at his waist, came around the corner. Arianna leapt forward, grabbed an arm, and they stumbled together as the guard struggled, bumping against the wall. Arianna shifted, shoved an elbow to his throat, then stepped around to jump on his back. The guard grunted, reaching for his weapon as Arianna whipped her cord around his throat and yanked. Neythan, for a moment, just watched as the man gagged, clawing frantically at his neck as the cord bit into the flesh like a butcher's porkstring.

"*Neythan*," Arianna hissed, straining at the cord.

Neythan stepped in and planted his blade beneath the ribs as the man reached for him, eyes bulging sickeningly. Neythan watched as the man's strength drained away, his grasp of Neythan's arms slackening as his gaze rolled loose, turning slowly inward as he slumped to the ground.

Arianna checked the fallen man's pulse to be sure before shoving past Neythan, mouthing angrily – *what were you waiting for?* – and then turning to make her way back up the stairs. Caleb was still crouched there when they reached the top, crossbow in hand, watching the guards at the other end of the corridor. Neythan took the crossbow from him as he settled beside him on the steps, lying on his stomach with the weapon poised as they got ready for what was next.

"You're not right," Arianna whispered to him warningly.

"I'm fine."

"Better be. And you better not mess this up." She snatched the crossbow and handed him her bow instead. "Best if I do it, I think. You don't look ready to run. Be sure you do not miss." She motioned to Caleb to hand her the shortsword, and then nodded at Neythan once more. "Do not miss."

The corridor was about fifty feet from end to end. Neythan rose to his knees to set the bow, positioning the nock carefully against the bowstring and allowing the fletching to rest against his finger, just the way he liked. Setting his aim to the guard nearest the wall, he breathed in as he pulled the string, and then exhaled slowly. He could feel Arianna ready next to him, could feel, in spite of it all, the gathering stillness of his sha as he sighted the man's throat, just as he'd been taught, his mind settling into the familiar worn grooves of execution. He murmured "Go" to Arianna.

She bolted, light-footed, her soles skimming the stone floor like a sprinting cat's. She was a quarter of the way there before the men, distracted by their own complacency and, perhaps, sheer tiredness, even noticed her. Neythan loosed the arrow as the nearest guard began to turn, the shaft slipping across the distance as smooth as breath and hammering through the man's chin, abruptly jerking his head before he fell to the ground. Arianna, sliding to her knees, aimed and fired the crossbow, spearing the second guard's neck. The man gagged, made a strange fitful motion with his hand, before sliding against the wall on the other side to slump to the floor.

Neythan and Caleb were racing toward the chamberlain's door almost before he'd hit the ground as Arianna, already sliding her tools into the lock, felt for the subtle push of weight as she flicked the counterbalance free. The door clicked open. Neythan discarded the bow, Caleb taking the crossbow as Arianna and Neythan drew their shortswords before stepping in.

Inside was dim. An oil lamp, low on its wick, sat on a table against the back wall, the flame petering out as it drank at the last dregs of oil. A few rolls of vellum lay beside it along with the occasional scrap of reed paper, scattered over the wood like fallen leaves. They crept further in, stepping around the chairs and upended chests that littered the ground. The place was a mess – stools, more scrolls, what appeared to be a broken ink well, a claypot filled with styluses lying on its side, all strewn across the floor in a slovenly jumble.

Neythan prowled through the lounge as Arianna moved ahead beyond it, slowly stepping beneath the arch of a wide walk-through toward the bedchamber on the far side. Caleb found a vessel of oil to refill the dwindling lamp and was tipping its mouth toward the filling hole in order to light the room when a figure reared up from the shadows.

The man leapt up, gripped Neythan at the wrist, trying to wrestle the blade free. Leaning back, Neythan pulled, threw an elbow with his free hand and kicked out the man's ankles to send him across the room in a sprawl as Caleb levelled the crossbow, lifting the lamp to get a better look. Arianna came back through from the bedchamber at the sound of the commotion and, seeing the old man on the floor, smiled.

"Well, well."

The old man looked up at her from the floor. "You."

Arianna came forward to look the old man over as Neythan took him by the collar and shoved him onto the table. His wrinkles seemed deeper than she remembered, tracing long thin creases along the sides of his leathered face, but other than that he was the same. The same fluffy halo of bright white hair, cresting the tanned pate of his head, and the same overgrown nose and ears, right down to the tiny network of capillaries around his eyes, tracing their puny branches of faint blue and red.

"We know you are part of it," Neythan said simply.

The chamberlain coughed. "Part of what?"

Arianna slapped the old man backhanded. "Let's not play this game, Elias. It won't go well for you, and we don't have the time."

His gaze rolled balefully toward her. "Part of what?" he repeated sneeringly.

Neythan stepped in again, jolted him by the collar, bouncing his head off the table's solid oakwood. "I saw you. Just as you are now. But in a place and *time* you shouldn't have been."

The old man smiled and tutted. "Neythan, Neythan. It sounds as though you have been dabbling in things you ought not."

"You're going to tell me what you were doing there."

"I don't know what you are talking about."

Neythan conjured a penblade from his pocket and pressed against the man's cheek, just beneath the eye. "I think you do. I think you know all of it." Neythan pressed the blade in a little more, letting the tip lean into the feeble withered skin. "Perhaps a man doesn't need both eyes in his old age, failing as they may be."

Elias shuddered, straining back against the table as though willing it to give out beneath him.

"Just tell us, Elias," Arianna said.

"You are too late to stop it now anyway. It is almost here."

"*What* is almost here? What are you talking–"

The night outside exploded, a blast of light detonating from beyond the window and tossing them across the room. Neythan landed hard and skidded across the floor.

Dazed, ears ringing, the room swinging beneath him like the deck of a windtossed ship as he tried to roll onto his elbows and knees. Dust everywhere, the whole room filled with it, clogging his throat and eyes as he tried to orient himself. The table had been thrown onto its side, and the lamp with it, dashed to the far corner where its dregs had spilt against a wooden chest and ignited. Beyond the clogged space Neythan could see flames in the night through the window, pockets of fire shimmering upon rooftops along the moonlit skyline of towers and housing. People outside screaming, smoke rising up off the buildings to blot out the stars and dirty the night.

"Bones of gods…"

"*Neythan*." Arianna, coughing as she pushed herself up from the floor onto her knees. Blood on her arm and across her temple. Neythan scrambled across the room to help her, then looked to the table. Elias was gone. Another blast detonated outside, shaking the building and convulsing the walls.

"Neythan." Caleb. In the walkway before Elias's bedchamber, the chamberlain's arm hooked around his neck and Caleb's heels skidding and scrambling for purchase as the old man yanked and pulled him along.

Neythan got up and limped after them. Caleb was reaching out to him, hissing and grunting from the squeeze of the chamberlain's arm as it hooked his throat whilst bars of firelight ran across them from the scenes beyond the window.

He limped closer, arm outstretched, reaching toward them, his dagger ready, fingertips touching Caleb's, and then gripping, nearly there, about to pull him free and then take his dagger and thrust it into…

Elias spun suddenly with his hand out, the skin of the palm somehow glowing, strobing neon bars running along the creases of his skin like some kind of membranous deep-water fish. He flung it at the air, striking at the nothingness between them with the heel of his palm. Neythan grunted with the impact, somehow smacked back across the room and through the walkway into the antechamber, crashing onto one of the upended chairs. He groaned, slowly rolled from the smashed pile of wood onto an elbow, squinting back across the dusty space to Elias and Caleb where the walkway now seemed filled with light. Because it was, Neythan realised: light from the chamberlain, swimming along his limbs from beneath his skin as though his blood was channelling the sun.

He reached out to shade his eyes as he pushed himself up. The chamberlain gripped Caleb tighter, clamped against his chest with the crook of one arm, and then motioned with his other hand, the light from his hand seeming to linger in its wake as he traced signs through the air until both Elias and Caleb began to quake.

"Caleb…"

Arianna had pushed onto her seat now. Neythan could feel her next to him, had a vague sense of her trying to help him up whilst Caleb, calling out to him, reached desperately with his free hand as the floor began to shudder and tilt and then…

Abrupt snap to the air, just like before, the room jumped as though the whole building had just been shoved and… and then… they were gone. The space where they'd just been moments before, empty, the dust sizzling in the void that had been left in their wake.

"Wha… Caleb?" Neythan blinked in shock. "Caleb!"

He tried to move, crawl across the floor to the bedchamber where they'd been standing just a moment ago.

"No." Arianna at his shoulder, holding his arm, pulling him away and back toward the corridor.

Neythan was trying to shrug her off when the building shuddered again, shaken by the dull thudded weight of something hammering against the palace wall below.

"We have to get out of here," Arianna said. "We have to go." She pointed to the window again. The city outside was ablaze. Fire everywhere. Neythan pushed himself upright to make for the door with her. And then went back to the upended table, kneeling to sweep some of its scattered contents from the floor beside it and into his sack before reluctantly following Arianna out. They staggered back along the corridor the same way they'd come. There were people everywhere now – maids, servants – scurrying along the upper level hallways in a panic trying to make sense of what was going on. Neythan and Arianna hit the stairway at a gallop, Neythan still limping, then skipped down the steps two at a time, past the body of the guard still slumped against the wall and all the way down to the ground floor. They persisted through the cluttered passages into the southern wing's gallery, before climbing out of one of the windows back into the courtyard.

Smoke clogged the air, thick and bitter, hanging low as fog across the cobblestones. They ran to the yard wall and hauled themselves back up. More people – running, shouting, shrieking: a man standing atop a flattop bollard on the corner of the road with his arms to the sky, shouting up into the sooty fog like a supplicant before his gods as a pair of loosed donkeys scampered up a street on the opposite side.

"What is this?" Neythan shouted. "What's going on?"

Several firelit arrows streamed across the sky above them. Somewhere to the east they could hear the vague sounds of fighting, a swelling melee of shouts and screams and clanging metal.

They went south, away from the main road and the marketplace. The city was big, but if they kept headed this way they'd eventually reach the gates, and the watchtowers, where they'd perhaps get a better view of what was happening, or at least be able to make their way out. People were moving south with them, spilling from their houses into the streets half naked, baskets and sacks of provision clutched under their arms.

The ground shuddered again as something thudded heavily in the distance behind them. The sounds of buildings collapsing. *How? Why?* Neythan was about to turn to others in the crowd to ask when he heard it. A noise unlike any he'd known before. He turned around, back toward the palace and the surrounding square of whitewashed terraces. There, atop one of the high walls of the palace's eastern wing, perched a… *creature*. A hulking shape the size of several houses, backlit by the flames and smoke. Neythan could see its breath: slow measured puffs, calm, almost meditative, disturbing the slow drift of the smog as it wafted up from the flames.

"Gods and fathers…"

Arianna turned around to see as it tipped its head back and bellowed at the sky, a long loud bearish squawk, before leaping down from its perch atop the wing's roof, disappearing into the dark and mist of the chaos beneath as more buildings began to lean under the assault of those dull, inexorable and anonymous thuds.

"*Neythan…*"

"Did you see that, Ari? Did you see that thing on–"

"Neythan."

He turned back to Arianna, and then to the street ahead where her gaze had now fixed. Fire, consuming the housing and a long wooden shelter harbouring the vendors' marketcarts. A horse on fire, running and bucking at the end of the street as it whinnied and shrieked in a mad jumping fit.

"We'll go around to the next street."

"*Look*, Neythan."

And that's when he saw her – small, fragile, walking out from amid the blaze as if it was little more than a gentle rain shower. Long dark hair. Slim. Pale skin. Small. A child. A mere child, walking to the middle of the road and then turning square to face them.

TWENTY SIX

DOMINION

"The season changes," the girl said.

To which there was no ready answer. The girl, like the voice in his head she'd once been, was apparently given to cryptic and strangely timed sayings. Not that it mattered. Joram had always liked as a boy to listen to the voice's soft honeyed words, pouring out its melodious bouncing murmur, that gentle chivvying tone redolent of a world hidden, a realm to which he was yet to graduate, dangling its furtive fruits to his childish mind beneath. There but not. Out of reach. Just like memory. Especially *his* memories.

He wasn't sure anymore when he'd first heard it, or how. He'd always been prone as a child to playing games with imaginary friends. There'd been Ousama, a large Haránite cook he'd seen once at a banquet in Qadesh that he'd later imagined to be his friend. Even now he could still recall those short and plump fussy lips and little brown eyes, bombastic buxom and jutting hips, chatting idly as she wielded a spoon about the pan, her every tale bent to the private calumnious whim of the gossip, given as she was to lewd jokes and ribald laughter. Just like some of Father's special friends who'd come drunk to the palace after dark. And then there was

Shamyla, who Joram had always liked to call Sham for short, with her long, plaited hair and brightly coloured lips, the way Father sometimes painted Joram's when they went to the upper rooms to play their games. Joram would speak to them often, these fictional friends, and sometimes hear them speak back, until one day the voice he heard told him that it alone was his true friend and that he should have no others, before insisting he show Ousama this by chopping the head and limbs off of a pet mouse and leaving its dismembered remains in the cot beside where little Sidon slept. Which worked.

He never saw Ousama after that, and Shamyla disappeared not long after, leaving only that nameless voice, just a warm soothing whisper at first, and then later something stronger, tingling comfortingly along the edges of his spine like the busy hum of buzzing wasp wings whenever it spoke to advise or chide or teach.

When he was six it taught Joram to know he was clever, that he could do things other boys his age couldn't – like understand the intents and thoughts of men, read them on their faces like words on a page, there in how they breathed, or blinked, or stood. When he was nine it taught him to know he was strong, and that he didn't have to do the things Father wanted him to. But that was the day Father became unhappy with him. Which was the one thing the voice didn't warn him of. But it didn't matter. It was all for the good, it said, things would be alright. One day he'd return to the throne Father had pushed him away from. One day he'd reclaim what had been stolen. And on that day Joram would become a better and stronger king and Sharíf than any who'd ever been.

So, when the girl, or god, Markúth, turned to him as she stood at the edge of the bluff overlooking the long plain before the crown city, and said, "Today is that day," no other words were needed. Joram understood. Joram knew.

But it wasn't until they were in the plain, the Swift glinting milky-silver alongside them to the west beneath the clear night's moon, that he saw Markúth's steeds, the creatures the voice had been speaking to him of all this time and revealing to him in his dreams.

"Wait here," the girl told him. But both Joram and the people following him had already stopped, staring up in awe at the huge winged beasts circling the walls of Hanesda overhead, three huge phantasmal shadows against the night. The girl turned to him then, gazing up through her greasy long dark hair to read Joram the way he'd learnt from her to read so many others; those cold grey-blue eyes staring intently into him, channeling the weight of millennia like light from a distant star.

"I will go ahead," she said. "When you see the flames begin to reach above the walls, then you will know to enter."

She turned and walked away in small measured steps to the city gates, parting them with a touch and continuing into the city. From there Joram, and the people with him, just watched. They watched as the cityguard and watchmen scurried down from their haunts within the city wall, then watched as they were set alight as they neared her. They watched houses, carts, shingles, and scaffolding spontaneously combust, instantaneously engulfed in flames. Then watched more flames ignite further up the street, flaring to life wherever and whenever the child turned her attention with the smallest gesture of her pale little hands. And throughout it all they all remained silent – Joram, Ola, Djuri, Marin, the entire multitude – stunned wordless with awe and fear as they watched the beasts – Markúth's steeds – swoop down from on high, gathering fleeing panicking people up in their savage jaws as the girl continued to walk through the streets of the city, rendering her devastation. In the end it was Djuri who nudged Joram from his stupor, nodding up at the watchtowers either side of the open city gates where fires flickered through the slim peeping gaps. Joram nodded, lifted his arm, holding the torch for the gathered multitude to see. And then motioned them forward, walking toward the open gates of Hanesda, toward the destiny he'd spent his whole life waiting for, and into the home he'd come to reclaim.

Inside was carnage. Bodies everywhere, fires licking at the charred remains lying prone in the street whilst others staggered around, arms flailing as flames consumed them. A brace of horses, yoked together to a now wheel-less cart, chased along the main road, fleeing the heat from the fire burning the cartbed they were dragging in their wake. Men and women crouched by the open cisterns that flanked the main street, scooping water with buckets whilst others dug holes through to the channels of sewage beneath, shoveling the dirt with their hands to douse the fires they saw burning everywhere. Through the thick smoke, Joram could barely see down the street ahead of them, and almost didn't notice the glint of armour through the chaos and heat and mist as a battalion's worth of cityguards began to fill the street and rush toward the open gate, toward *him*, and the troop of Kivites who were following behind.

Joram drew his sword and lifted it over his head, shouting to signal the affray, and then, at the roar of the men behind him, ran forward into the blazing tumult to meet the onrushing cityguard. He slowed of course, allowing those at his back to come past him and beat him to the clash, then squinted at the splatter of blood as it exploded from the almighty collision of flesh and metal and bone ahead of him as the two armies crashed together.

The crush of bodies squeezed in around him, the ranks of Kivites pushing and shoving their way to the front with maces, axes and swords as Joram tried to work his way free of the bedlam. Eventually he stumbled clear and found himself in an alleyway off the main road. He glanced around, doubled over with hands on knees, coughing from the smoke.

And here, standing aside in the street as the warriors of his tribe scrapped and hacked at the armoured men of Hanesda, he couldn't help thinking how nice it would have been to have the others come with him to where he was about to go. Because in truth, none of this was the way he'd imagined it would be – the heat, the bitter suffocating waft of the endless smoke, funnelling out from every conceivable corner and alley so that he could barely see his own hand in front of his face. And there seemed to be fire everywhere, embers of it floating and drifting on the thermals as men chopped and hacked at each other on the main road.

Joram tried to survey the street, calling to mind the visions the voice had given him before leaving him to enter the pearl, and the directions it had provided, but there was too much smoke. He glanced back, orienting himself by the citygates behind, and set off in what seemed to be the general direction of the royal concourse.

He passed through a narrow street and onto a wide dirt lane running west, stumbling out onto a road filled with droves of fleeing people, faces black with soot and running as one in a continuous tide south, probably heading for a cattlegate to try to escape the city.

Debris littered the ground. Shards of wood and broken chunks of rock and sandstone from blasted buildings nearby. Beneath the gables of the houses the upper edges of some of the walls had been scorched, smeared in streaks of black from where flames had ripped along the brickwork, combusting roofs and flipping out the contents of their kitchens – logs, skillets, pans, skewers – and tossing them onto the streets beneath.

Joram joined the crowd, moving past the smouldering frontages along the road until he began to near the city's centre. To his right the charred remains of market stalls lay in the square: crispy poles of wood, some frosted with the dusty white of ash and draped with tattered ash-stained rags, prodding at the air in uneven angles like exposed, upturned ribs. He turned toward it, jogging through the low-hanging smog that continued to linger over it all, hanging there like the newly exorcised ghost of what the street had once been.

As he turned the corner the tops of the crown palace edged above the tenements to the east like a signpost. Joram almost felt like weeping as he glimpsed those familiar high, thick walls, the jagged shape of the ramparts and parapets, like the prongs of a king's crown, pointing at the night as though to herald the terror above. And then as he looked, his gaze was drawn further, beyond the bulwarks of the palace's upper levels to a pillar of hot white light shining there, channelling down from the sky to some hidden point of convergence amid the rows and terraces beneath, like some god had straightened a fork of lightning and frozen it in place between the earth and the increasingly cloudy firmament above. *Some god*, he thought. *What was Markúth up to?*

He ducked into an alley at the sight of soldiers scrapping with Kivites in the street ahead. And then turned again into another narrow passage between two house walls. And then, almost unthinkingly, he knew he was there. This was the place. He'd seen this before, the tall-walled aisle Markúth had shown him. He moved further in, found the door hidden behind a jumble of seared timber, and then looked back along the alley to be sure he hadn't been followed. He then knocked on the door, the same complicated rhythm he'd seen in the vision, and waited.

Rough scrape of a shutter sliding open, and then the solid clack as it swiped shut and the fidgeting jangle of chains and locks being unlocked before the door slowly hinged open, revealing a muscular, thick bearded man.

"Inside," he urged.

Joram stepped tentatively across the threshold into a confined and poorly lit space. The walls were black with grime, and opened to similarly dirty passages on every side. There were others here, sat on stools or leaning against the walls. A girl and a boy, a few men.

The doorkeeper fastened the complex medley of locks at the door and then pointed to the passage on the right. "That way, please."

So Joram obeyed, wondering what this place was, wondering where the passage led, wondering why Markúth had told him to come here and what it would all mean. The tunnel kinked and twisted several times down a stairway before arriving at another door where Joram knocked again, and was welcomed by an armed guard who nodded him in through a drape of beaded ropes and leather into another similarly cramped space. The stale mingled stench of sweat and smoke clogged the room, and the place was filled with more people he didn't recognise. A man sitting in a low-riding wicker chair against the near wall. Another standing by a stool in the opposing corner, and then, beside him... Joram froze. The woman's ornately patterned robes were smudged with dirt and slag but the sense of familiarity was unmistakable. Her slim, carefully poised frame. Her long dark hair, tassled and messy with dust and fragments of stone tangled in it. And her face, lined around her mouth and eyes, and yet still...

"Mother…" The word tumbled unwittingly from his lips, like a confession.

The woman's face – a face he thought he'd forgotten – broke into a wild flurry of expressions: smiling, weeping, joy, grief. She came across the room so quickly she almost knocked him over, winding him as she flung her arms out around him, sobbing.

"My boy," she gasped, chugging the words out between her choppy sobbed breaths as she clung to him as though he was life itself. "My boy… my boy."

Slowly, Joram lifted his arms to hold her. And it was then he felt it, a small brittle something inside himself, a forgotten space deep within, now cracking. Millions of hours imagining, *here*. All those countless days as a child, desperate and hungry in the Reach, and alone. Those nights sheltering with beggars in woods and caves so cold and dark he thought he could taste the stuff of it in his teeth, feel it in his bones, deep and dense enough to snuff the breath from him in his sleep. And all that wandering amid desolate scrublands and dry creeks and barren plains, watching constantly for raiders and vagabonds because his skin was too dark, every hour of sleep a risk, until he managed to fight his way into the tribe of Shurapeth and claim shelter. A decade of distance too wide to measure.

He was still clutching her, eyes stinging as he blinked back tears, when he noticed him, standing sheepishly against the far wall where the woman, *Mother*, had been moments ago.

"Sidon?"

He couldn't be sure. He looked so different, the jaw strong and square where it had once been small and chubby and round. And the eyes were so much more watchful now, and of course he was so much bigger, becoming a man even. How old would he be now? Fourteen? Fifteen? And yet there was a certain wry bent to the lips, a searching look to the eyes that Joram recognised.

"Brother?"

The boy flinched at the word.

Joram reached out his hand for him to approach, to embrace, as Mother had. For that was why they were here, wasn't it? This was why Markúth had sent him along the burning streets above to find this bunker, to offer him this miracle. But Sidon didn't move.

Mother was recovering herself now, finally releasing her embrace as she turned to face her other son across the room. "This is why I brought you here, Sidon," she said. "Why I brought both of you here. I could not risk either of you knowing. It would have confused you to know, compromised you."

Sidon was affecting a small scowling smile, a mild curl of his lips. After the explosions his mother had appeared with her guards, cajoling him down here to this hidden bunker in the heart of the city via a series of winding underground tunnels Sidon had never seen or known of before. Even then, as she'd led them, she'd seemed to him a little too calm, too expectant, as though the attack and the calamity above wasn't altogether a shock. And now, here was this stranger, embracing her, whom she'd apparently been expecting too, and she was just standing there, teary-eyed and smiling, expecting Sidon to swallow it all, to be a good boy, to fall into the paths of whatever convoluted scheme she'd now laid down. "You're saying this is Joram?" he asked dubiously. "You're trying to tell me this is truly him?" He smirked, incredulous. "No, Mother. My brother is dead. That's what *you* told me." He jutted his finger at her bitterly. "Because what kind of Mother would tell her child his brother is dead unless it is true?"

"A desperate one, Sidon. There was no other way to save him, and also you. Elias told me this would be the best way."

"The chamberlain?" Sidon's eyes flitted between them – mother and son – roving from one to the other like a twitchy pendulum. "What does *he* have to do with this?"

"I am here by the hand of Markúth, Mother," Joram objected.

"You are here because…" She pulled on the collar of her robe, tugging back the fabric to reveal to him the skin beneath her collarbone by her shoulder.

Joram fell silent. Five dots of ink, arranged at the points of an invisible pentagon. Joram looked down and lifted his own wrist, turning it palm up to show the identical minimalist ink mark there, just beneath the root of the thumb.

"Yes, my son," Chalise answered. "It is the mark of the disciples of Markúth. Elias put it there so you could be watched over, when it became clear you would have to be sent north, away from your father. You will not remember. We put you to sleep first, so you wouldn't know."

"You sent him north?" Sidon cut in. "Where?"

"Your father sent him north, exiled him to the Reach, once Elias had sown the seed in his mind."

Sidon just stared at her, his head shaking in raw disbelief.

"We had to do it," she said.

Sidon laughed then, hatefully, eyes teary. "Just like you *had* to kill Father?"

That stopped all of them, Joram included. He'd known Father was dead, of course. But the rumours that had worked their way north had told of the great Helgon the Wise being brought down to the grave by sickness. He looked at his mother, who was staring at Sidon, stunned.

"Yes," Sidon spat the word. "Did you think I wouldn't find out? Of course, you didn't. We are no more than pieces on a board to you. There to be schemed with, manipulated."

"No, Sidon. That's not–"

"Don't *touch me*." He jerked his hand away from her fingers and stepped back. "You stole my brother," he growled, jabbing at the air toward her. "You killed my father. You are *poison*."

"I had to," she whimpered, her eyes manic with grief. "But now we are free of him. Now we are finally together, after all these years. We can be a family."

Sidon balked. "You *had* to kill Father?"

"To protect you."

"Protect me? From my own *father*? Father loved me! He never lied to me, like you! Never schemed against me, never treated me like some–"

"He was lying to you with his every breath from the day you were *born*. You do not know the things he did to your brother. Unnatural things. Things he was readying to do to *you*."

"What are you talking about?"

But Joram knew. He understood. There were times he felt the fringes of it, tugging around the edges of his memories like a restless child at a loose thread from a hem; those nights during the new moon festivals when all would be loud outside and Father would come drunk to Joram's bedchamber with his special friends, a secret he was to keep and never tell, that's what Father always said. That was Father's law. Joram took hold of his mother's arm. To comfort her. To warn her. Because he didn't want to break that law now, not anymore. He didn't want all he'd worked to fold away and bury undone and spoken aloud, made real, brought to life in the mind of another, especially not little Sidon.

"Well?" Sidon demanded, glaring angrily at Mother.

Joram pressed his fingers to her arm, shook his head, only slightly, only so she'd know, and he could see that she did, could read it all in her eyes in that one swift moment as she looked at him and even nodded back, telling him she wouldn't tell, telling him she understood, that he was safe now, she'd protect him, always protect him.

"Well?" Sidon barked again. "What? Why did you *have* to kill Father?"

But Mother said nothing, just stood there holding Joram like the son she'd always wanted and the son that he, Sidon, could never be. And so he moved toward the door, striding across the room to leave and return along the passage and up the stairs to Josef, Daneel, Tamar and Noah. Joram reached out and snagged his arm as he tried to pass.

"Brother, wait…"

But Sidon couldn't, the lies, the disregard, the neglect, and his father, rotting in the ground because of bloodless selfish Mother. And suddenly it was all so clear. How Joram had been Mother's favoured son. How Sidon had been Father's. And how her grief at the loss of her firstborn had twisted and turned to resentment of him. And now he, Joram, was standing here, the favoured son, resurrected, calling him brother as though he could ever expect to understand the word, as though he hadn't in his way abandoned him too. So he shrugged his arm loose from Joram's grasp and turned and glared at him, glared at them both, seeing the way they were still clinging to each other with an affection that Sidon had never been able to know, an affection that now sickened him and turned his blood. "You are not my brother," he said coldly. "My brother is dead." And then Sidon walked out of the room without looking back.

TWENTY SEVEN

DIVINITY

You never expect to see a small girl come walking out from a blazing wall of fire, even less for that same girl to reach up and channel light down from the sky. And yet that was what this girl, fragile and slight as she was, appeared to be doing, her thin white arm reaching up to the increasingly tumultuous skies above as though to summon the elements themselves.

Neythan and Arianna cursed in unison as they stood in the middle of the street, a hundred feet away, and watched along with the other denizens who'd fled this way. All of them now frozen to the spot as the child stood there, her clothes and hair whipping up to the gust of some strangely localised blizzard all around her as the brilliant beam of luminescence shone down along its perfectly straight axis from the expanse overhead.

"What is she doing?"

"I don't know," Neythan answered. "But it can't be good. And it can't be good to allow her to do it."

"Neythan?"

But he was already moving forward, walking up the street toward her. Blade drawn, limping with fatigue, the ever-present sag of the shadow on his sha dragging within him. The earth seemed to be gathering into a mild tremor, the skies rumbling, flickers of lightning igniting in strange shapes among the night's clouds. The city's south gate would be three-quarters of a mile beyond where the child stood in the street barring the way. One long straight road, bracketed by tenements and the flamboyant sprawl of the richer districts to the southwestern quarter, with their wide houses and expansive grounds. Neythan could see the look on the child's face now, a concentrated grimace, her eyes closed, her pale body trembling slightly from the strain of whatever she was doing. The light was all around her, her skin glistening with it, her limbs fine lambent rods of alabaster. And Neythan could feel the resistance of it, whatever she was doing, an invisible tension in the air he had to *push* through. Like trying to walk uphill, or into a gusting wind. Somewhere behind him he could feel Arianna, following, trying with him to press a way to the girl to… what? What would they do? Strike her? Try to kill her? Politely ask her to stop?

He could see some of the buildings on the periphery beginning to shudder, as though mirroring her strain, trying to remain upright and intact against the pressure and weight of whatever she was trying to do.

And then Neythan heard the strange squawk-roar of one of the giant winged creatures somewhere overhead, circling back around, and the windswept shout of Arianna behind him, probably trying to beckon him back, or warn him. And it was then he realised, there at the eye of it all, amid the shudder-gust intensity of the light, the little girl was now looking at him, her body still fixed in place, unmoving, a slight tremor along her outstretched arm, but her eyes – icy blue, cold, spiteful – peering out from the whip-slap frenzy of her windblown hair across the chasm of energy between them, watching him approach. She shifted her arm, did something with her hand, relinquishing her hold on the sky and the intensifying shaft of light that had been gathering around her. Everything stopped – the tremors, the light, the sizzle of thunder that had begun to swell among the clouds above – all of it shuddering to a halt so sudden it seemed to make some of the buildings, released from the forces that had been gripping them, recoil and slacken back into place.

"You will never learn, will you," the little girl said, eyes locked on Neythan's. "But then each is taught in his own way. And, as I once tried to teach my sons, if a soul cannot hear…" She looked up, allowed her eyes to roll back in their sockets and closed them again, exhaling slowly, "he must *feel*."

"Neythan, look out!"

He turned, swivelling to face Arianna, who was scrambling to the side of the street as the monstrous bulk of one of the creatures filled the thoroughfare, swooping down and gliding along its length toward the crowd still gathered there, toward *him*.

"Everyone down!" Neythan shouted. But it was too late. The beast's wingspan scythed like the edge of a giant axe into the terraces that flanked the street, crumbling the walls, spraying dust. Neythan saw several men too old to run cut down as the beast flew low, its long belly parallel to the ground and its horrifyingly immense jaws hinging open, revealing the slick black flesh of its throat.

Neythan screamed and dived to the ground as the creature swept past, its wings passing over his head like a wave. He rolled and tumbled, dragged along the dirt in the after-draft of the massive wing's wake as the beast reared up, climbing back into the night sky with the little girl now clinging to the furred girth of its neck, riding it.

"Neythan!"

Arianna was climbing to her feet. Blood and gore littered the road behind them where several men had been halved at the waist, their entrails spilt and scattered across the ground. The rest of the people were screaming, running back the other way to get out of the street as Arianna took hold of Neythan by the arm and helped him up.

"Quickly. That thing is circling back around."

A few archers had gathered at the street's other end, others on a mezzanine overlooking the road from the east, trying to sight the beast as it arced high and swung across the moon to turn around.

It split the night with another cry, gathering speed as it descended back toward the narrow straight of the south road. Neythan and Arianna were limp-skipping toward the end of the street but they could already tell it would be too far. Neythan could hear the rip of the wind as the beast's wings began to skim the rooftops behind them, preparing to lower further to scythe and decapitate with its wings. Some of the archers ahead had begun to loose their arrows, aiming low, unsure how to measure the distance with the creature's rising speed.

"Do you see that?"

Arianna beside him, jogging with his arm across her shoulder as she pointed toward the end of the street – the archers still there, but a few paces beyond them and still walking, a figure, moving toward them along the middle of the road whilst the people fled in the opposite direction to exit it.

"Who is—"

The crash of broken stone behind them. The beast was in the street, the blade-sharp edge of its wings once again scraping along the walls as it flew headlong toward them.

"Let me go."

"Neythan, what are you—"

He shrugged her off. "Let me go. We won't both make it. I can't run." He turned, sword held low, and stepped toward the middle of the road to face it. Arianna turned to join him instead of running to escape as Neythan wanted, but there was no time to argue now.

They watched it come, and for the first time Neythan could see something of the beast's shape and countenance as it sped low toward them – the shoulders of its wings, thick long limbs with talons of black bone protruding from the joint. The broad girth of its neck, furred with coarse chunky bristles, probably more like fingernails or scales than hair, covering the vast musculature of the breast and neck like armour. The malicious sneer of its snout, something between a giant wolf's and a shark's, creaking open as it neared to reveal the black oily flesh and drool of its throat. Its huge skull bobbed slowly with each subtle row of its wings, almost gliding now, its flight barely hindered as the bony edges of its pinions sliced and bumped along the walls of the housing, issuing sparks with every contact as the beast continued to drive forward with the weight and speed of its gathered momentum. Neythan found himself cringing and flinching at the sound – like the magnified grind of steel on whetstone – as he tried to still his sha and bring himself more fully to the moment.

He gripped his sword two-handed, digging the toes and heels of his sandals into the dirt, and stood side on, knees slightly bent, poised to meet victory or death as the beast only seemed to accelerate further with its mouth now stretched wide to show its teeth, long serrated blades of enamel several rows deep, ready to snatch and puncture and grind. And Neythan could feel himself trembling now, a shivering weakening churn along his every sinew and through his organs as he leaned into the pureness of the moment – here with his sword, Arianna at his shoulder, just the two of them again like those days back in Ilysia sitting atop the Great Dry Lake's edge as though they alone were the world's last remaining survivors and witness, and now in a way perhaps they were, here in the heart of the crown city, standing in the middle of the main south road as the vast hulking frame of death incarnate raced toward them on the wind to–

The flash came from nowhere, whiting out the road – the night, for a moment, radiant, the surroundings lit bright as the noonday sun. A dazzling burst of fluorescence detonated on the beast's chest like a bolt of lightning. The creature roared in agony, and then abruptly pulled up, favouring its left wing where the flesh beneath the shoulder sizzled and glowed, its singed fur smouldering like the dying remains of a furnace as the beast groaned and flapped to haul itself clear. Neythan shielded himself from the rise of dust as the creature ascended, and then spun around to see the hooded figure on the street, standing a few feet behind them. Amber eyes aglow, gleaming like hot metal as she removed her hood.

"You have *got* to be kidding me," Arianna said as she looked on.

Neythan said nothing, stunned silent. He took a step closer, to be sure of who he was seeing, and then frowned as the questions raced through his thoughts. How could she be here? Where had she been? How did she just do what she'd just done? But instead the only thing that came out was: "*Nyomi?*"

Nyomi got them out of the city, guiding them to waiting horses by the forum before leading them through sidestreets and alleys to navigate around the continuing pockets of fighting and exit through the trade gate at the eastern wall. Once out of the city she took them several miles east into the mountains where they made camp. From there they looked down on the landscape at Hanesda, shimmering in the night like a miles-wide lantern sprawled across the plain as the fires and fighting continued.

"Your skin," Neythan said. He'd been staring at it for almost the entire way here.

Nyomi sat by the fire with her cloak over her head, her scalp wrapped in a coloured headscarf beneath it as the hot amber gleam of her eyes slowly dimmed to something approximating normality.

"It's different," Neythan added.

Arianna followed his gaze and saw that he was right. Nyomi's hands, resting on her lap as she sat cross-legged before the fire, were no longer their usual chestnut brown, but instead blanched. Patches of white skin dappled her fingers and knuckles and wrists in blotchy patterns, and the same seemed to have happened on her face, flecks of pale skin speckling the area around her forehead and merging into larger jagged patches that ringed her eyes and cheeks like the shorelines of small continents.

Nyomi grimaced as she reached toward the fire to warm herself. She was breathing heavily, clearly weakened. "It is the mark of my blood," she said wearily. "My ancestry. I will be able to hide it again as I regain my strength."

"Because of what you did back there?" Arianna asked.

Nyomi scowled in pain as she adjusted. "It has been many years since I last had to… uncover myself that way. Decades actually. But there was little choice. You could not be harmed. The time…" she inhaled deeply, it was as though she was struggling to breathe, "it grows short. So short…" She trailed off, glancing back to the plain beyond the exalted crack of rock she'd settled them in.

"What *are* you, Nyomi?"

Her gaze reeled back in from the cold dark of the horizon and settled on him. There was still a glint of the luminescent amber of earlier as the fire reflected in her gaze. "In Súnam, there are those whose skin is this way. Dark, and light. There are others whose skin is pale only, though they are born of the Summerlands. Although many do not understand why these things are, I do. I always have."

"You are… some kind of mystic?"

She laughed, then wheezed. "A little more than that perhaps, Neythan." She looked up at him then, fixing him with that tigerish yellow gaze. "What I am about to tell you will mean you will no longer have a choice, either of you. You cannot know what I am unless you remain bound on this course. I tell you this because there will be things to come that will make you want to depart from the way upon which you are now set."

Neythan exchanged glances with Arianna, then shrugged. "After all we have seen, Nyomi, I don't think there is any going back for us."

Nyomi looked at each of them to be sure this was true, and then nodded to herself. "I am the firstborn child of a god," she said, then returned her gaze to the flames to continue warming herself.

"Hmm, yeah sorry, see I'm confused," Arianna answered. "You're saying you're the daughter of a *god*. Like… a *god*."

"Centuries ago some left their world to come here," Nyomi said, "to abide among men, to relinquish the garments of light and be clothed in the flesh of dust. They transgressed laws to do so, to establish kingdoms for themselves. They sired offspring with your men and women, sons and daughters of flesh *and* light, children of divinity. Some in the Reach, some among the lands you now call the Sovereignty, some further south in Súnam, like me… You could say we were… *different*. Like men, yes. Mortal. Some more easily killed than others. But also divine, touched by the light of our forebears, and inheritors of some of their nature, some of their strengths."

"Wait," Arianna said. "So… how *old* are you?"

"Centuries. Although I will say displays like the one I was forced into tonight are unlikely to help me remain for many more. Many of my brothers and sisters are dead because of their profligacy with their light. We are mortals, not gods. These powers were never intended to abide in the flesh of men; it is too weak to withstand their cost. But when we were young, we did not care for these things. Many of my siblings used their strengths to become rulers and champions among men. Pale kings, they called us then, and so we were. Drunk with greed and pride because of the things we could do. In the end, it is what betrayed us."

"Why did you not tell us any of this before?"

"It is as I said, you are bound to the light that has been shown to you. You cannot unknow what you have been told, and once you have been told, you cannot turn away. You will not understand these things now, you are only human. We do not hide these things from you, we hide them *for* you. They come to you as they are ready to be received. This is a law, the way of all light. But as I say, you are only human."

"You're saying there's more, other things you haven't told us?"

"There is always more, there is no end to finding out. But not all things are mine to tell. Some things are Filani's to tell. And some will come by the hand of others."

"She remains alive?"

"She does. For now, at least. When I lost you at the shrine, I returned to Jaffra by night to see her."

"They didn't tell us that," Arianna said.

"They didn't know. I did not announce my presence when I went… She was weak though, when I saw her… it is unlikely she will recover." Nyomi coughed, leaning away from the fire, and then wiped her mouth with a sleeve.

"Are you alright?"

"I shall be, given time."

"Why did you do it, Nyomi?" Neythan asked. "Why did you save us?"

"You are part of a battle that began before you were born, both of you. A battle for bloodlines and territories and things beyond what you will at this moment be able to understand... What you can and should understand is that that little girl you met back there in the city was not really a little girl."

"*That* I can believe," Arianna replied.

"She is Markúth, isn't she?" Neythan said.

Nyomi regarded him. "You knew what she was?"

"I suspected... I'd been having... I don't know... visions, of her. The girl."

"What visions?" Arianna said. "You never told me."

"I didn't want to worry you."

"As I recall, I asked you *specifically* about things like this."

"I didn't know how to make sense of it myself. I didn't understand. Not until I saw her."

"You are seeing the worlds within the world," Nyomi remarked soberly, "and they will know it now too. They are able to look at you just as you look at them."

"Who are?" Arianna asked.

"The gods: the Fathers, the Mothers. This is why I came for you. Why I *had* to come for you. You are a key. There will be others, but you are the one they can see now. Perhaps the only one. They will be seeking you because of this."

"What do you mean, a key?"

"The girl you saw. She is Markúth's to make himself flesh – to abide here, in this world. Now that he has succeeded, others will be able to try. He is the father, you see. He had to be first. But he is not the only one who has been seeking to enter. There are others who hope to do the same, some who belong to him, some who oppose him."

"You're saying things like *that*," Arianna pointed vaguely back in the direction of the crown city burning in the plain below, "are going to be happening *more*?"

"If we do not stop them, yes."

"And how are we supposed to do that?"

"The scroll. You still have it?"

"Of course." Neythan patted his sword sleeve on the ground beside him, which was where he typically kept the scroll, strapped to his back in a pocket of the sleeve beside his blade.

"Good. It will help us. The secrets of how to defeat them are hidden on its page, and also the pages of the others."

"Others?"

"There are five Magi scrolls in all, Neythan. You have one of them, the Earth Scroll. The Brotherhood were thought to have another, but as for the rest, they are hidden. We hoped, Filani and I, that you would be able to help us find them, once you'd read your own. The scrolls were written knowing these days would come; that once the priesthoods fell, the way for the gods to return would be made open. Qoh'leth, the author of your scroll and the father of the Shedaím, did not want to turn on his own kind and help to destroy the priesthoods. He did so because he knew they had become corrupt, embroiled in conflicts with each other that threatened to tear apart every known land. But he also knew that their right purpose was to ensure there would be no return to what had come before them: no return to the Godswar. So, he and others collected and created relics, distilled them, and put them in order to be included in these scrolls – all the knowledge needed to bring about the downfall of the gods when they returned. They must be found, and their secrets learned, in order to prevent what is coming. It was for this purpose we began the Fellowship of Truths."

"The Fellowship the Shedaím tried to destroy?" Neythan asked. "You started it?"

"I helped to, together with Filani and others. That the gods chose to use the Brotherhood to try to keep us from discovering the scrolls is precisely why we must find the others and learn to read the one you have."

"I *have* learned," Neythan said. "It's why we came to Hanesda. I saw Elias, the Sharíf's chamberlain, in a vision one of the stones in the scroll showed to me of Karel, the first Sharíf. Elias was there. At the Battle of Banners nearly three centuries ago, he was there."

"Then he also is a descendant of the gods, as I am, but working to help them."

"He took Caleb, Nyomi… We have to find him."

"I agree."

"You do?"

"You are surprised."

"I thought you would tell us to find the scrolls first."

"Elias will likely have answers concerning them. We must find him."

"I guess the only question that leaves, for now at least, is how," Arianna put in. "We have no way of knowing where he has gone."

Neythan reached for the satchel they'd filled with the contents of Elias' table and emptied it out between them on the ground by the fire. "We took these from his room, in the palace."

Nyomi shuffled closer to examine the items – letters, scraps of writing on torn pieces of vellum, a stylus, what appeared to be some kind of signet ring. Nyomi lifted it, inspecting the jewel – a small sapphire seated in a gold fixture. "You say you learned to read the scroll," Nyomi said.

"Yes?"

"You may be able to read this jewel the same way."

"Are you sure? The priest at the shrine warned against reading things that are untreated."

"I will guide you. If you follow carefully what I tell you to do, you may be able to dip into the jewel for a short time, like a gull taking fish. A jewel like this, that has perhaps been bound to a man for many years, will carry something of his sha within it. If it is not too old, the shift will be very clear. You will be able to see its memories well."

Neythan hesitated, looked to Arianna, who answered with a noncommittal shrug. "What do I need to do?" he asked Nyomi.

She nodded and shuffled on her seat again, turning herself square to him. "Imagine that you are Elias. Imagine, from your sha, not with your mind, what it is like to be him."

"But I do not know him."

"I said not with your mind, Neythan. You don't need to know him. Just close your eyes. Breathe."

And so Neythan obeyed, stilling his sha, closing his eyes.

"You will follow what I say. Do not think. Do not try to understand what I say. Only follow. Are you ready?"

Neythan nodded.

"Good. Now. Think on Elias, the chamberlain, and imagine that it does not matter whether you know him well or not. Imagine he is a perfect stranger." Nyomi paused, allowing Neythan to settle into his breathing. "Imagine all you need to know is already present within you, waiting in your sha. Because it is. Trust that. Trust your sha. Lean into the not knowing. And let yourself fall into the truth that you already do know him, as all men know all…"

Neythan breathed deep, and then let go, allowing his mind to follow whatever notions of the man it conjured.

"I'm going to put the jewel into your hand, Neythan. And you're going to imagine yourself frightened, fearful of the future; the things you planned are failing, all you have built is dying. You need a safe place, free of the weight of things. You need somewhere to go and understand what is to be done next. Imagine how much you need that place, Neythan. Think on it as you touch the jewel."

Neythan did, and felt the pull instantly, an abrupt whip-like gravity, stronger than before, tugging on his bones and drawing him inexorably inwards with the sudden thrust and snap of a recoiling bowstring.

And suddenly he is… elsewhere. Outside. Daytime. It's the stillness he notices first, the warm calm air close to his skin, and then, as he turns, the wide blunt horizon, an unending scape of green marshy lowlands, punctuated here and there between the long reeds by pools of murky water as the land stretches away beneath the clouded sun for as far as his eyes can see. He watches the sun's light where it pierces the bright scuds of cover overhead, watches the way it parades in slow broad patterns across the windless terrain whilst dead trees stand erect amid the slough like giant antlers, still as a picture, their barren branches arcing up to cradle the sky. The ring is on his hand now, its gold band snug to his middle finger and the blue jewel winking in the cloudy brightness. He tries to wipe the mudsplatter from the stone but it only smears, and there's more gathering on his arms and clothing, kicking up as he treads ankle deep through soft squelching earth toward a single living tree up ahead. From what he can tell, it is the last living tree for several miles in any direction. And the one he knows he is meant to go to.

It puzzles him to look at it, a tall bold cypress, standing there surrounded by the flimsy buzz of mayflies and the sodden earthy stench of the grass: because it seems – this tree – so lonely and fragile, and yet so powerful too, its defiant height pushing up from the vast, mushy landscape as though to embody some ancient law. He finds, as he looks, that he admires this tree, he likes the way the fluffy gossamer blossoms trail down from the gnarled boughs like hung ghosts. And it's only then he notices he's not alone. He sees the figure: there, beneath the tree, waiting within its thin, broken shade as he continues to plod toward it. And he knows they are there for him. They've arranged to meet like this. They will share some needful secret to guide and instruct him. This is where he needs to be. Which is why he is stunned, as he watches the figure begin to step forward beyond the tree's plaited shadows to show themselves, when it all begins to collapse – the tall bold cypress with its spectral blossoms, the shorter dead leafless trees that surround it, the milky sky with its pale muted sun, distant and hidden above the clouds like a coy stranger – all of it sliding into a dimming blur and coming apart piece by piece like beams of scaffold until there is no more day or marsh or unending bright cloudy horizon, all of it brushed aside like a common drape to reveal the world as it really is.

Neythan blinked awake to find the night around him and Nyomi and Arianna gazing at him from across the dwindling campflame. He hadn't collapsed this time, which was interesting. Perhaps he was beginning to get used to these visions, developing his own special tolerance for them.

"What did you see?" Nyomi asked.

And so he told them, explaining the details of the land and the tree and the shadowed stranger waiting beneath it.

"I know this place," Nyomi said. "It is an altar, deep in the

Sumerian Riverlands. Maybe a day's travel south from here."

"You are sure?"

But when she turned to Neythan to answer she seemed distracted, her gaze and thoughts already drifting beyond them to somewhere else. She nodded vaguely. "Yes. I am sure."

Neythan watched her for a moment, and then nodded. "Alright. Then that is where we shall go."

SOUTH OF THE FORK,

BY THE CRESCENT PASS

AND WEST OF THE

RIVERLANDS.

The month of Gan. Second year of Sharíf Sidon.

"So peaceful isn't it, the dark."

"That's not quite how I'd put it."

"No? Well, perhaps you haven't thought it through."

"That's rich. I agree, you say I understand. I disagree, you say I haven't thought it through."

"The dark removes things, takes them out of the way, allows you to think. Allows you to see."

"Is that what you teach your disciples?"

"I cannot teach them that, I can only tell them, like I'm telling you. Whether they learn the truth of it or not is down to them, and how well they think on what's been said."

"Could be because you're Súnamite, your love of the night."

"How so?"

"Talagmagon, the Mother of Mothers, she is goddess of the moon isn't she, the light that governs the night, which I find strange by the way: that the Summerlands, where the sun barely ceases, should have for its god of gods one who lures the moon, when Markúth, to the north, is god of the sun."

"But that *is* why. In Súnam they say the Mothers drove the Fathers north from their lands in the godswar, and that the sun shines brighter there because Markúth is trying to woo Talagmagon back. That's why the moon remains still by night, whilst the sun moves with each hour by day. It is Markúth, giving the best of himself as he searches to reclaim his bride and sister, to be reconciled again, and make the day one with the night once more."

"If that's how they tell it in Súnam, how was the story told here, in the Sovereignty?"

"That always depended, as with most things, on who was doing the telling – Harán, Sumeria, Calapaar; they each had their own tales, but in each they all said the Fathers drove the Mothers south, rather than the other way around."

"Convenient."

"It is, isn't it. And it's also why here, all royal lineage is carried through the sons, whilst in Súnam, it is daughters who are born to rule."

TWENTY EIGHT

HISTORY

Terror. That's mostly what Sidon felt as they smuggled him beneath the walls of Hanesda, scurrying through tunnels and bunkers he'd never seen before whilst the cacophony of the city's destruction hammered and rumbled through the stone above and around him like an especially chaotic storm. Josef went at the head of the guard, the waning light of an oil lamp in his hand as he led them along narrow subterranean passages, following the painted signs on the walls – a pair of Sidon's bodyguard at his shoulder; Daneel and Noah bringing up the rear. They'd get beyond the walls, emerge within a stone's throw of the fishing villages lying south of it along the Swift, and hope there were still horses there. It remained a rule for a royal caravan to be kept in every settlement surrounding the city for exactly this purpose, but it was anyone's guess whether that would be the case now. No telling how loyal men might remain when faced with the sights and sounds of fire and battle from within the crown city's walls. In the end, they would have to go on hope.

They eventually reached the dark at the end of the tunnel, climbing up limestone steps to rejoin the night a half mile out from the walls of Hanesda. The Swift to the west, the city behind them, a short journey to the nearest fishing village ahead. Sidon, unable to help himself, turned to look at the city as they climbed out and stood there, awestruck and heartbroken, staring at the glow of fire riding on the rising smoke as it lifted above the southern wall and watchtowers, and then the immense shadowed shapes of those alien winged beasts against the flame-lit smog: long-tailed and leather-winged, soaring in slow circles overhead like giant vultures deciding which carcass to swoop down for next as the cries and shouts from the battle within continued to echo into the night.

"Come, Sharíf," Josef said, placing a hand on his shoulder and then guiding him away by the elbow. "We cannot linger."

The first fishing village was empty when they reached it; the pens and stables deserted, the granaries ransacked and the few houses and sheds that there were, abandoned. Josef and the guards wandered the riverbank for boats and rafts whilst the others scavenged for food and provisions among the housing. The shore was empty, only the cut bindings of the dock ropes floating in the water near the moorings. By the time they stalked back up from the banks the others were ready to continue on. Maybe they'd find better at the next village; which they would need to, Sidon knew. If they were forced to journey the whole way to Qadesh on foot it would likely take them the remainder of the night, and there would be little cover between here and there if they were to be pursued.

Painfully, Sidon parsed it all out in his mind. Hanesda taken, half-destroyed. The crown city, the jewel of the Five Lands and the only home he'd ever known, usurped by creatures from another world accompanied by Kivites in their thousands and the claims of an apparently resurrected brother. He imagined his mother – Chalise, daughter of Sulamaar of the house Saliph, Sharífa of the Sovereignty, wife and killer of Helgon the Wise and perhaps partly responsible for the attempt on Sidon's own life too – now sitting in the throneroom, or whatever was left of it, with her favoured firstborn upon the ivory and bronze seat they'd come to steal like thieves in the night.

"How can this be happening?" Sidon murmured, and then turned to look at Josef walking beside him. "How?"

They walked for an hour through the night, the quiet drift of the Swift beside them and the silvery flicker of the moon bouncing over its gently shifting current as Sidon continued to try to map it all in his mind.

"Are you alright, Sharíf?" Josef asked.

"Yes... No..."

"We *will* reach Qadesh, Sharíf. We'll get horses, warn the cityguard, then journey on to Sippar, or perhaps even Qalqaliman by the South Sea Gulf. Far away from here. Where we can consolidate, gather forces."

Sidon looked at him. "Tell me, Josef. Have you ever seen creatures like those we just saw over the city?"

Josef somehow managed to look even more sober than usual. "No, Sharíf."

Sidon glanced to Josef's brother, Daneel, walking and chattering agitatedly with Noah and Tamar on the path ahead. "Yet you are unmoved."

"I must remain calm to do my duty, to serve you as I ought."

Sidon looked at him again, and then to Daneel, trying to recall memories of his own brother as he watched him – the vague image of Joram as a child, sitting cross-legged in front of him in the grass on a sunny day and handing him a spoon he was trying to teach him to hold, both of them smiling and giggling each time it slipped from Sidon's stubby fingers. "You're so different, the two of you," Sidon murmured, his eyes still on Daneel, walking and chattering ahead. "It has always been that way?"

Josef followed Sidon's gaze to his brother. "Ever since we were children."

"But you love him."

Josef hesitated, apparently thinking about it. "He is my brother, Sharíf. He will always be my blood."

"Yes... I suppose he will, won't he."

"The crown city will be retaken," Josef said, leading them back onto more familiar ground. "We will go south and gather men."

"And how many men must be gathered to destroy those winged... whatever they are?"

"Daragaurs," Tamar said over her shoulder ahead of them.

"What?"

"Those creatures. That's what they're called."

"You know of them?"

"I do. All my people do. You speak to the right scribe you can even read about them. Although those writings are not so simple to find as they once were. Almost all of them are now destroyed. The work of the Cull. Dumea is probably the best place to go to find what remains of them now."

"That would be over a week's journey to the west, along the straight," Josef answered.

Tamar shrugged. "Do as you please, but you want to know where they can be studied, that's the place."

"How is it you know of them?" Sidon asked.

"My mother and father told me of them from when I was a child. Used to tell all of us by the fire each night, a different story each time, but we'd hear plenty about daragaurs in most of them… From Eram, my people, by the southern coast. We know true histories there," she decided to add. "Not the tales you get taught here in your cities."

"Tales…" Sidon said.

She shrugged. "You people wouldn't know true histories if they came and slapped you in the face, which I suppose you could say is half the reason they just have."

Josef was stepping forward to take hold of her for her impudence when Sidon lifted his hand, gesturing calm. He'd spent almost his whole life being told how things were, and how they were meant to be, and now Hanesda was lost, his mother was a betrayer, his uncle too, and his brother, apparently alive, was attempting to usurp his throne. "I want to hear what she has to say," Sidon decided.

Tamar shrugged again. "There's not much more *to* say. Daragaurs are joybloods, the seed of Markúth, taken and mixed with other beasts."

"I thought Markúth was just a story."

"What just happened back in that city look like just a story to you? What you want to worry about is the others he'll be bringing after him."

"What do you mean?" Sidon asked, frowning. "What others?"

"You know. The others. All the names you've learned to think belong to children's tales, the names you use to mark the months of your year. Yirath, Gilamek, Talagmagon, Adramelec, Armaros… they're all coming, birthing themselves into the world to finish their war."

"War?"

"The first and last war. The Godswar. The war the old stories all speak of." She glanced to Noah and Daneel beside her. "This is like speaking to children. Are you taught anything here?"

Again, Sidon lifted his arm to ward Josef off. "So, what would you do," he asked, "were you Sharíf for a day, or more?"

Tamar pulled a face, her eyebrows lifting, and glanced again to the others before answering. "Well. I don't know much of anything about things like that. But me, I'd want to get safe. I'd want to learn all that could be learned about the gods and their fiends – daragaurs, other joybloods and so forth – seeing as you're all sorely lacking in your knowledge. And then I suppose I'd want to wrangle out whatever means I could to get rid of them. All things I'd have to go to Dumea for though, or maybe further south to Súnam. They have priesthoods there, especially in the crown city, Nubassa. But both are a fair way from here whichever way you slice it."

Sidon nodded, almost walking beside her now as they continued along the road in the dark. "I appreciate your counsel," he said, and then turned to Josef. "What do you think?"

"Only what I have said, Sharíf. Once we reach Qadesh you will be able to strengthen. You have friends there. You have friends to the east, as well as to the north."

"But how many friends? My mother is the daughter of King Sulamaar of Calapaar. What guarantee he will remain loyal to *me*? My uncle, Játhon, is husband to Queen Satyana of Hikramesh, the daughter of King Jashar of Harán. There is no way to know how far my mother's influence reaches now. They could have been planning this whole thing for months, maybe even years. Mother's hand may stretch to the High East as far as Kaloom for all we know. No. I cannot trust them. Not yet. Qadesh, Qareb, Sippar, Qalqaliman – they will remain loyal, that much I know. But the others are a guess at best, for now at least. And who knows how many of the governors will have even made it out of the city? Many of them had remained following the Feast...

"We will go to Qadesh, as you have suggested, and send word south from there. What they have done to Hanesda will be to our advantage. It is the jewel of the Five Lands, the home of much of our trade. The merchant towns to the south will not abide its destruction quietly."

They continued south along the Swift, passing through further empty fishing villages on the river's other side before eventually sighting the Bulapa lake and the walls of Qadesh as the sky began to lighten beyond the mountains to the east. Sidon exhaled in relief, exhausted, feet aching as they glimpsed the light of the watchmen's fires winking through the peepholes of the twin watchtowers flanking the city's northern gate.

Even as they neared, they could hear the disquiet within the walls. The inhabitants of the evacuated villages along the river behind them, and the escapees who'd made it out of Hanesda's south gate, all cramming their way into Qadesh's comparatively modest environs. The word from the crown city had probably spread to the various surrounding villages, drawing their settlers to the city in search of refuge.

Daneel glanced up at the tall wooden doors of the gate and sniffed. "Sounds busy."

"That it does," Josef replied, then turned to Sidon. "We should ask for the governor?"

"Assuming he made it out of the crown city."

The gatekeeper, haggard and irritable, came down after a brief exchange with Josef from his perch above, the doors hinging open for him to inspect the latest in what had clearly been a long line of new arrivals. The man went from bored and surly disinterest to fretting flustered obeisance when he saw Sidon close up and was shown the Sharíf's signet ring.

"Majesty. Forgive me… Your clothes… and here on foot… We get so many pretenders. Tonight especially, there's been so many, and–"

"It's fine. If you could have a horse and carriage brought…"

"Of course, my king. Right away. Right away." He turned, gesticulating and shouting for the gate to be opened and for transport to be brought.

A few moments later Sidon was sitting in the back of a carriage with Josef – Daneel and the others in another – as their caravan carried them along the main road of Qadesh. As he glanced out of the window, Sidon couldn't help thinking about the last time he was here, rolling through the streets of Qadesh to the governor's house ahead of his planned wedding to a rich merchant's daughter from Tresán. The streets had been pleasant then, lightly peopled with drunken fishermen coming in from the lake beyond the walls, sprawled along the sides of the roadways singing and japing as the royal caravan slowly rolled by. Now these same streets were thick with villagers from beyond the city, clustering along the paving or sitting on walls with blankets on their heads like shawls or wandering aimlessly about the city's cobbled lanes – families, elderly stragglers, agitated men and women clutching bedrolls under their arms – ambling aside to allow the caravan through as it made its way down the curving thoroughfare toward Qadesh's municipal borough.

The crowds had thinned by the time they reached the governor's house, marshalled by cityguards and footmen who'd arrived from the crown city.

Surprisingly, it was Yassr, the governor himself, who came out to greet them as they slowed to a stop.

"Thanks to our fathers, Sharíf, you are alive." He hurried panting to the caravan as Sidon stepped down to alight from the carriage. "I'd feared the worse. I'd thought of every worst thing when I saw the Forum fall." He came to a halt before Sidon, breathing hard, as the servants came out to take what little belongings Sidon and the others had managed to bring with them from Hanesda. "You are well. That is all. That is everything now. You are well."

"As are you, thankfully, Yassr."

The governor glanced at the others with him, eyeing the scruffily clad Tamar and Noah in puzzlement before turning back to Sidon to usher him forward into the building. "And your mother?"

"She remains within the city," Sidon said tonelessly.

Yassr seemed to read meaning there and swiftly moved onto other things. "Tubal and Sufiya are here, and Malkezar was able to escape also, but he has gone on to Sippar to prepare the city. Elia too is here, she plans to go on to Qalqaliman to make preparations also."

"That is good. I may well be travelling with her. I plan to go south to gather our armies there. I would speak to the governors here before I do. And then I must rest."

"Of course, Sharíf."

"Has there been any word of the general?"

"Gahíd? No. Not yet. But if there is any man who will have found a way out of that mess it is him."

"Let us hope so, Yassr."

Sidon waited until they were through the tiled lobby of the governorhouse and out of earshot of the others before stopping and turning to face Yassr. The older man carried on for a few paces before noticing that Sidon had halted. He walked back to him, puzzled. "Sharíf?"

Sidon looked into the man's eyes. "Did you know what was coming, Yassr?"

"*Know?* Majesty… I am sorry for what I did. Truly. But I could never… An attack on the crown city. The destruction… I could never have any part in such a thing. I cannot believe the queen mother could knowingly involve herself in such a thing either."

"You may come to find yourself disappointed then, Yassr. It was she who took me down to the bunker when the fires and fighting started. Not only did she know what was coming, she knew by whose hand."

"You are certain?"

"Yes. She had the invaders' leader brought to the bunker, and then stood with him."

Yassr became even more confused. "The invader? He was brought to you, by the Sharífa? Does he yet live, this man?"

"He does. Because of who he is."

"I don't understand, Sharíf."

"He is a man I was told was dead, as were we all. But my mother knew different. The one who has invaded the Five Lands, who has brought ruin to Geled, Çyriath and now the crown city itself, calls himself my brother, Yassr. He calls himself Joram son of Helgon, and he seeks to take my throne."

TWENTY NINE

SHRINE

Neythan had tried to ignore it but it had been getting harder of late – that dull aching fragility skimming along the edges of his thoughts like a cold breath: the irrational and random bouts of fear, and the strangely vertiginous sense of peril they evoked within him, as if his increasingly brittle sha had been teetering precipitously at the edge of a cliff, buffeted now and then by sudden gusts of wind. He breathed deep, squatting amid the sedge and rushes with Arianna and Nyomi as they surveyed the scruffy township, trying to contain the private storm within, trying to focus on the matter at hand.

The marshland spanned the length of the village along its northern side, stretching west toward where the waned sun sank beneath the hills and peeked between the thin striated bars of cloud. Neythan glanced up at the evening sky to watch its colours, often one of his favourite things about this time of year; the summer days waiting to tip toward something cooler, and the evenings, as though to salute the season's shift, splaying their colours across the expanse in a diffuse haze like some crazed painter's dream. But even that seemed different now, tinged by that same shadow – the sky's patterns shorn of their wonder, imbued instead with a grim and vague menace, as though the night was watching him, hiding some secret miasmic presence waiting to find him out.

"Neythan?"

He started, glanced aside to Nyomi crouching next to him as she watched the edge of the village from the reeds. It had taken a few days to reach the Riverlands, and then almost a whole day to arrive here from its borders, navigating the sodden earth and the half-mile wide patchwork of bogs and ponds whilst Nyomi, still drained from her exploits in Hanesda, kept falling asleep on the way. She turned groggily toward him now, placing a hand on his shoulder as she looked into his eyes.

"You weren't listening, were you?" she asked.

"Listening?"

Her eyes flitted to Arianna and then back to him again. "Is something wrong, Neythan?"

"I'm fine. Just a little tired. The journey…"

"You're sweating."

"It's the journey. I'm fine."

He turned his attention back to the village and tried to ignore the concerned exchange of glances between Nyomi and Arianna as they leaned back behind him. Arianna had taken to watching him like some kind of invalid of late – her eyes drifting toward him as they sat around the campfire in the evenings, or glancing over at him for no apparent reason as they'd journeyed west across the fields after crossing the Swift. It was like she could sense the shadow clinging to his sha, corrupting him from the inside, emitting its drab sapping presence like creeping decay.

"This place," Neythan said to change the subject. "It doesn't look like what I saw in the vision, when I touched the ring."

"That's because the village has been here for less than two centuries," Nyomi answered. "It was settled back when Kaldan the Quiet built Qareb by the Amber. What you saw in your vision, what the jewel chose to show to you, was from a long time before that, back when these lands were unsettled and wild… The tree you saw lies that way," she pointed north, "just beyond the village's border."

Neythan looked to where she pointed, gazing doubtfully at the low and messy skyline of shanty housing. "You're sure?"

"I am. It is a bloodtree. It's why it was the only one in your vision that you saw alive."

Arianna looked at her. "Sorry, what? A *bloodtree?* Here?"

"The Shedaím were not the first to practice the ways of the sha, Arianna. Many of the disciplines were begun by the very priesthoods the Brotherhood was founded to destroy."

"You're saying there are bloodtrees beyond Ilysia?"

"Not many. But yes, there are some. Including the one here."

"And how do *you* know this place?" Neythan asked. "How do you know of the bloodtree?"

"I just do."

Which was typical. *Just* like Filani, Neythan thought to himself, looking at Nyomi; that same infuriatingly cryptic habit of saying as little as possible, and of turning the little she said into some kind of obscure riddle, as though she was a teacher of things they didn't deserve to know. Neythan turned to her. They'd come too far for secrets now, they'd seen too much. "I will not play this game anymore. You must speak plainly with us now. No going back, remember? That's what you told us. Well, it must go both ways."

Nyomi held his gaze, saying nothing.

"You need to tell us how you know about the bloodtree."

For a moment she didn't answer, just matching him with her gaze, as though stubbornly waiting him out, and then she sighed with a little shake of the head and looked back toward the village. "I know, because… it was my bloodtree, Neythan."

Arianna almost choked. "*What?*"

"There is a shrine here. Very old," Nyomi went on. "The villagers who first settled this place used it as a monument to their fathers, a place to pray to them. But it's not the purpose for which it was first built. This place is sacred. Marshland, to those who understand it, almost always is – the priests used to call it nature's bridge, a way to mark the boundary between earth and water, just as it marks the edge between this world and the next."

"What are you saying?"

"I'm talking about why Elias is here… This shrine, this whole village now perhaps, it is a birthplace. Elias has come here to attempt to pass over, or help someone else to."

"Pass over?" Arianna said.

"Yes, enter the Aeon, or help someone exit it to come here."

"*Someone.*"

"The Aeon is not the dwelling place of mortals, Neythan. We can only assume that Elias plans to invoke a god." Nyomi glanced at the sky, considering the waning light and taking another deep breath. She'd been doing a lot of that, as though permanently fatigued. "We should hurry. The sun is low but he cannot start until nightfall. If we reach him just as he begins, he will be vulnerable." She turned to them. "I will not be able to do as I did in Hanesda. I'm still weakened. But we can stop him…" She glanced once more at the sky. "Come. There will not be much time."

She strode toward the dirt track that bordered the township, partitioning it from the brief strip of green that edged into the marshland surrounding on all sides. There were people walking up the lane – a crew of crab farmers in leathers, behind them a pair of young boys, bared chests, scrawny and bronzed, carrying mosquito nets over their bony shoulders like strung capes and letting them drag in the dirt behind them. Neythan and Arianna followed Nyomi as she led them up the lane and into the glut of housing, shanty sheds of barkwood and thatching, some daubed with pitch, presumably to seal out the ever-present stench of the marsh. The houses sat closer together the further they went in, clustered in disorderly rows with narrow backlanes running between them like gutters, the furrows of moss and grass worn into twin grooves by the wheels of whatever barrowcarts daily pulled or pushed along their lengths.

They turned into another dirt lane of pebbles, grit and flattened weeds, and continued toward a matrix of alleys walled by rails of wooden spokes tethered by twisted yarn. It was as though the whole place had been pillaged of stone, left almost entirely devoid of any brickwork.

"We are close," Nyomi said. "Just beyond this lane."

They rounded an open-walled shack full of tools and chopped timber and came into a brief clearing of clayey dirt, the houses set back from it in a circle like onlookers around a stage, and a shrine of painted stones and charred wood in the middle, and then, facing them, stood Caleb and Elias, waiting expectantly.

Confused, Neythan slowed. Of all the scenarios they'd expected to discover upon finding Elias, him standing there with Caleb, shoulder to shoulder like a pair of companions and Caleb completely unfettered or restrained, had simply not been one of them. Neythan looked them over warily.

"Caleb?"

The little man just stared dull-eyed at Neythan as if he were a stranger, his arms hanging loose and relaxed on either side. Glancing at the others, he almost seemed to sigh, as though disappointed, before returning his strange hollow gaze back to Neythan. "You should not have come here, Neythan."

Neythan scanned the periphery, checking angles. The clearing was a glorified enclosure for all intents and purposes, a few narrow dirt lanes leading off from it to the north. An ideal place for an ambush.

"There is no trap," Caleb said. "But you should not have come. You should go."

"We've come here for you, Caleb. To free you."

"I am already free. I have decided to remain with Elias. You should go back while you can. I won't be coming with you."

Neythan, stunned, just looked at him.

"He has made his decision, Neythan," Elias said. "You should respect it, and make yours."

"What have you done to him?" Arianna asked.

"Ah, you see? So easy to blame others, isn't it?" Elias replied. "What a soothing balm that must be. For every displeasing thing to be the work of another."

Emerging from the alleys skirting the clearing on either side, a pair of hooded figures stepped beyond the shadows to flank Caleb and the chamberlain, facing Neythan, Arianna and Nyomi.

"And here was I thinking you could learn the lessons of your past," Elias said. "That is what all this is about, you know, Neythan. Learning. You should be grateful; not all are offered the opportunity. Not all are granted a choice."

It was growing dark, the sky an indigo shroud overhead, dimming away from the gentle golden hue lining the horizon to the west where the sun was still setting behind them. As he removed his hood, Elias took up a torch from the low wall of the shrine behind him, his crinkled features shining beneath the flames as he held it before him.

"Although when it comes to you, I suppose blind persistence should be no surprise. But I think tonight you shall learn the depth of that flaw."

Had to be something to do with the shrine, Neythan decided. They'd used it perhaps, found a way to somehow twist Caleb's thoughts. Neythan eyed it – the way the boulders were laid up in a sort of curved circular wall with a gap at the front, the whole thing resembling a small roofless hut. Effigies of wood and stone sat stacked against the back of its interior, mixed with what looked like animal bones, long bars of dirty enamel leaning in disorderly angles amid the assorted lumps of timber and straw. Someone had created stick figures to sit at the front, limbs and spine joined together with yarn, and the heads built from straw-stuffed parcels of wool. Neythan paced slowly, surveying it all as Arianna, to his left, began to fan out, eyeing the hooded figures as she widened her angle.

"Caleb, whatever they have done to you can be undone," Neythan said.

"You will pretend to care for him then," Elias answered, "after the way you have treated him? Yes, that's right. Caleb and I spoke about that," Elias shook his head in mock disapproval. "A sad thing, to fail to keep a promise to a friend. Can you really blame him for finally tiring of it? You see, we haven't *done* anything to Caleb, Neythan. We simply helped him to see the truth and offered to help, to bring him the rest and justice he and his family have so richly deserved.

The justice you were unwilling to fulfil your vow to him to dispense. In return, he has agreed to help us."

Neythan looked at Caleb whose head was now bowed, willing him to lift his gaze to meet his, to provide some tacit sign, a hint to refute what Elias was saying. "No," Neythan answered, speaking to the chamberlain. "You're lying. Caleb wouldn't…"

"Wouldn't what? Wouldn't grow tired of waiting? Tired of your broken promises? Your Brotherhood murdered his *family*, Neythan. Killed them like dogs. And he came to you for help. And you chose not to."

"I was going to," Neythan said, eyes still on Caleb. "I *am* going to."

"*Are* you?" Elias asked back. "When? Next week? Next month? A year from now? How long should a true friend wait for help from the ones who claim to care for him? How long had you made him wait already?"

"Caleb. Please…"

"For what its worth, I understand," Elias continued. "Truly, I do. Yes, so they murdered his family. Yes, you made a covenant to help him. But sometimes there just isn't time, is there. Sometimes there are other priorities, more important things. Sometimes it cannot be helped. I sympathise, Neythan. Truly, I do. I see how difficult these things can be. But you should not blame Caleb, or me, for your failure to keep your promise."

"Caleb, listen to me–"

"But I am tired of listening, Neythan," Caleb finally said, halting Neythan in his tracks. "I am tired. I only wanted to know my family's killers, and see them punished. That was all. That is all I have. There is nothing else…" He lifted his head to meet Neythan's gaze, his eyes watery. "You should go now."

And with that, Caleb turned away, rounding the low walls of the shrine to walk toward the back end of the clearing.

Neythan was moving forward to follow when Elias stepped into his path, blocking his view. "He has chosen, Neythan. Time for you to choose too."

"There is nothing to choose."

"Ah, come now, Neythan. That's only because you haven't thought it through. You think you must do as you have been bid, by the Watcher, by a scroll." He shrugged at Nyomi, standing quietly to the side of him. She appeared to be struggling for breath now, taking furtive gulps of it from the air. "You even think you must do as you've been told by her and her liar of a friend, Filani. But you see they've kept things from you, refused to show you the options. But I will not, Neythan. I will be honest with you, as I was with Caleb. All you need do is see our side."

Neythan drew his sword, moving to step around Elias and the hoods to go after Caleb. One of the hooded figures stepped with him, again blocking his path.

"Ah, that's right," Elias said. "Rude of me. I haven't introduced you all have I?"

The figures removed their hoods. Two women. One a Súnamite, the other Sumerian, or perhaps mixed.

"Zora and Shimeer. Shedaím of course, and very eager to meet the pair of you, the famed betrayers responsible for destroying the Brotherhood."

The women unsheathed swords from beneath their cloaks and began to approach.

Neythan glanced aside. "Nyomi?"

Elias scoffed. "You look to her for counsel? Better to lean on a splintered staff than trust this one, Neythan. She has kept so much from you, she lies to you even now. It's why we have been so willing to be patient, forbearing. I would have been sad for you, after all your chasing, knowing you would have died here having not learned the truth, having not been offered a chance to choose it."

Neythan, glancing beyond them to the withdrawing Caleb, lifted his sword as he locked gazes with the chamberlain, pointing to enunciate his words. "That's funny. Because when I kill you, I will feel nothing at all."

"Kill me?" Elias inclined his head and smiled. "Are you still so foolish, Neythan?" He gestured to the women. "Zora, Shimeer, deal with the Súnamite. I've decided I will have a little fun after all."

The women turned and moved toward Nyomi as Elias placed the torch back in its sconce on the shrine's wall. He smiled again at Neythan, and then began strolling across the brief space toward him, unarmed.

Arianna came rushing in before the old man had made it halfway across the clearing. She swung her sword, slamming it toward Elias's gut as though to chop him in half. Elias stepped in and caught her wrist, then pivoted, turning his back to smack an elbow into her chest as he yanked the blade from her hand. Neythan moved forward as she staggered, his sword thrusting at the chamberlain's gut. Elias danced aside, swatted Neythan on the arm with the blade, and then turned, lightning quick, to whip his fist into Arianna's ribs with a swiftness that ripped the air. The blow sent her skywards, spinning slowly as she crashed through the wall of a shack on the far side.

The chamberlain turned slowly back to Neythan as he climbed to his feet. "You know what separates youth from the wise, Neythan? An acquaintance with limits – one's own, and those of others. A lesson you remain too stubborn to learn." The old man glanced down at the hand he'd just struck Arianna with, flexing the fingers. "I know what you're thinking," Elias continued as Neythan stared at the wall forty feet away that Arianna had just been thumped through. "There will be a way to defeat me. Surely, there will be a way. But you are wrong, Neythan. Just as you have been wrong from the very beginning. I will teach you that tonight, acquaint you with your limits... And then I shall make you watch as I teach your friend, Arianna, too."

Neythan came rushing forward, sword flurrying. The chamberlain leaned back, swaying one way and then the other as Neythan's blade struck futilely at the air around the old man's ears. Neythan feinted with his blade, and then turned to throw a kick. The chamberlain caught it easily and swept Neythan's ankle, tossing the caught heel contemptuously aside and flinging him onto his back.

"Really, Neythan? That's the best you have to offer?"

Elias paused, as though waiting for an answer, and then swung a shin into Neythan's gut, lifting him from the dirt and propelling him into the wooded wall of a shack on the opposite side. Neythan hit shoulder first, scraping down the shingles into a heap. He rolled, struggling to breathe, and tried to get up, but couldn't, something pinching and trapped inside. He shifted onto his other flank, wincing from the pain of what was probably a cracked rib, and turned in time to see one of the women slamming a spinning sidekick into Nyomi's chest, sending her onto her back, skidding in the dirt.

The chamberlain was walking toward him now, strolling leisurely across the square with one hand behind his back like a court cleric.

"You should join us, Neythan. There is a war coming. Not everyone has been granted the chances you have to pick a side."

"The war has already come," Neythan croaked, pushing himself up onto his knees.

Elias just laughed. "That little display in Hanesda? Please. That was mere play. There is a new age dawning, Neythan. One that shall be unencumbered by the kind of sickly attachments you've allowed yourself to be ensnared by. An age of *kings. Real* kings." He grabbed Neythan by the scruff of the neck. "Come. You will need to see this." He dragged him on his belly back to the clearing. Nyomi was on the ground now, bloody but still breathing. "Zora, Shimeer, stop playing with her. It's time for Neythan to be freed from the things that hinder him."

Neythan rolled his head as the women stood over Nyomi. He watched as one, heeding Elias's call, began to walk away from the prone woman and toward him, then watched as the other turned and stood over her, Nyomi's body between her feet. The woman axel-gripped her sword and lifted it.

Neythan reached out his hand. "No!"

But the woman ignored him and plunged down with the blade, driving it through Nyomi's chest and then staying there, leaning on the pommel of her sword to watch as the Súnamite's impaled body stiffened, and then slowly relaxed, until all the life had leaked away.

"Always so dramatic, Shimeer," Elias quipped. "Take care of the girl over there by the wall. Zora, come, hold Neythan in place."

The woman handed Elias her sword and took Neythan by the hands. Neythan screamed, his cracked rib burning and stabbing within him as she dragged him across the dirt to a wooden pole by the shrine and shackled his wrists around it, leaving him stretched out on the ground.

"Why are you doing this?" Neythan gasped, looking up at Elias. "Why help these gods? You are as much a son of man as you are of them."

"You think this is about *them?* It is about the way things are, Neythan. It's about nature, beginning again. Not all will be destroyed. Just enough for things to be cleansed. There will still be men when it is over."

"You'll have destroyed the world. You will have set the race of men back centuries."

"Back? You see, that is what blinds you, Neythan. You think that time is a tower. That the more that is added the higher we go; you think that you are better than your fathers because of it, but you are not. Time is no tower, Neythan. Time is a circle. As man endures, so does what is in him. All that is has been, and will be again. Just as day follows night, just as the seasons of the year follow from one to the other. It is nature. There is no escaping it, just as there is no escaping yourself." Elias turned square to Neythan, tilting his head as he stared down to meet his eyes.

"I've seen it, Neythan. It's a truth that only lifetimes can truly teach. You see the generations spread out and realise there is no change in man; for all he learns, however much his knowledge grows, however advanced the societies he builds become, he is still the same. The same greed, the same lusts, the same fears and hopes and pride. The same weaknesses that keep him from obtaining what is before him and becoming what he should. They will always remain, unless he is cleansed."

"Destroying cleanses nothing."

"Wrong. Destroying cleanses *everything.* Like a wildfire, Neythan. When the days are dry and the wind is right it can devastate a forest in hours. But that devastation is only for now. After, what was destroyed is made more fertile than what it was before, and flourishes in ways far richer and greater than the forest that preceded it. I have seen it myself, Neythan. That too is what lifetimes teach you."

Elias squatted down in front of him, leaning on the point of his sword.

"You see? I am not *destroying* the world. I, and others like me, are *saving* it. We will gift man the chance to begin again, this time with the guidance of the Fathers. He shall become far more than what he could ever have been any other way. He shall grow beyond the corruption that plagues him. Because that is what it is, Neythan. A plague. Its reality is as undeniable as its symptoms are predictable. It's what has allowed me to do what has been done. It is the very means by which we are here, in this place.

"You see, we all *want* things, Neythan. That much cannot be denied, not even by me. I want for my god and father, Yirath, and his brothers, to be returned to the world that wronged them. But I knew they could not be returned before their father, Markúth. He had to be allowed to enter first. That is a law of the gods. So I simply used the wants in men, the corruption I've been speaking to you of; wove together the threads of it like a tapestry, because I *could* Neythan. Because man is what he is. All you see now coming to pass was rendered by the fabric of *their* corruption and the skill of my hand. One could not act without the other."

"You are lying."

Elias smiled and leaned in. "Am I? This began *years* ago, Neythan. I plotted for *decades*. Skillfully. Patiently. And predictably, because I learned to look at man for what he is, and not, as you do, for what you hope him to be. This is what Caleb understands and you do not, that even the best of you are corrupt, slaves to your wants…

"Chalise, the queen mother herself, wanted her son, Joram, away from the Five Lands, out of reach of her husband, and was willing to do anything to make it so. Joram, the true heir, would always want his throne back, and comfort from the pain of his exile. And Játhon, well, he wants to be Sharíf. Always has, always will. An unoriginal ambition but an endlessly useful one just the same. But how to get what we want, Neythan? How to take the throne when the Shedaím are in the hand of your enemy who sits on it? How to send away your son from the crown city when your husband is the Sharíf? And so I come, I take their wants and I help them; *and* I use them, for what *I* want…

"Consider, Neythan. It was your own elder, Gahíd, who suggested Yannick's decree, you know. A simple way to distract the throne in order to initiate a coup, all because he *wants* for there to be a man on the throne in place of a feeble child. Of course, he couldn't have predicted how I might use this little want of his to destroy his Brotherhood and thereby remove an enemy. And from there the rest was easy. I'd told Chalise to gain more influence among the council, to position herself as regent in order to oversee the return of her son, Joram, to the throne. I continued to whisper to Játhon of his right to rule, stoking the flames of his own ambitions for power so he would agree to using your pursuit of Arianna as a distraction to help him gain it. I gave Elder Safít names for those belonging to the Fellowship of Truths, so that we could destroy them whilst destroying the Shedaím, removing every enemy that would withstand us. And then, in choosing your friend, Yannick, to be slayed by Arianna, we ultimately chose *you*, Neythan – the strongest and most open of your sharím, knowing how you would break with the disciplines of your order in pursuit of her, because you are all, inescapably, driven by your *wants*."

He smiled again and straightened to his feet. "Do you see, Neythan? Even you are part of this, part of the ineluctible plague of corruption I speak of; like the others, author of the very revolution you are now here seeking to prevent… But… There is still hope for you, a means of redemption, which is why I am here, telling you these things."

Elias nodded across the clearing.

Neythan rolled his head to see.

"It is time to be set free, Neythan," Elias murmured. "Time to die to all that holds you back from what you must choose, and for all that holds you back to die to you."

The Shedaím, Shimeer, had found Arianna's senseless body and dragged it into the space before the shrine. Neythan could see her rousing back into semi-consciousness as the woman tossed her down in the dirt.

"No... No..."

Zora was holding him down now, his hands still shackled by the pole as he struggled, his rib prodding sharply at his innards as he yanked and strained to pull himself free. He didn't feel the raw bleeding skin around his wrists as the chains scraped against them, biting and rolling against the joints of his thumb and the bones in his hands as he tugged viciously, willing them to crunch and squeeze and shrink against each other to set him loose as the woman, Shimeer, flopped Arianna onto her back and then stepped around to stand over her. He saw Arianna's head turn toward him then, her eyes, now open, blinking wearily across the short distance to meet his.

"No! No! *No!*"

The heat in his throat and chest, the savage kneedling of his rib against his failing lung as he bucked and screamed, eyes wide, willing Arianna's dazed prone body to rise and fight or flee. And he could see her lips moving, whispering silently toward him, saying words he would never hear as the woman standing over her hefted the blade as before, shifting it into that double-fisted axel grip and lifting it overhead.

"No! Please! *Please!*"

But it was as though the whole world was deaf to him, his impotent pleading words dissipating into the night like vapour as the woman thrust down and plunged the blade into Arianna's gut and stayed there, just as before, leaning her weight over the pommel of her rooted blade as she stared down at her victim, watching Arianna's life leak away.

Neythan grew still, slackening as though the blade had plunged through him instead. And then Elias's face was there, the old man squatting in front of him.

"You will hate me now, Neythan. But you will thank me later. Now you will be able to make the choice you should have made from the beginning, and that you foolishly spurned. Now you can take hold of your true destiny and become the vessel to augur the new world to come. You will be the House of Brothers now. They will abide with you. And you will know power and life like you have never known before. Now you understand man's corruption, and see the futility of your own attempts to undo it. Now you understand the salvation we seek to bring. Now, you are free of the encumbrances that held you back from taking what I now offer. Take my hand now, Neythan, and I will bring you to the shrine, and you will know life like you've never known before. Spurn it, and I will finish what Yirath and his brothers began in that temple in Ilysia, and you will die, right here.

"The choice is yours, Neythan. Death… or life."

The chamberlain held out his hand and waited as Zora undid Neythan's shackles. Shimeer was standing there too now, her dreadlocked hair hanging across her face as she stared down at him on the ground.

"Well?"

Elias was still squatting there, waiting, allowing the weight of his offer to press in, his eyes glittering hungrily in the half-light as he held out his palm like an expectant creditor.

And it was then that Neythan felt the futility of it all, here on the brink of annihilation as the death and life of Elias's ultimatum swung back and forth like a shifting pendulum. Because the chamberlain was right. Why fight? Why try? Why do any of it? He lay there, Elias's face looming over him from out of the night like a ghost, his features seeming to shift in the play of shadows as the flame from the torches began to falter. It was beginning to rain now. The light dying, starting to wink out just as Arianna and Nyomi had.

And it was then that he knew what he would choose, and knew, as he looked up at the chamberlain, that the old man knew it too. He watched as Elias's smile wavered, and then finally flattened. Glancing to the others, the chamberlain shook his head and straightened once more to his feet, dusting his shift down with his hands and smoothing out the creases.

"Shimeer."

The woman came forward again, still working a whetcloth over her blade to presumably clean the blood of the work she'd already done. A meticulous executioner.

"Make it quick," Elias said, his eyes turning toward the periphery. "The villagers are rousing. We will have to leave soon."

Shimeer glanced down on Neythan pityingly, and then nudged his thigh as one might a wounded animal, checking to see what was left of his strength. When she stepped over him, planting her feet either side of his hips, Neythan knew he was ready. So tired, and ready. The pain had already begun to subside with his acceptance, wilting beneath the deadening torrent of grief as his eyes met hers. He breathed, giving himself to the moment, watching the almost ritualistic flourish of Shimeer's hands as she shifted once more into the axel grip. The point of her blade glinted in the guttered light as Neythan looked beyond it, and beyond her, up into the sky above, the night leaning in to offer itself for his perusal this one final time. And that's how he stayed, gazing at the stars through the rain as Shimeer plunged down with her blade, burying the cold steel into his gut as the others watched on. He felt the white-hot pain of it surge through him, blossoming out from the planted sword in his stomach to his flanks and spine like a spreading fire, trapped within. And then he felt it begin to wane and fade, cooling along his limbs as a rapid black chill filled him from the inside out, taking him with it, out beyond Elias and the Shedaím and everything he'd ever known or would as Shimeer leant over him like she had the others, watching him die.

"I am sorry," she whispered, and then straightened, allowing him to leak away into the cold black night, fizzling out by degrees like the drenched torch as the rain began to hammer down.

THIRTY

STARLIGHT

He knows this place, or at least he thinks he does. The arboreal shadows dappling the ground. The autumnal slats of light, casting their amber haze through the immured gloom of the canopy above like beams from another world. Even the way the ground slopes, its curves and dents so familiar, dipping and rising down the hill's steady decline between the gnarled trees. And yet the place seems so different too: altered, worn. The grass is the wrong colour, tinged yellow and brown in place of the rich lush green he remembers, as if the dirt has been dried out from beneath. He can feel the hardness of it underfoot, and a brittleness to the soil, patches of it showing through at his feet like a balding scalp as though the whole place is dying around him. So he turns to survey the rest of it, the familiar jagged row of shelters that foot the slope, cordoned by the thin stream barring the village below from the slanting forest above. From here the settlement seems sparser somehow, emptier, shorn of the usual bustle of people that he would expect to find at this hour.

"Neythan."

He turns to meet the voice and finds a tree instead, broad-trunked and high, its branches stretching out in every direction to offer its thick foliage to the sky. The sun winks down through the boughs and greenery overhead, brightening the pale bark. The trunk's broad girth, the thick sinewy twist of the roots where they knead the earth below, all of it seems too pronounced and vivid somehow, as though the very air is thinner, more clinical, trimmed of the myriad flora of dust and seeds that should be floating meanderingly through it.

"You don't recognise it do you?"

And then she is there. The white, golden-eyed owl perches on one of the lower boughs, staring at him. Her plumage, flecked here and there with silver, ruffles gently in a breeze he can't feel, glinting like armour in the sun. Proud tufts stand atop her head like ears, and her pupils, dilated, and hemmed by the shimmering ring of gold that marks her gaze, stare out to him, containing the world, containing him.

"It is yours, Neythan," she says.

He glances up at the tree once more, bewildered by the towering immensity of it, the scale and span of its shade, reaching out to claim the cloudless expanse above.

"But it is dying," she adds.

It's then he sees the climbing wire of black within the bark, a vein of liquid shadow encased within the wood and running up from the root to clasp the branches. Already he knows what it is, what it will do, and yet his hand, unthinkingly, is reaching out toward it, drawn as though by gravity to feel the heat or cool of the dark and toxic current as it scythes up through the wood. He watches as the vein blots beneath his poised fingers, spreading into tiny black capillaries as though knowing he is there, reaching toward him, trying to get out...

And then, abruptly, he is elsewhere, standing on a vast twilit shoreline, the sky a deep aqueous blue and riddled with stars, like luminous dust scattered across the expanse. The moon is low, and too big, dominating the vista as it hangs above the still sea like a toe waiting to test the waters.

"I've been here before," he says, transfixed by the horizon, his gaze locked to the moon.

"You have been everywhere before, Neythan. At least everywhere you will go. It is like that for everyone."

"That makes no sense."

"Are you still waiting for things to make sense? Even now?"

"I want to know what is true," Neythan eventually answers. "I want to understand."

"Then do so."

"How?"

"A thing's path lies in itself, Neythan. It is the sha that knows all things. If you wish to know, then you must look to it."

"But I can't… I don't know how."

"It is a discipline of the sha. Is that not what you were taught?"

He tries to think about it but is distracted by the water. Strange how the ocean, as vast as it is, can be so still, and yet it is not silent. He can feel the power and surge of it roiling, a constant brooding weight buried within its depths, like the waves and their tumult have been entombed deep below the surface. And for a moment it's as though the sea is speaking to him, furtively offering up its answer through the loud stillness of its water, showing the truth back to him like a cloudy mirror.

"I don't know how to trust what I was taught anymore," Neythan says, still gazing at it. "Everything is different now. Everything is gone."

"Everything goes, Neythan. And nothing does. That is the secret within every seed. All it shall be, it already holds. Everything is new. Everything is old."

Neythan tries to take hold of the words and believe they are some kind of answer, that they can somehow make sense of the bone-deep loss aching along the hollows of his soul, but he can't; the words are like oil to him, slipping away and leaving their elusively smooth residue like a footprint in his thoughts. He breathes, trying to still his sha as before and reach after it, trying to find an answer or whatever the Watcher will give.

"Did you know it would be this way?" he asks.

"Your path is within you, Neythan."

"If my path is within me then why have I failed?"

"Failure. Victory. These are childish thoughts. There is only the seed."

"But I don't understand what that means."

"You must look to your sha. You must look to the seed."

"But why? Why does any of it matter?"

But she says nothing, her presence lingering at his shoulder like a waiting judgement as he gazes out at the night and the waters and that great pale moon. And the moon seems to be speaking to him too, mourning silently.

"I'm dying aren't I," he says finally. "I can feel it. There is only… loss… it is all I can feel, all that there is."

"That is the shadow that speaks, Neythan. It clings to you even now, even here. You will find no truth in its whisper. Look and see for yourself."

His gaze drifts downwards and sees it there, creeping slowly up his ankles from where the water laps gently at the shore. A bruise, a shadow beneath the skin, slowly rising up his body from inside as it emits its bleak dark chill. And suddenly it all seems so meaningless, to have heeded the Watcher, to have read the scroll, to be here, now, hovering in this nebulous nexus between life and death. For what?

"Why am I here?" he says. "Filani is gone. Nyomi is gone. Arianna is gone. Caleb is gone. *That* is truth. That is loss. All you offer are questions without answers." He turns from the ocean to face her then and sees her there, standing on the shore with him, facing out to the waters. He is jolted by the immensity of her, a magnitude beyond scale, transcending size, like she is denser than everything else, heavier even than the high imposing cliff that backs the beach behind her. As she turns to look at him, her hair seems to tinkle, a long white dreadlocked mane clinking against her shoulders, arms and waist as though made from crystal. And that same golden-eyed gaze, glinting like distant flame as she towers a full head above his height and stares down.

"Questions, when understood, *are* answers," she says. "But that is not why you are here. You must seek what can be known."

"I want to know why you came to me in the first place. Why choose me?"

"But we do not choose. It is you who must."

"Choose what?"

"Whatever this place seeks to tell you. You have been here before, just as you have said, and yet you fail to heed its voice. There is a void that cries through you, Neythan. There are laws between you and I."

"That is what you say to keep from speaking plainly."

"No, Neythan. It is what keeps you from understanding what I speak. The laws do not belong to us, they are in you. The babe in his mother's arms does not understand her ways or her speech. He must grow to do so, as must you, if you wish to understand. You must learn what this place seeks to speak. You must relive the pictures that have come to pass."

So he looks again to the ocean, his gaze tracking the horizon and calling to mind his every previous encounter here. The Watcher by the waterfall. The thing that had taken him in the inn. Always bringing him to stand or sit before an unending vista to view the sea as it meets the sky. But that too makes no sense, offers no message or lesson, and what does it matter now anyway, seeing as he is going to die? Just like Mother and Father, just like the Brotherhood, just like Caleb and Filani and Arianna and…

"There is only death," he says. "I was told it would be this way, that they would do what they have done and take everything and everyone from me, piece by piece, one by one." The god's words echo back to him on the stirring sounds of the water's subaqueous sift. "I am not some hero in a story," he says. "It is all as I was told it would be… And now they are all gone, everyone I cared for, and it is my fault."

He is about to turn from the sea back toward her when he notices the rain, starting in fine drops but not in a way he understands. He watches the spits of water, rising instead of falling, ascending in slow tiny globules like reversed snowfall, as though time itself has dilated and rolled back on itself.

"*What... you...*"

He scans the horizon: more drops drifting sluggishly up toward the sky, some of them, if he stares hard enough, even hovering still in the air, just hanging there like motes of dust snagged by a warm draft, held still for inspection, his very gaze a fissure through time. Above it all the clouds and sky shudders and quakes whilst the moon continues to glare steadily through the surreal tumult like a giant shining eye. And then even the moon too seems to respond, touched by his gaze – wires of light flashing across its broad pale globe in bolts of tiny electric blue. And it's as though the firmaments are alive, trembling under the weight of some new unseen pressure whilst the shore he stands upon maintains its solid still calm.

"What is happening?"

"The time is short. You must seek what must be known, Neythan. To seek aught else is meaningless."

The moon's light blinks brighter as she speaks, touching the sea and igniting the water, its light spreading slowly out from the horizon like liquid wildfire.

"But why? Why me?"

"The blade is not *chosen* for battle. The blade is *for* battle. Its path and its purpose are one. Like a bloodtree and the one to whom it belongs. It lives only to measure the road to the secret within its seed; the truth within its blood. It shall tell the story of the one to whom it is bound. Because every story is one story. The oldest story of all. All is one. One is all. Everything is old. Everything is new. You must learn the secret of your seed."

The light on the water swells, consuming the horizon, moving toward them where they stand on the shore as the horizon detonates, flinging gouts of blazing sea skywards in the distance to obscure the moon. As Neythan staggers back from the shoreline he sees the stars begin to fall, a billion tiny lights cascading down the dark blue expanse as the rain continues its slow floating ascent.

Neythan turns to the Watcher beside him, standing like an alabaster tower, fluorescent against the night. "What is happening? What does it mean?"

"It means it is the end, Neythan," she says, then turns to face the ocean as it explodes, its gleaming waters leaping into the sky to wall off the moon and everything else as the buried waves finally break free, sweeping the shore to devour beach and Watcher and all else.

EPILOGUE

DAWN

"You said we'd be gone by now."

"I said we'd leave when the time came."

"I think it has come and gone several times over since we've been here. And you've still not told me what we are waiting for."

"I told you, all waiting is learning."

"And I'm telling *you* that *that* is ridiculous."

"Because you don't like waiting."

"Because it's pointless."

"Nothing is pointless, Yasmin. Not when seen truly."

She watched as Sol dipped the skillet to the fire, making the strips of rabbit flesh hiss in their pan as the fat sizzled and cooked. They'd been here weeks now, studying the pages of her dead brother's letters and writings, learning the traditions and tales of extant faiths and forgotten mystics whilst the shaven-scalped black man prodded her with his smug aphorisms and questions to test her. Still, it would be worth it to find her son, Noah. And Sol had said he would still be alive somewhere. He'd promised that, and by some unknowable sense within her, Yasmin could feel he wasn't a liar.

They sat on worn flat pillows of cotton-stuffed hemp, their bedmats rolled neatly to one side, watching the plain beyond the river as the smell of the cooking meat drifted with the breeze in the other direction, moving toward the gurgling, frothing current of the Crescent behind them. Better that way, she supposed, away from any predators on this side. But Yasmin still felt nervous about being here. The craggy outcrops of rock, breaking up the landscape to the north with their shadows, and the sparse vegetation along the stretches of dusty plain beyond the river, a haunt for snakes and scorpions or perhaps other prowling things worse than those. Several nights ago, she'd spied the glinting eyes of a watching something from the night beyond the campfire, twin coins of yellow light, hovering in the dark – a jackal perhaps, maybe a wolf – staring hungrily at her from the darkness whilst the black man slept. The week before, they'd heard the howling bellow of a bear from the other side of the river, and before that the growling hiss of a rattlesnake in the craggy pockets of stone surrounding their camp. All of which made Yasmin uncomfortable, like the land around them was agitated by their presence, telling them they shouldn't be here, that they didn't belong, whilst the black man spoke only of waiting.

She glanced toward the rugged country west of them where the land sloped away, showing through to a forest in the distance lining the riverbank.

"Why do we have to camp up here anyway?" she asked. "Where the whole land can see us, and smell us, not to mention everything we catch and cook."

"As I said, Yasmin. Nothing is pointless, and… it seems your reason is finally here." He nodded to the east behind her, gesturing for her to turn and see for herself.

A lone figure on horseback, picking slowly through the narrow rubbly path of the valley leading into the plain.

"Don't worry, Yasmin. They are friends."

"Friends?"

Shading her eyes from the sun to look more carefully, she saw there were two of them, each on horseback, each hooded, loping steadily up the incline.

It took a half hour for the figures to reach them. Which Yasmin could well understand having taken that route with the man herself the week before, coaxing her horse nervously up the slanting loose terrain to reach this greener crest along the river.

The pair of strangers removed their hoods as they arrived. Two women, both Súnamite. They climbed down from their horses as Sol rose to greet them. And then each removed their cloaks as they came to sit by the cookfire and, beginning with the leader, offered Yasmin a smile.

"Hello again, Yasmin."

Yasmin nodded, still, even now, a little nervous of her. "Imaru."

"You have not met Luavese," Imaru said warmly, introducing the slimmer, younger girl as she folded her legs to sit.

"What news from the city?" Sol asked.

Imaru settled and gazed soberly across the campfire to her master. "It has begun."

"So soon?"

"We'd left before it happened," Imaru replied, "but even from a distance the fires over Hanesda could be seen. We will not have long now."

"And what of the Sharíf?"

"We think he was able to escape, but we cannot be sure. But of the rest, we were able to persuade him. He learned of the plot against him and accepted our counsel. Just not soon enough to prepare the land for what has now begun."

"No matter. It's good you were taken into his confidence. If he survived, he may still prove useful."

Imaru took the dish of bean rice Sol passed over to her, and then shared it with Luavese, who dipped her head in thanks before offering Yasmin, when she saw her looking, another toothy smile. "What of your errands?" Imaru asked.

Sol shrugged, noncommittal. "They've been fruitful enough... for now at least. The boy was on the road south from Çyriath, headed to Hanesda. After that he became harder to see." He gestured lazily at the air, as though half-heartedly shooing away a fly. "A cloak shrouds the child now. Another seer, perhaps."

Imaru slurped, slipping a fingerful of rice into her mouth from the dish with the quick flashing dexterity of a lizard's tongue as she glanced at Yasmin, observing her response. "But he is alive?" she asked carefully.

"Of that I have no doubt," Sol responded. "And his strength grows. I feel him to the south, but precisely where he is remains more difficult. Cloudy."

"You plan to follow him then?"

"I do."

She slurped again at her fingers, bobbing her head to the lifted dish as she took a final swipe at the salty spiced grain. "What about us?" she asked, still chewing. "Perhaps Luavese and I should come with you. Things will be different now the door has opened."

"No. You should return to Súnam, join your mother in Nubassa to help prepare the city. We will be able to meet you there soon enough once we have found the child."

"And what if he is not alone?"

Sol shrugged, smiling thinly. "Well. I am not so old just yet, young one."

Yasmin looked away to the east as they talked, back to the valley the women had journeyed up to join them from. The sun had begun to wink from behind the mountains, scything through the terrain to signal the dawn. She always felt alone when they were together like this – all of them Súnamites; and she, a High Easterner by birth, the lone citizen of the Sovereignty, which, despite the contrast in complexion, remained a thin mark of difference that often only became noticeable in aggregate, when there was more than one of them with her at a time. Even then it was only in little things – the things they would laugh at and why, and, often, even the *way* they laughed, their whole bodies opening to the sound like instruments of music as they rolled and howled and giggled as though possessed by whatever had become the object of their fun. And then there was the way they'd speak sometimes when they were all together, their heavily accented words accelerating, and their gestures becoming as fluid and pronounced as a dance; or the way they would playfully argue when in disagreement, how their eyes would bulge as they shouted and smirked, the whites widening as they moved their hands through the air and then inevitably broke into laughter afterwards.

It made her miss family, those whose humour and ways, through long-ingrained routine, had become shared, and safe. But most of all, it made her miss Hassan. No matter how many times she tried to persuade herself that seeing his body had been for the best, in the small hours, when everything was still and the silt of grief had resettled to the bottom of her, the lie became easier to doubt. She'd lay her head back on the pillow, watching the memories stalk through the shadows like ghosts; Hassan, half-smiling as he gazed toward her that first time in Hanesda. Or laughing with Noah as he played with his pigeons beyond the city walls. Or scribbling by lamplight in one of his many scrolls, his tongue pushed against his inner bottom lip in that earnest childish way of his as he leaned to write. And then afterwards she'd quietly weep from the way each memory panged and twisted so vividly inside her, often lingering long enough for her to forget, for a moment, that Hassan was no longer alive.

There'd been a whole day when she'd thought it had passed. Until, in one of the villages on the way here, she'd seen him striding along the dusty broadwalks as she weaved through a small crowd to catch up. Those thin square shoulders, that long swanish neck, the black sleek neatly cropped hair just the way he always wore it, only for him to turn and reveal himself a stranger, a face she didn't know, and thereby plunge her back into the depths of her bleak sorrow once more.

She would fail to sleep that night, which, thinking back on the memory, probably remained the one thing which she was grateful to be out here for, in the middle of nowhere, away from any crowds and, as a consequence, the risk of evoking the aching flutter that ran through her heart when she'd thought she'd seen her husband, alive from the dead.

Perhaps it was because of this Yasmin felt compelled to stare and wait for several moments before turning to Sol to share what she was seeing in the valley to the east. "Seems you have more of your friends on the way."

Sol broke off from speaking with Imaru and Luavese to gaze to where Yasmin was pointing. Judging by the look on his face, he hadn't been expecting further visitors. So they all sat there, watching tensely as the lone hooded figure continued to drive a cart through the valley pass and then up the shallow incline and along the Crescent toward them.

By the time the figure reached the top, cresting the craggy path before stopping a few paces off from the camp, they were all standing. Yasmin watched Sol, as she often did, and tensed when she observed the stillness of him, his hands hidden dangerously within the folds of his cloak, probably clutching weapons, and his dark face as calm and fixed as stone as the lone figure, still yet to acknowledge or greet them, rummaged in the cartbed before pulling out what looked like a long and unwieldy swaddled weight – the size of a *body* – and heaving it onto their shoulder before lumbering across the short stony distance to join them. The figure knelt to place the body down and then rose again, removing the hood to reveal themselves. Another woman: again Súnamite, but this time older – probably around Yasmin's own age although she couldn't be sure. She always found it difficult to tell with them, and the woman had strange blotches of pale skin interrupting the smooth chestnut brown of her complexion, on her hands, her face, perhaps elsewhere beneath the heavy dark shawl she was clothed in.

"Nyomi?" Sol said, loosening from his stance and stepping forward.

The woman smiled faintly, wearily, and glanced around at the others as she stood on the small ridge of stone that edged the camp. The woman's gaze, as it passed over Yasmin, unsettled her a little: the impassiveness of it, the emptiness, her eyes resting on her for a moment as though Yasmin was more a thing to her than a person, and then moving on to assess the others before returning once more to the black man standing opposite.

"How did you find me?" Sol said.

"Shimeer."

"*Shimeer?* You saw her?"

"Yes. With a man called Elias, a chamberlain in the crown city and adviser to the Sharíf, although I doubt he is still trying to dress himself as that now. In truth, I almost didn't recognise her. She has grown so much."

Sol gestured for her to sit but she wouldn't, which caused all of them to remain standing – the four of them arranged in an untidy crescent opposite this visitor whilst the campfire smouldered at their feet.

"We assigned Shimeer to the chamberlain to watch him," Sol said. "Not something you would approve of, I know. But the times have changed, become desperate. It is natural that our own measures have been forced to do so also."

"Let's not speak of our differences now, Sol. There is no need, not anymore. It's been such a long time." She glanced down at the swaddled body on the ground. "And there are more important things."

She stepped back then, returning her gaze to Sol expectantly, who in turn came forward to kneel beside the body-shaped bundle of cloth the woman had apparently traversed tens of miles of open terrain to bring to him atop this obscure rocky crest by the river. It felt strange to Yasmin, observing the exchange, and then seeing Sol, so often calm and assured – even, at times, recklessly so – now hesitant. She watched the halting way he moved toward the body; the slow, pondering reluctance with which he reached out to the veil of swaddling that had been draped across the face, and then the quiet stillness that came over him as he removed it, the sight of the dead man's face he'd revealed locking him there, engulfing his thoughts. He stayed like that for what seemed a long while before finally straightening to his feet, allowing Yasmin to see the face for herself – youthful, dark olive skin paling to caramel over the bloodless tissues beneath, black kinked hair and, around the eyes and the shapes of the cheeks, a certain familiarity – even… a resemblance?

"You brought him here for me to bury," Sol murmured quietly, glancing back to the woman. "I am grateful, Nyomi."

She bowed her head. "I would have done that... But that is not why I brought him here."

As Sol turned from the body to face her, Nyomi took hold of her shawl and parted it, revealing a blood drenched swathe of bandaging running across her stomach. "I am here because Shimeer was ordered to kill me, Sol. But didn't. The blade of her sword retracted into the handle as she struck her blow – an invention of yours, as I remember." She winced, lowering her shawl again. "Broke the skin but not much further. It was only then that I saw that it was her, as she leant over me, whispering, telling me what to do and where you were to be found. She did the same with Arianna, in the cart back there."

"Arianna is here?"

"She sleeps. She has other injuries, but she too will live, I think. But as for Neythan, Shimeer could do nothing to save him. Elias was standing over her, watching as he asked her to lift the blade." The woman had turned to face the plain now, away from the body on the ground, gazing out across the gently undulant land before them as the sun finally breached its haunts to the east, rising fully above the valley's peaks to gild the landscape and cast long shadows from the stubby outcrops of stone littering the ground. "He is a key now, Sol. He is important."

Sol frowned, reading something in her words. "What are you saying?"

"I'm saying I'm tired, Sol," Nyomi answered. "I begin to feel my time has come..." She turned toward him. "I came here because you know the ritual. And the boy... he cannot be allowed to remain as he is."

"Nyomi... You are asking–"

"I *know* what I am asking. I know... Filani lies in Jaffra, dying. I came to you because you are the only other person I have taught to perform this."

"And you are certain this is what you want?"

"We all have our season, Sol. Remember? The life is in the blood. I have all that is needed with me, in the cart."

When he turned back from the woman to face them, Yasmin thought it was almost as though Sol had forgotten they were there, blinking and glancing, somewhat startled, to each of them rapidly, before again kneeling beside the body on the ground whilst Imaru and Luavese reverently watched on in silence.

"It has been only two days," Nyomi said then. "If you begin tonight, it can be done. But he will need you now. He will not be the same. The old will have gone. All will be new."

Later that night Yasmin sat by the campfire with Sol, resting from working on the ditch they'd spent the remainder of the day digging following Nyomi's arrival and request. The woman sat by her cart out on the ridge now, staring at the night as Imaru and Luavese continued to dig.

"Who is she?"

The way Sol looked at Yasmin across the firelight unnerved her. He seemed drained, withdrawn, his long dark face, for the first time, seeming to show his age as he looked back to the flames and prodded at the pile of chopped timber being consumed by them. He drew some of the ash out and picked it up, rubbing it between his fingers before sprinkling it into the small mortar before him and grinding them in with the rest of the contents the mysterious woman had brought with her. "She carries godsblood," he said finally, "a strong strain of it… She is a firstborn daughter of the Mothers… Perhaps the last one left."

Yasmin, taken aback, studied the woman as she continued to sit there on the ridge, leaning a shoulder against the cartwheel as she quietly surveyed the sky. "Which Mother?"

"Ishmar. She would never tell me that. She probably still won't, even now. But it became obvious after a while. The things she'd speak about, the things she knew."

"How old is she?"

He smiled a little. "She wouldn't tell me that either. A woman's prerogative, she would say… I'm not sure she will even know herself

350

now. Not exactly. But if I were to guess, I'd say she is more than four hundred years old. Maybe even five hundred."

Yasmin sat back, trying to imagine it, a life spread out across centuries, straddling the reigns of sovereigns. The woman was older than the Five Lands itself. "And she was your master, as you are Imaru's and Luavese's?"

"Not master, no. But she did teach me things. And she was… She is one of those with whom we began the Fellowship of Truths, along with another – Filani."

"But you did not continue together, the three of you. You divided."

But Sol just sprinkled something from the woman's pouch into the mortar without answering, and then continued to grind the pestle in.

That night Yasmin tried to watch as much as she could without prying. She helped to finish digging the pit, then sat propped up against a rock with Imaru and Luavese, exhausted, listening to the babbling drift of the river behind them until Sol finally rose from his seat to perform the rite. She watched him sit on the ridge with Nyomi away from the fire, feeding spoonfuls of the mix he'd made into her mouth as they sat and murmured to each other beneath the full moon and clear black sky, of things Yasmin dared not draw any nearer to hear. And then she watched as he drew the blade down her numbed forearms, propping her elbows on pillows before placing the clay bowls under her wrists to collect the blood. She saw him make an unusual gesture then, one she hadn't seen before, touching the knuckle of his thumb to his forehead and then his chest as he bowed his head before her.

After that they waited, staring at the flames of the campfire and listening to the usual scratch and call of the various animals that liked to come out in the dark, as the woman's life slowly eked away.

Death is merely a door, Sol had told her once, a frontier to unknown places to be feared or loved but always revered, and which men, without noticing, pass through many times before arriving to that final rest. Yasmin thought on that as they lowered the woman into the pit and began to shovel the dirt back over her. They'd placed the girl the woman had brought with her by the fire by then, laying her head on a pillow and wrapping her in blankets – Arianna, Sol called her, kneeling to cradle her head as he mingled Nyomi's blood with water and tipped it to her lips to strengthen her.

By the time they came to Neythan's bundled body it was midnight. The dark was chilly but still, and too thick for the plains or river to be seen beyond the meagre halo of the shrunken fire. Sol stripped him to the waist and sat with the boy's cold rigid body in his arms as he opened his mouth and slowly dripped the godsblood in before pouring some out over his wounds. He remained with the boy that way for hours, whispering and pouring, the blood, remarkably, only occasionally dribbling from the boy's lips to run out as Sol carefully, methodically, tipped and waited, allowing the mingled blood and water to somehow soak into the young corpse from the inside until he'd emptied out the pint-sized vessel. After that he lay the boy down again, covering him in blankets and placing him on his own bedmat whilst he lay beside him on the open ground.

Later Yasmin dreamed she was hovering above it all, suspended like vapour as she watched the seasons pass in a hurried manic dance, buds sprouting from stems and blossoming in one sped moment as the clouds raced across the sky. She saw a fruit fall from its sad crooked bough and land in the dirt, eating away as the decay consumed it, the plump ripe flesh crumbling and rotting down to the seed and then the seed itself bulging to splinter from the inside. Its thick dark shell scythed apart to birth the tiny wrangles of fresh pullulant vines from within, tiny fingers of pale green tissue rapidly searching and spreading and grappling with the soil as they burrowed their way down.

It was the sun that woke her, its light grazing and warming her face as it pushed above the valley to repeat its inexorable ascent and wash away the night.

When Sol saw her wake he nodded to her. "Help me, Yasmin." He was crouched over the boy again, propped on his knees across from her and the ashy pile of wood and kindling, leaning over him as he reached down to lift his head. "Hand me the other skin of blood. Over there."

So Yasmin pushed herself up and wandered sleepily over to where Sol had stashed the remainder of what he'd drawn from Nyomi the night before. Hobbling back with the slim, stiff wineskin, almost stumbling in her grogginess before handing it off. Sol received it gratefully without noticing, his motions ragged and rushed now, divorced from the methodical care of the night before as he fumbled the cap loose and again tipped the skin to the boy's lips. The hastily administered blood ran down the sides of the youth's mouth and across his jaw like dirty tears. Which confused Yasmin, considering how judicious Sol had been with it the night before. She was, against her better judgement, about to ask him why when the boy coughed. And then coughed again. Yasmin froze, stunned silent as she watched him gagging on the blood in his mouth as Sol helped him roll onto his side to spill the rest of it out onto the ground. Sol rolled him onto his back again, gasping, his mouth grabbing at the air like a beached fish, his eyes wide, blinking frantically as Sol held him.

"It's alright, Neythan. It's alright."

Finally the boy looked up at him, seeing him for the first time, and settled. "Uncle…" he croaked. And then, his eyes dancing over the sky above, shocked by the light and the air, he began to slow his breathing. "Am I dead?"

Sol looked down on him, softly cupping his jaw in his palm, and smiled. "You were. But now you are alive. You are reborn, Neythan… Everything is going to be different now."

ABOUT THE AUTHOR

MICAH YONGO is a Manchester-based journalist, writer and videographer. When he's not writing articles he can be found lamenting the often rainy weather in his beloved hometown of Manchester (England), working on his true passion – fiction writing – or blogging about the varied things that make the world, and those living in it.

ACKNOWLEDGEMENTS

'It was the best of times, it was the worst of times…' So said one especially talented storyteller way back when; words, in more ways than one, to sum up what has been an amazing but incredibly challenging journey over the last year or so, for all sorts of reasons I won't get into here. Suffice to say, to have also experienced the privilege, pleasure and toil of writing a second novel over this same period is a sort of miracle I still can't quite figure out how I managed, and one that wouldn't have been possible without the support and help of a few special someones along the way.

So, a huge thank you to my family – my mother, Shimeer; my brother, Daniel; my sisters: Iveren, Iember and Hannah, and to my beautiful nephews and nieces whose smiles are so achingly contagious it's hard to believe they don't have supernatural origins… then again, they do. This story is for you, little ones. I hope you get to it later.

Big thanks too to Penny Reeve, for managing to be a spectacular human being, awesome at what you do, and for making this whole being-an-author thing so damn fun. You are a rare and special breed. Nick Tyler, whose effortless suave and wit is so devastatingly charismatic it's almost intimidating. You should actually be a character in a novel… oh wait, now there's an idea…

A special thank you to my editors Simon Spanton Walker and Paul Simpson, savants and oracles both of you. Thanks too to Gemma Creffield, publicity manager extraordinaire; and Eleanor Teasdale for steering this thing through to fruition. And huge thanks to my agent, Robert Dinsdale, for your tireless support and guidance and for generally being every shade of awesome under the sun – I salute you.

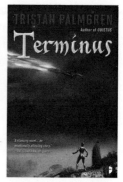
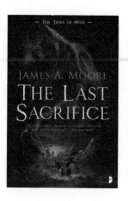
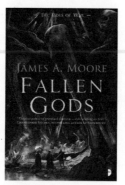
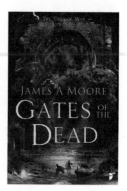

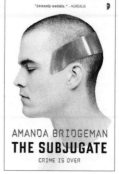

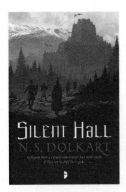

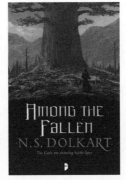

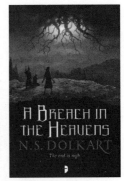

SILENT HALL
N. S. DOLKART

AMONG THE FALLEN
N. S. DOLKART

A BREACH IN THE HEAVENS
N. S. DOLKART

Science Fiction, Fantasy and WTF?!

THE BULLET-CATCHER'S DAUGHTER
ROD DUNCAN

UNSEEMLY SCIENCE
ROD DUNCAN

THE CUSTODIAN OF MARVELS
ROD DUNCAN

@angryrobotbooks

PAIGE ORWIN
THE INTERMINABLES

MOONSHINE
JASMINE GOWER

AN OATH OF DOGS
WENDY N WAGNER